Also by James V. Viscosi

Available Now

Night Watchman
A Flock of Crows is Called a Murder
Long Before Dawn
Television Man
Father's Books

The "Strings" Duology
Shards
Ravels

Anthology Appearances
New Traditions in Terror
edited by Bill Purcell
featuring "The 66th Vampire"

Crossings
edited by Megan Powell
featuring "Draw"

www.jamesviscosi.com

"That was my doll when I was little," Beth said. **"Can I see her?"**

Janice looked at her new best friend as if getting permission, then nodded and handed Candy over to her mother.

"So that's your doll?" Richard said. "I wasn't sure."

"Of course she's mine. Who'd you think she belonged to? You?" Inspecting the doll from various angles, Beth said, "Dad took her away from me when I was like six. He told me he was going to take her out in the woods and bury her. He said she'd be out there under the dirt forever, and it was my fault for being bad. I guess he didn't really do it."

"Nope," Janice said. "I found her in the basement when all the lights went out."

"You were in the basement when all the lights went out?"

"Uh-huh. It was dark. I was scared."

"I'll bet," Beth said. "Richard?"

"Beth?"

"We'll discuss this later."

"Great," Richard said.

Suddenly, a sound like a gigantic electrical spark ripped through the kitchen. After a moment, Janice announced: "Candy says that was the man from the electric company."

The three of them went to the front porch. A worker was sprawled on the ground near the damaged pole. The paramedics were working on him; onlookers had gathered to kibitz about the injured man's prospects.

"Candy says he's gonna die," Janice said.

Copyright © 2020 James Viscosi
ISBN-13: 978-0-9861048-8-6
All Rights Reserved

Cover Art by Émilie Léger
www.emilieleger.com

Father's Books

a novel

by James Viscosi

PART ONE

1

THE OLD MAN LINGERED BEFORE he died.

That was what they told him when he arrived at the hospital. He walked in the door and asked the woman at the front desk what room Walter Bartoski was in, and she directed him to ICU; but when he got there the old man was already gone. The nurse who had been assigned to him said he had passed away just after midnight and had been taken down to the morgue. She shook her head, pursed her lips. The poor man had hung on for hours after the stroke, calling out *Victor, Victor!* We couldn't understand him at first, she said. Over and over again, he kept calling, but nobody came; and then the calling stopped, and he died.

He didn't respond, just stood there thinking, looking around the room, and eventually she asked him: Was that you? Was he calling out for you?

He said he doubted it.

He was the old man's only son, and his name was Richard.

The nurse called someone to escort Richard Bartoski to the morgue. It was in the basement, of course, as morgues were, down an elevator and a long, gently sloping corridor that looked dirty but reeked of antiseptic, finally coming to a room whose cement walls were buttoned with shiny metal doors to refrigerated chambers. Like a baton in a relay race, Richard was passed to an attendant who sat at a counter near the front, then to another attendant who sat at a desk in the back. The second attendant checked some paperwork and took Richard to one of the doors, checked the paperwork again, took him to a different one. He opened it and rolled out the metal drawer from inside. A breath of icy air came with it. The shallow tray was lined with some kind of thick paper, the body covered by an opaque plastic sheet. When the drawer banged to a stop, one bony arm slipped free and swung down, thin and fragile-looking, covered in wispy white hairs. Nothing like the sturdy, inescapable arms Richard remembered from his childhood, arms that could seize you and drag you off and put you where they wanted you to be and make you stay there.

The attendant muttered something and picked up the arm and put it back into place. It fell off again, swept back and forth, a stiff pendulum counting out the seconds of the old man's death.

"Rigor," the man said. "Damn thing won't stay put." He took hold of the plastic and unrolled it as if unwrapping a candy bar. Richard watched his hands, which were obviously practiced in this peculiar art. He was wearing thick latex gloves. Richard could see the outline of a big wristwatch through the opaque material.

"Is there going to be an autopsy?"

"Above my pay grade." Now that the corpse was naked to the waist, the attendant lifted the old man's body slightly, swept the errant arm beneath it, and lowered the cadaver so that its weight held the limb in place.

Richard stared at the body, a pinched and shriveled thing, the abdomen sunken, the ribs showing beneath a dusting of ash-colored hairs. And the face, the old man's face; his mouth hung open in a silent, twisted shriek, as if he had died in terror, with the Devil himself rising up before him, reaching out with red-skinned hands to drag him down to hell.

"Why does it look like he's screaming?" Richard said.

"Dislocated jaw." The attendant demonstrated, gently pushing the old man's chin with a gloved forefinger to illustrate its looseness beneath the papery skin. "See the scrapes along his cheek? He probably fell and injured himself when the stroke hit. You can talk to his doctor about it if you want to. Or a grief counselor. We have—"

"No," Richard said. "It's not important."

"Okay. If you're worried about people's reactions, get a good funeral home with a good makeup artist, they'll make him look like a movie star. Or just go closed-casket."

"It doesn't matter," Richard said. "There's not going to be a funeral. Nobody would come."

The attendant gave him a funny look, then wrapped the body up again and closed the drawer. He sent Richard back upstairs, where there was some paperwork to sign, some belongings to claim. Stupid little details. Richard took care of them and left the hospital. A warm, thin drizzle had turned the lights in the parking lot into big yellow spheres, reflected as fuzzy circles on the damp pavement. The trees that bordered the lot looked jaundiced, pasted in from an old sepia photograph. Their leaves fluttered in the breeze that swirled the specks of rain around the lamps, as if they were waving goodbye.

He got in his car, started it, turned up the heat; he was unaccountably cold, even though the air was warm. The chill in the morgue seemed to have crept into his bones. His stomach felt tarry from the vending-machine coffee he'd gotten in the hospital lobby. The machine had had buttons labeled *Sweet* and *Light*. He'd pushed both, causing the machine spit out a paper cup, into which it puffed identical hits of powdery chemical substances that bore no resemblance to sugar or cream before urinating a stream of black stuff that bore only a passing resemblance to coffee. He'd gulped it down without tasting it then, but he was tasting it now as he sat there, unsettled, unable to explain to himself why he had driven all the way down here on account of the death of a man he hadn't seen or heard from in years. He should've just gone to the liquor store on the corner for a bottle of champagne and celebrated that the world was one asshole poorer. But no, he'd rushed to Bentonville like the concerned son he wasn't, and had arrived too late to say goodbye, or fuck you, or whatever he'd thought his parting words might be.

He looked at the clock. Three in the morning. He could be home a little after dawn if he drove fast enough. But he was so tired, he'd probably wrap his car around a tree. He needed some sleep. Maybe he could go to a motel. Was there one nearby? He had no idea. He hadn't thought to look into it before he'd left home. Surely somebody at the hospital could make a recommendation. He reached for the door handle, intending to go back in and ask, but the rain chose that moment to intensify into a barrage of atmospheric machine gun fire and he let his hand drop. His gaze strayed to the key chain that dangled from the ignition of the car, focusing on the tarnished brassy yellow key that he'd never removed. He wondered if the old man had changed the locks.

Probably not. The old man never changed anything.

Richard drove out of the parking lot, following the *thump-thump* of his windshield wipers into the night.

The house was more or less as he remembered it—two stories of white clapboard with a fake chimney on one side and a real chimney on the other—but the grounds had been neglected. A low and unkempt neck beard of bushes grew all around the foundation and spread into the yard. The trees in back and to either side had filled in, maple and pine and ash saplings grown into adolescents, underbrush plugging the gaps between them. The windows were dark, which was to be expected at this hour; the other houses in the neighborhood, the ones that were occupied, had dark windows too. All the decent people were asleep.

The streetlight out in front was on the fritz, flickering and dim. Richard didn't find this surprising. He turned into the driveway just past it. Broken asphalt ground under the tires as he drove up the steeply sloping blacktop. From this angle, the house looked like a big ship bearing down on him, ready to smash his car to scrap metal and keep going. Behind the house, the driveway widened into a pond of pavement, with the garage and the house baring their teeth at each other from opposite shores. The garage, dating back to the days of smaller vehicles, might have fit a Model T or a horse and buggy without the horse, but not much else. The old man had always used it as a shed, parking his car under a latticed awning that extended off to the right. It sat there now, nestled into its nook, the chrome rear bumper streaked with rain, shiny in Richard's headlights. He sat there holding the steering wheel and staring at the old man's license plate as his car hummed and the wipers flapped in a desperate attempt to achieve liftoff and refrigerated air from the remotest frontiers of the dashboard fought to keep a thin fog from creeping up the windshield.

He almost fell asleep there a few times. Maybe he did fall asleep. At some point he realized that the rain had stopped but the wipers were still going. He cut the engine and got out and went to the back door. His key turned easily in the deadbolt. Same old locks. He opened the door and went into the mudroom, an oblong cubby where visitors were expected to abandon their dirty footwear and wet overcoats and damp umbrellas. It had once been a back porch, before being enclosed with wood and glass. Richard clicked on the light. A single pair of boots stood beneath the wooden bench on the left, leather galoshes, old and cracked and stiff with dried mud, reddish-brown, caked around the soles and partway up the sides.

All that space, and just two boots.

Richard turned off the light and opened the door to the house proper and proceeded into the kitchen, cramped and narrow and faded. The archaic refrigerator whirred and hummed and occasionally coughed in its eternal quest to waste as much electricity as possible. It stood in a silent face-off with the stove, the top of which hosted a diluvian patina of spattered grease dotted with small, charred islands of gristle. An automotive calendar from 1993 hung over the sink; here in the old man's kitchen, time had stopped two years ago. The faucet was dripping into the metal basin, sheening a teardrop-shaped rust stain. *Ping. Ping. Ping.* Richard turned both knobs. The cold water one moved a little and the dripping stopped.

He went into the dining room. It was smaller and darker than he recalled. A table the size and shape of a personal trampoline was shoved off to the side, near the window. Its dusty surface was cluttered with small cardboard boxes and wrappers and paper towel cores. Newspapers were scattered around, mostly old ones, yellowed like maps to buried pirate treasure. Richard picked one up and looked through it carefully, trying not to tear the brittle newsprint. Four years old. He didn't see anything in its urine-colored pages to suggest why it had been saved. The masthead named it the Bentonville *Herald-Journal*. Hadn't the *Herald* and the *Journal* once been two different papers?

He put the newspaper back where he'd found it and went into the living room, which took up this entire side of the ground floor and, unlike the rest of the house, seemed bigger than he remembered, more spacious. Maybe that was because most of the furniture was gone, sold or stored or thrown away. The only survivors of whatever purge had occurred were a wide, lumpy couch and a tattered recliner and, directly opposite those, a squat, square television sitting on top of a card table that looked a little too spindly for the task it had been given. More newspapers lay strewn around the floor, as if the old man had intended to repaint but had only gotten as far as partially covering the carpet.

Richard scuffed through the papers and on into the front hallway, where stairs led up to the second story. Beneath them was the door that led to the basement. Richard put his hand on the basement door, but didn't open it. Instead he peered at the darkened space above, remembering the room where he had slept as a child, the narrow dim hallway, the creaking floorboards. Memories clung to everything like mildewed wallpaper. He pressed the wall switch to turn the lights on above. The hallway had two ceiling fixtures, twin globes of rippled sepia glass, one at the top of the stairs and one at the opposite side of the house. Only the far one lit up, its light feebly visible at this end; the one above Richard's head stayed dark, black and dead, like a knobby bowling ball attached to the ceiling. He wondered how long it had been burned out, how long the old man had been trudging up and down a half-lit hall.

He shut the upstairs light off and went back to the living room and examined the couch. It was a new one, in the sense that he hadn't seen it before, but it was hardly fresh from the showroom, not with its collection of stains and cigarette burns and its stale, closeted odor, reminiscent of a damp towel that had fallen behind the washing machine and been forgotten. He kicked off his shoes and lay down on the sofa and stared up at the ceiling for a while. The paint was yellowed, stained darkest above the recliner, with another shadowy blotch above the sofa. He imagined the old man shuffling back and forth between the two pieces of furniture—probably the only exercise he got—him and his cigarettes, the smoke slowly coating the formerly white paint overhead. He turned to look at the television. It had a glossy shell, black like a beetle's. He found the remote between a couple of the cushions and used it to turn on the TV. He flipped through the channels until he came to a round-the-clock news network. He turned the sound low, background noise to screen out the things he didn't want to hear, the echoes; then he decided it was too quiet and turned it up again.

Lulled by the rhythmic babbling of the television anchors, he put the remote on the back of the sofa and rolled over and covered his eyes with his arm, and waited to fall asleep.

~~~

Every time Pedro Ortiz drifted off, he found himself back in front of the house next door, watching Mr. Bartoski stumble out the door and fall down the steps.

The dream, and the reality, both went like this: Pedro was walking the family dog, an ancient half-blind chihuahua mix that spent most of his time curled into a sleeping doughnut, nose to butt. The evening was pleasant enough, clear sky, light breeze, warm, a hint of rain hanging in the air. He was standing there holding the leash while the dog nosed around the telephone pole in front of the old man's house, communing with all the other dogs who had ever stopped by. The street lamp lit them up like they had just come on stage to perform a routine. Everyone put your hands together for Pedro and the Pooch!

Suddenly, sounds emanated from the old man's house: Crashing, banging, yelling, as if people inside were fighting, even though Mr. Bartoski lived alone and always had for as long as Pedro could remember. He looked up the walk just as the noises stopped. The front door opened and a skinny form staggered out into the yellow glow of the porch lamp. He was saying some garbled thing, and saying it loudly, more words than Pedro had ever heard come out of his mouth before. He just couldn't understand them.

It wasn't like Pedro *knew* the old goat; nobody did, not really. You saw him on the street and waved to him or said hello, he looked at you like you were throwing earwigs at him. But something was clearly wrong with him now. Pedro headed up the walk, dragging the dog along behind him; it resisted, not wanting to tear itself away from the pole, then had to piston its little legs to catch up. "You okay?" Pedro called. "Hey, Mr. Bartoski, are you okay?" Mr. Bartoski, clearly not okay, clutched at one of the columns that supported the porch roof. It seemed to be the only thing keeping him on his feet. He managed to stay upright until Pedro got halfway up the walk; then his arms went slack and he let go, sagged to his knees, slumped forward. He didn't so much fall down the stairs as flow down them, a limp collection of arms and legs tumbling to the bottom of the steps. He ended up on his back at Pedro's feet, staring up at his own house with wide, terrified eyes. He was still talking, the same word now, mumbled over and over again, slurred by his flabby, nerveless lips, by the odd hang of his jaw. Pedro couldn't make out what he was trying to say. The

15

fat old half-blind dog bared his little teeth at the fallen man and snarled. The attempt at fierceness seemed sad and ridiculous, like a senior citizen picking a fight with the opposition's quarterback at a high school football game.

Suddenly the old man turned his head and gave a slurred shout. "Quiet!"

And Pedro sat up in bed, the echo of the cry chasing him back to waking. He leaned forward, rubbing his temples with his fingers. If only he had turned right from his house instead of left, somebody else would've found the old man and called the ambulance. Or maybe not. Maybe he would've lain at the foot of the stairs until morning. Was it wrong for Pedro to wish for that, instead of being the one to have found him?

Probably. But still.

He threw off the sheets, padded over to the window, lifted the shade. The driveway, which ran alongside the house to the garage around back, moated him from the miniature forest that surrounded the old man's house on three sides. The wooded area grew in a slight depression, trees sloping down from Pedro's house and then up again before giving way to Mr. Bartoski's yard. He could see the upper part of the old man's house from his window, the second floor and the attic, a dark shape rising from a sea of green. He remembered watching from here over the weekend as the Weiss place—the next house past the Bartoski residence, on the far side of the woods—had burned to the ground. Pedro had walked by the next morning, joining a group of gawkers on the opposite side of the street; they hadn't been able to get too close because of the barricades put up by the city, closing the road for part of the day. The house had been reduced to a smoldering ruin, blackened and jagged, investigators crawling over and around. The foliage on the trees nearest the house had turned an odd shade of brown, killed by the heat, but not burned. The fire department had hosed them down to keep them from igniting, and the force of the water had broken some of the smaller branches, blown a lot of the leaves off, like an early fall. Coppery mud had sheeted the sidewalk and driveway where torrents of water had run out of the woods and into the gutter.

He'd still been skulking around when they'd carried a small body bag out of the wreckage. Seeing that had made him feel like a ghoul, and he'd left. He remembered passing Mr. Colosseo, who lived next door, and the look the guy had given him, and how he had muttered something about returning to the scene of the crime. As if he thought Pedro coming to check it out meant *he* had burned the place down. Every other neighbor was there, too, or at least most of them. Did Mr. Colosseo think they had all taken turns tossing matches?

Pedro's brooding was interrupted when a light came on in the second-floor hallway of the old man's house, a dim and dun-colored glow behind the dirty window. Somebody was over there. Who could it be? A friend? A relative? Did Mr. Bartoski have either one? Pedro didn't know. Maybe it was a burglar. That was probably what Mr. Colosseo would say.

A shadow slid across the window, roughly human-shaped, moving in from the left. Then it stopped there, motionless. Pedro couldn't see who was casting it. Someone standing some distance away, he supposed, out of direct view, although the angle didn't seem quite right. He found its utter lack of movement vaguely disturbing. What kind of person would step out into the hallway and then just stand there?

The light only stayed on for a minute or two and the shadow stayed put until it went out and the window turned black again. Pedro imagined he could still see it in the inky glass. It made him not want to move, in case the shadow should take note of him. Of course that was ridiculous, but still, he stayed there a little while longer, watching the old man's house being all dark, before he carefully lowered the shade and slunk back to bed.

The sound of mumbling disturbed Richard's sleep. A light fell across his face, disturbing it more. He opened his eyes.

The light came from the open archway to the front hall. A figure stood just inside the other room, aiming a flashlight at Richard. He pushed himself up to a sitting position and shaded his eyes, trying to see who was there, but he couldn't make anything out through the glare. The person seemed to be the one mumbling. Richard couldn't make out any words. "Who's there?" he said. "What do you want? I can't hear you."

Instead of speaking up, the shape clicked off the flashlight. Purple spots faded from Richard's vision and he could see that the front door was open, admitting a cold, harsh illumination that revealed the foyer was empty. The murmurs he'd been hearing were louder now but he couldn't make sense of them. He stood up and stumbled into the foyer. The voices were very loud here. It sounded like an argument that didn't really concern him being conducted in a language he didn't understand. He couldn't see a thing outside. Freezing air flowed in. He closed the door on it. The intensity of the muttering didn't change and he realized it was coming from behind him. As he turned he heard heavy footsteps pounding up the cellar stairs. He spun around as the basement door burst open and a rank wind gusted out, pushing a swirling noisome fog, thick and moist and dense and cloying, filling up the room, his nostrils, choking him.

It smelled like the old man's house.

Richard opened his eyes again.

He lay on the floor next to the sofa. The cracked, discolored ceiling swam overhead, blurry and indistinct. Morning light filtered through the Venetian blinds. The television was dark, although he didn't remember turning it off. He sat up, then stood, feeling lightheaded and sick. A few pages of newspaper were stuck to his back like shabby angel wings. He pulled them off and tossed them aside. He sat back down on the edge of the sofa and hung his head toward his knees until he'd shaken off the lingering scraps of sleep. His clothes felt tight and filthy, as if they had absorbed the loathsome funk from his dream. But had he brought anything to change into? Of course not. When he'd jumped in the car to drive down to the hospital, he'd given no thought to the possibility of being here for more than a few hours, let alone of sleeping in his childhood home. He hadn't packed a suitcase, hadn't even thrown an extra pair of socks or underwear into a bag. His mother would have been appalled.

He couldn't bear the thought of driving back home in these dirty clothes and filling up his car with the smell of the old man's sofa. He would wash what he was wearing, he decided, and while his clothes were getting clean he would take a shower, scrub off the cruft he'd brought back with him from his dream, rinse it down the drain along with the past that this house represented.

And then he would get the fuck out of here, forever.

The washer and dryer were in the basement: Not Richard's favorite part of the house. It was no surprise the noxious fog in his dream had oozed up from there. He stood for a little while in front of the cellar door, bracing himself to face whatever monsters might surge up at him after he opened it. When he finally did, nothing lurked behind it; there was just the staircase, narrow, unfinished, descending into darkness. He reached in and flicked the switch on the wall stud just inside the door. The incandescent bulb swaying at the end of a loose wire overhead flared, popped, and went out, blinding him like a flashbulb in the face.

He turned off the switch and, once he could see again, unscrewed the bulb and shook it, listening to the filament jingle around inside. He considered it for a moment, then screwed it back in. Replacing light bulbs in the old man's house was not his job.

Leaving the door open to admit light from the front hall, Richard descended. The stairs groaned and creaked beneath him, just like they used to, only louder. The air down below was cool and damp and musty; the general dankness that suffused the place bloomed here, in the peeling, discolored, lasagna-wavy floor of wood and dirt and old linoleum, and wicked up into the rest of the house via capillary action. The basement consisted of three rooms, one vast and two tiny, like solitary confinement cells to hold particularly troublesome prisoners. The dark, empty doorways to the little rooms faced the steps, beckoning him to step inside, look around, see if he found anything familiar.

No thanks.

He flicked the switch to turn on the overhead lights. Naked fluorescent tubes struggled to life, starting with faint, oddly musical plinking sounds, like someone plucking the strings of a tiny, mistuned ukulele, then transitioning to a high-pitched electromagnetic buzz before finally coughing up a hideous pinkish phlegmy illumination that made his skin look mottled and corpselike. He let his gaze wander over all the crap that cluttered the big room: A pair of floor-standing lamps that would have been hip twenty years ago, crumpled and unlabeled boxes, heaps of stained clothing, overstuffed plastic bags and wooden crates, the skeletal remains of broken furniture. The walls, plastered cinderblock that had once been white, were now tattooed with brown spirals of unfriendly-looking mildew. There were a few windows up near the ceiling, but bushes grew so close and thick on all sides of the house that very little daylight got through to alleviate the awfulness.

The washer and dryer were jammed into a nook under the stairs like a pair of frightened pigeons huddling together for comfort. The work area was cluttered and filthy, with off-white powdered detergent strewn across the tops of both machines like the detritus of a weeklong cocaine bender. Small, tacky splotches of blue liquid fabric softener collected hair and lint and dust that would never again float freely on the soft cellar winds. He stripped off his clothes and threw them all into the washer together; separating darks from lights was a time investment he was unwilling to make.

Once the machine had filled and started churning, he went back upstairs. He picked up the ancient black phone in the front hall to dial Tony, his partner in the accounting office. Tony answered after the seventh ring. "Hello?"

"Tony, it's Richard. Sorry to call you at home so—"

"Richard? What number is this? I almost didn't pick up." Then, after Richard had explained the situation, Tony said: "I thought you hated that old bastard."

"I do. I mean, I did."

"So why are you down there?"

"I don't know."

A grunt. "Glad to hear you're self-aware as always. How's Beth taking it?"

"Beth's not here."

"She let you go all by yourself?"

"She doesn't know anything about it."

"Because why?"

"Because I didn't tell her."

A pause. "Are we playing twenty questions, Richard?"

Richard sighed. "If I told her, she would've thought she had to come. That means she would've had to bring Janice. Janice doesn't need to be in this house."

"Uh-huh. You understand how pissed Beth is going to be at you for keeping her in the dark, right?"

"Yeah, I know. I'll deal with that after I get back."

"Which will be when?"

"Tonight."

"So you'll be in the office on Thursday?"

"Definitely."

"Okay. See you then. Have fun explaining to your sister how you left her out of your little adventure for her own good." Tony hung up. Richard cradled the phone and made a face at it, then headed upstairs. He hoped there would be enough hot water for both the shower and the washing machine to run at the same time.

But of course there wasn't.

In the light of morning, Pedro's grim thoughts about the house next door, the shadow in the window upstairs, seemed remote and fabulous. He did wonder who was there turning lights on in the middle of the night, though, and felt he needed an explanation, so after a quick breakfast of milk and crumbled chocolate sandwich cookies, his system flush with sugar-induced energy and confidence, he decided to go have himself a look.

He went out the side door and across the driveway and into the trees. There was a path there, sort of, with relatively firm soil and somewhat less underbrush than the rest of the tiny woods. It had rained last night and the forest was damp. He could smell the water on the leaves, the moist bark, the old pine needles, the pockets of ruddy mud that squished underfoot and got all over his sneakers. The path ended near the back of Mr. Bartoski's house, not far from the shed-like garage and the plastic-roofed awning that didn't do a very good job of keeping the old man's car shielded from the elements. There was another car parked in the driveway, a little foreign job, expensive-looking, but dilapidated and kind of sad, as if it had been bought used and hadn't been taken very good care of since. It had a license plate frame from a dealership Pedro had never heard of. He glanced at the big old house, then back at the unknown car, then back at the house.

So there *was* someone else here. Unprecedented.

Curiosity satisfied, he started to turn away, but then a flash of white from the driveway-facing window caught his attention. He turned and saw a girl behind the glass, with a smudged face and long dirty-blonde hair, watching him with huge eyes the color of the deep end of a pool. She wore a smock-like dress or night shirt, streaked with dust and what might have been mildew. Who was she? Did she belong to whoever owned the car? It seemed likely, except he had the feeling he had seen her before. Not at school—she wasn't old enough to be in the building he had just graduated from—but around the neighborhood, maybe. He paid little attention to the crop of younger kids that roamed the local sidewalks and yards; they came and went as families moved around and he didn't really interact with them. Yet something about the girl, the way she stood there staring at him, kept him from leaving. Unsettled by her unflinching gaze and the oddly desolate look on her face, as if she knew a terrible secret but had no one to tell, Pedro tried a smile and a wave. Her expression didn't change. She backed away and vanished into the dim interior of the house, and now he realized that the blinds on the window were drawn, dusty and cobwebby and studded with the desiccated husks of long-dead insects. They hadn't been opened in months, maybe in years.

So how could he have seen the girl?

He backed away from the house. It stretched out above him, seemed to curve over and toward him, its dark windows glaring from dirty white ruffled clapboards, angry, threatening. He saw a pale shape behind one of the sheets of black glass, but it vanished when he tried to look at it directly, evaporating like breath-fog from a mirror.

By the time Pedro got back to his own driveway, wheezing from his panicked sprint through the forest, he had decided that he really wasn't very interested in the old man's visitors after all.

This had to be the most uncomfortable shower Richard had ever taken.

The bathtub, up on spindly legs, made strange creaking noises and shifted every time he moved; he was afraid it would dump him out like dirt from a bucket loader if he moved too far to either side. The soap—some godawful off-brand brick he had found under the sink—smelled like rendered animal fat and felt like it was impregnated with sand, and had been moldering for so long that the label remained visible even after he'd removed it from its wrapper. The water's low pressure made it like standing under feeble dribbles of enlarged-prostate pee, while its temperature kept swinging between icy and volcanic extremes without ever pausing at something comfortable.

Richard washed away the last of the slightly oily lather as best he could, turning this way and that until it was more or less gone. There was no shampoo to be found; he considered rubbing the bar of soap in his hair, but decided that would only make it greasier and settled for a thorough rinse instead. The plumbing made odd groaning noises after he turned off the water, reminding him of the sounds made by quarreling bears in nature documentaries. Maybe the pipes were starting to go. Maybe the whole house was on the verge of collapse, and would decompose into a pile of timbers and shingles as he pulled out of the driveway, flipping it the bird in his rearview mirror.

What a satisfying departure that would be.

The tiles were slick and icy underfoot. There had once been a bath mat, but it was gone now. Maybe the old man had taken it for his own bathroom. Maybe it had rotted away to nothing. The towel bar was still there, the fake chrome worn off to reveal patchy dull grey stuff beneath. It was long enough for two towels side by side but there was only one, which Richard had taken from the linen cabinet in the hallway. Scratchy and threadbare, it had faded from its original color to a pale ochre. As he reached for the towel, the last of the water gurgled out of the tub. It sounded almost like a voice, choking on his name. *Richard Richard Richard.*

He froze, listening, the old stiff towel inches from his hand. Sunlight streamed through the bubbled glass window. The drain made one last sound, a weak belch. No words there, no veneer of meaning.

Richard shook his head, pulled down the towel, sandpapered himself off. Wearing the towel around his waist in the manner of a hotel guest returning from an illicit skinny-dipping excursion to the pool, he headed down to the basement to move his clothes into the dryer, then returned to the living room. Unwilling to have his skin in direct contact with the furniture's noisome upholstery, he stood and watched the morning news until he heard the dryer buzz, loud enough to make the floor vibrate. He dressed right there in the basement. The cool cellar air raised gooseflesh on his skin, but his hot clothes quickly counteracted the chill.

As he was buttoning his jeans, he heard a sound from one of the little rooms, a sharp, quick intake of breath and the scuffing of feet. He turned just as a pale shape emerged from the furnace room and darted for the stairs. He barely had time to register what it was before it was gone: A young girl in a white dress, long blonde hair streaming behind her. She was up the steps and gone before Richard's jaw had even finished dropping. "Hey!" he called. "Hey, come back!"

She did not, of course, come back, and when he started to go after her he stumbled over a box and fell down hard on the floor. By the time he got back to his feet and made it upstairs, the girl was nowhere to be found. He went through the house, living room to dining room to kitchen. No sign of her. The deadbolt was still set on the front door and he didn't hear the floorboards creaking upstairs, so he went out the back door, stood on the warm concrete patio in his stocking feet, looking around like a confused dog that was sure its favorite toy was around here somewhere.

Where had she gone? Was she still in the house?

Had she ever actually been there?

The more he thought about it, the less sure he was of that. What would she have been doing down in the basement? How would she have gotten in? Wouldn't he have heard the cellar stairs complaining as she ran up them?

He really should go back inside and do a thorough search of the house, top to bottom, to assure himself that there were no small girls hiding there. Instead he noodled out into the driveway and took a good long look at the house. In the daylight, it was really no different from any other old place in the neighborhood: Clapboards slightly warped, roof bowed a little in the middle, bricks in the chimneys beginning to shift and erode. He remembered playing detective with Beth when they were kids, rubbing their fingertips in hard circles on the bricks until they were covered with a pinkish powder that smelled like damp stone, then pressing them to a piece of paper to transfer the patterns. Confess, criminal. We've got your prints.

There had been other changes to the grounds, especially to the wooded side and back lots. Coming in last night he'd thought that the trees seemed taller, denser, but had chalked it up to the effects of darkness and exhaustion. In the daylight, though, he could see how the forest had grown and filled in to become a thicket surrounding the house on three sides. It hadn't been like that when he was younger. Then, the spaces between the trunks had been clear, and he could run among them in any direction. He wouldn't be able to do that now, not unless he wanted to get a faceful of brambles. In winter, when the trees had lost their leaves and the underbrush had shriveled to bracken, they must be like skeletal hands waving and clicking, bending inward, hoping to grab a piece of the house and anyone inside.

Richard closed his eyes, opened them again. Trees and bushes. Being here was making him morbid, if not downright paranoid. He checked his watch. Ten o'clock. If he left right now, he could be home by early afternoon. Beth would still be working. He could drop in on her, tell her what had happened, where he had been. She couldn't very well kill him in front of the customers, could she?

Yeah, that was what he should do. He should go back inside, put on his shoes, get in the car, drive away. And yet he stood there in the driveway in his stocking feet, gawking, at the house, the decrepit garage, the old man's car, gunmetal grey, shiny beneath the streaks of dust, tucked beneath its protective awning. He remembered helping build the overhang, making a framework of posts and crossbeams to brace it up under winter snows, anchoring it to the existing garage, laying down a roof of yellow and green corrugated plastic. His role had mainly consisted of fetching tools and boards and fasteners, enduring taunts about his incompetence as an assistant, dodging then retrieving the occasional hurled hammer or screwdriver or hand saw when his father reached a critical level of frustration, which occurred with increasing frequency as the project progressed.

Some nice bonding time, that had been.

The garage door was closed and looked like it hadn't been opened in years. He wandered over to the side door and peered through the dirty window at the gloomy interior. He could make out dim heaps of clutter within, reminding him of the basement, as if the house were a ruminant with two stomachs and they were both full. He tried the knob. Locked.

A noise from behind him drew Richard's attention. He turned to see a station wagon slowly crunching up the slope of the driveway, reflected trees and sunlight and blue sky traveling across its windshield as it moved.

Beth's car.

Oh, shit.

He stepped out of the way as she guided her wagon into the wide spot in the driveway, parking it next to his car. In the shadow of the house her windows turned translucent and he could see her behind the wheel, or at least, her shock of copper-red hair; she was looking at the house, not at him. Her daughter Janice sat in back on the passenger side, a little clone of her mother, from the color of her hair to the current position of her head.

Still looking at the house, Beth cut the engine; then she removed her seat belt, got out of the car, and came over to where he stood. She stopped in front of him and folded her arms and said: "Richard."

"Beth." He glanced at the car. "I thought you were never going to bring any child of yours to this awful house."

"That was while Dad was alive. And now he's not. Right?"

"Right."

"And you were going to tell me about it when?"

He shrugged. "When I got back."

She shook her head. "I can't believe you came all the way down here without even calling me and letting me know what was going on."

"I didn't think you'd want to come."

"You mean you were afraid I *would*."

"Well, I—"

A loud rapping from the wagon's rear window interrupted him.

"Hold that thought." Beth went to the rear passenger door of her car and opened it. Janice came tumbling out. The little girl ran around the car and gave Richard a hug, then pointed at the house. "Mommy says you used to live here. Are you going to live here again?"

"No fu—um, no, definitely not."

"Good. I don't like it. Mommy, I'm hungry."

"You ate on the way," Beth said.

"That was *hours* ago."

Beth looked at Richard and rolled her eyes and mouthed *it was half an hour*, then said, "What's Dad got in the fridge?"

"I don't know. I didn't open it. Body parts, maybe."

"Richard!" Beth said.

"What?"

She indicated Janice with a tilt of her head.

"Sorry," he said. "But I wouldn't eat any food in that house if you paid me."

"You don't have to eat it," Beth said. "Just watch Janice eat it. Come on."

She led Janice up to the back door. He stood there and watched them go. When she got to the square of concrete that formed the back patio, she stopped and glanced back at him. "Are you coming or not?"

Richard sighed. "Yeah, I'm coming." He went to the door and opened it and stood aside so Beth and Janice could precede him into the mudroom.

As they passed, Beth looked down at his feet.

"By the way," she said, "nice socks."

The kitchen was a lot drearier than Beth remembered, like a narrow, dingy, poorly lit corridor in which someone was storing battered old appliances pending a trip to the junkyard. An old refrigerator took up a good chunk of the right wall, rumbling and muttering to itself in its nook among streaky green cabinets. The left wall was occupied by the sink, counter, and stove, with another set of cabinets and drawers painted the same sad shade of spoiled mint. The counter's fake marble surface had split and peeled in many spots, especially around the sink basin, where shoddy repairs had been attempted with yellowed packing tape, its internal filaments brown and swollen with moisture. The old gas range and nearby countertop were grimed with spattered grease and bits of blackened stuff she couldn't identify. At the far end, beneath the octagonal window, a small table stood. It was flanked by three mismatched chairs, one of which was considerably more worn than the other, string tape holding the seat back and cushion together in multiple spots. Beth could remember sitting at that table, years ago, on cold winter mornings, basking in the heat from the stove; their father was always parsimonious about running the furnace, so this was often the warmest spot in the house. Obviously finding a warm spot wasn't a problem now, in the murky depths of August, with no air conditioning.

Richard, arms folded, leaned against the door to the mudroom while she rummaged through the cabinets in search of nonperishable or unexpired child-friendly food items. Janice, meanwhile, sat on the table, eyeing Beth's activities with suspicion, kicking her feet and picking at the tape despite repeated admonitions to stop doing both.

"It smells funny in here," Janice said. "We don't have to stay, do we?"

"Not for long, honey," Beth said. She had located cereal boxes and was assembling them into a line on the countertop "Just for a little while." She surveyed her finds. All were conspicuously high in fiber and low in sugar, adorned with pictures of older adults, active and cheerful because their wise breakfast choices kept their daily bowel movements so regular. She didn't even bother offering any of them to Janice, and moved on to the refrigerator. Bottles clinked against each other as she rifled its contents. Finally she pulled out a carton of eggs and some dilapidated bacon. "These only just expired. I'll cook them all."

"One cholesterol special, coming up," Richard said.

Beth gave him a sidelong glance. "And what have *you* eaten today, big brother?"

"Nothing. I haven't even had coffee."

She tilted her head at the droplet-spattered coffee maker near the sink. "Make yourself useful, then. I need caffeine."

While Richard got to work on his assigned task, Beth returned to the cabinets and crashed around in them to find a usable skillet, then fired up a burner on the stove. Little blue flames danced happily in a ring until Beth squashed them with the pan. After a few minutes, the smells of brewing coffee and frying bacon engaged the general miasma and air of resignation that hung in the kitchen in a valiant battle for supremacy.

"What exactly did you mean, before?"

She glanced at Richard. He was staring at the coffee maker's transparent reservoir as the water slowly drained out of it. "Before when?"

"About being here for a little while. What's *a little while* mean?"

"Oh." She stirred the contents of the pan with a plastic spatula she had taken from a crock on the back of the stove. "I was thinking a few days. A week, tops."

"A *week*? Why?"

"Well, we have to at least stay for the wake."

"What wake?"

"Stop being obtuse."

"I'm not being obtuse. Who's going to hold a wake? Who would show up to pay their respects to that old bastard?"

Beth glared at him over her shoulder, then shot a glance her daughter's way. Janice was bouncing up and down, staring at the brownish light fixture in the ceiling, giving no indication that she was paying them the slightest amount of attention. She turned back to the stove. "He was our father, Richard."

"Yeah, that old bastard was your father," Janice said.

Beth gave Richard an *Are you happy now?* look, then said, "Janice, that's not a nice word."

"I don't care, you bastard."

"*Janice.*"

"Sorry, mommy."

"That's all right. Just don't say it again." The eggs, expanding on a lake of bacon grease, began threatening to surge over the sides of the pan. Beth fought them off with the spatula. She looked at Janice over her shoulder. "Chair, kiddo." The little girl slid off the table and onto a seat.

"If you're going to insist on staying," Richard said, "don't stay *here*. Get a motel room or something. This is not a healthy place."

"The past can't hurt us, Richard. Not unless we let it."

"Say that again when the past starts gnawing on your leg."

She stabbed and slashed at the eggs. "He's dead. We can get past that now. We can close that whole chapter and move on."

"That was a very important chapter," Richard said. "I think I'd prefer to keep reading it."

"Now *that's* a healthy attitude." Beth turned off the heat and deposited a steaming yellow-white heap onto a plate, topping it with crispy strips of bacon, then brought it to the table and put it in front of Janice.

Her daughter examined this offering with a skeptical eye.

"I hope that old bastard has ketchup," she said.

While Beth went to the hospital to talk about the old man's final hours and see about his postmortem arrangements, Richard stayed at the house with Janice. Entertaining a little girl in a house devoid of toys, picture books, puzzles, or games presented a challenge that Richard solved with daytime television. As she watched some cartoon involving superhero dinosaurs who talked like teenagers, Richard sidled into the kitchen and dialed the office.

"Richard," Tony said. "What's up?"

"Beth's here," he said.

"Yeah? You called her?"

"No, the hospital did. She's unlisted so it took them a little while to track her down. They finally got her at work. Anyway, the reason I'm calling is, she wants to stay here for a few days, and—"

"She does? I thought she hated that bastard even more than you did."

"That's not possible. We hated him equally. Anyway, she wants to close that chapter and move on by having a wake or a service or something. So I won't be back today after all."

"You're staying too?"

"You don't think I'm leaving her here by herself, do you?"

"She's a big girl, Richard."

"She's still my baby sister."

"Uh-huh. And she's not there right now or you wouldn't dare call her that." Another pause. Richard pictured Tony checking his calendar. "Look, I have to go; the Schwartzes will be here in ten minutes to talk estate planning. Why don't you just forget about rushing back and take the whole week off?"

"I'm not staying here for a week."

"Who says you have to stay there? Go have some fun. Go to Vegas and get laid. Go to the Caribbean and get laid. Hell, go anywhere and get laid. God knows you could use it."

"Tony, I—"

"Gotta go. I expect to see a signed affidavit on Monday that you had sex and are feeling a lot less uptight."

Click.

Richard glared at the receiver, as if it might capture his lethal gaze, transmit it up the line, and melt Tony's phone into a puddle on his desk; then he hung up and headed back to the living room. "So, kiddo, have the dinosaurs saved the world yet?"

Janice didn't answer.

This was because Janice was not there.

Richard called her name, got no response. He stood there for a second, pondering where the kid might have gone. She hadn't come into the kitchen, and he hadn't seen her in the dining room as he'd passed through. Just to be sure, he turned around and looked under the table. Nope. That left the front hall. He went to it. She wasn't there either, but the cellar door was ajar. He opened it the rest of the way, peered down the stairs. Would Janice have gone down there by herself, in the dark? Probably not; probably the door hadn't quite closed properly when he'd charged upstairs chasing after that imaginary girl. He was about to close it when he detected noises from below, the sound of furtive movement among the boxes: Janice, he thought, going exploring and trying to be stealthy because she knew she shouldn't be doing it.

Richard flicked the switch for the stairway light, then remembered, when nothing happened, that it was burned out. He went down the stairs and stopped at the bottom. The basement was dark and gloomy and cluttered as the tomb of a hoarder who had taken it all with him. He flicked on the fluorescents. They went through their sputtering startup routine as they dragged themselves back to life. He still couldn't see Janice anywhere in the maze of junk, but there were plenty of places to hide, if that was the game they were playing.

"Janice?"

No answer.

"Hey, kiddo, are you down here?"

More no answer.

From above, he heard hinges creaking as the cellar door swung shut.

A moment later, the lights went out, leaving the basement even darker than before he had switched them on.

"Shit," he said.

From the darkness, a tiny voice echoed: "Shit."

At the hospital, Beth learned that her father's body was going to be cremated, as per a document that they had found in his pocket, neatly folded, with the words *in the event of my death* scrawled on it in a shaky hand. If Richard had bothered to go through Dad's personal effects, or even to ask a few questions, he could have saved her a trip down here; but, typically, he had done nothing except drift through the hospital, as passive and constrained as a paper boat in a stream.

They showed her a photocopy of the document. It wasn't a will, just some notes about the arrangements he had made, along with his children's contact information. Richard's was correct but hers was at least three phone numbers and two addresses out of date; each change represented another time she had begun to receive angry phone calls and threatening letters from her ex-husband after he somehow tracked her down despite living on the other side of the country.

She asked about the body, and learned that it was currently undergoing an autopsy somewhere in the bowels of the hospital. If she wanted to come back in a few hours, they said, the procedure should be finished, and she could see him then. She thought about it and finally declined; it would be easier to deal with a pile of ashes hidden in an urn than with a stitched-up cadaver. She did take a copy of the copy of the note, though, as it had the name and address of the crematorium that would be performing the old man this final service. Then she went out to her car, got in, stared for a little while at the paper in her hand—succinct documentary evidence of how all of their lives had gone wrong—and spent about fifteen minutes sobbing into the steering wheel, a good long therapeutic cry in a place where no one would bother her. Not grief for her father; he didn't rate grief, just regret and contempt and, perhaps, a measure of pity. No, this was something else: Longing for what might have been, but hadn't; wishing things had been different when they weren't, and couldn't be, and all the wishing in the world wouldn't change one second of one day of any of their lives. She knew all that, of course, everyone knew it, but it didn't stop anyone from longing and wishing and thinking, *If only I had done this; if only I hadn't done that.*

What had she hoped to accomplish by coming here? Not just to the hospital, but to the town, the house? It had all seemed to make sense in the morning, when she had run home from the store to throw some clothes into a couple of suitcases, scooped up Janice from school, and set out on what she'd hoped would be an expedition that would end at that elusive goal, closure. But maybe, in order to get there, things needed to reopen first.

When she finally wore herself out, she discovered she had twisted the note up like a Christmas cracker. She sat back and looked at her red, blotchy, tear-streaked face in the mirror. What a frightful apparition. If she hoped to avoid a million questions from Janice, she was going to have to make herself presentable before she went back.

Leaving the old man's note crumpled up on the passenger seat, she got out of the car and went back to the hospital in search of a ladies' room.

Richard flicked the switch for the fluorescent lights up and down a few times. Nothing happened. The few shreds of noontime light that made it through the bushes along the foundation made the basement a maze of grey and black piles. You would think that his niece, with her pale skin, would stand out like a ghost among the tombstones, but he knew from experience that the kid was good at hiding, squeezing into spaces you would swear were too small for her, melting into shadows and disappearing.

"Janice? Are you down here?"

For a few seconds there was no response; then he heard, from somewhere out in the trash heap, "Uh-huh."

All the junk down here, the boxes and clothes and crates, muffled and misdirected sound, so he couldn't tell where her voice was coming from. The last thing he needed was to flail around looking for her and knock a box of hammers onto her head. "I'm going to go upstairs and find a flashlight. You just stay put, all right?"

"Okay, we will," she said.

"We? Who's *we*?"

There was a long pause before Janice said, "Nobody."

"Are you sure? You haven't got a mouse in your pocket?"

"No," she said with a little giggle, as if this were the silliest thing she had ever heard.

"Okay," he said. "I'll be right back."

"Okay."

He went upstairs, half expecting to find the cellar door bolted from the other side, though of course it wasn't. He played with the switch for the overhead light in the foyer, flicking it off and on and off and on. Nothing happened. Blown fuse, maybe? He headed for the kitchen, where his father used to keep a huge, ancient flashlight on a shelf under the sink. He hoped it was still there, and that it still had batteries. He tried other light switches as he passed them along the way. None worked; the entire house had lost power. This wasn't that unusual, but normally there had to be something to knock out the lines: A thunderstorm, or high winds, or sleet. Nothing like that had happened today. Maybe a transformer had exploded somewhere.

In the kitchen, Richard knelt down in front of the sink, opened the cabinet. The space within was moist and smelled of mildew and rodents. Off to the right was the little shelf, and on it he found the flashlight, lying on its side, a foot and a half of metal with a glass dome on the end. He took it out, hefting it like a club. It was rustier than he remembered. He tested it out. Despite the pits and scratches, the big lens sprayed whatever he aimed it at with a firehose of light.

Very fresh batteries, then.

Armed with this formidable artifact, Richard returned to the front hall and descended the creaky stairs to the cellar. At the bottom, he clicked on the flashlight. A wide circle of illumination lit up the shabby walls, the crumpled boxes, the naked supports. He took a few steps into the wreckage of the old man's life, then put his foot down on something that rolled out from under it and fell into a pile of boxes. They all toppled over, some spilling backwards, some forwards, disgorging the contents of multiple containers onto him. He stifled a shriek as long, musty, clingy things fell over his head and neck and shoulders, wrapping around his mouth and nose.

Scarves. Moldering knit scarves. That's all they were. He gathered up the scarves and stuffed them back into the box. They all seemed loosely constructed, trailing strands of material like the tentacles of yarn jellyfish or simply coming apart in his hands. A vague memory surfaced: His mother, sitting in the living room near the fireplace, long needles working furiously, knitting items that, as far as he knew, she never completed. Certainly neither he nor Beth had ever worn anything she had made. Finishing them probably hadn't been the point.

Once he had repackaged the knitwear, he looked around for the flashlight. It had found its way behind an old pair of ski goggles and shone through the amber plastic lens, staining everything in front of it with a urine tint. He picked it up and waved it around the cellar. "Janice?"

She didn't answer. Maybe he had scared her with all his crashing around.

"It's okay, Janice. You can come out. You're not in trouble. Uncle Richard just tripped, that's all."

Still no answer.

Great.

He aimed the light into the windowless solitary confinement cells. He picked his way over to them, starting with the one on the left. It was so crammed with junk that not even Janice could have found a nook to hide in. The remaining open space was barely as big as a closet. He moved over to the utility room. This one was weirdly empty, although stained outlines and drag marks along the dusty floor suggested that it had once been stuffed just as full as the rest of the basement. Richard went into it all the way to the far wall, took a few deep breaths, then leaned forward and aimed the flashlight into the corner between the water heater and the furnace. The open sump, eternally full of water, gleamed blackly, like a troll blinking in the face of unaccustomed illumination.

Janice wasn't there.

Relieved, Richard returned to the basement proper. Sweep, sweep, sweep went the light, sliding over the workbench, piled with boxes of nails and screws and other fasteners, hacksaws, big-headed mallets, screwdrivers of various sizes and lengths; over ceiling-high shelves stocked with broken small appliances and junk packed into shoeboxes and mason jars and plastic tubs; over heaped ribbons and clotheslines and ropes, bolts of fabric and soiled clothes and shoes, scraps of wood and asphalt shingles and buckets stacked inside each other. So much stuff down here, the sediment of decades. Only gasoline and a match would get it properly cleaned out.

He turned in a circle and finally spotted something, a little foot in a little sneaker sticking out from behind the washing machine. Richard edged in that direction like a spelunker in a fragile cave. He found Janice sitting on the floor in a barrow between the stationary tub and the washing machine, mostly shielded from view by a pile of boxes leaning against an old quilt rack. She was clutching something, a large red-haired porcelain-faced doll with plastic hands and dull black shoes and a pleasant, vacantly idiotic face. It looked familiar. Had it belonged to Beth? He thought so.

Janice's eyes were closed, her little lips moving, like she was talking silently to herself, or maybe to the doll.

Richard said: "Janice."

She didn't answer. He nudged her foot.

Her eyes opened.

She shrieked, "Quiet!"

Janice brought the doll upstairs with her. She said its name was Candy. It was her new best friend. "I only went down there because Candy called me," she said, as she stomped up the steps in front of him.

"She called you?"

"Uh-huh."

"What did she say?"

Pitching her voice chipmunk-high, Janice chirped, "*Help! Help!*"

"That's what she was saying?"

"Uh-huh."

They came out into the hall. Richard could see flashing lights through the blinds on the tall windows that flanked the front entrance. He shut the cellar door and reached to set the latch. "Why did she need help?"

"On account of she was tied up in the basement. I untied her and then we hid."

Richard froze with his hand on the latch. He took a breath, then another, then set the latch. No more unauthorized rescue operations into the cellar for Janice. "Who were you hiding from?" he said. "Me?"

She shook her head.

"Then why didn't you answer me when I was calling you?"

"Candy said not to. She said we had to be quiet like a mouse."

"Because why?"

"Because of the other person who's down there."

A strange chill tickled Richard, somewhere between his lungs and his heart. "What other person?"

"The one who tells people what to do."

"Mmm, I see. And what does this person want people to do?"

Janice held the doll out at arm's length in front of herself, staring into its porcelain face. "To finish the job."

"What job?"

Janice shrugged. That, apparently, was information she didn't have. He put his hand on her head. "Well, I'm glad that you have a new friend, but I don't want you going in the basement by yourself again. Or with Candy, either. No matter who's down there calling for help. Okay?"

"Okay."

"Good." He ruffled her hair, eliciting a little squeak of protest. "Let's find out what's going on out front. Want a ride?"

Janice grinned and nodded. He hoisted her onto his shoulders— she plopped Candy down on his head like a hat, the doll's plastic-shoed feet hanging down by his ears—and carried her out onto the porch, ducking low so as not to scrape her off on the doorframe. The front yard sloped down to the street. At the edge of the yard, a blue sedan had jumped the curb and smashed into the telephone pole that stood in front of the house. At least one of the power lines had fallen on the vehicle, draped over it like a jungle vine across a boulder. The flashing lights belonged to two police cars, an ambulance, and a fire truck, but none of them were getting too close to the accident scene; the cops were out in the street directing traffic and keeping a knot of onlookers away from the scene, while the firefighters were making sure nothing ignited. The paramedics just looked bored.

"Candy says the electric company will be here soon," Janice announced.

"She does, huh? Well, she's probably right."

"Yeah. They'll get the wires off the lady's car, but one of them will get a shock."

"That's not a nice thing for you to say, Janice."

"*I* didn't say it. Candy did."

"Well, tell Candy it's not nice."

"I don't have to, she already heard *you*," Janice said.

Unable to think of an argument to counter that, Richard descended the steps and went partway down the long walk, stopping well back from the street. He drew some disinterested glances from the authorities, who didn't seem to care about his presence as long as he stayed well clear of the incident, and some very interested glances from the small crowd of onlookers, who seemed to care about his presence quite a bit. He could imagine their surprise at having real live people emerge from the old man's house; it must be like going to a wake where the coffin banged open and someone other than the deceased climbed out of it.

Janice said, "Something smells bad."

"The top of the car is burning," he said. "See?" He pointed at the wisps of smoke drifting from the roof of the car where the wire lay; it sported one of those silly vinyl-covered tops and it had begun smoldering a little.

"It's stinky."

"Sure is. Come on, let's get upwind." He carried Janice across the yard to the driveway and then, because she was no longer the weightless tyke she once had been, put her back on her own two feet. He took her hand and the two of them walked down the driveway towards the crowd. One of the bystanders detached from the others and intercepted him at the edge of the group. It was an older fellow, a man in his seventies, maybe. He looked familiar, but Richard couldn't quite connect the face with a name. Something that started with a C, he thought. Conrad, Conner, Conroy?

"It's Richard, isn't it?" the man said. "Walter's boy?"

"That's right," Richard said, shaking the proffered hand. Cunningham, Carter, Collins?

He hoped the man would introduce himself, but he didn't; instead he crouched down in front of Janice. "And who's this? Your daughter?"

Janice clung to Richard's leg and half-melted around behind him, clutching Candy with her free hand, staring at the elderly neighbor as if he were some sort of chattering apparition.

"This is my niece, Janice," Richard said.

"Oh, your sister's kid? Elizabeth, right? Is she here too?"

"She's at the hospital."

"I hope she's all right."

"She's fine. She's just talking to them about the—uh, about Dad."

"Oh, yeah, poor old Walter." The man stood. "When the good Lord sees fit to take me, I should so lucky."

"Lucky?"

"Don't get me wrong. It was a terrible thing. Terrible. But at least it was quick. Not to spend weeks in the hospital with a tube up his nose? And to have a good neighbor right there to find him and dial 911? Sure, I'd call that lucky." The fellow reached into the clutch of onlookers and somehow plucked a teenager out of it, like an employee in the seafood section plunging his arm into the lobster tank and coming up with just the right one. "This here is Pedro. You wouldn't know him, his family moved in after you kids left, but he's the one got the ambulance. Didn't you, Pedro?"

Pedro looked and sounded nonplussed at being hauled into this conversation. "Didn't I what?"

"Call the ambulance. After Walter's stroke." Turning to Richard, the neighbor said, "Pedro went right into your house, picked up the phone, called for help, he did. Didn't think twice about it."

Pedro's eyes widened and he looked at Richard. "*Your* house?"

"That's right. Richard here is Walter's son. He's staying in the house with his sister and his niece, wrapping up Walter's affairs."

"You are?"

"Well, sort of. I mean, we're there for now, but we haven't lived here in years. It's not *our* house."

"If it's not yours, then whose is it?" the neighbor said.

"No idea. For all I know, he left it to Pedro." He turned to the kid. "You want it?"

"Um, no thanks," Pedro said. "So, it was nice meeting you, but I've got to, um, you know …" He trailed off and hurried off up the sidewalk, making a right turn into the driveway of the next house past the thicket.

The older guy watched Pedro until he was gone, then leaned over and said, in a stage whisper, "I'd go through Walter's things if I were you, see if anything's missing."

"What?"

"I'm just saying. Who knows what that little punk took before he called the hospital?"

"Oh, come on," Richard said. "There's nothing in that house that anybody would want to steal."

"Those people will steal anything. You know how they are."

"No, I don't." Richard hoisted Janice back onto his shoulders. "And I don't think you do either."

He turned and headed back across the yard toward the house.

"Fine, don't listen to me," the guy hollered after him. "You'll be sorry when the family silver turns up missing!"

Beth returned shortly after the electric company arrived. She came in through the back door, toting several bags of groceries, complaining that the police had made her park way down the street and she'd had to traipse up the sidewalk and then go up someone else's driveway and cut through the trees because the sidewalk was blocked by a cherry picker from the electric company, and what on earth was going on, anyway?

Richard explained about the accident while Beth put the groceries away. When he was finished, Janice piped up. "Candy says they'll be done soon."

Beth paused in the act of stowing bottle after bottle of Janice's favorite ketchup—Richard wondered what her weekly condiment budget was—to look at her, then at Richard. "Who's Candy?" she said.

A big grin on her face, Janice produced the doll from under the table, where she had stowed it when they'd heard Beth at the back door. Beth seemed startled, but then a wan smile flickered across her face. "That was my doll when I was little," she said. "Can I see her?"

Janice looked at her new best friend as if getting permission, then nodded and handed Candy over to her mother.

"So that's your doll?" Richard said. "I wasn't sure."

"Of course she's mine. Who'd you think she belonged to? You? Goofball." Inspecting the doll from various angles, Beth said, "Her name was Polly. Polly Porcelain, to be exact." She sat down, settling Candy in her lap, smoothing the wrinkled, discolored blue dress and the tousled hair as if holding a real child who had come in all mussed up from playing outside. "Dad took her away from me when I was like six."

"Why?"

"He was punishing me for something. I don't remember what. I still remember what he told me, though." She leaned forward and said, in a low voice, "He told me he was going to take her out in the woods and bury her. He said she'd be out there under the dirt forever, and it was my fault for being bad." She sat back and was silent for a moment, then said, "I guess he didn't really do it."

"Nope," Janice said. "I found her in the basement."

"Really." Beth's gaze flicked to her daughter, then to Richard. "In the basement."

"Uh-huh. Then all the lights went out."

"You were in the basement when all the lights went out?"

"Uh-huh. It was dark. I was scared."

"I'll bet," Beth said. "Richard?"

"Beth?"

"We'll discuss this later."

"Great," Richard said.

Suddenly, a sound like a gigantic electrical spark ripped through the kitchen. After a moment, Janice announced: "Candy says that was the man from the electric company."

The three of them went to the front porch. The wires were off the sedan, but a uniformed worker was sprawled on the ground nearby. The paramedics were working on him; the onlookers, their patience rewarded with an injury, had gathered on the near side of the street so they could kibitz about the injured man's prospects. Then the paramedics spoiled the show by loading him into the ambulance and zooming off, siren screaming.

"Candy says he's gonna die," Janice said.

Beth took Candy away after that.

Janice cried and pouted. It wasn't Candy's fault, she said; Candy didn't *make* it happen, she just knew about it, and that wasn't the same thing. Candy needed her. Candy was her friend. Candy was lonesome. Candy was scared. Candy didn't want to go back downstairs. On and on and on she went, until finally Beth sent her up to bed early, then gave the doll to Richard and told him to do something with it, she didn't care what, just as long as Janice didn't get hold of it again while they were here. He was pretty sure Beth was planning to take the doll home with her when they left; after that, managing its interactions with Janice—for instance, preventing any more spooky predictions—would be her problem.

So now Richard stood in the basement, at the foot of the stairs, directly under the long greenish fluorescent bulbs, clutching the doll, his only companion on a subterranean adventure through a scary old dungeon. Though it wasn't so scary now that the power was back on. He went to the box of unfinished scarves he had knocked over earlier and tucked Candy into it. The sickly fluorescent lights gave the doll's porcelain face a baleful cast, as if expressing its tiny fury over being relegated to the cellar again. But it wasn't as if she was being taken out and buried in the dirt. She was safe and warm in a bed of hand-knit softness. Not so bad, right? No reason to be angry.

Still, he tucked a little skein of yarn over her head before he left her there, just so she couldn't glare at his back as he walked away and shut off the lights.

2

THEY WATCHED THE NEWS AT eleven; Beth wanted to see if the man who had been electrocuted out front had really died. Richard slouched on the sofa alongside her, barely able to stay awake through the coverage of local political squabbles and the tales of community interest and the weather forecast and the *blah-blah-blah* of the commercials. Then, somewhere in the middle of the sports scores, Beth muted the television and elbowed him back to alertness. Richard was afraid she was going to bring up Janice's adventures in the basement, but instead she said, "You haven't asked what I found out at the hospital."

Realizing just in time that *I don't care* was not the correct response, he said: "What did you find out at the hospital?"

"Dad had already made arrangements to be cremated. They had to perform an autopsy first, which they were doing when I stopped by this morning, so we can figure he went into the oven some time this afternoon." That turn of phrase gave Richard a deeply uncomfortable feeling, as if they were talking about a pie or a gingerbread man. "They'll have the ashes at the Magee Funeral Home on Orchard Street. We can pick them up there tomorrow."

"Pick them up?"

"Well, we can't just leave them there."

"Why not?"

"Richard."

He sighed. "Okay. But what'll we do with them?"

"Anything," Beth said. "They told me there aren't any laws. Well, I mean, there are laws, but nobody enforces them. We could use the ashes as fertilizer if we wanted to."

"That'd probably kill the plants."

"He's dead." Beth turned the sound back on. "Let it go."

There were still some more local stories to sit through before the perky anchor said, "An Eastern Electric worker was killed today freeing a car from downed power lines." The screen cut to video of Potter Street, where the cop car, the ambulance, and the electric company truck all jostled for space in the road. Up on the hill, the old man's sagging white house squatted, a spectator eager for blood.

"The telephone pole was struck by a car, knocking out power to the block," the anchor said in voice-over. "The driver of the car, who has not been ticketed in the incident, told police that—"

Beth turned off the television. "Janice was right. How could she have known he would die?"

"Let's not lose our perspective. Janice didn't *know* anything. She was just shooting off her mouth."

"Yeah, yeah, of course. But she's never said anything like that before. Why start now?"

"Her grandfather just died. Even though she didn't know him, that's got to have some effect, right?"

"But after Mom died, she didn't—"

"She was a lot younger then. Besides, being in this house, it would make Santa Claus morbid." He looked at the silent television, then back at Beth. "Speaking of morbid Santas, I ran into Mr. Colosseo today."

"Who?"

"Mr. Colosseo. Lives down the street? Used to give us peppermints every Christmas when we were little?" She shook her head. "Okay. Well, don't feel bad about it. I couldn't remember his name for a while either. Anyway, he introduced me to the kid who called the ambulance for the old man."

"He did?"

"Uh-huh. His name is Pedro. He lives next door."

"Next door? Where the Martins used to live?" Then: "Duh, it would have to be there, since the house on the other side is gone."

"It is?"

"Yeah, it burned down. Looks recent. You can still smell the smoke. Don't tell me you didn't notice." Richard gave a little shrug;

he hadn't, of course. Beth shook her head. "You're hopeless."

Richard knew better than to dispute this.

She started chewing on her lower lip the way she did when she was thinking about something. "Next door, huh? Maybe I'll take a walk over there tomorrow."

"You really want to know all the details about what happened?"

"I'll never get another chance to find out, will I?"

"I suppose not. I don't think he really wanted to talk about it, though, so good luck with the interrogation, girl detective."

"Are you calling me Nancy Drew?"

"All you need is a cardigan and a flashlight. And I know where you can get a flashlight."

She took a playful swing at him with her right arm, which he caught by the wrist, so she took a swipe at him with her left. Dodging this attack caused him to fall off the couch, pulling her with him. They both ended up on the floor, Richard on the bottom and Beth on top of him, straddling his waist, punching him in the right shoulder with her free hand until he managed to grab that wrist too, stopping her from pummeling him. Laughing, she squeezed his hips with her knees, immobilizing him, leaning forward, hair hanging down toward his face, telling him to confess and she might let him up. Before he could think of anything to confess to, though, a voice said: "Mommy?"

They both turned. Janice, sleepy-eyed, stood in the archway to the front hall, looking at them. "Why are you on top of Uncle Richard?" she said.

He and Beth looked at each other. Feeling his face flush, Richard let go of her. She stood up hastily, her own face and neck bright red, which only made him blush more. He scooted back onto the couch and tried to look casual. "We were just wrestling," Beth said, running a hand through her hair to flip it back over her shoulders. "Like when we were kids. What are you doing awake?"

"I heard a big thump."

"That was Uncle Richard falling off the sofa."

"Like when I fall out of bed?"

"Yes," Beth said. "Just like that."

"But it was louder."

"Well, that's because Uncle Richard is so much bigger than you."

"But it was from upstairs."

"That's just the house playing tricks on you."

"But—"

"No more *buts*, kiddo," Beth said. "It's late." She went over to her daughter and picked her up. "Come on. Back to bed with you." Then, over her shoulder: "Good night, Richard."

"Good night," he said, as she exited the room. He heard the stairs groan as she ascended, then the floorboards squeaking overhead as she moved along the hallway to her old bedroom.

After the sounds had stopped, he sighed and turned on the television, hoping to find something distracting.

Richard was awakened by the wind outside the house, beating on the walls, making them creak and sigh. He could hear the bushes swishing and rustling against the windows. The curtains billowed inward from the windows, the sheers rippling like gauzy banners. He didn't remember opening a window. Maybe Beth had come down and done it, to air the place out. Good idea. Doomed to failure, but good idea.

He closed his eyes again and listened to the distant thunder, low and rumbling, far away, rushing through the darkness with its cargo of rain and wind and lightning.

The floorboards creaked overhead. Somebody was walking in the hallway upstairs, going to the bathroom, maybe.

Creak.

On the stairs now. Not going to the bathroom, then; coming down to the first floor. Maybe it was Beth. Maybe she couldn't sleep. Maybe she wanted to talk. Maybe she wanted to wrestle some more.

A flash of lightning penetrated his closed eyelids. Thunder rolled through the room. The storm was closer now, moving fast, coming toward the house. The floor in the front hall gave a little groan of protest as Beth stepped off the stairs. He listened, pretending to be asleep, as she walked slowly across the living room floor, deliberately, as if she was afraid she would trip over something in the darkness.

Lightning. Thunder. The storm had arrived impossibly quickly. The wind kicked up to a howl and the old house rocked and groaned and muttered. Something started banging on the kitchen wall, the sound echoing throughout the place, *thump-thump-thump.*

The footsteps kept coming. It seemed to be taking Beth a long time to get here. Finally she reached the couch and stopped. He could feel her looking down at him but he wasn't going to open his eyes, not until she said something.

Why didn't she say something?

Lightning flashed. He waited for the thunder, but it never came. At last he opened his eyes. The curtains flapped madly, streaming inward from every window, even though they were all closed. The storm flashed and raged, turning the glass into sheets of dazzling light through which nothing of the outside was visible. And beside the couch, with deep wells of darkness for eyes and a chin glistening with drool, the thick opaque plastic shroud from the hospital morgue draped over his shoulder down to cover the lower half of his body, stood the shriveled, pasty form of his father.

In a hoarse, bubbly voice, the old man said, "Wake *up*, Richard."

As he spoke, a single gleaming drop of saliva fell from his trembling lower lip. It splashed onto Richard's cheek.

Richard sat up on the couch, sweating, the room still and dark and quiet around him. No storm. No wind. No old man. Just himself, and the dissipating fog of his nightmare.

He flopped back and lay there, staring at the ceiling. Beth's bedroom was directly overhead. Was she asleep? What was she dreaming about? Probably not their father wandering around the house wearing his death-wrap toga. She hadn't seen him in the morgue, didn't have that memory to float up and haunt her.

Sleep wouldn't return, which given his recent track record with dreams was maybe just as well. He lay on the couch until the windows began to lighten; then he got up and went to the front porch to peer out at the waking world. Orange and yellow sawhorses surrounded the power pole that the car had crashed into. It had been reinforced with boards and angled braces until it could be replaced. He wondered if the electric company worker had been taken to the same morgue where his father had ended up.

He went back inside. He needed to wash his clothes again, but with Beth and Janice around, he could hardly strip down and throw everything in the laundry and hang around naked until it was finished; and so, once again victimized by his own lack of forethought, he climbed the steps to the second floor to raid the old man's wardrobe.

The upstairs hallway ran the length of the house, a long empty passage between two large windows, one at either end. He recalled once seeing a bird fly in through one of them, glide along the corridor, and exit through the other. He wasn't sure if this was a legitimate memory or only a story someone had told him once that he'd incorporated into his history, but he hoped it was true. It gave hope of escape, that lucky bird, just passing through rather than being mired here like the rest of them.

It was a long walk down the corridor, along those squeaking floorboards, past his old bedroom on the right, Beth's on the left; past the two spare rooms, growing space for a family that hadn't grown; past the door to the attic, narrow as a cruel, pinched nanny from a cautionary fable; past the bathroom where he had showered yesterday. He paused beneath the glow of the hallway's only working light, just outside the door to the master bedroom and suddenly he was a child again, eight or nine, and he was standing right where he was standing now, and his mother and father were beyond the door screaming at each other, threats and insults rendered incomprehensible to Richard by his parents' sputtering rage and his own fear. Beth crouched next to him, clutching his arm, fretting and crying as the flying word-weapons drew blood. This was the first fight that he remembered, but over the years the ferocious arguments would become a near-nightly ritual, growing increasingly intense until finally the last one ended with Mom storming out, grabbing Beth and Richard as she went by, not saying a word then or ever about their eavesdropping, hustling them down the stairs and out to her car, the old man following, hurling threats and entreaties in equal measure, as if he couldn't tell the difference between them anymore.

Up to his knees in the bubbling tar of the past, Richard had to remind himself that he wasn't a kid anymore, that Beth wasn't clinging to him for safety, that there was nobody on the other side of the door, no screeching argument, no sound of thrown objects thudding into walls. His mother had never explained what had finally driven her to leave when she did, and he had never asked, and now he would never find out. Not unless Beth knew what had happened. But he would have to ask her before she would tell him. He knew he wasn't going to do that. And what did it even matter anymore? They were dead, both of them, dead and gone. No more time for insults. No more time for accusations. Or for apologies, either, if anyone were inclined to apologize.

He shook the memories off and opened the door and went inside.

Almost everything was covered by something else; thick curtains hung over closed blinds on the windows, a tattered woven rug sprawled across the patchily varnished floor, somber grey sheets smothered the bed, faded streaky paper clung to the walls. There were no pictures, no snapshots of Mom or Beth or Richard, no old family portraits, no paintings. He crossed to the window and peeled back the curtains. Dust cascaded out of the folds, swirling through the streams of light that pierced the old wooden Venetian blinds; when he raised those, clickety-clack like flat bones, the streams became a flood, rushing in and filling up the room. Through the dirty panes of glass he could see the driveway below, his and Beth's cars, the garage, and beyond it the woods running up the slope, ending far away at the fenced backyard of another house on a street that ran parallel to theirs. It might as well have been a parallel universe. He unlatched the window and tried to lift it, but it wouldn't budge. Stuck, or painted shut, maybe. He could come back with a screwdriver and a hammer, break the seal, lift the window, let in the air the same way he had let in the light, chase away the stale odors of sweat and cigarette smoke and cheap cologne that filled the room.

He could, but he wouldn't.

Richard turned away, looked around. He imagined he could feel the space straining against the light, resisting, trying to push it back out; like the rest of the house, the old man's bedroom was accustomed to the dark, and enjoyed it. He went to the dresser and the wardrobe, a matched set built from the same plain, murky wood, made dull and streaky by a layer of dust. He opened the wardrobe. Cedar-lined, it smelled incongruously pleasant inside; he was almost tempted to climb in and shut the door and inhale the outdoorsy scent for a while. A wooden cane leaned against the left wall inside the wardrobe. He took it out, looked at it, turned it over in his hands, trying to picture the old man hobbling along, leaning on a third leg. He found that he couldn't summon the image and put the cane back, then began sifting through the clothes that hung from the crossbar. He had difficulty finding anything wearable, but eventually came up with an old flannel robe in red hunter's-cap plaid. He decided to wear that while his clothes went through the wash again.

As he took the robe down, the telephone rang explosively, making him jump. The phone, a big old rotary model made of dull black plastic or maybe even Bakelite, sat on a brown table next to the bed; when its bell trilled, he could feel the floor shake a little. He blinked at it for a second, wondering who could possibly be calling, then picked it up. "Hello?"

There was a moment of silence, then a *click* as the line went dead.

"Same to you," Richard told the phone, dropping the handset in the cradle.

Later, over a breakfast of cereal and toast, Beth asked him who had called. When he told her the caller had just hung up, she said, "Don't you think it's strange that we haven't heard from anyone about Dad?"

"Not really. I mean, I doubt he was anyone's favorite neighbor."

"Well, yeah, but still, you'd think *somebody* would call or stop by and at least pretend to be sorry. Even if it was just to find out what we've been up to for all these years."

"Most of them probably have no clue who we are. And anyway, I did talk to Mr. Colosseo. I'm sure he keeps everyone well informed."

Beth snorted. "Yeah, whether they want to be or not."

Just then the doorbell rang. This was so unprecedented that conversation halted as Beth and Richard stared at each other.

"Ding-dong," Janice sang.

"Speak of the devil," Beth said.

"And he appears." Richard stood. "I'll go see who it is."

The back door had no real bell, just a rotary knob that made a mechanical, vaguely musical grinding noise when turned, so Richard headed for the front hall. When he got there and opened the door, he found a man he had never seen before, wearing a neatly pressed ivory suit with a matching hat. Glossy silver hair, glossy black shoes, glossy white teeth. Too tall to fit beneath the dangling wrought-iron fixture on the end of its long dusky chain, he stood off to one side of the door. "Good morning," the man said, touching the brim of his hat.

"Can I help you?" Richard said.

"Oh, no, sir." The tall man reached into the pocket of his jacket and produced an ivory card, which he held out towards the door. "I am here to *offer* help, not *seek* it."

Richard opened the screen door and took the card, which had *Robert James, Antiquarian* printed on it in a handsome purple script. He looked from the card to the visitor. "This is you?"

"Ah," the man said, "a trick question. The card is not me; it *represents* me, as in the days when upper-class visitors would place their calling cards upon silver trays borne by their host's servant. Sadly, such niceties are now the etiquette of a bygone era." He touched the brim of his hat. "Robert James, at your service."

No one who talked like that could possibly *not* be selling something: Knives, encyclopedias, the secret to getting into heaven. Richard looked at the card again, then tucked it into his shirt pocket. When he returned his attention to the front door, he found a big hand waiting for him. He took it and a firm handshake ensued, after which the antiquarian failed to let go.

"Mr. Bartoski—I presume that you are the son of the late Walter Bartoski? Yes?—Mr. Bartoski, I would like to ask you to consider something. When a loved one dies, innumerable decisions must be made, not least how to dispose of the loved one's possessions. There are—"

"Are you kidding me?" Richard tried to tug his hand free, but James held onto it.

"Kidding you? No, not at all. Not in the least. Your father has done business with me in the past, and when I learned of his—"

"What sort of business?" Richard tugged on his hand again. James didn't seem to get the message.

"He sold; I bought. And I listened. He *needed* the money, but he *wanted* the listening, I think."

Robert James, antiquarian slash amateur pop psychologist. At least now Richard knew what had happened to the missing stuff, assuming the man was telling the truth. "Well, I appreciate your, uh, offer, Mr. James, but we don't know who's inheriting what or if there's even a will. So we certainly can't sell you anything. I'm sure you understand."

"Of course. But now we have arrived at how I can help you. Your father kept a set of ledgers, in which he recorded various information, including our transactions. The items I had already purchased, the dates, the prices, as well as a list of items he intended to sell in the future and the prices we had already negotiated for them. He was having a bit of memory trouble, you understand, and he needed the ledgers as a reference." James finally let go of Richard's hand. "You said that you were looking for his will?"

"No. I said we didn't know if there was one."

"Ah, that's right. Shades of meaning. Well, allow me to suggest that you seek the ledgers. If he had last wishes to express, he may have done so in them."

"All right," Richard said. "I'll keep that in mind."

"Very good. I would ask that you hang onto my card and keep *me* in mind as well. And please, allow me to extend my sympathies to you during this difficult time." He tipped his hat and executed a shallow bow, then turned and departed; Richard watched him amble down the long concrete sidewalk toward the street, where a shiny black sports car waited. It had windows so dark they might have been made of metal. James circled around the wedge-shaped hood to the driver's side, folded himself into the vehicle, and drove off.

Richard shook his head. What a phony. But was he telling the truth about the ledgers and the will? Richard took the man's card out of his pocket and looked at it again. It was a nice enough card, stiff ivory paperboard, lavender lettering, but there was no phone number, no address. Maybe it would help him keep James in mind, but how was he supposed to get in touch? Mental telepathy? He tore the card in half—this required more effort than he expected; the thing was surprisingly sturdy—and dropped it in the living room wastebasket on his way back to the kitchen.

"Who was that?" Beth asked.

"Some guy named Robert James," Richard said. "He's an antiques dealer or something. He knew Dad had died and wanted to stop us from throwing away any valuable junk."

"That was nice of him."

"Yeah." Then: "He claimed Dad had sold him stuff before. Do you think that might be true?"

"Mmm. I guess it would explain the missing furniture. Although I don't remember us having any antiques."

"Me either, unless you count the car. But that's still here."

Beth snorted. "Of course it is," she said. "Dad would've sold you and me both before he'd have sold that car."

Sitting at the tiny, scratched table at the far end of the kitchen, a cup of coffee slowly cooling in front of her, Beth stared at this one spot on the wall where the thick paint had bubbled and peeled away, uncovering a white splotch of plaster that looked like a person's head. Almost, anyway. A vague profile, hair and forehead and nose and lips and chin. Could be anyone. Could be Mom; could be Dad; could be Jesus; could be her.

Once upon a time, the kitchen hadn't been so run-down, so depressing. She remembered sitting where she was now, staying out of the way, watching Mom—always Mom, never Dad, who couldn't make toast and was proud of it—at work in the kitchen, mixing and measuring, and good smells emanating from the oven, sweets and desserts, spice cake and cookies and apple pie, the kind of treats you liked best when you were a kid.

Yeah, sitting where she was now, holding Polly Porcelain. She hadn't been able to pronounce *porcelain* properly then; it always came out *Polly Pollen* or *Polly Pusslen* or something like that. Then her father had abducted poor Polly and told her he was going to bury her out in the woods. Beth had believed him, and had spent many fruitless hours out there with one of her mother's little garden shovels, digging little holes, trying to find Polly's little grave, never suspecting that she had been imprisoned in the basement the whole time. And there she had stayed until Janice had found her and rescued her and rechristened her Candy. In a strange, irrational way, Beth felt like she had failed Polly, and that was why Polly had renounced her and taken up with Janice instead.

Someone stepped into the kitchen, too small to be Richard, so it must be Janice, returning from a loudly announced trip to the bathroom. "Did you wash your hands, kiddo?" Beth said. When she didn't get an answer, Beth glanced at the doorway, and froze.

Not her daughter.

It *was* a young girl, but older than Janice, taller, slimmer, blonder, and altogether more bedraggled than Beth would ever have allowed Janice to get. She was barefoot, wearing a smudged white frock that looked like a bed sheet. She stood near the front door, watching Beth with these huge blue eyes that seemed as big around as golf balls.

After a momentary shocked silence, Beth said, "Hi, honey. What's your name?"

No response, just staring.

"Where'd you come from?"

More staring.

Beth started to stand up, and when she did the girl pivoted and vanished into the dining room, silent as a mouse in moccasins. Beth reached the doorway a few seconds later. There was no sign of the mystery child. Her *own* child, though, had just entered from the living room, still adjusting her suspenders, making sure the princess and pony clips were correctly oriented and exactly where they were supposed to be. She saw Beth and stopped and said, "What?"

"Did you see anybody in here just now?"

Janice wrinkled her brow. "Like who?"

"Like anybody."

"Like Uncle Richard?"

"Somebody besides Uncle Richard," Beth said.

Janice shook her head.

"Nobody at all?"

Janice shook her head again.

Beth leaned against the wall.

"Are you okay, Mommy?"

"I'm fine, honey. Just tired, I guess."

Janice gave her a solemn look and said, "Maybe you need to take a nap."

Richard stood on the ratty woven throw rug and waited for the dryer to finish. His pants were still a little bit damp, but he figured a few more minutes would finish them off and then he could get the hell out of the old man's robe and put his own clothes back on. Then he would go shopping, buy a pair of jeans, a shirt or two, pajamas, or at least sweats. Something that was meant to be slept in. Maybe that would help with the weird dreams, the nightmares.

What would *really* help was getting the hell out of the house, but he couldn't leave Beth and Janice in this place alone.

The dryer buzzed and stopped churning. Richard opened it and felt his clothes. Hot and dry and a little bit stiff; the cheap fabric softener sheet hadn't done a thing except get stuck in his underwear. He quickly got dressed, then went upstairs. When he came out of the cellar, Beth was sitting at the foot of the stairs to the second floor, smoking a cigarette and staring at the ceiling. She didn't look at him as he closed and latched the basement door, but he could tell she was waiting for him. "Where'd you get the cigarette?" he said.

"I found a pack in the kitchen," she said. She inhaled, blew smoke through her nostrils. "You want one?"

"I quit."

She tapped some ashes onto the stairs.

"You quit, too."

She looked up at him. Inhaled. Blew.

"You weren't going to let a weed control you, remember?"

"The weed's not controlling me," she said. "I'm controlling the weed."

"How do you figure?"

Instead of answering, she said: "Have you ever seen a blonde girl around here? Big blue eyes? About twelve?"

Richard stared at her for a moment. "Why do you ask?"

She looked at him then, cigarette held off to the side, like some sort of noir *femme fatale*. "Holy shit," she said. "You have. You *have*, haven't you?"

"Yeah. Just before you and Janice got here. Where *is* Janice, anyway?"

"Bathroom. Again. Don't change the subject. Where did you see this girl?"

"I was in the basement washing my clothes. She came out of the furnace room and ran upstairs. I went after her, but—"

"But you couldn't find her."

"Right."

"And you didn't think to mention this?"

"What was I going to say? Watch out for Alice in Wonderland?"

"Well, I saw her just now, in the kitchen. She was there, right in front of me. She ran away when I started to get up and then she just … Disappeared."

"Really?"

Beth nodded, turned away. She took another drag on the cigarette; grey curls drifted toward the ceiling.

"I would've heard her running around up here. A hamster couldn't walk across these floors without making them squeak."

"I know that."

"So what—"

The sound of a toilet flushing gurgled down from upstairs.

Beth sighed. "Break's over." She squashed her cigarette out against the step, leaving a black smudge in the wood, then dropped the crumpled remains through the slats in the nearby floor grate and stood. Noticing his raised eyebrow, she said, "It'll give the place some character."

"Character is the one thing this shithole has in spades," Richard said.

Under Janice's expert supervision, Beth and Richard played a game of Rock-Paper-Scissors to decide who had to go pick up the old man's ashes at the funeral home. Richard lost. Beth gave him directions to the funeral home and sent him off, grumbling, to retrieve the cremains.

After he had left, Beth took Janice out the back door and into the driveway. The old path through the trees was no longer obvious, and she didn't quite remember where it was. As they searched for it, Janice said: "What are we looking for?"

"A trail."

"A trail to where?"

"Next door."

"Are we going next door?"

"Yes, honey."

"How come?"

"Because I want to talk to somebody who lives there."

"Who?"

"Nobody you know," Beth said.

"Why don't we go that way?" Janice pointed at the sidewalk.

"Because I want to go this way." She had finally spotted the path, back by the corner of the garage, almost fully obscured by encroaching undergrowth. She led Janice through the gap and into the woods. The way had become tight and overgrown, underbrush plucking at them with little fingers, low-slung branches bending toward them, leaves waggling as they went by. Beth could smell the woods, a blend of living and dead foliage, water, earth. Janice's small hand was warm in hers, holding on tightly. The dense trees shut out her view of the street and the surrounding homes. She could have been deep inside an endless primeval forest. Birds twittered as they fluttered from limb to limb; squirrels crashed and snarled overhead, dropping broken twigs and small branches in their wake.

She could tell when they had reached the midpoint of the path, because that was where the old iron bench was. Severe and straight-backed, adorned with curls and flourishes and a fleur-de-lis in the center, it stood beneath a rotting, incongruous garden arch: A sad remnant, perhaps, of a time when this little woodland had been part of someone's lawn, had been tended and cared for. Beth had found the bench while questing for Polly Porcelain and had adopted it, rubbing off the rust, clearing away the brambles, repainting it with cans of spray paint she'd sneaked out of the garage. She remembered sitting out here and talking to Polly, as if the doll could hear her in its unmarked grave.

The poor bench had fallen back into a state of decay since Beth had been gone; its once white surface was heavily marred by bubbles of corrosion and rust, and it was once again entangled in creepers and swelling brush. She had wanted to see it again, but now she was sorry they'd come this way. She would rather have remembered it as it had been.

She heard stealthy movement and noticed a chipmunk perched on a moldering stump next to the arch, keeping a wary eye on them. She nudged Janice and pointed the creature out. It vanished when her daughter reached a hand out towards it. Poof. Gone, like magic. That got her thinking about the hamster she'd once had, and what her father had done to it, right in front of her.

Ugh. This place. The memories. Things she hadn't thought about in years.

She started walking again, pulling Janice away from the chipmunk's erstwhile perch, and before long they emerged onto the driveway of the house next door. She went to the side entrance, rang the bell. No answer, except from a little dog; she heard its nails scrabbling along the floor inside, followed by a series of tiny rough-voiced barks as it tried to scare them off. Janice whimpered softly and tried to pull away. Beth glanced down at her daughter, then off to the right, where a rather dilapidated convertible sports car sat near the garage. Fuzzy dice dangled from the rear-view mirror. She hadn't been aware you could still get fuzzy dice. Anything that retro had to belong to a teenager.

She tried the bell again. The dog continued to provide the only response. She stepped back and looked up at the house just in time to see a curtain drop in an upstairs window. Someone was home, all right, but they weren't coming down.

Beth sighed. So that was how things were going to be, eh?

She took Janice's hand and led her daughter back into the woods.

Through the gap between the curtain and the window, Pedro watched the people from next door disappear back into the trees. Although he had never seen the woman before, he recognized the little girl from when old Mr. Colosseo had dragged him over to meet Richard Bartoski, so he figured this must be the sister they had mentioned. That little chat, brief as it was, had been excruciatingly awkward, leaving Pedro keen to avoid another one. Good thing his parents weren't home or they would've answered the door, invited the visitors in, offered coffee and snacks, and sat in on the conversation making comments and suggestions. God. How horrible would *that* be?

Pedro finished getting dressed, then went downstairs, grabbed a stale doughnut from a box his mom had brought home from work, and exited through the side door. Munching the doughnut while trying to clip his name tag to his shirt, he headed for his car, not really paying attention to his surroundings until the bushes rustled and the lady from next door emerged, little girl in tow. "Hi," she said. "I'm Beth Bartoski. I used to live next door. Are you Pedro? You met my brother Richard yesterday?"

"Oh. Um. Hi." Crap. She had been lying in wait for him. "Yeah. I'm Pedro."

"Do you have a few minutes?"

"I was just leaving. For work." He pointed to his department store badge, crookedly affixed near his breast pocket. "I'm running late."

"Just one minute?" Then, when he didn't answer: "Please?"

"Okay. One minute."

"So, uh, you found my father. After his stroke."

Pedro just looked at her. It wasn't a question, so it didn't seem to require a response, and he was sort of hoping that if he acted all uncommunicative, she would go away.

"Did he say anything to you?"

"Nothing that made sense."

"So he said *something*, then."

"Well, yeah. He said something." She didn't ask him what it was, and after a moment he opened the car door, and slid into the driver's seat. Beth came over and stood next to the car on the passenger side. All he could see of her daughter was the top of her head. "He said *quiet*."

"Quiet? That's it?"

"Yeah. That's it. That was all I could understand, anyway. His mouth was kind of messed up. I think he hit it when he fell." Pedro started the car; Beth backed off, looking crestfallen, as if she'd thought maybe the old man had given Pedro a deep and meaningful dying message to pass along. Feeling sorry for her now, and like a bit of a shit for ignoring her earlier, he added: "Look, I have to go, but I'll be home around four. If you want to talk about it some more, you can come back then, okay? Or I can come over there."

She nodded and stepped back, hoisting her daughter up onto her shoulders. Pedro released the brake and rolled out of the driveway, probably a little faster than he needed to. As he backed out into the street, she still stood where he'd left her, in the shade of the the trees, holding her daughter's hand, staring after him with a puzzled expression on her face.

By the time he cut the wheel to get his car pointed in the right direction, they were gone, vanished into the woods.

Idling at a red light that was taking forever to turn green, Richard glanced at the cardboard box on the floor on the passenger side. It was a rather attractive package, colored a soft pastel lilac, unobtrusively decorated with a string of lilies along the borders. The box could have contained a cake, but it didn't; it contained a mass of purple tissue paper and styrofoam peanuts and a small stainless steel urn with a locking airtight lid. Not particularly decorative, but functional. It was the sort of canister in which you might want to store coffee or sugar, if it didn't already contain a plastic bag full of cremains.

Cremains. That was his new word for the day. Come to Bentonville, grow your vocabulary.

He was having trouble reconciling the size of the canister with the body he'd looked at a few days ago. Hard to believe that the long, thin, stiff body of a man—a body that had occupied an entire drawer in the hospital morgue—could be reduced to something that fit into such a little container. It put him in mind of those silly cartoons where someone would sprinkle out a teaspoon of powder and put a drop of water on it and it would reconstitute itself into a steak or a cheeseburger or whatever. He found this idea disquieting and tried to put it out of his head, but now it was lodged there and wouldn't go away. Damn it.

Somebody behind him leaned on their horn; the light had changed while he'd been woolgathering. He returned his attention to the road, but soon found himself glancing at the box again. It was sealed with filamented packing tape, just like the split countertops in the old man's house. He couldn't decide if that was ironic or not.

A few blocks later, nearing Potter Street, he noticed a small shopping mall on the left, where an abandoned textile mill and associated worker barracks had once stood. He thought he remembered the decrepit buildings being demolished around the time they'd moved away. A department store anchoring the near end beckoned to him, the parking lot invitingly empty on this weekday morning, reminding him that he really needed to pick up at least one change of clothes. Would it be terribly gauche, he wondered, to take a detour on your way back from the funeral home and visit the mall while your father's ashes sat in the car?

Well, the old man needed to get out more anyway.

He turned into the lot, found a spot near the department store entrance, and went inside.

Quiet.

Beth sat with Janice in the middle of the wooded eastern third of her father's lot, where it was quiet indeed, and contemplated the old man's last words. Who had he been talking to? What had he heard that he was trying to silence? The pounding of his own unleashed blood? The accusing echoes of memories? The approaching thrush of death's black wings?

Death's black wings. God. It was like she was going back into her Goth phase. Maybe she needed to pick up dark purple tights and mauve lipstick and bruise-black nail polish and draw some gloomy sketches in a notebook with a skull on the cover.

Beth shifted around on the bench. The corrosion made it rough and scratchy. It needed a good sanding, a repainting. And a haircut: She had to keep brushing away an insistent vine that kept falling across her shoulder like an infatuated bus seat-mate who wasn't getting the message.

"Mommy, why are we sitting out here?" Janice asked. She had started fidgeting a while ago.

"Because I'm thinking."

"What are you thinking about?"

"Your grandfather. Some of the things he did to us."

"On account of he was an old bastard?"

"Janice, it's not nice to call somebody an old bastard."

"But Uncle Richard said—"

"Uncle Richard is a grownup. Sometimes grownups use words that little girls shouldn't. And he was angry. It's not polite to talk like that and he's sorry he did."

"He didn't *say* he was sorry."

"Well, sometimes people are sorry without saying so."

"Oh." Pause. "Was grandpa sorry without saying so?"

Beth smiled thinly. "I don't know, honey," she said, "but sometimes people do things that are so bad, they *have* to say they're sorry, and even then that's not enough to make it right."

"Really?"

"Yeah. Sometimes."

"What did grandpa do?"

She wasn't about to answer that one. "I'll tell you when you're older."

Janice heaved an enormous and elaborate sigh.

Beth said: "What?"

"You *always* say that."

"You're not older yet."

"I'm older than I used to be."

"Yes, you are. But you're still not old enough, kiddo."

Janice folded her little arms and harrumphed like a miniature schoolmarm. "I'll ask Candy what grandpa did. *She'll* tell me."

"How would Candy know anything about it?"

"She knows lots of things. She told me grandpa would come into the basement and talk to her and write in his book. Then he would go back upstairs and leave her alone in the dark again. He did that a bunch of times while she was there. Even when she was asleep, he would wake her up and make her listen."

For some reason, this throwaway fantasy raised the hairs all along Beth's neck. She could immediately picture the scene, the old man sitting at the bottom of the stairs, scratching away in a weak pool of light, talking to imaginary creatures in the dark. "When did she tell you that?"

"Last night."

"But Uncle Richard took her away."

Janice gave her a withering look. "Only because *you* told him to." Then: "She still came and visited me. We played while you were sleeping."

"What did you play?"

"Hide and seek. Tag. Patty-cake."

"Uh-huh." Beth was starting to tune her daughter out again.

"Then we had a tea party and she told me how she hit her head and died and burned up in the fire."

Beth processed that for a second, then said: "What?"

Janice didn't answer; she just smiled inscrutably, kicked her legs back and forth, and started humming.

Beth said: "Janice, what fire?"

"I'll tell you when you're older," Janice said airily.

Pedro had just finished racking some sport coats when he spotted Richard Bartoski wandering into the store. Crap. What was he doing here? Had his sister sent him to ask more questions? She knew where he worked, had seen his badge with the name of the store on it. He himself had made sure of that.

He ducked behind a nearby pillar as Richard passed by, keeping it between them until he was sure the man was searching for clothes and not answers. If he was putting on an act, it was a good one; he moved slowly, looking around in the vaguely unfocused manner of somebody who knew that what he wanted was probably nearby, but not exactly where to find it. Pedro shadowed him through the department, wondering what sort of attire an offspring of the strange and reclusive Walter Bartoski would choose. He riffled through the shirts in the clearance rack, selected two of them, moved on. He picked up underwear; he picked up socks; he picked up jeans. Nothing out of the ordinary. Not that they *had* anything out of the ordinary for sale here anyway.

Relieved, Pedro headed back to his station, where a customer stood at the register holding some argyle support hose. "I was starting to wonder if I should just leave my money on the counter," the guy said, waggling the package at him like courtroom evidence. Pedro apologized several times but the guy stayed pissy, even though he couldn't have been waiting more than a minute or two.

Richard Bartoski turned up after the sock man had left, while Pedro was straightening up a display of ties next to the register. "Hi," he said. "It's Pedro, right? You work here, huh?"

"Correct on both counts," Pedro said, tapping his name tag.

"I'm Richard Bartoski. We met the other day." As if Pedro might have forgotten. He nodded but didn't speak and after a second Richard said, "So, um, where are the dressing rooms?" Pedro pointed them out and Richard thanked him and headed off in that direction. Good. Keep things on a purely customer service level. No need to discuss other stuff. That was how the Walter Bartoski incident was to be filed: *Other Stuff, Not-To-Be-Discussed.*

Pedro glanced under the shelf of the counter, where a bank of small televisions granted a godlike view of the menswear department, if God had black and white vision: Leftover winter jackets, relegated to the hinterlands for summertime, way back in the corner; underwear racks, screened from the aisle by a rack of colorful tee shirts, because someone had once complained that it was intimidating seeing big men paw through packages of colored briefs; and, of course, the entrance to the dressing rooms, a wide maw in the wall, with racks on either side full of clothing that had been tried on and rejected. He watched as Richard Bartoski walked into view, looked around, and headed for the booth nearest the front. He went in and closed the slatted door behind him.

Safe at last.

Pedro looked away from the screens, then stopped, frowning, and looked back. Just as he'd turned his head, he could have sworn someone had entered the dressing room hallway, seemingly through the emergency exit to the parking lot, which was impossible, because it only opened from the inside, and if anyone had gone in or out that way an alarm would have started squawking. He certainly didn't see anyone in there now, although jagged, angular bands of interference were flickering across that particular screen, marching left to right, obscuring the image of the hallway. Some sort of malfunction with that monitor or camera, maybe. The others were fine. He reached down and thumped the unit a few times, even though they weren't supposed to do that. It didn't help. He switched it off and back on; that didn't help either.

Eyeing the static, he thought he detected a pattern in it, a grainy shape made of dots and fuzz and static that was independent of the drifting streamers, moving slowly forward, sometimes drifting left, sometimes right, progressing towards the front of the hallway. Almost like a person, lurching with an unsteady gait, checking each dressing room as it went, as if searching for something.

Or someone.

The nearest fast food joint was a five minute drive from the house. Janice kept chattering about this and that, pointing stuff out through the windows, talking nonstop, asking questions and never waiting for an answer. Beth only half listened. If she tried to pay attention to every single word that fell out of her daughter's mouth, she'd be ready for the loony bin in a week.

But once in a while … Once in a while the kid came out with a real zinger. Like that question about her grandfather. Was he sorry and he didn't say it?

Beth had never imagined the old man to be capable of remorse or regret; she had always thought of him as a sort of human bulldozer, plowing straight ahead on whatever path he chose, flattening anything in his way, never looking back. But maybe he *had* looked back, after it was too late, when she and Richard and their mother had all been running the other way.

Suddenly she realized that Janice was saying, repeatedly and with increasing vehemence, "Mommy!"

Beth looked at her daughter in the rearview mirror. "What?"

Janice pointed a small accusing finger back up the road. "You passed the restaurant!"

So then Beth had to find a driveway to turn around in, and of course she chose one that belonged to some old crank who came out on his porch and screamed obscenities at her for wearing down his blacktop—lots of new words for Janice to add to her burgeoning vocabulary—before they finally arrived at the burger place, with its welcoming aroma of meaty grease and fried potatoes. She went up to the counter and ordered the artery-clogging usual for herself, a meal with a toy in it for Janice. The teenager behind the counter asked her which toy she wanted, directing her attention towards a museum-style display case full of plastic figurines, characters she didn't recognize from a recent movie she hadn't seen. She turned to Janice and said, "Which one do you want, kiddo?"

Janice wasn't there.

Beth turned and scanned the seating area.

Janice wasn't there, either.

She moved away from the counter to get a look at the seats behind the fake potted plants and the festively painted trash containers.

No Janice.

She hurried to the exit, barged through, swept her gaze across the parking lot.

No Janice.

She told herself to relax, that Janice had to be nearby. She was pretty sure she'd had hold of her daughter's hand when they entered the restaurant. When had she let go? Probably when she'd stepped up to the counter and opened her purse. Beth turned and went back inside.

The kid behind the counter was leaning forward and looking at her. "Everything okay, ma'am?"

"My daughter—"

He pointed toward the restrooms. "She went that way."

Oh, thank God. Beth hurried up the dingy hallway to the ladies' room and pushed the door open. Single stall, sink, odor of disinfectant and cheap hand soap. Nobody inside.

"Janice?" she said.

Silence.

She went into the cubicle-sized chamber. The stall door hung open; someone had used the toilet and not bothered to flush. Lovely. Beth spun and hurried out of the restroom and there was Janice, standing in the hallway looking around. She snatched the little girl up and gave her a big hug, eliciting squeaks and squirms. Beth set her down, then said: "You shouldn't go off without telling Mommy."

"I told you I had to go to the bathroom."

"No you didn't."

"I *did*. In the car." She put on a pout. "You weren't listening. Again."

"Okay. I'm sorry. I'll listen better next time, all right?"

"All right."

"Good." Beth took Janice's hand. "Come on, let's go pick out a toy."

As they headed back towards the counter, Janice said: "That was a funny bathroom."

"Funny how?"

"There were two big white things on the wall. They were full of water and had little round things inside."

Beth looked down at her daughter.

"I think they were fountains," Janice said.

The jeans Richard had picked up fit pretty well, which he found worrisome, because they were larger than what he usually wore; the store didn't have his size so he had gone up one, expecting them to be nice and roomy, but they weren't. Tony was always trying to get him out to the gym. Maybe he needed to go.

He put on one of the shirts he'd selected and stood in front of the dressing room mirror. It was one of those multipart ones where you could look at yourself from multiple unflattering directions, as if there were six of you, all facing different ways, all equally out of shape. He shifted himself from foot to foot, turned sideways, searching for an angle from which he looked fit and trim and, while he was at it, five years younger and with better hair. He kept not finding one.

What was that?

Richard paused, peered at the vertex where two panels of the mirror joined, creating strange dimensions of reflectivity. He thought he had spotted something where the shiny surfaces met, some unexpected sight in the glass, but now it was gone. He moved a little closer, tilted his head left, tilted it right. The shape he had seen in the depths of the junction didn't return.

Wait.

There it was.

He had to look at the mirror sidelong, using his peripheral vision. A third of his reflection was on one pane and a third was on the other; the remaining third was missing. In the glass between the two incomplete pieces of himself was something drawn and grey, far off in the deep vertex, an extended amorphous thing, a face bent in on itself. He looked over his shoulder. Nothing was behind him, no face, no figure, just cheap streaked wallpaper and a hook screwed into the sheetrock, with the other shirts hanging from it. Maybe that was what he had seen: Shirts, swaying a little, doing a little dance, turned into a phantom by bad lighting and a quirk of reflective interplay.

Maybe.

He turned back to the mirror and the thing he had seen was closer now, so much closer, and it wasn't shirts, it was a person that had been folded in half. Its stubby arms were outstretched, its head lolled on rounded shoulders. The lower part of its body was a wrinkled shapeless mass, like bunched plastic, and suddenly he recognized it: The old man, still in his garb of plastic from the morgue, coming forward as if to embrace him, delighted at a chance meeting. *Richard! Hello! It's been so long!*

He reflexively scrambled backwards, away from the mirror, realized that meant he was moving closer to the thing reflected behind him, tripped over the shoes he'd left on the floor, and fell over. He hit his head on the wall, saw stars, closed his eyes, opened them again.

The shape in the mirror had disappeared. He was looking up at the buzzing fluorescent light. Somebody was knocking on the dressing room door and asking him if he was all right.

Richard pushed himself to his feet and started putting his own clothes back on. "Yeah," he told the door. "Yeah, I'm okay."

"You sure you don't need help?"

"Yeah." He recognized the voice now; it was Pedro. Always turning up when Bartoskis fell down. "I'm fine."

"I can call—"

"I'm fine." Fully dressed in record time, Richard opened the door. The kid was standing just outside, a concerned look on his face, glancing all around, as if searching for blood spots on the dressing room walls.

"Okay. You didn't … Nothing weird happened just now?"

"No. Nothing. I got tangled up putting on pants and fell. That's all." He gathered up the clothes he'd been trying on, pushed past Pedro, hurried out of the dressing rooms. "I'll take all of these. Can you check me out?"

"Uh, sure. Yeah, of course." Richard followed Pedro to the checkout, where he paid for the clothes and left.

He didn't wonder, until he was back on the road, why Pedro had asked him if anything weird had happened, and if he should have told him the truth.

Returning from lunch, Beth parked around back, in the shade of the house and the trees, guiding her car into the same spot she'd been in before. Richard's car wasn't there. She wondered, idly, why it was taking so long for him to get back. It wasn't like the hospital was so very far away. He'd probably gotten sidetracked by something, as usual.

She let Janice out of the car and started walking toward the back door, but Janice hung back, looking fearfully at the house. "Come on, kiddo," Beth said after a moment.

Janice, eyes wide and focused on something over Beth's shoulder, shook her head slowly.

"What's the matter?" Beth asked.

"Candy says we shouldn't go inside. There's something bad."

"Janice. Candy is a doll. She can't talk. She can't tell you things. She isn't even here."

Janice pointed. "She's at the window."

Beth looked. Was that a flicker of movement through the dining room blinds?

No. Nothing.

She turned back to the car. "Janice, listen to me. The only bad things in this house are memories. They can't hurt us. They're just memories." She knew she was talking over Janice's head now, but at this point she was speaking as much to herself as to her daughter.

Maybe more so.

"But Candy says—"

"I don't care what Candy says. Come on." Beth took Janice's hand and pulled her toward the house. The little girl dug in her feet and started shrieking and after a moment Beth stopped. Janice was sobbing. Marvelous.

"Okay, honey. Shh, it's okay. You can wait in the car. All right?" Beth shepherded Janice back into the wagon, started the engine, turned up the air, engaged the locks. Then she backed off and shut the door. "You stay in here until Mommy comes out," she said through the closed window. "Don't unlock the doors for anyone except me. I'll get our things and then we can go to a hotel. Okay?"

"No! Don't go!"

Beth turned her back on the car and walked to the house.

"Mommy, don't go!"

She hesitated at the step, glanced behind her. Janice had her little hands pressed flat on the glass, her face up against it, her breath making amorphous fog patterns that the air conditioner obliterated; they formed and faded, formed and faded, like a flickering ghost.

Beth shook her head. A flickering ghost? Really? Richard was right. This place made them all morbid. No wonder he was still out there noodling around doing whatever he was doing instead of coming back like he was supposed to.

She crossed the mudroom and entered the kitchen. The house was quiet, except for its usual faint creaks and groans. Funny how quickly she had grown accustomed to its wheezing, its sighs, the half-remembered background noise of her childhood. The odor of stale tobacco remained pungent. She moved into the dining room, circled the table to the window. The blinds were drawn. She opened them and debris cascaded out, dust and dead bugs, an icky harvest of bad housekeeping. The car was only a few yards away. She could see the top of Janice's head inside. The kid had slouched down in the seat, sulking, she hoped; a nice quiet sulk was always preferable to an unhinged meltdown. She wondered what had set Janice off, why now was the time she planted her tiny flag and refused to come inside. It wasn't like the place had changed since yesterday, when she'd been happily swinging her feet off the edge of the table in the kitchen. Maybe taking Candy away had been a mistake, reducing it from a physical presence to a victimized doom-whispering phantom that lurked in shadowed windows. When Richard got back, she would have him retrieve Candy from her hiding place—which, as per Beth's instructions, he hadn't disclosed, lest she be tempted to go and retrieve the doll—and negotiate with Janice the terms of her return.

For now, though, the best thing she could do to assuage the kid's fears would be to emerge from the house unscathed.

Beth closed the blinds and headed into the living room, which was exactly as they had left it, like a shabby smoker's lounge. No bad things here, either, no monsters slouching on the sofa watching obnoxious daytime TV with the volume up too loud. She continued on to the front hall. Empty. The cellar door was closed and latched. She frowned, wondering for the first time why it had a latch on this side. Did the old man think there were scaly creatures in the basement that might come slithering out at night? She undid the latch, opened the door, looked down into the dark. The air wafting up smelled like mildew and dampness and old paper.

As she stepped back to shut the cellar door, she noticed the front closet was open a little. Had Richard been poking around in there? Abandoning the basement for the moment, she went to the closet and opened it the rest of the way and peered inside. A couple of musty coats. A few pairs of shoes. A smell of mothballs. Dirty girl-sized sneakers the color of strawberry cotton candy sat on the floor, shoved back into the corner. She didn't remember them, but they must have been hers. Had their father grown sentimental and kept old footwear around for nostalgia's sake? Did he make them pretend-walk around the house? Beth didn't want to know. She backed out and shut the closet door, turned around, leaned back against it, regarded the empty silent foyer and living room and staircase up and staircase down. She was starting to feel ridiculous. Why was she even hunting around for Janice's nonexistent bogeyman? When she got back to the car, if the kid asked if she had found something bad in the house, she could just lie. Went through it top to bottom, honey, didn't find a thing. Candy doesn't know what she's talking about.

Beth pushed off the closet and climbed to the second floor to collect their things. The stairs went creak, creak beneath her feet. At the top, she stepped into the long hallway that ran from one end of the house to the other, window to window. She looked through the one behind her, at the crowns of the trees spreading close to the house, a canopy of green just beyond the glass. Her own face was reflected in the pane, a faint transparent image superimposed over the foliage. The distant hallway light formed a fuzzy nimbus around her head, as if she were one of those benevolent spirits in an old religious painting.

Richard's old room was to her immediate left. Devoid of furniture or carpeting, its only remaining features were the curtains hanging over the windows. She went inside. Richard's bed had been there, his dresser there. She eyed the closet, once full of clothes and shoes and boyish junk; now its door hung open on a vacant space. Not even a single wire hanger swayed on the wooden bar. No sneakers sat on the floor, but she spotted a grimy baseball back in the corner, covered in dust. On the right, the red brick fireplace stood as it had when she was a girl. Its stones were discolored from smoke and soot, though she had never seen a fire in it; the hearth was stopped up with wallboard on which she and Richard had drawn a happy watercolor fire, eternal and unchanging. Somehow, now, it seemed more pathetic than cute.

She continued up the hallway, past the spare bedroom, as thoroughly empty as Richard's room, without even the benefit of curtains. She stopped at her old room. A couple of dressers, neither of which she remembered, were jammed together in a corner, along with a coffee table up on its side. The old sleeping bag that she'd brought occupied most of the floor space, and their suitcases—hers black, Janice's pink and decorated with ponies—occupied the rest. She noticed a scrap of yellowed paper sticking out from behind one of the dressers and went to retrieve it. It turned out to be one of her old pencil drawings, a sketch of a pop band she'd once liked, all spiky hair and sensitive eyes. The walls of her room had once been festooned with such artwork, but it had been ages since she'd drawn anything. She didn't even know where her old portfolio was, thank God. She could only imagine what embarrassments it contained.

Beth hesitated, her gaze alternating between the stuff she was supposed to be gathering up and taking to the car and the door at the far end of the hallway. Finally she folded her arms and moved on. Past the bathroom, empty and quiet. Past the door to the attic, always kept locked. Ending up outside her father's room. The door was closed. She stopped in front of it, hugging herself.

Was the old man sorry? She would never know.

She turned the knob and pushed the door and followed it as it swung inward. She went to the middle of the room, stood right in the center of the big discolored woven rug. "I'm leaving," she told it. "*We're* leaving. We're leaving and we're not coming back. What do you think of that?"

The room sighed then, a long, creaky sound, the house settling into its foundation, the floorboards adjusting to her weight. Like she had told Janice, the only bad things here were the memories that they brought with them.

She went to the window that overlooked the driveway. The window was unlatched and she tried to lift it, but it wouldn't move. Painted shut, swollen with moisture, jammed in a frame that was no longer square. The car sat directly below. She couldn't see into it, just the roof and the windshield. Wisps of vapor drifted from the exhaust; water condensing from the air conditioner trickled away from underneath it.

Beth heard a thump from behind her, a hollow, wooden noise, like someone slamming a heavy book down on a table. Startled, she turned around. The room looked exactly like it had when she came in. Nothing had moved. Nothing had changed.

Thump.

The sound had come from near the bed. Was there an animal in here? A squirrel, an opossum, a rabid raccoon?

Thump.

Suddenly Beth wanted to be out of this room. Out of this house. Out of this town. Why had she even come here? Why had she brought her daughter? She looked at the bedroom door just as it swung closed as if blown by a wind she couldn't feel. She was there an instant later, scrabbling at the knob. It refused to turn. She backed up a few paces, staring at the door, muscles tense. She knew all about busting doors down; she had been inside of more than one room, watching it happen. You didn't charge shoulder-first like a battering ram. You kicked as hard as you could, right next to the knob, and you kept kicking until something gave way. The hinges were on this side, which made things more difficult, but the door itself was flimsy, hollow. She could break it.

As she prepared herself to deliver the first blow, she heard the sound again from behind her. *Thump.* But this time it was followed by another sound, a softer one. Something sliding.

She turned to face the noise.

There was a dark little table beside the bed, a phone stand with a single wide drawer. The drawer had opened. Inside she could see a book, a blue book with a gold design on the cover, drawn like a maze. The pattern reminded her of the surface of her mother's old electric hot plate, concentric resistors inscribed under glass. The inlay was damaged, though, burned and scraped, as if someone had taken a soldering iron to it or it had shorted out.

She didn't approach the table. Whatever was in the book was nothing she needed to read.

Then she heard the shriek of old, dry wood surfaces grinding against each other as the window overlooking the driveway slid upward, all by itself. There was no screen. August air rushed into the room, bringing the smell of trees and leaves and rain. The book lying in the drawer skipped to the bed. Its blue covers parted. The pages began riffling, as if in a powerful wind.

A voice whispered, *Elizabeth.*

"No," she said.

Elizabeth.

"No!"

Elizabeth!

She put her hands over her ears and screamed, "Quiet!"

By the time he reached the old man's house, Richard was thoroughly disgusted with himself. He'd acted like an idiot in the store—that mirror thing, falling down and hitting his head, rushing out with his bags like he was being chased by a pack of hounds. God. That Pedro kid must think he was nuts.

The driveway crunched and crumbled under his tires. As his car climbed the hill and came around the curve, he saw the back end of Beth's station wagon. She had talked about maybe taking Janice out for lunch but apparently hadn't, or else they were back already. But when he got closer he saw something on the windshield, a big dark shape that shouldn't be there.

He parked behind her car, got out, feeling something in the pit of his stomach, something like sharp icicles, growing and pushing and pricking his guts. He slowly approached the vehicle. He heard muffled crying from inside. Janice was curled up in the back seat, sobbing. And Beth lay face-down on the windshield. Her head was twisted around impossibly far on her neck. The windshield had cracked beneath her. A little bit of blood trickled from her mouth, onto the glass, following one of the cracks down to the hood, along the rain channel, where it disappeared. He imagined it might eventually find its way down to drip onto the driveway, just like the faucet in the kitchen had been doing into the sink. *Ping. Ping. Ping.* But there was no knob he could turn this time to stop the flow.

Beth.

Dead.

Beth dead?

Behind him, he thought he heard the house laughing.

3

RICHARD STOOD BESIDE BETH'S CAR and waited for the police to arrive.

He had gone inside to call 911 from the phone in the kitchen, and then he had turned around and come right back out again. Not unlike what that kid, Pedro, might have done when the old man died, except that this wasn't some grumpy neighbor he hardly knew. This was his sister.

911 had told him not to touch anything as long as the engine was running and the air was on and Janice didn't appear distressed. Distressed? Ha. Yeah, Janice appeared distressed all right, but it wasn't because of the temperature. She stayed hunkered down in a little ball in the back seat and wouldn't even acknowledge his presence as he spoke to her through the glass and told her that it would be okay, the police would be here soon, everything would be fine.

Yeah, sure. Everything would be fine once the cops would arrived with their resurrection machine and brought Beth back to life.

He kept feeling a gaze on his back. The old man's wintry eyes, maybe, his restless, plastic-shrouded ghost roaming the creaky halls and derelict rooms, peering out at him from every dirty window as he shuffled by. Richard refused to give the house the satisfaction of looking at it. He stayed at the passenger side instead, trying to calm Janice down, without success. Not surprising, considering that she was stuck in the car with her mother's dead face staring at her. So he stood there and told Janice useless lies until finally two uniformed officers walked in from around the side of the house, a man and a woman, accompanied by a nondescript guy in a loose brown sport coat with matching slacks and a woman lugging a hefty box. Richard wasn't sure how long it had taken them to get here. Seemed like forever. The costumed crime-fighters went over to the car, walking around it, not touching anything, while the woman set down the box and removed various pieces of photographic equipment as if preparing for a fashion shoot. The guy in the sport coat came over to Richard and got out a little spiral notebook. "Hi," he said. "Arthur Leeson, homicide. You're the one who called this in? The brother? Richard Bartoski?"

"Yes."

"To all three?"

"Yes. All three."

Leeson nodded and wrote something in his pad, then shooed Richard away from the vehicle so the woman could take unobstructed pictures of the car from all different angles. When she was finished, the detective ambled over to Beth's body and felt her wrist. He stood there a moment, then frowned slightly and scribbled something in the notebook. He let go of Beth's wrist and reached into his pocket and pulled out a thermometer and leaned it up against the wheel of the car, then walked back over to Richard.

"Tell me, Richard," he said, looking at the thermometer, "has your sister been in the shade since you got here?"

"Uh, yeah," Richard said. "I mean, I think so. I don't know. I wasn't really paying attention to the lighting."

"Of course." More information went into the little spiral-bound pad. Then he stood there quietly and watched as his two companions investigated the car and the photographer blew several rolls of film taking pictures of everything in sight: The house, the garage, the trees, the driveway. After several minutes Leeson bent over and looked at the thermometer, pocketed it, and wrote something else in his journal. At about the same time, an ambulance rolled into view, lights flashing but siren off. A set of paramedics tumbled out. Leeson, now studying the house, didn't appear to notice the new arrivals, but the uniformed officers went over to have a hushed conversation with them, gesturing at Beth. The paramedics looked disappointed. They started rattling around in the back of their vehicle, getting their stuff together, but not with any particular urgency.

"What, uh, what do you think happened?" Richard said.

"Well, it looks to me like your sister fell head-first from at least the second floor." Using his pen instead of his finger, he pointed at the nearest edge of the roof. "From up there." Below the eave was a tiny octagonal attic window. Leeson moved his pen to aim at that, hesitated, then said, "Nope." He lowered it further, to the window to the old man's room. "Or maybe from there."

"That window's painted shut," Richard said. "I tried to open it this morning and couldn't."

Leeson grunted and fell silent for a minute, then aimed his pen at the second story window and said: "Can you take me up to that room?"

"Sure. But can we get my niece out of the car first, please?"

"Oh. Yeah. I don't see why not." He called over the female officer. "Sherry, would you do the honors?"

Sherry snapped on a pair of latex gloves and tried the handle, then looked their way and shook her head.

"Do you have a key to your sister's car?" Leeson said.

Richard didn't. After attempts to persuade Janice to open the doors from the inside failed, Sherry resorted to using some police implement, a long flat ribbon of metal which she slid down into the door through the window gasket to snag and release the locking mechanism. As soon as Sherry opened the door, Janice rolled out, scrambled over to Richard, and fastened onto his leg. He pried her loose and picked her up, rocking her and mumbling blandishments in her ear. After a few minutes of this, Leeson caught his eye and tilted his head towards the house. Richard nodded and started forward, but Leeson made a little *uh-uh* noise, pointed at Janice, and shook his head. Richard, unsure of what he was supposed to do with Janice if Leeson didn't want him bringing her in the house, stopped and stood there feeling thick and stupid until Sherry came over and collected her. Janice had gone limp, apparently having fallen asleep while Richard had been holding her. All that crying had worn her out.

"After you," Leeson said.

Richard went inside, Leeson following him through the mud room, the kitchen, the dining room, the living room. The house echoed around them. They went into the front hall and up the stairs to the second floor, where Richard paused and said, "Do you think somebody pushed her out the window, Detective Leeson?"

"I don't think anything yet. And please, call me Art."

They proceeded down the hall to the old man's room. Richard reached for the door but the detective waved him away and pulled on a glove before trying the knob. It turned silently. Art pushed the door inward, then stood there looking around. The room was just the way Richard remembered it, except someone had closed the drapes again. Beth, maybe, but Beth wouldn't have had any reason to come in here and do that. He couldn't see her idly tidying up while Janice sat in the car.

Something else was different, too, but he couldn't figure out what.

Art went to the curtained window, the one he thought Beth might have fallen from, and threw open the curtains. The window was closed, the blinds raised. He tried to open the window. Richard watched him strain for a moment, then looked at the other wall. He noticed a faintly lighter spot on the paper where a picture had once hung. He remembered it: A family portrait, him and his mother and his father and Beth. He shut his eyes and tried to imagine a world where the family hadn't fallen apart, where that picture was still there. In that world, Beth would still be alive. Their mother probably would be, too, and maybe even their father. But would there be a Janice?

"Hmm, what's this?"

Richard turned. Art was crouched on the floor near the window. "Did you find something?"

The detective glanced at him. "Huh?"

"Did you find something?"

"Oh." Art pointed to a smallish black blob on the floor. "Purse."

"So she *was* in here."

"Well," Art said, "her purse is." He dug his fingers into the bag, took out her wallet, looked at the license. Richard saw the green and white of money, the yellow and red of plastic. "I guess we can rule out robbery."

Richard sat down on the edge of the bed. They could rule out robbery. And they could rule out suicide, at least from here, because the window didn't open, and even if it did, even if she jumped from it, she couldn't have shut it behind on her way out, couldn't have closed the drapes. So, what, then? The roof? What possible reason could she have had to go up there? And if she had, why was her purse in the old man's bedroom? None of it made any sense.

Yet there she was, with a broken neck on the hood of her own car.

The smell. That was what had changed in here. The room smelled like leaves, like grass and rain, as if fresh outdoor air had gotten in. But that would mean the window had been opened, which it couldn't have been. It was painted shut, stuck in place. Unless maybe the house was holding it shut, keeping it closed, the way a clench-jawed kid refused to take her medicine or eat his peas. Maybe the house had opened the window like a mouth to spit Beth out and then closed it up tight again. He almost said something to the detective, but stopped himself before he spoke. Nobody would thank him for voicing an insane theory like that.

Suddenly Richard realized that Art had come to stand nearby, looking down at him with an expression of mild concern. "You all right, Mr. Bartoski? You look like you're going to be sick."

"I'm okay," Richard said, but his voice sounded unfamiliar to his own ears. Distant. Weak. Unconvincing.

The detective seemed unpersuaded. "Maybe you should wait outside, get some air. Come on, I'll walk you out."

And so Richard found himself being escorted through his childhood home like a terminated employee being shown to the door by security. As they started down the stairs, Art said: "I do have a question and a request. First, the question: Is there any access to the roof from inside the house?"

"To the roof? You can go out my sister's window and climb the drain pipe. We used to get up there that way." He thought of all the times he and Beth had done that, so many years ago, swarming up the rusty old iron like a couple of rats.

"Drain pipe. Uh-huh. And is this something an adult who was not a ninja could do?"

"Um, probably not. But there are also a couple of dormer windows in the attic that you could squeeze through if you were small enough."

"Was your sister small enough?"

Richard thought about it, trying to scale the openings from the size his child-self remembered. "Yes, I think so."

"Am I?"

Richard thought about it some more. They were passing through the living room now. The sofa where he and Beth had been sitting last night sagged and glowered. "Maybe."

"Are you?"

"No."

"Okay. How do I get into the attic?"

"The skinny door in the upstairs hallway. It's probably locked. It always used to be, anyway. But we knew where the key was hidden."

"We can open it without the key," Art said. They had reached the mud room, and here, Art stopped him. "Okay. Now, the request. I know this is going to sound cliché, and I don't want you to start getting paranoid or anything, but I'm going to need you to stick around for a while."

"Stick around? You mean here, in the house?"

"In the house? No. You'll just get in our way. Stay with a friend, get a hotel room, it doesn't really matter. We'll contact you when we're done processing the scene. Just make sure we know where to reach you." Art turned and headed back into the kitchen.

"I don't have any friends in Bentonville anymore," Richard said.

"Then a hotel room it is," Art said, shutting the door behind him.

Rosalie Mancuso was staring at her computer and trying to choose a synonym for *feckless* when the assistant editor for local affairs, Alan Akins, appeared and sat down on her desk. He looked at her screen for a few seconds, noted the highlighted word, and said: "Incompetent."

"*Incompetent* is accurate, but not exactly what I'm going for. And get off my desk."

Alan grinned and stood up. "Listen, can you drop that for a little while?"

"Because why?"

"Because we just got wind of a developing situation. A woman jumped or was pushed off a roof. She landed on her own car and died right in front of her six-year-old daughter. I need somebody to go check out the situation."

She stared at him. "For God's sake, Alan. I don't work on stories like that. Send one of the ghouls."

"The ghouls are busy. Roy is at a conference and Steve is in

Albany and Alison is at the State Fair, and we are not the *New York Times*, so that leaves you."

"I see." She closed the file she was editing, a series of mostly anonymous interviews with the employees at the Bentonville mayor's office regarding the behavior of their boss, who was being investigated by the state for instigating or participating in various flavors of cronyism, chicanery, and crooked schemes. Allegedly.

"Where?"

"136 Potter Street."

"Potter Street?" She drummed her fingers on her desk. "Where that house burned down the other day?"

"Yep. Right next door. Also where an EE worker was electrocuted yesterday afternoon. And where the occupant died of a cerebral hemorrhage Monday morning. Picture the headline: *Street of Death Claims Another Victim*."

She rolled her eyes at him.

"Too much? What if we just focus on 136? *House of Death Claims*—"

"Please, just stop."

"Hey, like I said, we are not the *New York Times*. But we do need to sell papers. Which means we need to report on news. Which means you need to take a little drive. You should get out more anyway. You're too pale."

"I like being pale. Pale is healthy."

"Pale is tubercular."

She stuck her tongue out at him, then started looking for her purse. "So the police are there now? Do we know who's running the scene?"

"We do. I think you're familiar with him. Arthur Leeson."

She looked at Alan for a moment, then sighed and said, "You could have just led with that, you know."

"What fun would that have been?" Alan gave her desk a couple of quick raps with his knuckle, then left, pausing to look back over his shoulder. "Tell your dad I said hello."

Richard stood in the mud room for a minute or two after Art had returned to the house, contemplating the single pair of boots, the chipped paint, the dusty glass of the windows. He wasn't the only one who didn't have any friends around here anymore. Finally he went outside. A sheet lay across the windshield and hood of Beth's car, the outline of her body visible beneath it. Yellow police tape stretched around the perimeter of the wide spot in the driveway. On the right, it was wrapped around one of the supports of the awning that the old man had built; it ran from there to the trees, where it followed a zigzag path to the edge of the house. On the left, it started at a young maple growing near the garage and then went along the side of the driveway, cutting over in front of Richard's car to the house. The male officer was just securing the final length of tape to a rusty garden hose faucet. Richard watched him tie it off and then step back, apparently admiring his handiwork. "Sorry, I didn't catch your name," he said.

The cop looked at him. "Officer Michael Sheets." He had an official-sounding voice, deep and pleasantly confident; Richard imagined him finding a career as a departmental spokesman if he ever got tired of the beat.

"Where ... uh, where did the ambulance go?"

"They had another call that took priority," Sheets said.

Richard felt an irrational annoyance that some other patient was considered more important than Beth, even though there wasn't anything the paramedics could do for her besides zip her up in a bag. "They'll be back, though, right?" he said.

"Yes, sir. Don't worry. Someone will come for your sister."

Of course they would. "Do you know where Janice is?"

"Officer Smith is interviewing her inside our vehicle."

Interviewing a six-year-old. Like she was looking for a job. Sorry, kid, you're not qualified for anything.

Richard heard something open above him and, turning, saw Art's head sticking out of Beth's bedroom window, neck craned around to the right. Looking for the drain pipe, probably. Richard looked for it himself and discovered it wasn't there anymore; all that remained was a vacant downspout and a long, ruddy vertical smear of rust along the wall. Art's head swiveled and then he was looking down at them, Richard and Officer Sheets and Beth's car and body. His gaze moved back and forth a few times. Richard could almost see geometric figures materialize in the air as Art judged distances and trajectories. He was no expert but it was obvious that Beth couldn't possibly have come flying out of that window and landed where she had; the window was too far away, and the angle was all wrong.

"Mike," Art called, "can you come in here for a minute?"

"Excuse me, sir," Sheets said. He went into the house.

Art pulled his head back inside, but Richard could see him skulking near the window. Keeping an eye on the scene, making sure nobody disturbed the evidence. After a little while he disappeared from the window, and a little while after that, he came out of the house. Richard said: "Find anything?"

The detective shrugged. "The window in your father's room looks like it hasn't been opened in twenty years. I got some prints off it that seem to match the prints Sherry took from your sister. I've also got unknown prints that I assume are yours or your father's. I'll need samples from you, okay?" Richard nodded. "Thanks. The door to the attic was locked, like you thought it would be. Your sister's window was locked until I opened it. The drain pipe you remember has rusted away or been removed."

"Yeah, I noticed just now," Richard said. "Beth always says—said—I'm not very observant."

Art shrugged. "Most people aren't."

Officer Sheets emerged from the house, passed them, headed for the garage. Richard watched him.

"I thought maybe a ladder was used to gain access to the roof," Art said, "and tasked Mike with looking for one."

"Oh. Okay. If she used a ladder, wouldn't it still be up against the house?"

"It would, unless someone put it away."

"Ah." Richard thought about this. "But nobody could have carried her up a ladder."

"Not likely. She would have had to have gone willingly. Maybe she was called up to look at something. A tilted chimney, damage to the shingles, a nest of squirrels. Whatever. It's a steep roof; she could have slipped and fallen. The other person could have panicked, climbed down, put away the ladder."

"I wasn't here," Richard said after a moment. "I was at the store."

"I know. I'm just saying." Pause. "Is there any other way onto the roof that you can think of?"

"No. Not really. Maybe she climbed one of the trees?"

"There were no obvious marks on her clothes consistent with climbing a tree. Though it's a little early for me to speculate on that subject. Forensics will need to take a closer look."

While they were talking, Officer Sheets had given up on the garage doors and gone to the smaller one on the side. He spent a moment jiggling the handle on the side door of the garage, then took a step back and stared at it.

Art said: "Who has keys to the house?"

"Huh? Oh, as far as I know, just me and my sister. I still had mine from, uh, before, and she took a set we found here. We didn't ... I mean, we weren't close to my father. We wouldn't know if he had given one to anybody else. But we haven't lived here in over ten years and my key still worked, so that tells you how old the locks are."

Art grunted and made some more notes in his little book.

The sound of breaking glass from the garage drew Richard's attention. Sheets had smashed a window on the side door with his nightstick. As Richard watched, he cleared away the remnants of jagged glass and reached through, trying to open the lock from the inside. "I might've been able to find a key for that," Richard said.

"We'll reimburse you for the window. Just file a claim." Art put his hand on the hood of Beth's car. "Since the girl was in the car and the engine was running, I figure your sister was planning to leave when it happened. Any idea where she might have been going?"

"Maybe to get lunch? Janice is hungry, like, all the time."

The detective chuckled a little. "Yes, I remember how six-year-olds are." Then: "How do I get into the basement?" Richard must have made a face, because Art raised an eyebrow and said, "There *is* a basement, right?"

"Oh, yeah, there's definitely a basement. The door's in the front hall, underneath the stairs to the second floor. Do you need me to show you?"

Art smiled with half his mouth. "I think I can probably find it."

"Okay. Be careful. The light in the stairwell is burned out, so it's dark until you get to the bottom and turn on the fluorescents."

"Noted," Art said. He hung around until Office Sheets came out of the garage before going inside. Just after he left, a white and red van pulled up the driveway and stopped with its nose barely touching the crime scene tape. A replacement ambulance, not in any hurry, come to take Beth away.

Bye, Beth.

~~~

Detective Leeson stood at the bottom of the stairs, looking around. Richard Bartoski hadn't been lying; it was dark as hell down here, even with the fluorescent lights doing their flickery best, which, to be honest, wasn't very good. And man, was it jammed full of crap. Boxes and clothes and old lamps and sawhorses and all kinds of other stuff. The fire department's worst nightmare. Funny how the upstairs parts of the house were nearly barren, while down here was an overstuffed cheese danish of junk: A cheap psychological metaphor just waiting to be explored.

He made his way to the two dark, narrow doorways in the wall opposite the bottom of the stairs, starting with the one on the left. He switched on the light, looked inside. It was a little clone of the large room: Crates, bubble wrap, filthy small appliances, threadbare blankets, an old ironing board, wooden folding chairs, so tightly-packed it looked like someone had shoved it all in there with a bulldozer. He turned off the light and moved to the next room, which was oddly barren, a virtual dungeon cell, dank, windowless, mildew creeping along the walls. Furnace, pipes, water heater, gas line. He smelled stagnant water and guessed there would be an open sump. Drawn by the incongruous void, he went in and peered around. It was as empty from the inside as it had appeared to be from the outside.

Wait. What was that?

Art sidled between the furnace and the wall to reach the corner, emerging with moist grey streaks across his shirt and pants. Now he was in a sort of nook between the furnace and the water heater, where a big grey pipe came in through the ceiling and disappeared into the concrete next to the sump. Peering in through the gap behind the furnace, he'd thought he'd seen something else in this little open space, a small shape sitting on the floor with its back against the pipe, but the only thing there was a coil of yellow rope lying on the floor near the pipe. Must have been a trick of the shadows.

He stood there, regarding the rope, which looked nearly new. It looped around the pipe a few times and was kinked in a couple of spots, as if it had once been knotted. What was it doing here? He frowned, his gaze moving from the rope to the pipe to the rope again.

He had just about decided that he should collect the rope and have forensics test it when he heard something from the doorway at his back, a low murmur, like someone talking under his breath, then a little patter of soft laughter. No, not really laughter; more of a chuckle. It had a distant, hollow quality, like a weak radio transmission.

Art pushed his way out past the water heater, which looked like less of a tight fit than the furnace route but wasn't; he almost got stuck between it and the wall. He sucked in his gut and let out all his breath and managed to squeeze through to the other side. No one stood in the doorway or out in the basement, but someone was muttering nearby. He reached beneath his jacket and put a hand on his gun, just in case, then called: "Is anybody there?"

The muttering stopped immediately.

"This is Arthur Leeson from the Bentonville police department," he said. "I'm here investigating a suspicious death. Whoever you are, come out now."

A hollow, whispering voice said, *Arthurrrr Leeeesonnnn*. Stretching out his name, tasting it, pulling on it like taffy. He stood there as the whisper rolled in through the open doorway like a breath of fog, filling up the tiny room, surrounding him, clinging to him, icy and fetid. Then, suddenly, there was something next to him, a grey presence, black eyes and skin like cobwebs. It fell against him. He reeled for a moment under the blanket of the voice, the fog. The room blurred, the walls sagged like melting wax. He felt a sharp tug at his holster and he reflexively spun away, jerking his pistol free to get it away from whatever was grabbing for it. A moment later something cold touched the underside of his chin and he realized it was the business end of his sidearm. Good God. He aimed the gun away from himself. The safety was off. How had that happened? He stepped away from the wall. The basement was utterly silent. Nobody was in here with him.

Feeling displaced and unsteady, Art set the safety, then holstered his weapon. He went back to the niche with the pipe and the rope, but the rope was gone. He stared at the spot where it had been until he noticed something dirty and yellow just below the surface of the sump. He got down on his hands and knees and lifted the end of the rope out of the water. It was saturated and filthy, as if it had been in there for months. Baffled, he let go of it. It fell back into the water like a dead snake. Sensing a presence in the room, he stood and turned, half expecting to see a shrouded figure with eyes like cigarette burns looming behind him; but, no, nothing, nobody. He was the only one down here. He had always been the only one down here.

He heard a gurgling chortle from directly behind him, as if a sneering perpetrator lurked in the sump, his face just breaking the dank, oily surface of the water. He looked at the floor and saw a long, wet handprint on the concrete, right between his shoes. Even as he stared at it, it faded away to nothing.

Art scrambled out of the nook, out of the furnace room. The stairs were only a few yards away. At the top, the cellar door stood open. Daylight spilled into the basement from above. He plowed through the trash-laden cellar to the steps, warped slabs of unpainted wood with ratty rubber mats nailed down for traction. He climbed them fast, not even pausing to turn off the fluorescent lights.

And if he heard something giggling in the cellar behind him, he pretended that he didn't.

Richard, still standing at the edge of the driveway, glanced at the back door as Art emerged from the house. He seemed kind of pale, shaken. Richard wondered why. Art dusted off his jacket, looked around, focused on Richard, motioned him over, and went back inside. Richard followed him into the kitchen, then to the tiny breakfast table. Art pulled out a chair and dropped into it. He pushed the opposite chair out with his foot. Richard sat down. "You all right, detective?" he said.

"Yeah." Art rubbed his eyes. "Working too hard, is all."

Richard raised an eyebrow. "Are there that many homicides in Bentonville?"

"You'd be surprised," Art said. "Can we go over again how you and your sister ended up coming back here?"

So Richard re-explained the situation to him: Why he and Beth were at the old man's house, how long they had been here, what they had done, where they had gone, whom they had talked to. No, they hadn't seen any suspicious characters lurking around. He didn't mention the disappearing girl. No, Beth didn't have any enemies. Her asshole ex-husband? He had moved to New Mexico a while back and, as far as Richard knew, she hadn't heard from him in at least a year. Art wrote it all down in his little notebook. Finally he closed the book and put it away and looked around the kitchen and said, "So what are you going to do with this palatial estate, Richard?"

"Oh God. Am I allowed to burn it down?"

"I'm afraid not. But if you do, make sure no one is inside. That way I won't get the case."

"Deal." Art seemed back to normal now, pallor gone, gaze steady, confidence restored. The routine of question-and-answer had clearly gotten him back on a proper footing. But what could have happened to rattle him so thoroughly? Surely the old man's basement wasn't the worst place he had ever been. Richard almost asked, but decided if it was something Art thought he should know, the man would tell him. Instead he offered to make coffee. Art accepted and Richard got to work locating all the necessary raw materials, which Beth, being Beth, had neatly put away in places Richard didn't know about. He was just pouring water into the reservoir when the doorbell rang. He automatically turned to go see who was there, but Art stopped him. "I'll get it," he said. "You carry on making coffee. That's an important job you've got there."

Richard nodded and went back to work, while Art got up and exited the kitchen. He returned shortly with Officer Smith and Janice in tow. Janice immediately ran to Richard and latched onto his leg.

"Hi, kiddo," he said, stroking her hair, the exact shade of red as her mother's. She kept her face pressed against Richard's chest, occasionally making a choked squeaking noise.

"How's she doing, Sherry?" Art said.

"About as well as could be expected," she said. "Not very talkative."

"Mmm." Art looked at Richard. "You and Janice stay here a minute, okay?"

"Okay."

Art and Sherry disappeared into the dining room for a hushed discussion, presumably about important police things that Richard wasn't supposed to know about. After a few minutes Art returned, alone. The coffee was ready and he poured himself a cup, then said, "I'd like to talk to the little girl, Mr. Bartoski. Bring her into the living room, please." He turned and went through the archway. Richard carried Janice to the couch and sat down with her still in his lap. Art and Officer Smith weren't there. Art's coffee cup rested on top of the television, letting off wisps of steam. The house was quiet, except for Janice's snuffling.

Suddenly the telephone beside the sofa emitted an explosive mechanical ring that made Richard jump. Cursing under his breath, he picked up the handset. "Hello?"

"Hello. Mr. Bartoski? This is Robert James. I was wondering if this would be a good time for—"

"No," Richard said. "This is not a good time. This is literally the opposite of a good time."

A pause. "I see. Has something happened? This morning, I thought we had made a connection that—"

"Well, you were wrong. We didn't, and we aren't going to. Don't call here again."

Richard slammed down the receiver just as the front door opened and Art appeared in the foyer. The detective came into the living room and eyed the phone. "That sounded friendly. Anybody I should add to my list?"

"You already know about him," Richard said. "It was that antiques dealer I told you about." He looked around. "Christ. He keeps calling. I don't even know who owns all this shit yet."

"Well," Art said, "I'm no probate expert, but unless there's a closer relative you don't know about, or a will that says otherwise, or a lot of back taxes to be paid off, I can't see it going to anyone but you."

"That's just great. I lose my sister and I gain a broken-down house full of worthless crap."

"Hell of a trade, huh?"

"Yeah," Richard said. "Hell of a trade."

Rose parked her car on the street, right behind a police cruiser, and sat there a minute peering at the house. She had to admit that it *was* kind of creepy: Tall and narrow, dirty chalk-colored clapboards, dusty panes of glass, a small expanse of trees on either side. The upward-sloping lawn rose to meet the edifice, overgrown grass tufted with unkempt bushes, through which a stained white walkway led to a small front porch, bearded by shrubbery, within which lurked a front door like a small mouth waiting to bite.

There wasn't anyone in the cruiser. Her father's mustard-yellow sedan was parked farther up, blocking the entrance to the driveway. That usually meant no further emergency vehicle arrivals were expected. She got out of the car and took a picture of the place; the readers of the *Herald-Journal* would doubtless want to see what a Death House looked like so that they could either avoid it or come and stare at it. The slanting rays of the sun struck orange fire against the second-story windows. Rose lifted her second camera and took another shot, color film this time. Black and white tended to reproduce better in the paper, but sometimes the boss liked to pretend he was running a glossy magazine, with the full spectrum at his disposal. To her eyes such attempts always came out looking like one of those old 3D movies viewed without the benefit of blue-and-red glasses, but whatever.

Before moving into the yard itself, Rose glanced up and down the street. It was a few hours after the incident but there were still some gawkers present, mostly older men and women standing in groups of two or three along the street, keeping a respectable distance from the scene. A cop moved among them, talking, writing things down. Hunting for witnesses, gathering statements.

Rose was drawing looks from some of the bystanders, who would naturally assume she was with the police department. She started up the front walk. The reflected glory of the sun shifted as she moved, the windows becoming dark, revealing the outlines of the rooms within. As she neared the front door, she saw movement in one of them, a vague shape in the dimness beyond. An occupant? A police investigator? She stopped and eyed the window. It was on the right side of the house, partially hidden by a tree; from the street, a spreading canopy of leaves and branches obscured it from view, and she had only just reached a position where it was visible. She saw the movement again and a moment later a little blonde girl rushed up to the glass. She wore a simple grey smock or shift, streaked with grime, as if she'd crawled through a heating duct that needed a cleaning. As Rose watched, she put both her palms flat on the window, traced its frame with her eyes, then reached up and started fumbling with the window latch. What was she doing? To get a better angle, Rose took a few steps toward that end of the house, raised the camera with the black and white film. Her finger came down on the shutter release just as the window slid silently upward.

Click.

As the girl wriggled halfway out of the window, Rose slowly lowered the camera, realizing she meant to jump. Rose said, "Don't —", but her voice got tangled up in her throat as a new figure appeared behind the girl. It was roughly person-shaped but strangely ill-defined, and its proportions were off in a way that Rose couldn't quite define. She lifted her camera again, but she was too slow; arms seized the girl and yanked her back inside before she could get a shot. And then the window was closed. It didn't slide back down; it just wasn't open anymore. Rose ran closer to the house, her gaze never leaving the window, but there was nothing to see. Just black glass, blank and reflective. No girl. No shape. No nothing.

"Excuse me, ma'am?"

She turned. The officer who had been talking to the neighbors was coming up from the street. Rose didn't recognize her.

"This is a possible crime scene, ma'am. May I ask what you're doing?"

"I'm a reporter from the paper," Rose said. "I'm here reporting."

"Can I see some credentials?"

Rose handed over her identification. The cop looked at it, then at her, then gave it back. "Well, press or not, you can't be wandering around the property right now. I'm going to have to ask you to return to the sidewalk and not enter the yard again without permission. Okay?"

"Could I talk to the detective on the scene?"

"He'll tell you the same thing."

"I'd like to talk to him anyway."

The cop looked at her, then shrugged and said, "Follow me." Rose trailed her around the left side of the house, up a length of steep and rather decrepit blacktop, through the narrow gap between a little foreign car and the house, then around the back left corner to a spot where the driveway ballooned out into an asphalt aneurysm. She knew better than to try to take a picture, so she surveyed the scene, memorizing details she might use in an article: Old house, old trees, old garage, old carport with funky antique sedan underneath. Old old old. A station wagon was parked near the house; it would have looked out of place even without the damage to the windshield and hood. A man was on his hands and knees, peering beneath the wagon, shining a penlight at the undercarriage.

"Detective Leeson, this woman would like to speak to you."

The man withdrew, squinted up at Rose, and sighed.

"Hi, Dad," Rose said. "How's the investigation going? Any bad guys under there?"

The officer said: "Dad?"

Art clicked off the penlight and tucked it into one of his many pockets, then sat back, wiped his hands on his trousers, stood, and looked at the officer. "Every time the hounds at the paper get wind that I'm investigating something they think might be newsworthy, they send my daughter. As if I'm going to slip up and tell her what's in the soup, so they can pass it along and get the citizenry all hot and bothered."

"Hot and bothered is our bread and butter."

"You sound like your pal Alan."

"He's not my pal. He says hello, by the way."

"I'm sure. Sherry Smith, this is Rose Mancuso, née Leeson. Rose, Sherry."

"Pleased to meet you, Sherry," Rose said, shaking Officer Smith's hand.

"So you're Rosie Reporter?" Sherry said. "I should have had somebody show me a picture."

"I'm surprised they don't have it posted at the station," Rose said.

"Now there's a good idea." Art turned to Sherry. "Got anything for me?"

"Not much." Sherry gave Rose a little side-eye and waited for a nod from Art before continuing. "Nobody heard any arguing or raised voices. Nobody saw any vehicles coming or going. Nobody saw anyone carrying a ladder, or anyone on the roof, or anything else unusual."

"You think she fell off the roof?" Rose said.

"Either that or from a beanstalk. Don't put that in your story."

"*Looking for a giant,*" Rose said, pretend-writing on her palm with her finger. Art snorted. She put her imaginary notebook away. "Hey, is there a girl in the house?"

"Yeah. The deceased's daughter."

"Blonde? Ten or eleven?"

He shook his head. "Redhead. About six."

"She's the only one?"

Art gave her a funny look. "What's with the fishing expedition? There's no other girl present. Just the daughter." He turned as the door to the house opened and a man came out, carrying a child in the crook of his arm. An officer Rose had seen around but never spoken to came out after them and shut the door. "That's her right there."

Rose examined the girl. Definitely not the one she had seen upstairs in the house trying to open the window. Not old enough; not blond enough; too well-dressed. She clung to the man, arms around his neck, face buried against his shoulder. Rose turned her attention to the guy. Was he the big shape she had seen? She didn't think so. He was much broader than it had been, and properly-proportioned. He carried a little pink and purple suitcase in his free hand. The bag was festooned with stickers of cartoon ponies. Rose's acute journalistic instincts told her it belonged to the girl, not the man.

Art pointed at the suitcase. "Going somewhere?"

"To a motel. Assuming we can leave."

"Sure you can leave. Like I said, just let us know where you're going."

"And you are?" Rose said.

The man glanced at her, then back at Art. "Who's this?"

"That's my daughter, Rose, the reporter. She was just leaving."

"Are you related to the victim?" Rose said.

"I'm her brother, Richard. This is her daughter, Janice. We're not giving interviews today."

Art said, "Sherry, would you mind escorting Rose back to the sidewalk?"

"Not at all."

"I can escort myself," Rose said, just as the little girl lifted her head, looked around blearily, and asked for her mother.

"Hush," Richard said. "Mommy's not here."

"Where's candy? I want candy."

"We can get candy later."

"I want candy *now*."

"I have lollipops." Rose fished around in her purse. The confections had settled to the bottom. She pulled one out and offered it to the girl. "You like grape?"

"Thanks, but she means her doll," Richard said. "Candy is its name." To Art: "Can I go get it? It's in the basement."

Art exchanged a glance with the officers. Rose knew that look. Police telepathy. If they let this guy—civilian, relative of the deceased, automatic suspect—go back into the house and take something from it, that would tell her a lot about what they thought of the incident.

Finally Art said: "Okay. Officer Sheets will go with you. Don't touch anything you don't need to touch."

"Right. Thanks. Does somebody want to, uh …" He tilted his head at his niece. Sherry went over. Richard transferred Janice to her, then went back inside with the other uniformed officer. Sherry hoisted Janice up onto her shoulders and started giving her a horsey ride around the driveway. Rose thought she saw the kid eyeing the lollipop that she still held in her hand, so she unwrapped it and held it up in the air. Janice snatched it, Pony Express style, the next time she and her steed went by.

Rose sidled over to her father. Speaking from the side of her mouth, she said, "So you don't really think this is a crime scene? What are we looking at, then? Suicide? Was there a note?"

"No comment," Art said. Then: "You carry lollipops around now, huh?"

Rose shrugged. "You want strangers to talk to you," she said, "sometimes you have to give them candy."

Richard, escorted by Officer Sheets, went back to the basement to retrieve the doll.

He didn't really want to be down there again, and took the steps slowly. Carefully. Listening. It was quiet as a coffin. He paused at the bottom of the stairs, looking at the junk. It had been disturbed since his last visit. He supposed Art had done that while he was down here looking for … Well, whatever he had been hoping to find. A hidden perp. A ladder. A signed confession.

From behind him, Officer Sheets said: "You do know where this doll is, right?"

"What? Oh. Yeah. Sorry."

Candy's new resting place in the box of scarves was near the washer and dryer, under the stairs. Sheets sat down on the bottom step to wait as Richard went around to the machines. There was the tower of boxes, scarves on top. He pawed through them, half expecting the doll to have mysteriously vanished, but she was still there, nestled in her bed of fabric, little doll eyes closed, little plastic doll face frozen in an eternal imbecilic smile, dreaming pleasant doll dreams.

He picked her up. Her bright blue eyes opened.

But they were painted on, not the type that rolled from asleep to awake.

Richard stared at her for a few seconds. He held her horizontal, then vertical, then horizontal, then vertical. The eyes stayed open. He must have just imagined it. Tucking Candy into the crook of his arm, he made his way back to the stairs. When he got there, he discovered that Officer Sheets had disappeared. Where had he gone? Up the stairs? No, Richard would have heard them creaking, and on top of that, the stairs themselves had changed. Now, no door—open, closed, or otherwise—stood at the top to allow egress from the basement; the steps ended at blank drywall.

As Richard stood there staring up at the non-exit, something started chuckling in one of the little rooms behind him. He began to turn, to see what might be standing in the doorway looking at him, but just then Candy twitched to life and jumped out of his arms. Her little feet landed with a quiet plastic *click* and she darted off into the rubbish.

Unthinkingly, Richard chased after her.

He hadn't gotten far before his shin thunked into something much more solid than most of the boxes down here. Moving aside a threadbare curtain and a mildewed trench coat, he discovered a sturdy wooden chest. The dry, faded exterior was bound together with tarnished bands of scalloped brass, as if the old man had dug it out of the sand at some sheltered buccaneer cove. It had a big hasp on the front, held shut by a staple that was turned sideways and secured with a padlock. Crouching down, he gave the lock a half-hearted tug. God knew which of the old man's treasures would require such heavy-duty security. Well-thumbed copies of pornographic magazines? The nonexistent family silver whose theft Mr. Colosseo had postulated? Richard dropped to his knees, lifted the lock, looked at the keyhole in the bottom. He thought of the keyring Beth had found and wondered if it contained one that would fit.

Thump.

He looked up sharply. It sounded like something inside the chest had banged on the lid, hard.

Thump thump.

He backed up a pace.

Thump thump thump.

The padlock bounced and rattled as the chest vibrated. He put his palm on the lid, feeling a powerful thudding from within, as if a little man with a little hammer was trying to cudgel his way out. What could possibly be moving around in there? An animal? A leprechaun? A battery-powered toy, inexplicably come to life?

Suddenly Candy rose up from behind the chest, touching it with her little ceramic hands, painted blue eyes locked on Richard's. He had the feeling she would tell him something, if only her brush-stroke lips could move. "Did you want me to find this?" he said, then felt like an idiot. Asking questions of a doll. What would be next? Arguing with his reflection in the mirror?

Richard. Welcome back.

The whisper came from everywhere and nowhere. The doll withdrew and vanished. Richard jumped to his feet and looked around, but didn't see anyone or anything.

Then the light in the utility room came on.

It didn't come from the incandescent bulb in the ceiling; this was a pale, cold, dusty light, like radioactive talc, giving the room a bluish-white color. He could *hear* the light, almost, a sound like sand falling, falling on stone, bouncing, skittering across a chiseled surface. Something slithered out from there, up the wall, undulating across the ceiling. A rope. Yellow nylon. Cheap, but strong. He knew what was coming, but it was if he were already trussed up tight; he couldn't move, could only watch as the rope wound its way along the brown beams, the pipes moist with condensation, until it was right above him. He lifted his head as it dropped on him, striking like a tree snake. It landed on his shoulders and looped down behind his back, catching and binding his wrists; it sent its other end down his legs, twined around them, whipsawed back and forth between his ankles, tied itself in knots. Then the rope jerked his feet out from under him, wrenching them up towards the ceiling. The cellar spun around him as he fell. The back of his head hit the floor. The ceiling disappeared in the glare of a dozen popping bulbs.

The next thing he knew, he was stuffed into the corner of the utility room, between the furnace and the water heater, lashed to the cold rough pipe. The lights were out, the room black as the inky depths of a cave, but he would never mistake this location: The smell, the feel of the pipe against his back, the floor beneath him. The fingers of his right hand trailed in the icy water of the sump.

Being here meant he was being punished. But for what?

It's your fault Beth is dead.

"No," he said.

You let your sister die.

It was the same voice he'd heard when the rope had come for him. "I didn't," he said, his words disappearing into the darkness. "I didn't."

Of course you did. Were you here when she needed your help? Were you there for your mother? You as good as killed them yourself.

"I didn't."

You did. If you'll just admit it, I'll untie you. I'll make you forget all about what you did to them.

"I didn't do anything!"

That's right. You didn't do anything. You never do anything. And that's why you belong down here, Richard.

"Quiet."

And this time you'll never leave.

"Quiet!" he shouted.

And that was what he got: A sudden, utter, watchful quiet.

So stubborn. I'll just leave you alone here in the dark for a while so you can think it over. The voice withdrew, becoming distant. *And we'll see how long it takes you to change your mind.*

Pedro stood in front of his window, buttoning his shirt, staring across the sloping field of trees toward the roof of the old man's house. The cops had only just closed up shop for the night, leaving the house barricaded behind plastic sawhorses and yellow tape. The place had looked weird in the upward-slanting glare of the lights they had set up, as if it were telling scary campfire tales with a flashlight under its chin, but the gloom they left behind after being switched off was worse. In that darkness, anything could be happening.

He turned away from the window. He could still feel the night at his back. He pictured something grey and gaunt and tenuous sitting on the roof of the old man's house, clinging to the chimney, staring across the darkness at his room. Watching him. Waiting for him to come back. "I won't," Pedro whispered. "I won't come back." But the imaginary grey thing just kept watching him, placid and patient. It knew better, and it had all the time in the world.

He was going out tonight with Sandy and Pete, to a movie and then dancing. Sandy had a friend who would meet them at the movie theater, somebody she said she thought Pedro would like. He didn't have high hopes. He already knew who he liked, and was mainly concerned with keeping it hidden from everyone else.

Got him thinking, that did. Hidden things. Obvious things. Take the old man's house. To Pedro, it was obvious that the place was rotten inside, but that hadn't stopped Richard and Beth Bartoski from staying there. And then Beth Bartoski threw herself off the roof —Pedro's mother had told him all about it; somehow she always knew the local scuttlebutt even though she was never home—right in front of her own daughter. A few hours later, another ambulance had come and taken Richard Bartoski away. Nobody knew why the second ambulance had been needed, exactly, but his mom said the neighbors were atwitter about it up and down the street. Those Bartoskis, they're all crazy.

But were they? Maybe, having been children there, they were too close to the place to see what it had become. Maybe he should have said something to them, told them how it had felt when he had been in that front hallway, making the call to 911: The air of unwelcoming, of rejecting pressure, as if an invisible broom had been trying to sweep him out the door. He'd had multiple opportunities, had taken none of them. Did that make it his fault, what had happened to them? Was he responsible? Could he have made a difference?

A horn tooted out in front. He checked himself in the mirror to make sure he looked presentable, then ran down the stairs, through the living room, out the side door. "Don't stay out too late!" his mother called after him.

He didn't.

Sandy's friend didn't show up for the movie, and he couldn't get into the show, being the extra person sitting next to Sandy and Pete and holding onto everyone's popcorn. The friend was already at the Palm Beach Under 21 Club when they got there—apparently there'd been a miscommunication about the plan for the evening—and she'd already hooked up with some guy and spent the night dancing with him while Pedro sat in a folding chair flanked by a piece of plywood painted like a coconut tree and a plastic kiddie pool filled with sand. Then Pete's buddy Glenn wandered in, declared that the music sucked, and convinced everyone, including Sandy's friend and her dance partner, that they should try another club down in the valley. Pedro begged off and they dropped him at the curb in front of his house. He said goodnight to Pete, collected a kiss on the cheek and a whispered apology from Sandy, and trudged up to the front door as they honked and drove away. And that was when he discovered that he had forgotten his house key.

Could this night get any more perfect?

Not wanting to ring the bell and wake his parents up, Pedro went back to the driveway. The trees, rustling in a gentle night breeze, seemed to be tittering at him—*He forgot his keys, he forgot his keys!*—as he walked around back to the rock garden, small but lush, with succulents and creepers and ivies twining over stones ranging in size from eggs to bowling balls. During the day, flowers bloomed in variegated waves and transient explosions of white and blue and red; now, most of them had closed up shop for the night. Pedro dug under the ivy, pulling it aside like a mat. Many small rocks lay beneath, giving it form and texture. He lifted up one of the rocks and fished a house key out of a slot in the underside. He kept telling his parents they weren't out in the country, they shouldn't leave a house key hidden in a fake stone, but he had to admit that it was nice to have it there when you were locked out.

He straightened up, key in hand, and headed back toward the side door. Along the way, he stopped, looking at the dark opening in the woods, the trail Elizabeth Bartoski had walked along to come see him. He had tried his best to brush her off. A few hours later she was dead.

How did something like that happen?

And then, before he had time to think about it, he was walking into the trees along that same dark trail where the streetlights didn't reach and the moonlight gave up the struggle somewhere in the foliage overhead. The metal bench at the midpoint of the path glowed like a skeleton in the dim light. The ground sloped upwards from here to the edge of the old man's driveway. Police tape stretched across the end of the trail, wound from tree to tree like the velvet rope outside the club. He stopped and stood at the edge of the woods, looking up at the house. The place slept, dark and quiet. He eyed the driveway. The station wagon was still there. They had erected a pop-up tent over it, protecting it from rain, he supposed, though he didn't think there was going to be any rain tonight. The other car sat behind the wagon, uncovered, exposed to the sky. Its windows were slick with condensation that fuzzed what little weak and sickly illumination managed to stumble around the corner from the streetlight at the end of the driveway.

He waited for something to happen, waited until he was satisfied that there was no grey thing on the roof, no little girl with a haunted face peering out from a darkened window, no bony shade wrapped in plastic lurking beneath the awning. The house hadn't done anything to anyone. It was just a house. He couldn't have saved the Bartoskis because there was nothing here to save them from. Any thoughts otherwise were the product of stress and imagination and lack of sleep.

Pedro backed away, then turned and moved quietly along the path, back to the safety and quiet of his own house, where he let himself in with the spare key and locked the night out behind him.

In the morning, Rose gave Alan her write-up about the events on Potter Street. Alan liked it, but the senior editors, shrinking from the whiff of sensationalism, trimmed the piece down to an inch-high square in the police blotter section. No pictures. No interviews. No byline. The bulk of the article went into the morgue and the photos went into storage and that was that.

Almost.

Rose rescued the shot of the girl trying to open the window, because it hadn't come out right.

There was no person in the picture, no girl, just a vague smear of grey, as if someone had used an eraser to rub away that portion of the photograph. She took the print back to one of the developers in the basement and tapped the smear with her finger, and he looked at it and said it was probably a flaw in the film, or maybe it had been exposed to light. She asked if it could have happened when the film was being developed, which earned her a lengthy and condescending explanation of the way they did things here in the developing department and why it couldn't possibly have been their fault and how she had probably exposed it improperly somehow. He was still pontificating about their standards and practices when she waved him off and took the picture back to her desk, where she now sat, hunched over, examining her smudged picture through a magnifying glass, searching for features in the smear. A suggestion of eyes, a hint of a mouth, anything. She thought she saw them, striations in the grey, but she knew people were great at seeing patterns that weren't there: Jesus in a water stain, the Virgin Mary on a pancake, a dog's face in wood grain.

But still. She knew what she had seen at the house. She knew what the film should have captured, but hadn't. Was she going to doubt her own eyes? Was she going to doubt her ability to load and unload a camera? To take a picture? Was she going to doubt her father when he said there was no such girl in the house? That series of questions had led her to ask two more: What was that grey thing in the window? What was the shadow gathering in the room beyond it?

She concluded, after much rumination, that what she had here might—just might—be a picture of a ghost.

It wasn't a matter she had given much thought to before. A haunted house? Like the things she used to go to when she was a kid, the corridors of a school or factory converted into a chamber of horrors? Skeletons, vampires, devils, zombies, guys in sheets waving their arms and going *whoo, whoo*? No. If real haunted houses were like that, everybody would know about them. A real haunted house would just sit there quietly most of the time and only show its secret face now and then, when it had a reason.

So what was the reason this time? Had she seen an echo of some prior event, or something recent? What had the girl been trying to do? Rose remembered thinking she was going to jump, before the shadow stopped her. Why would a ghost be trying to escape from the house it haunted, and what would be able to prevent it from doing so?

That house seemed to be a dangerous place to be. The father's death looked routine enough; she'd gotten hold of the autopsy report, which confirmed both the stroke and the sorry state of his lungs and arteries. Next there was the man from the electric company who'd been killed by the power lines that had been downed by the woman crashing into the pole: Unusual, but it happened sometimes. After that came Elizabeth Bartoski's death—suicide, as far as anyone could tell, even though they hadn't figured out how to place her in a spot from which she could have jumped and landed where she did, as hard as she did—followed by whatever had happened in the basement that had sent Richard Bartoski in the hospital, which the police officer who had been not ten feet away had neither seen nor heard.

What was the phrase Alan had used? *House of Death*? She was starting to think maybe he hadn't been that far off in his assessment.

But before that, he had called it the *Street of Death*, because of what had happened at the next house up. It had burned to the ground just prior to the elder Bartoski's demise. That fire had killed a—

Rose's eyes widened.

She slipped her ghost picture underneath her keyboard, then got up and headed off in search of files about the fire up the street from the House of Death.

The plane circled around for its final approach, banking to align itself with the runway. Through the tiny, scratched window, Hank Pritchard watched the ground get closer, fields of tufted green becoming trees, grey capillaries becoming roads. The wheels touched the earth. The plane jerked, bounced, landed, jerked again. He closed his eyes and waited for the ride to end. He felt sick to his stomach and he was probably as pale as the plastic wall next to him. Fucking puddle-jumpers. He hated them.

They finally stopped rolling and he opened his eyes. Ground crews were outside, pushing over a big metal staircase on wheels. For God's sake. Climbing down rattling metal steps to the asphalt like a refugee? Welcome to the Third World.

Hank unfastened his seat belt, stood, and retrieved his suitcase from the overhead bin, and a few minutes later he had Bentonville ground under his feet for the first time in a decade. He stood on what passed for the tarmac, surrounded by little planes and dinky baggage carts being dragged around by hand. The terminal, a wooden building about the size of a minor Interstate rest stop, stood a few dozen yards away. Next to it was a squat control tower that resembled a mushroom with dark windows. Through the tinted glass he could just barely see shapes, the outlines of people and equipment. At least, it looked like equipment. It could just be a bunch of orange crates mounted for effect. This podunk town still didn't have a real airport and never would.

Hefting his carry-on bag, Hank headed for the rental car office near the terminal. They had a sedan for him, dull green, filthy from being out in the rain. God knew how long it had been sitting around waiting for some poor chump to fly in and need a vehicle. He made them wash it before he would take it. Couldn't pick up the kid in a dirty vehicle, could he?

Once he had the car back—still not really clean, but better than it had been—he drove to the nearest motel to check in; this joke of an airport rolled up the runway once it started to get dark, so he was going to be stuck here overnight. The motel lobby had maps of Bentonville in a rack, along with brochures for the sad handful of shitty attractions in the area. Hank grabbed a map and took it to his room. The cops had told him Janice would be at the main police station, over on Brookhurst Street, which was not one he was familiar with; apparently they'd built themselves a new headquarters after he moved away. The directions they'd given him didn't take him down Potter Street, so he plotted his own route that did. He wanted to get a fresh look at the old man's house, see where Beth and the old man had died, pay his respects, maybe piss on the porch, if he could get away with it.

He drove slowly, looking at the houses and the roads and the businesses along the way, comparing what he saw to what had existed when he'd lived here. There were a lot of shuttered storefronts and abandoned industrial properties, but also a few renewal type projects converting factories to lofts or shopping areas. After passing a new mobile home park in an area that he remembered as a swamp, he came up to Potter Street from the eastern end, driving alongside the cemetery. The grounds had grown to cover nearly the entire hillside, the forested fringes cut back leaving just a few of the biggest, choicest trees to spread their shade over grassy slopes. There were only a few headstones in the new sections, leaving plenty of room for expansion. No matter the economic conditions, you could always count on the local population to keep dying.

He turned left onto Potter Street, putting the graveyard in his rearview mirror. A few hundred yards later, there it was, 136 Potter Street, where Beth and Richard had spent their formative years being molded into the neurotic, messed-up adults they would become. He had never liked the place; there had always been a noxious and unwelcoming air about it, and now it was even worse, sad and menacing at the same time, like some run-down country hideaway inhabited by a crazy inbred family of fallen aristocrats. The yard had grown unkempt, overrun with crab grass and dandelions and out-of-control shrubbery. A couple of police sawhorses blocked the end of the driveway, reminding him, in an odd way, of Walter Bartoski and his always unwelcoming posture; the old man had hated visitors in general and Hank in particular, so every time Hank, as a teen-ager, had come over to hang out with Richard back when he and Richard had still been friends, or, later, to pick up Beth for a date, their father would invariably find a way to lurk in some corner where his glaring eyes could follow Hank as he entered and passed by. Hank figured the rest of the family already knew the old man was malevolence wrapped in a bathrobe, so he never bothered to mention it to anyone; he just glared back, matching the implicit threat with one of his own. If you let an asshole like that intimidate you, he would just keep pushing things until you laid him out.

His gaze strayed to the forest off to the left of the house. He remembered doing some heavy petting on the bench out there in the wooded area, Beth and him, panting and straining against each other, and in the middle of it the old man's voice booming from the house. *Where are you, Elizabeth? Get your ass in here now!* Hank had tried to turn that around—*yeah, let me get in your ass here now*—but Beth, genuinely terrified of what her father might do, had pushed him away and run back to the house, leaving him and his boner alone in the woods. He'd tried to service himself on the bench but then he'd heard a distant smack and a yelp from Beth, then the crunching of leaves and branches as the old man came out into the woods, and he'd fled, zipping up his pants as he went. Talk about a mood killer.

That was Hank's last date with Beth before his family had moved away up north. Years had passed before he crossed paths with Beth again, by chance, on a beach at a mountain lake. By then Beth was eighteen and she and Richard and their mother had moved out of Bentonville, finally driven away by the old man. Beth had stayed behind to sunbathe while the other two were off playing mini-golf at a sad little amusement park up the road. Her bikini-clad body had caught his attention before he recognized the copper-penny sheen of her hair. He'd gone over and plopped down onto the sand next to her to catch up, and before long the two of them went back to the motel to finish what they'd started on that bench so long before. After that, he'd tagged along for most of their family activities—going out in the canoe on the water, renting ATVs and roaring around the fire roads—and the two of them had stolen away when they could, taking long hikes to nowhere, fucking out in the woods. He could tell Ma Bartoski and Richard weren't thrilled about his presence, especially when he and Beth ran off to get married right at the end of their overlapping vacations, but that just made everything more fun.

Hank hadn't been all that surprised when, a few years later, Ma Bartoski had swallowed an entire bottle of acetaminophen and died of liver failure, or when Richard had cracked up and vanished into the psych ward for three months, he *had* been surprised when Beth had packed up Janice and just disappeared in the middle of the night. Sure, maybe that last fight of theirs had been a little more intense than the one before that, which had been a little more intense than the one before that; and maybe it wasn't the first time the cops had paid them a visit and taken him for a little ride in their car so he could cool off; but it *was* the first time he'd come home to an empty apartment. No Beth. No Janice. No note. Just the blue fabric-covered ice bag sitting in the sink. He had unscrewed the cap and poured it out and seen that there were still a lot of cubes inside, so he knew she couldn't have been gone for that long. He had taken up a position at the door, waiting for it to open when she came slinking back, but she never had.

That was how the Bartoskis were. You couldn't count on them to stick with anything.

This fucking place. This fucking family.

Hank stepped on the accelerator and left the old man's house behind on his way to get the kid.

It felt like Richard had been tied up for days in the dark after the voice went away. He'd expected it to come back, taunt him some more with his failures as a son and a brother, but it never did. The old man had never left him in the basement for this long. Not for days. Not even overnight, except that one time. When he didn't show up for breakfast in the morning, he had heard his mother's raised voice through the ductwork, shouting at his father, threatening to start making phone calls, and—

Wake up, Richard.

There it was. The voice again.

Come on, Richard.

What did want this time?

Richard, if you don't wake up right this minute, I swear to God I'm going to make you personally handle every call we get from the IRS for the next ten years.

Wait. What?

Richard mumbled, "Nuh-uh."

Tony's voice came back: "Hey, I think he hears me."

"I'm not surprised." This speaker was a woman. "You're speaking very loudly."

"So his ears are working."

"There's no physical reason they wouldn't be. We found no evidence of head trauma. Pupil response is normal. He hasn't even got a bruise. His catatonia has, I believe, a psychological etiology."

"Yeah, that's just what I was going to say," Tony said. "You hear that, Richard? I've got confirmation from a medical professional that you're nuts."

"That's not what I said."

"I'm paraphrasing."

Richard cracked an eye slightly, just enough to get a blurry image of the room around him. It was well-lit, and seemed to be clean. It wasn't cold. It wasn't damp. It didn't smell like mildew and yarn and old cardboard. So it most assuredly was not the old man's basement. In fact, it didn't look like any part of the old man's house.

He opened his eyes fully, blinked away the blurs. The smears of light and whiteness resolved into a hospital room. Sunlight poured in through a window to his left, laying streaks across his bed and an empty one to his right. He checked his wrists; they weren't bound after all. Neither were his ankles. His hands and feet still tingled with pins and needles. He made and released fists, rolled and unrolled his toes, making sure everything still worked. Tony and a tiny woman dressed in white stood side by side at the foot of the bed, observing all these activities without comment.

Richard spotted a cup of water on a stand next to the bed. He fumbled it into his grip, only spilling a little. He took a sip, then another; he was going to take a third, then decided to pace himself and put it down. Finally he pulled himself up into an almost-sitting position and said, "Tony? What are you doing here?"

"What am I doing here? Your buddy Detective Leeson called me, that's what I'm doing here." He scratched his nose. "Always fun to get cold-called by the police. I was afraid it was going to be about parking tickets. Luckily it was just about you."

"You didn't have to come all the way down here."

"Who else is going to look after you, huh?" Then: "They told me about Beth. You, uh, you remember what happened to her, right?"

"Yeah," Richard said. "I remember." He vaguely recalled someone offering to make him forget, but everything he'd experienced while unconscious was already evaporating, the way dreams did after you woke up.

"Okay. I'm sorry."

"Me too." He looked at the doctor. "I have a headache. You got anything for that?"

The corner of her mouth twitched. "I think I can scrounge something up." She pivoted on her heel and exited like a triumphant attorney surfing out of a courtroom on a wave of acclamation. Richard watched her go. So did Tony. After the door had closed behind her, Tony leaned in close to Richard and informed him that he was going to marry the doctor.

"Are you?" Richard said. "I've heard that one before."

"I'm serious this time."

"I've heard that one before too."

The door swung inward and Leeson entered. "Good morning," he said, stretching out the *good* like an announcer on a game show. "I was just on my way up and bumped into the doctor in the hallway. She told me you were awake. How are you feeling?"

"Not too bad. Where's Janice? Is she all right?"

"She's fine," Art said. "We've got someone looking after her. We almost never cut six-year-olds loose to fend for themselves. I do have news, though. We tracked down her father. He's not in New Mexico anymore. Now he's in Virginia. Still in the cave business, though."

"Cave business?" Tony said. "What is he, a guano scraper?"

"Public relations. Marketing and promotions and such."

Richard snorted. "Public relations? Hank? How is that possible? He's a creep."

"Creeps can be startlingly good at that sort of thing. Anyhow, Social Services contacted him yesterday. He's on a flight up right now." Art checked his watch. "Might have already landed, in fact. We'll be releasing Janice into his custody."

"I wouldn't give Hank custody of a goldfish."

"That won't be up to you or me. Parceling out children is outside my area of responsibility, thank God." Art looked at Tony. "Could you excuse us? Richard and I need to discuss something for a minute."

"Sure, no problem," Tony said. He paused at the door. "I'll be listening, just in case you start beating him with a rubber hose."

"I'll bear that in mind," Art said.

"I was talking to Richard." Tony went out. Before the door closed behind him, Richard saw him looking up and down the hallway, probably in search of the future Dr. Mrs. Tony Pellegrino.

Alone with Art, Richard waited for the detective to speak, but he just stood there at the foot of the bed looking thoughtful, like he was trying to make up his mind about something. Finally Richard broke the silence. "Did you find anything? At the house, I mean? To explain what happened to Beth?"

"No," Art said, "we haven't found anything yet, I'm afraid."

"Oh. So, uh, what did we need to discuss, then?"

"Actually, I wanted to ask you about the incident in the basement."

"The ... incident?"

"Yeah," Art said. "When you passed out. Officer Sheets didn't see it. Says he heard something moving in the utility room and went to check it out. By the time he turned around, you were on the floor in a pile of boxes."

"It sounds like you know as much about it as I do. The last thing I remember is picking Candy up."

"Yeah, you did succeed in finding the doll. In fact we had trouble prying it out of your grip so we could give it to your niece. So it's a blank for you after that, huh?"

"I'm afraid so."

"The doctor doesn't think you hit your head hard enough to knock yourself unconscious, let alone give yourself short-term memory loss."

"Well, I guess she's wrong." The room fell quiet. Faint noises came through the door from the hallway, people walking and talking, announcements coming over the loudspeaker. Art stood there, hands in pockets, watching him. "It's too stuffy in here," Richard said, after the silence had gone on a bit too long. He gestured at the window. "Do you mind?"

"Not at all." Art went to the window and turned the crank, opening a narrow side panel a few inches. Bird noises came in, the sounds of traffic; and air, soft and warm. "You're lucky you're in the old wing. In the new one, they don't believe in things like access to fresh air."

"Yeah, lucky, that's me," Richard said. Then: "Did Officer Sheets find what was moving in the utility room?"

"What? Oh. No. Nothing was there. I had searched it previously, then Officer Sheets searched it, then we searched it again after he made his report. It was just as empty each time."

"You looked in the corner between the furnace and the water heater?"

"We looked in the corner between the furnace and the water heater." Art eyed him. "Why do you ask about that location, specifically?"

"You can't see into it from the door."

"Is that the only reason?"

"I spent plenty of time back there when I was a kid."

"Hide and seek?"

"I wish."

Art nodded. "This time you spent back there when you were a kid," he said. "Would that have involved sitting on the floor tied to the pipe as some form of punishment?"

Richard stared at him.

"Figuring stuff out is sort of my job."

"Right."

"So that's it, then? You can't tell me anything else about what happened down there?"

"I'm afraid not. Sorry. But if I remember later, I'll let you know."

Art looked like he was about to say something else, but then the door opened and the doctor came in carrying a tiny tray with a thimble-sized paper pill bucket and a plastic cup the size of a shot glass, a manila folder tucked under her arm. She put it on the table next to Richard's bed. "Two aspirin," she said. "Take them and call me in the morning."

"Call you? You're kicking me out?"

"We typically refer to it as *discharging*," she said, "not *kicking out*."

"But don't you want to keep me for observation?"

"We don't need to," she said. "There's nothing physically wrong with you."

"Okay." Richard looked at Art. "Are we done?"

"Yeah. For now. We can talk more on the way."

"On the way? Are we going somewhere?"

"Yes. Back to the house, to pick up your car. I'll drive." Art headed for the door. "The clothes you bought are there in the closet. We sent them with you in the ambulance. You go ahead and get dressed. I'll wait outside."

After Art had left, the doctor handed him the folder. "Getting kicked out instructions," she explained. "Call 911 if you experience dizziness, nausea, vomiting, or excessive tiredness in the next couple of days. I don't think you will, though."

"Thanks," Richard said. She stood there watching him until he swallowed the aspirin and gulped the water, making sure he didn't choke or throw the medicine in the trash, he supposed; then she nodded and left. Richard slid out of bed and checked the closet. There were his new clothes, still bearing the tags from the store. He ripped those off and then got dressed. The rest of his belongings were in a brown paper bag with thin rope handles. It had his name scrawled on the side. He sat in the visitor's chair and went through the contents of the bag. There wasn't much in it: Wallet, wristwatch, keys, his belt—he took that out and put it on—a comb, and a ball-point pen. He clicked the pen a few times, wondering where on his person he'd been carrying it, since he could never find one when he needed one.

Tony came into the room as Richard was looking in his wallet, making sure everything was still there. "Quit counting your filthy lucre and let's go," he said. "I'm parked in an ambulance zone."

"You are not." Richard looked up. "Art said he would drive me."

"Yeah, I had a quick talk with him. He had to leave in a hurry. Something came up, I guess. But hey, if you'd rather wait for a ride in a cop car, that's cool. Maybe they'll let you run the siren and the flashy lights."

"Whee," Richard said.

"Rose, you taking lunch today?"

She shook her head and waved her hand, not looking up from her computer. Once whoever it was had wandered off, she opened her top drawer, removed her sandwich, took a bite, and hid it again. Eating at the desk was officially frowned upon, even though everybody did it, and she didn't want anyone to stop and remind her about the rules and get a look at what she was doing. On her desk, hidden under an interoffice memo envelope, was the file folder for the house fire story, with pictures of the scene and of the family, name of Weiss, that had lived there. All three members of the family were dead, but only one them had been a victim of the fire: The daughter, a twelve-year-old girl named Cassandra. Cassandra Weiss had been reported missing three days before the fire, yet afterwards her body was found in what had been a closet on the second floor.

The house had burned so fast, the investigators were sure accelerants had been used; it was arson, no doubt about that. The only question was who had set the fire. Suspicion was focused on the parents, who had been found dead in their idling car in the cemetery at the end of Potter Street, out on one of the new loops of road in a section that had only recently been opened for burials. The car had a length of garden hose duct-taped to the tailpipe; it ran through a slightly rolled-down rear window, pumping the passenger compartment full of exhaust fumes. The obvious conclusion was that the missing persons report had been bogus, that one or both of them knew where their daughter was the whole time, and that the guilty party or parties had subsequently set fire to the house with the girl inside. Whether it had been a single homicide with a double suicide or a double homicide with a single suicide was open to debate; that their daughter had been murdered was not.

The file contained a snapshot of the dead child. Because her own picture showed nothing but a smear, Rose only had her memory to go on, her recollection of those few seconds when she had seen the girl in the window. Although she might not have been able to pick the face out of a photo book, she saw nothing to eliminate Cassandra as a match. The age was right; so was the hair.

But if Cassandra had died in her own house, why would her ghost be lurking in the one next door?

Maybe there was another dead Bartoski that Rose didn't know about, or some other tragic backstory to that place. She needed to eliminate possibilities. To do that, she needed to acquire information. And that was why she was spending her lunch break sitting at her desk staring at her screen. About four months earlier, the paper had finally finished a project to create an electronic archive of articles, editorials, columns, the works. The idea was to make everything more easily accessible for follow-ups and reprints and that sort of thing. Unfortunately, although the archive was stored on some fancy new piece of hardware—IT called it a *jukebox*, as if you could drop a quarter in and get your groove on—you still had to crawl through the ancient computer system to get at it, which was slow as death and twice as painful. She had told the thing to find her all the stories containing the words *Bartoski* or *Potter Street* or *missing blond girl*, and the progress bar had been stuck at ninety percent for nearly ten minutes. The first few times this sort of thing had happened, she'd decided the system had crashed and had shut her computer off with the power switch; this eventually earned her a visit from one of the tech guys, who had lectured her about orphan processes and how she had to have more patience with the system and blah blah blah. She had tuned him out until he stopped yammering, at which point she'd said okay and he had left, satisfied that she'd been properly chastised.

Finally the computer beeped and a list of articles appeared. Nineteen for *Bartoski*—thank God they weren't named *Smith*—eleven for *Potter Street*, and a shit ton of ones for *missing blond girl*. People loved to read about missing blond girls. The number of articles where the words intersected was, fortunately, much smaller.

She scrolled through the list, starting with the Bartoski ones. Nothing much there. An auto accident three years ago that shattered Walter Bartoski's hip. A police report from nine years ago regarding a domestic disturbance at the Bartoski residence on Potter Street. The other Bartoski articles were of little interest, most involving an apparently unrelated city councilwoman of the same name, who had died four or five years ago. Rose had forgotten all about her.

On to the Potter Street articles. A couple were about house fires; one was about a homeless encampment that had been cleared from a ravine that ran behind the houses on the opposite side from the Bartoski residence; another was about the problem of people dumping trash into said ravine; another was about the cancellation of a planned community cleanup day where those who lived nearby would haul said trash out of said ravine and dispose of it properly. That ravine got a lot of bad press. It needed a better agent.

She took a closer look at the articles about the fires. The first one, at 112 Potter Street, had occurred in July 1986, during the day. No one at home, no injuries. The second was the one at the Weiss family home, 134 Potter Street, in which Cassandra had been killed. The call had come in at one in the morning, the day before paramedics had scraped Walter Bartoski off his front sidewalk. Maybe all the excitement next door had been too much for him. Maybe he'd been stressed for other reasons. Maybe it was all a coincidence. Who could say?

She pulled out the file and looked at the snapshot of Cassandra Weiss again. In the background, out of focus, she saw what looked like an old farmhouse, surrounded by trees. The picture hadn't been taken on Potter Street. Rose didn't need any investigative skills to discern that; on the back, someone had scrawled *Candy, age 11* and, underneath that, *Visiting Grandma in Massalacqua.* That was a village about an hour northwest of Bentonville. Route 18, a local main drag, went through it. Rose thought she'd been there once or twice, on her way to someplace else, which was really the only reason anyone ever had for visiting Massalacqua if Grandma didn't live there. She flipped through the other papers in the file, hoping to find Grandma's name and address, to save herself a little trouble, but no luck.

Rose went and ran the snapshot through the color photocopier and put the copy back in the file. She kept the original, figuring that offering it to Grandma would be a good icebreaker when she tracked the woman down for a chat about her dead family. Lollipops probably wouldn't cut it this time. She returned the file to storage, then went back to her desk and made some calls to people she knew in various offices, and before long had the information she required. The grandmother was one Mrs. Gustav Arvidsson, and she lived on Wishbone Road in Massalacqua, and she either had no phone or it was unlisted.

Well, Rose could use a drive today. See the scenery. Take her mind off things.

A student intern collared her as she was heading for the stairwell to the side exit. "Mr. Akins is looking for you," he said. "He wants to know if that story about the mayor's office is ready to run."

Oh, yeah, that. How would the free world survive another day suffering under the Bentonville mayor's unfettered cronyism? "Not yet," she said. "Tomorrow, maybe."

"He said if it's not ready, I'm supposed to ask why."

She sighed. "Just tell him Rose is being feckless again," she said, and left.

PART TWO

4

TONY'S CAR ROLLED TO A stop in front of the house. He parked against the curb and cut the engine and leaned forward, looking up at the house through the windshield. "So that's where you grew up, eh? I expected something more awful."

"It wasn't the house that was awful so much as the person in it." Richard got out of the car and started up the walk, but stopped and turned around when he heard the car door close behind him. Tony was already halfway around the vehicle. "What're you doing?"

"Coming with you," Tony said.

"The hell you are."

"How am I supposed to keep you out of trouble if you leave me standing on the sidewalk?"

"When have you ever kept anyone out of trouble?"

"I'm an accountant. Keeping people out of trouble is my job."

Richard almost laughed. Almost. "Look, Tony, I just … I don't want anybody else in that house, all right? Your actuarial tables won't protect you here."

"Richard." The side of Tony's mouth quirked up in a little grin. "You're worried about me. I'm touched. Fine, I'll stay here. But if you end up in a heap on the floor again, I'm telling your buddy Art it was your own fault because you wouldn't let me go with you."

"I'm not going to end up in a heap on the floor again. I'll be out in a few minutes. Scout's honor."

Tony gave him a mock salute, then settled against the car, his gaze wandering over the property. Richard went up the driveway and around back to where the cars were parked. Beth's was under a pop-up tent, as if it were the grand prize in a craft show raffle. He looked at it for a moment, then went over to the garage. The broken pane on the side door had been patched with tape and cardboard; it reminded him of the counter in the kitchen, held together by adhesives and inertia.

He returned to the middle of the parking area and stood there looking up at the house, at the window to the old man's room, wondering where the police had gone. Maybe they were finished with the scene and just hadn't collected their tent and sawhorses and yellow ribbons yet. Maybe they were inside. He went to the back door and knocked, waited, knocked again. Getting no answer, he tried the knob. Locked. He used his key to open it and went in through the mudroom to the kitchen. The house was silent. Not a creak, not a groan, not a whisper. Even though the place was obviously empty, he called out, "Hello?"

No one answered, of course.

He went into the dingy dining room, then into the paper-strewn living room, then into the front hall. There was the cellar door with its incongruously shiny latch. The door was closed but the latch was open. He set it. Whatever was down in the basement could stay there. He went up the stairs, then to Beth's old room, stopping just inside. Beth's suitcase sat on the floor next to the sleeping bag. It was open, its contents in disarray; he supposed the police must have searched it. The mess didn't matter. Beth wouldn't be needing a change of clothes, not ever again.

Withdrawing, he looked up the hallway, at the old man's room, dark beyond the threshold. He shuffled towards it, noticing as he passed that the attic door hung open a few inches. Well, Art had said his people could open it. Richard continued on to the end of the silent hallway and stood there staring into his father's room and thinking of nothing at all.

Suddenly the phone rang, a massive, heavy, explosive sound that made the floor vibrate under his feet even though the handset was on a nightstand all the way across the room. He found himself walking forward, shambling over to the little bedside table. He picked up the handset and held it to his face but didn't speak, expecting it to be Robert James again. After a moment, though, someone else's voice crackled through the earpiece: "Is anybody there or what?"

"Yes. Who's this?"

"Richard? Is that you? This is Hank."

Hank. His old friend from high school. Beth's ex-husband. Janice's father.

That prick.

"What do you want?" Richard said.

"Hello to you, too," Hank said. Then: "I'm here at the police station. They told me you might be at the house. They suggested that even though I'm under no obligation to tell you a goddamn thing, it would be nice of me to maybe call you and let you know Janice is with me."

Fuck.

"Thanks," Richard said. "I appreciate it. Where are you staying?"

"Staying? What makes you think I'm staying?"

"What, you're going to grab Janice and leave?"

"Why wouldn't I? I'm her father. I can take her anywhere I want. The cops are done interviewing her. And I'm not needed as a witness to any suspicious deaths. Unlike you." Asshole. Richard moved the handset away from his ear so he could glare at it, then brought it back to his ear. Hank was still talking. "… flight out isn't until tomorrow at eleven, so we're leaving then."

"Where did you say you were staying?"

"I didn't. I don't want you showing up and making a scene, do I?"

"I'm not going to make a scene. I just want to say goodbye to Janice."

"Okay, hang on, I'll put her on the phone."

"In *person*, Hank."

"In person? Yeah? I guess I can let you do that, if you promise to behave. Do you?"

"Do I what?"

"Promise to behave."

Richard took a deep, steadying breath, then another, then said, "Yes. I promise to behave."

"Good. I'm in room 103 at the Pine View Motel. The address is —"

"Give me a second." Richard pawed around in his pockets for a moment before remembering that he had left the ball-point pen in Tony's car with the rest of his bagged-up crap. The nightstand had a drawer under the telephone, which he opened, revealing the usual assortment of bedside junk along with a blue notebook and a pencil. He took them out, opened the notebook, and jotted down the address on the inside back cover. He thanked Hank, who hung up without responding.

After getting off the phone with Hank, Richard examined the notebook more closely, wondering if it might be one of the volumes that Robert James had described. It did look like a diary or journal, bound in blue leather or something like it. Gold inlay decorated the covers, front and back, the twin patterns connected by two lines that ran across the spine, one at the top, one at the bottom. The maze-like designs reminded him of something electronic, down to the burn marks that interrupted the continuity, as if the circuit had shorted out. He flipped through it, back to front, turning thick off-white crimson-lined pages with nothing on them. No last will and testament; no inventory of furniture that the old man had sold or was planning to sell; no rambling screeds about the neighbors; no list of grievances against his family.

He stopped turning pages when he came to an unfinished sketch of Beth's room, drawn from the perspective of someone standing in her doorway. The layout of the room reminded him of how it had been when they were younger, the walls decorated with posters, plush stuffed animals on the windowsill, accessories scattered across the dresser. The lower part of her bed was visible off to the left, along with her legs and her feet, adorned with pom-pom sneakers, toes pointed downward, as if she was lying on her stomach while reading a magazine on her pillow. It was a pose Richard had seen many times when passing her room, back in the day. He stared at it and kept finding more little things hidden in the corners, in the shadows under the bed, almost as if details were being added before his eyes. Feeling vaguely unnerved, he closed the book and sat there tapping his finger on the back cover, wondering when his father had taken up sketchwork and why he had chosen that topic. Memories of his family? He would never have thought the old man would be sentimental about anything, including that. And the sure, steady hand applied to the drawing seemed incongruent with what little he knew about his father's recent condition. It must be an old sketch, he decided. Maybe there were more of them. He wondered if there was one of his room, too.

Well, he couldn't spend all day up here flipping through the drawings like a kid on summer break with a comic book; Tony was waiting for him outside. He decided to take the book with him. Surely Art wouldn't mind; it could hardly have anything to do with what happened to Beth. Journal in hand, he headed downstairs and exited through the mudroom. When he emerged from the house he found Tony standing in the driveway, peering at the cracked windshield of Beth's car. Richard stopped short on the little square of cement outside the back door. "What are you doing here?"

"You were taking too long. I came up to make sure you weren't passed out or something."

"I'm fine. The doctor said there's nothing wrong with me."

"That's because she doesn't know you very well." Tony eyed the notebook in Richard's hand, but didn't comment on it. Instead he pointed at Richard's car. "What's in the box?"

"Box?"

"In your front seat? Looks like it should have a cake in it, but probably doesn't?"

"Oh. That. You don't want to know."

"Sure I do."

"It's the old man's ashes."

Tony grimaced.

"I told you you didn't want to know."

"Yeah, you did. Are we just about done here?"

Richard stood there for a moment, then said: "Just about." He opened his car and put the notebook on the passenger seat, then picked up the box. Tony watched him, but said nothing, and didn't follow him as he carried the box into the house.

Box in his arms, Richard went down into the basement, then into the utility room. He sat down on the cold floor with the box in front of him, staring at it, while his thoughts drifted and re-formed and drifted again, dark recollections gathering into darker ones, like clouds before a storm. Finally he punctured the tape with a key and opened the carton. The purple tissue paper was bunched and twisted into a flower-like shape. Inside of that were the styrofoam peanuts, multicolored pastel ones, as if the box might contain a ceramic Easter bunny. He fished around inside and found the stainless steel urn and lifted it out of the package and put it on the floor. It looked just like the ones on display at the funeral home; having the old man's ashes inside hadn't corroded it, turned it black and sinister. Yet.

He spent a few more minutes looking at it. Hard to believe they'd managed to fit the remains of a person into such a small container. He could see faint machining marks on the canister, tiny scratches going around and around and around. He fiddled with the latch, stopped, fiddled with the latch again, unlocked it this time, lifted the lid. There was a faint sucking sound as the gasket disengaged, and then he was looking into the gleaming interior of the canister. Inside was a plastic bag containing a grey powder, like rough and dirty talc, with lumpy bits here and there. He regarded the bag for a little while, then took it out and brought it along as he squeezed himself through the space between the furnace and the wall. The corner was a lot more cramped than he remembered. He didn't really know what he intended to do back here until he discovered that he was pouring the ashes out into the sump, where they formed a scummy layer of grit and small particles. He shook out the bag, making sure to disperse all of it. A few larger pieces *plooped* through the floating surface, leaving little holes in the drifting sludge.

"See how *you* like it, you son of a bitch," Richard said.

Arthur Leeson emerged from the coroner's autopsy chamber, took off his surgical mask, and wiped his mouth with the back of his hand. When he'd gotten a call that the procedure was about to begin, earlier than scheduled—he wasn't sure how that had happened; it wasn't like anybody was canceling their appointment with the medical examiner—he had skipped out on Richard Bartoski to rush down here so he could lean against a wall and watch Mack "Don't-Call-Me-The-Knife" Connack slice open what he described for the voice recorder as a *well-formed female in her middle twenties*.

Well-formed. Yeah, she had been, once. Now, not so much.

Art often wondered if it was worth it, sitting in on autopsies. He had this worry, totally irrational of course, that the coroner might miss something that he himself would catch. Something vital, something to crack the case, solve the mystery, catch the bad guy. It hadn't happened yet, but maybe it would someday.

Today was not that day.

The autopsy had revealed nothing of note. There were no wounds except the ones she had suffered when she hit the car. No sign of a struggle, or of assault; no defensive wounds, no attacker's skin under the fingernails. Nothing on her shoes or clothes or hands consistent with the old tar shingles of the roof, or with climbing a tree, or with the ancient wooden ladder that they'd found hanging on the back wall of the garage, dusty and cobwebbed. All they had was her purse on the floor in the old man's room. But that window was stuck tight; it would take a crowbar to pry it open, and there was no evidence anyone had done so. It would take a while for the toxicology results to come back, but Art was pretty sure it would all be negative. And even if she was coked to the gills, that wouldn't explain what the hell had happened to her. Drugs might make you think you were flying, but couldn't actually lift you up into the sky and then drop you on a car.

The metal door behind him creaked open and Mack stuck his head out. He said, "You want a last look at anything?"

"No, I'm good," Art said. "Thanks."

"Okay. I'm just gonna put the bag of organs inside and stitch her back up." The door clanked shut.

Bag of organs. Jesus. Like the giblets on a turkey.

Happy goddamn Thanksgiving.

The Pine View Motel did, in fact, have a view of pines: Not especially remarkable around these parts, but truth in naming nevertheless. The motel stood near the crest of a hill on the north side of the valley, a swath of conifers spreading beneath it, sloping down into the suburbs and ultimately into Bentonville itself. The airport was a mile or so to the west, on a plateau with a slightly lower elevation, so you could see planes come and go if your room faced the right way.

Richard's room did not face the right way. What he saw as he stood there staring out his window was fifteen yards of asphalt driveway, then a wide, steep, downward-sloping meadow, then the trees. At the far end, where the meadow leveled out, the grass was dotted with heaps of dirt and a sign Richard couldn't quite make out. Future site of something-something, a developer name that started with a Q. The dirt piles were overgrown with tall grass and the sign had faded and begun to peel, so he suspected that the project, whatever it was, had stalled some time earlier and would likely never be finished.

Tony sat in a mustard-colored chair near the bed. He kept picking tufts of fuzz off the upholstery and flicking them away, as if afraid they would migrate to his clothes. Silence stretched out for a while, until finally Tony said, "So what's the deal with the cops, anyway?"

"The deal?"

"You know. The investigation. What do they think happened with Beth?"

"I think they don't know what to think," Richard said. "I know they're doing an autopsy—Art told me it's routine in a case like this —but the problem is, where did she fall from? How did she get there? And why? Autopsy's not gonna help with that."

"Yeah, I guess not. So after they're done with that? What then?"

"Then we have a funeral and bury her, I guess."

"Here?"

"Hell no. In Bentonville? No. Back in Nathan's Corners, with Mom. She has a plot with spaces for us."

"Burying Beth." Tony shook his head. "Hard to believe."

"Yeah." Richard continued to stare out the window, at the clouds gathering against the azure sky. He wondered if Beth could see the clouds from wherever she had gone. After a little while he noticed Tony glancing at his watch and said, "You probably need to get going, huh?"

"Yeah, I probably do. You'll be okay?"

"I'll be fine. I might take a nap. I could use some real sleep."

"Okay." Tony stood up, brushed imaginary motel lint off his slacks. "Give me a call if you need anything."

"I will. Thanks for coming down, Tony."

"It's the least I could do." He headed for the door, stopped, looked back at Richard. "You sure you're going to be all right? I could stop by the hospital, ask that cute little doctor to come over and take your temperature."

"I can take my own temperature."

Tony snorted. "Too much of that and you'll go blind," he said.

Rose approached Massalacqua from the south, where Route 18 ran along the edge of a high plateau. From up here, she might have been looking down at a bucolic painting instead of an actual town full of actual people. The village lay in a wide, shallow valley, occupying the flood plain of an ancient torrent that was now a concrete-hemmed creek. Oaks and maples and ash and birch linked arms to form a thick afghan of foliage, pierced here and there by sharp stands of dark green pine. An old white church steeple, complete with clock, protruded from the blanket; a few larger houses were visible, and some yards, and, in the middle of the village, a big green park topped with an ice cream sundae of a gazebo.

The road banked right and descended into the valley, taking her under the trees, greenery on every side. She stopped at a gas station and went in and asked the kid behind the counter—Roger, according to his name tag—for directions to Wishbone Road. He described the twists and turns required to get there, making each sentence sound like he was the one asking questions, then, as she turned to leave added, "You're too late for the estate sale, though?"

She turned back to him. "Excuse me?"

"The estate sale? It was this past weekend?"

"Sorry, whose estate are we talking about?"

"Old lady Arvidsson's? The only house on Wishbone?" The kid scratched his ear. "I used to deliver papers out that way? Two miles long and just her house at the end of it? And did she ever give me a tip?"

Rose guessed that no, she did not ever give him a tip. "Did she move, or … ?"

"She passed away, nine days ago, maybe ten?"

"I'm sorry to hear that." Interesting. It had been a rough couple of weeks in that family. Wondering if this death, too, had been suspicious, she said: "Do you know why?"

"Why what?"

"Why she died?"

"Old, I guess."

"That's it? Just old?"

"Well." He lowered his voice to a whisper. "I heard her head exploded?"

"I see. Thanks, Roger." She glanced at the stack of newspapers for sale next to the register. The banner across the top identified it as the Massalacqua *Mirror.* A local publication, about the size of the *Herald-*

Journal's Sunday magazine insert, but a little thicker. She picked up a copy and looked it over, gave Roger her money, then handed her change back to him to help make up for all those years of no tips from stingy old Mrs. Arvidsson. Then, holding up the paper: "Can you give me directions to where this is published?"

"Oh, sure," Roger said, and for once it didn't sound like a question. "Everyone knows where to find Ozzie."

Art stood in the driveway in back of 136 Potter Street, staring at the broken windshield of the station wagon. He'd been hoping the autopsy would give him something to go on, a blow to the back of the head or some other injury that the scene had been arranged to obfuscate, but it had not. So how could a woman plunge thirty feet— that was the coroner's admittedly inexact estimate of the minimum distance required for the injuries sustained—when she had no evident way to get to the roof and there was no appropriate means of defenestration? Even if that bedroom window could have been opened, the height just wasn't adequate to account for the force of the impact; it was almost as if she had been fired at the car head first. Maybe he should be looking for a perpetrator with a giant slingshot.

A perpetrator. He had no evidence that one even existed, and little prospect of finding any. They'd confirmed Richard Bartoski's story about stopping at the mall, and Beth Bartoski's credit card history showed she had been at a fast food place at about the same time her brother was shopping; Mack had found the remains of that meal in her stomach, barely digested. The kid who'd been working the register remembered her because she had skirted the edge of panic when she'd briefly lost track of Janice. He'd said they were alone, just mother and daughter. It was the same with everybody else they'd talked to. Nothing was the least bit suspicious. Yet Beth Bartoski was still dead.

And the thing was, it didn't matter. Absent unexpected developments, he was going to have to close up shop here soon. The brass had already pulled his site protection earlier this morning, without bothering to tell him they were doing it; he had only learned about it when he arrived and discovered the place was unattended and called in to ask where his officer was, and found out they'd sent him after a couple of cars drag racing on Cemetery Street. At least

Richard Bartoski had been thoughtful enough to put the sawhorses back across the base of the driveway after removing his car.

Art's cellular phone cheeped. He pulled it out of his pocket and flipped it open. "Leeson."

"Arthur. It's John."

John in Records. The Information Man. "Hi John. Got something for me?"

"Yeah, the skinny on the Bartoski clan. You ready for it?"

Art sat down on the splintered blacktop and got his notebook out, cradling the phone between his shoulder and his ear. "Hit me."

"Okay. Walter Bartoski, father. Welder. Several drunk and disorderlies back in the seventies. Two domestic violence calls, no arrests. Wife, Edna Bartoski, left and took the kids nine years ago. Walter kept a low profile since then, except for a car accident three years ago. He was walking while drunk and was struck by a vehicle. Hit and run, driver never identified. Walter's hip was shattered. Replacement was made but he never returned to work and retired on disability."

Art was scribbling away, writing it all down. "Okay. Next?"

"Edna Bartoski, born Edna Sayles. Married Walter Bartoski in 1963. Children: Richard Bartoski, born 1967, and Elizabeth, born 1970. Miscarriage at fifteen weeks in 1973. Like I said, she left Walter in 1986. Died of a massive self-administered overdose of acetaminophen, 1990. Brief note, to the effect of *Goodbye, cruel world*."

"Acetaminophen? You can kill yourself with that stuff?"

"Yep. Next, Richard Bartoski. Accountant. Never married, no children, no arrests."

"Okay. Nex—"

"Richard Bartoski mention his episode?"

"Episode?"

"He was involuntarily hospitalized for three months in 1992. Severe depression. They thought he was likely to harm himself."

"Or others?"

"Just himself."

"Okay. No, he didn't mention that. Next?"

"Elizabeth Bartoski. Worked the cosmetics counter at a department store in Nathan's Corners. Drapers. Must be a local place, I never heard of it. Married Hank Pritchard in 1988. Child,

Janice, born 1989. Separated from Pritchard in 1991, divorced him in 1992. Nathan's Corners PD states there were numerous calls made regarding Pritchard during their marriage and for a few months after their separation, but no charges were ever pressed. In 1991 he moved to Carlsbad, New Mexico, and eventually got a job with the park service in the caverns. Moved to Luray, Virginia, in 1994, and went to work for some other cave there."

"Scraping guano," Art said.

"What?"

"Nothing. Say, what are the chances that Pritchard crawled out of his cave and visited Bentonville yesterday to haul people onto rooftops and throw them off?"

"Zero. I inquired. He was giving a presentation at the time of the incident. There's videotape and everything. If you like him for this, you're going to be disappointed."

"Okay. Is that the whole ball of wax?"

"Those are the highlights. The full report can be found on your desk."

"Thanks." He closed the phone, put away the notebook. A cool breeze was blowing, rustling the trees. He noticed that the tips of the leaves were beginning to turn brown, like they were slowly rusting from the edges. He'd have to start raking his yard, such as it was, before too long. A month or so, tops. Maybe this year he'd pay the neighbor's kid to do it.

Art scissored himself to his feet and went in through the back door. The place smelled like a hamper full of old, wet clothes rolled in tobacco. He walked through the dining room and the living room and into the front hall. He paused at the cellar door. It was latched. Had they left it that way? He wasn't sure.

The doorbell bonged. He turned and opened the front door and found himself facing a tall guy in a white suit and matching hat. The man looked down at Art and smiled and said, "Good afternoon. Is Richard or Elizabeth Bartoski at home?"

"They are not. May I ask who's inquiring?"

"Robert James, antiquarian."

"Oh, yeah. Richard mentioned you."

"Only good things, I hope."

"Just your name and your trade. But I'd love to hear more." Art flipped open his identification. "Detective Arthur Leeson. Homicide. You can call me Art." He opened the screen door. "Won't you come in?"

"Homicide?" James said, as he followed Art into the living room. "Are you here in an official capacity?"

"I'm afraid so. I take it you didn't see the police barricade out front."

"I noticed the sawhorses, yes, but I supposed the driveway was being resurfaced."

"You supposed incorrectly." He dragged the recliner around to face the couch, then sat in it and gestured James towards the sofa. "Won't you sit down?"

"Are we going to be here a while, detective?"

"That depends. Please, have a seat." James shrugged and folded himself onto the sofa, taking off his hat and resting it on his knee. Art got out his notebook. "The reason I'm here is that Elizabeth Bartoski fell or jumped or was thrown from some high point on or in or near this house. She broke her neck. Landed on the car right in front of her little girl. We're looking at it as a possible homicide."

"Oh my." James looked thoughtful. "How tragic. When did this happen?"

"Yesterday afternoon. I don't suppose you have any light to shed on the subject?"

"Me? No, I'm afraid not. I was at an auction from around eleven until well after five o'clock. I didn't get back to Bentonville until eight or so."

"I see. Where was this?" James gave Art the name and address of the auction house. It was in the town of Marshall, about a hundred miles to the southwest. Art wrote it in his notebook. "So. Richard Bartoski tells me you're interested in the disposition of the estate, such as it is."

"Yes, that's right."

"We've been through the house, and, to be honest, I didn't see a hell of a lot that looked like it would be of much value to a pawn shop, let alone an, uh, antiquarian."

"The majority of the items here are mundane, but that's true of most homes. I am often interested in things that may appear unremarkable to the untrained eye. As I explained to Richard

Bartoski, his father kept a list of what I had agreed to purchase. A bill of future exchanges, if you will."

"Yes, Richard mentioned that you had had contact with his father before his death. How often did you stop by?"

"Not very often. If he was short of cash, he would telephone and sell me something. Other times he just wanted to talk. I considered it a form of elder care, really. He lived alone. He rarely went out. No one else ever called. No one else ever visited. It was a very lonely existence."

"That's quite charitable of you, to provide such a service. When was the last time you were here?"

"Oh, a few weeks ago. But when I heard about his death, I felt that I needed to come by and pay my respects to the family."

"And also to conclude those future exchanges you mentioned?"

James lifted his shoulders, let them drop. Business was business.

"Well, I appreciate your indulging me, Mr. James. I won't keep you any longer today, but could I get a number where I can reach you? Just in case I have more questions."

"Certainly. I'll give you my card." He produced an off-white rectangle from a leather case and handed it over. It said *Robert James, Antiquarian* in pale purple script. The other side was blank, no contact information. Art pointed this out. "Oh, of course. How stupid of me." James took the card back, scribbled an address and phone number on the blank side, and returned it. Art tucked it into his jacket pocket.

"Is that all, detective?" James said.

"That's all for now. Thanks for your time."

"You're very welcome, Mr. Leeson." James stood. "When you speak with Richard, please tell him my interest remains strong."

"I'm sure he'll be glad to hear it," Art said. He walked James to the front door and watched him leave. The man shambled down the long, sloping sidewalk, big shoulders swaying, hat perched on his head like a flying saucer that had crash-landed on an asteroid. He got into a small black car with darkly tinted windows and a nose like a doorstop and drove away. Art closed and locked the door, turned around, leaned against the thick wood, facing the stairs. The latch on the cellar door glimmered in the dim light. It wasn't dull and tarnished, like the faucets and the towel racks and the other bits of chrome in the house. Art found himself staring at the shiny metal. There was no way into the cellar from the outside, so what was the point of having a latch on it? What had Walter Bartoski thought might try to get into the house from the basement?

Art returned to the living room, looked at the stained ceiling, the ratty furniture, the scattered newspapers. No matter what Robert James said, he didn't think there was or had ever been anything here worthy of gracing the shelves of a shop run by someone who called himself an *antiquarian* and handed out business cards so fancy they didn't advertise his location. But then, why would James keep showing up? Art would have suspected drugs, but their one drug-sniffing dog already went through the place and the only thing it found was an old pack of smokes hidden under the sink. Art hadn't even known the dog was trained to look for tobacco. The handler had given him a little smile and said, "Bootleg cigarettes, Detective."

He would have someone check out Robert James's story about the auction, but he was sure it would hold up; nobody would make such a definitive statement of their whereabouts if it couldn't withstand scrutiny. And it probably didn't really matter anyway. He had nothing to turn this death into a homicide other than improbable velocities and angles and a weird spooky feeling of wrongness. The little girl hadn't helped, saying how her invisible friend had told her there was something bad in the house but insisting it wasn't a person. He couldn't build a case out of this. What was he supposed to do, arrest the boogeyman? The monster under the bed?

The place grew quiet, oppressive, the weight of its years pushing down on him, flattening him, squeezing the color right out of him and leaving him grey as an old photograph. He felt like he was missing something, failing the deceased in some way, but he couldn't figure out what or how. It was time to take a break. Get out of here, go for a drive, think things through, search for inspiration.

Art went out the back way, and locked the house's mysteries in behind him when he left.

The office of the Massalacqua *Mirror* was in a storefront on the village's main street, a central door bordered on either side by big glass windows with the name of the paper emblazoned across them in a yellow marquee font. Inside, Rose found a lobby with a light blue carpet matched by walls speckled in white. A table next to the door held copies of the paper. A few chairs stood along the wall, facing a counter and hallway leading further into the building. There was a little bell on the counter but no one behind it. She rang the bell and waited, sniffing the air. Something smelled delicious.

After a few seconds a big man lurched into view from the interior, a half-eaten meatball sub cradled in his arms like a blessed bundle of joy. He settled onto a stool behind the counter and said, "Can I help you?"

She showed him her press credential, told him who she was and that she wanted to talk to someone about Mrs. Arvidsson, and he responded that, yes, he could help her with that. First, though, did she want a look around their setup? Despite her protestations that this was unnecessary, the man and his aromatic cargo proceeded to take her on a voyage through the paper's inner sanctum, which consisted of the publisher's office—the nameplate on the open door said *Oswald Heckles*; another on the desk inside just said *Ozzie*—a loading bay in back, and a room that contained a computer, a scanner, a big laser printer, and a machine for collating and folding pages. He apologized for not knowing exactly how all the gadgets worked but seemed quite familiar with and proud of the paper and its operations, and she decided he was most likely the publisher as well as the principal photographer, reporter, and editor. Based on the presence of a small, tidy desk in one corner of the printing room, Rose further postulated the existence of an assistant, who most likely *did* know exactly how all the gadgets worked, and who was probably at lunch.

Once the grand tour was completed, her guide took her back to the publisher's office. She sat in a plastic chair while he settled in behind the desk to finish polishing off the meatball sub. Given the small scale of the operation, she was fairly impressed at how good the finished product looked, and told him so. He beamed and graciously credited that to his son Chris the computer whiz and to his assistant Susan, who kept everything running smoothly. Then he said: "So. Why are you interested in our Mrs. Arvidsson?"

Rose explained about the house fire in Bentonville, showed him the picture of Cassandra Weiss. "Yep, I've seen that girl," he said. "Not often, mind you. Mrs. Arvidsson never came into town much.

Once a week to church and the grocery store was about her limit on community interaction. But when the family came to visit, sometimes they would all turn up at the diner or the park. Everyone around here was shocked to hear what happened to them. If Enid hadn't passed away already, the news probably would have killed her."

"Enid?"

"Sorry. That's Mrs. Arvidsson. I'm kind of on a first-name basis with everyone in town."

"Everyone? Literally?"

"It's not that big of a town. You can test me if you want to."

"I'll take your word for it. So do you know what she died of? Enid, I mean? The kid at the gas station told me her head exploded."

Ozzie chuckled. "Young Roger watches too many movies. She had a stroke. Now maybe you could make the case that *does* mean her head exploded, in a sense, but the specific rumor amongst the impressionable folk is that there was an actual explosion, with bits and pieces flying all over."

"I would think young Roger would be old enough to know that's impossible except in the movies."

"Yeah, well, the closed casket wake didn't do anything to dispel the notion. And where the Arvidssons were concerned, there was not always a nice sharp line between the possible and the impossible."

"Oh?"

"Yeah." He took a big bite of sub. One of the meatballs fell out and rolled across the desk, leaving a trail of sauce behind it. It came to rest against his soda cup. Ozzie picked it up and stuffed it back into the bun. "Did Roger tell you about all the land Mrs. Arvidsson owned?"

"He alluded to it. He's still holding a grudge from having to go all the way out there during his paper route days."

"Ha! Yeah, he would be. Notoriously bad tipper, Enid was. Well, they owned about a hundred acres of woodland, and that's on top of the fields the family used to farm back in the day."

"What day would this be?"

"Oh, way back. Since the late eighteen-hundreds, early nineteen-hundreds. Even into the nineteen-sixties, Gustav Arvidsson—Enid's husband—still kept a small amount of land planted, gentleman farmer style."

"Why'd he stop?"

"He vanished. There one day, gone the next. Just like this." Ozzie plucked a meatball out of the sub and popped it into his mouth. "After it became obvious old Gustav wasn't coming back, Enid let the fields go fallow and they started reverting to forest. Except for ... Okay, here's a story that goes to what I said about the Arvidssons. You know how when old-time farmers first cleared their fields, they would move all the big rocks to one place, get them out of the way of their plows?"

"Uh-huh. They would pile them up or make fences out of them."

"Exactly. So out in the Arvidsson's fields, there was this really big flat-topped boulder. You could build a house on top of it, or a church, if you wanted to actualize a biblical metaphor. No way the early Arvidssons could move that thing, except maybe by dynamiting it to pieces, and who wants to go to that much trouble? So they just dragged up all the other rocks over and piled them up around it. After they stopped farming that location you got second-growth forest springing up all around it. No more field there, just woods and rocks. With me so far?"

Rose nodded, wondering where this was going and exactly how simple Ozzie thought she was if he figured he might have lost her already.

"Now, kids being kids, they like to have parties out in the woods, away from adult supervision. Every new crop of teenagers that discovers this location decides it would be a great idea to throw their little soirées. Up on top of the big rock, you can have your bonfire and not worry about the forest going up in flames. It's a local tradition from which the present generation is not excepted. So one night, my son and a bunch of his cronies climb up there and they spread out their blankets and they start their fire and they sit around it drinking their, uh, beverages, and roasting their hot dogs and making out and whatnot. They have their music going from their boombox." Here, Ozzie paused for an air guitar solo. "Night falls. The boombox goes on the fritz. No more tunes, just static. And then they start hearing voices in the static, lots of different ones. Talking, but nobody can make out the words. Laughing, but crazy laughing, not happy laughing. Crying. Babbling."

"Sounds like a good time to turn off the boombox," Rose said.

"Oh, they did. But the voices keep coming. So they—"

"Take out the batteries?"

"—Take out the batteries. But the voices keep coming. How is that possible? It's not. They were already more than a little drunk, and now they're more than a little scared. What do you do when you're drunk and scared?"

"Punch somebody?"

Ozzie saluted her with his cup. "Sure, if there's somebody to punch. Another option is, you take off. That's what they opted to do. They cleared out and left the boombox where it was, static-talking into the night. The next day the owner of the boombox—this would be my son—he goes back to get it. It's right where they left it. No noise coming out now. Whew. He sees the batteries are arranged in a little tower. Did he do that? Damned if he can remember. He loads them back up, turns it on, but the thing is dead. Doesn't work. He brings it home, plugs it into the wall. Nothing. The boombox never makes another sound." He took a sip of his drink, set the cup down. "The kids still have parties there, but my son hasn't been back for one since."

"Well," Rose said after a moment. "That's an interesting story."

"Isn't it, though?"

"Do you believe it? About the voices?"

Ozzie shrugged. "Hell, I don't know. But the boombox was toast. That part is a fact. I know, because I had to buy him a new one."

"Lots of things can happen to electronics that get left outside overnight. Maybe it got wet."

"Sure, that's possible. But strange things do go on in those woods. Come turkey season, you're guaranteed at least four accidental shootings."

"Come on. That happens everywhere. If hunters shooting each other means a forest is haunted, then the state is full of ghosts."

"Fair enough. Here's another thing: People have gotten lost in there for days. That property is just not big enough to get lost in for that long. You keep walking in the same direction, any direction, eventually you come to a road. Probably not even take you two hours. Yet I can give you at least three instances of search parties being called out."

"It's easy to get turned around in the woods and start walking in circles."

He tipped his soda cup at her, conceding the point. "Okay, one more thing. Route 18, it runs next to this forest, out the other side of town. Sheriff Thomas, he gets people, oh, three, four times a year calling to tell him they see things in the woods. Lights moving around, weird figures, pale faces just inside the woods staring out at them. Cyclists have reported being shadowed by figures they can't identify. Sheriff's department checks the calls out, but they've never found anything. Not once."

"That could just mean there's nothing to find."

"Yeah, it could. But you're still writing it all down."

She *had* been writing it all down, her pencil scratching away in her notebook as Ozzie spoke; figuring he had finally finished discoursing on the subject of the Arvidssons and their haunted forest, she closed it up and put it back in her bag. "Well, I've taken up enough of your time," she said. "Thanks for the information and the local folklore."

He waved a hand at the suggestion that he could have possibly had something to do besides talk to her. "You came all this way. What say we go out to Wishbone Road? I'll show you the big flat rock and the Arvidsson homestead. You can get a few shots for your story, at least."

She thought about it. She hadn't actually told Ozzie that she was working on an article, though of course he would have assumed she was here on assignment from the paper. Alan liked to say the *Herald-Journal* was not the *Times*, but from Ozzie's perspective, out here in the sticks producing his little five-pager out of what amounted to a garage, the Bentonville paper must seem like a metropolitan standard. No wonder he wanted to help her out. Dip a toe into the big leagues. Chase the story where it led. Which, in this case, was, apparently, to an empty farmhouse.

Well, why not?

Maybe she could get another picture of a ghost.

Once Pedro's shift was over, instead of going home, he hung around the mall for a while, playing video games in the arcade, wandering from store to store pretending to shop. It wasn't that he particularly liked being here, but he happened to know that Sandy was working today, and would be getting out a few hours after he did. When it got to be close to her quitting time, he positioned himself in the small food court, along the path she usually took to the exit. To make it all seem casual, he got himself a burger and fries. She didn't come by at the usual time, though; he finished the burger and there was still no sign of her, forcing him to drag out the fry-eating process, consuming them one by one, slowly, as if he was really, really savoring them, which he wasn't, because they had gotten cold. Nobody liked cold fries.

To keep himself from getting nervous and leaving, he occupied his mind with people-watching. The mall was always crowded on hot summer days, when everyone came to enjoy the air conditioning without spending their own electricity dollars to run it. School would be reopening soon, so there were plenty of families shopping with their kids, picking up supplies and new clothes for the coming year. His gaze strayed to the shoe place opposite the food court, which was full of customers tugging sneakers onto their feet, then walking around on the carpeting to see how they felt. As he watched, a girl with long blonde hair marched up to the big window that faced the hallway, stood there for a second facing the food court. That reminded him of the mournful girl he'd seen at the old man's house, or thought he'd seen, anyway, standing there in the dining room window, staring out at the world. But this girl was just out shopping with her family, and after a moment, she shook her head and turned around and marched back to her parents. No sale.

"Pedro!"

He looked up and there was Sandy Peterson standing right next to the table, looking absolutely smashing in a light sweater and black skirt and ridiculously complicated high-heeled shoes, hanging on with both hands to a big bag from a novelty store down the north wing of the mall.

"Oh," he said. "Hi."

"You're in the ozone, Pedro. I've been standing her for, like, *minutes*, waiting for you to notice me."

How had he missed *that?* "Sorry," he said. "I was thinking."

"About what?"

"Just, uh, stuff."

"Stuff? Sounds major." She brushed a strand of hair away from her face. "What're you still doing here, anyway? You got off work, like, an hour ago, didn't you?"

"Two hours. But our house isn't air conditioned, so I'm hanging out here until it cools off outside."

"All by yourself? Sad." She plopped down into the chair opposite him. "Lucky for you I came by."

"Sure is. What's in the bag? New shoes?"

"No." She lowered her voice to a whisper and leaned forward. "Props."

"Props?"

"Yeah. For a little thing we're doing tonight."

"A thing? What kind of a thing? A party?"

"Not exactly. A little get together at Pete's house. Do you want to come? I promise it'll be more fun this time."

"Yeah, okay, sure." He popped the last of the fries into his mouth.

"Cool." She flashed that grin at him. "I was going to call Pete to come get me, but maybe you can give me a ride instead?"

After he stopped choking on the fries, Pedro told her he of course he would.

As they drove along Route 18 on their way out to Mrs. Arvidsson's property, Ozzie started fiddling with Rose's radio, turning knobs and punching buttons as he traversed the staticky wasteland of the local airwaves. She glanced at his activities a few times, then said, "You'd better not mess up my presets, Ozzie."

"Just looking for—ah, there we go." He had found some local college station, a couple of young amateur DJs in the booth whose speech patterns reminded her of some people she surprised with interviews: Eager to talk, but not sure why anybody wanted to listen to them. Still, when they stopped jabbering and started spinning tunes, the music was quite all right. They continued on, serenaded by discordant alt-rock melodies, while the forested perimeter of Mrs. Arvidsson's property went scrolling by. She kept glancing at the woods but didn't spot any lurking shapes or phantasmal faces: Disappointing, but hardly surprising.

"Pull off here," Ozzie said. She eased onto the grassy shoulder. Ozzie pointed to a path, barely visible in the wall of the woods. "That goes to the party rock. It's about a half mile in. Up for a walk?"

Rose thought about it for a minute, then said: "Yeah, all right."

Ozzie led the way along the leaf-lined path into the quiet woods, the steady whoosh of traffic on Route 18 becoming muffled, then fading. The trees here were mostly young, slender trunks supporting light-colored crowns, second or third growth dating to when Mrs. Arvidsson had let the cropland go fallow. Curving arcs of brambles, saplings, and broad ferns occupied the spaces between the trees. The ground sloped down from the road before bottoming out in an old flood plain bisected by a deep-channeled creek. A log lay across the gap, serving as a bridge; the top had been planed and heavily scored with an axe to provide a relatively flat surface for walking. On the other side, the path turned sideways to climb a steep bank, cresting and disappearing over a sharp fold of earth.

"Coffee Creek" Ozzie said, gesturing at the stream. "So named for the color. Tannins leaching from fallen leaves turn the water—"

"I'm familiar with tannins," she said. "Is it much farther?"

"No, we're almost there." He crossed to the other side. Rose followed, but stopped in the middle to peer down into the sepia current. Although the stream was narrow, it looked fairly deep; she could just barely see the rocks at the bottom, outlines in the dark water. Her reflection wobbled on the surface, her pale white skin tea-stained, her eyes shadowed pits, her hair almost invisible, making it look like a skull was peering back. She could imagine decrepit hands reaching from below, closing over her reflection, pulling it down into a placid, eternal darkness.

From the opposite bank, Ozzie said: "There used to be a story, popular amongst the impressionable folk, that if you look at Coffee Creek for too long you might see a skull looking back at you, and if you do, it means there's going to be a death in the family soon."

She glanced at him, stood up. "Yeah? Does seeing the skull make the death happen, or was the death already going to happen and that's why you see the skull?"

"I don't think that's an answerable question," Ozzie said. Then: "So what did you see? Anything of interest?"

"Just my reflection. But I can see how the impressionable folk might think they were seeing a skull, if by *impressionable* you mean *drunk*."

Ozzie chuckled and put his finger to the side of his nose, then turned and continued along the trail. They went up the ridge and down the other side, through a stand of narrow pines, fallen needles making a spongy brown cushion under their feet. No significant brush grew between the conifers and she could see, a little distance away, the beginning of a rock-filled clearing. Just before they reached it, the trail they were on ended at another path that came in from their right; Ozzie told her that one led to the Arvidsson homestead. They turned left and followed the new trail to the field of stones. It occupied a broad, shallow depression, as if all the weight had bowed the earth. Along the edges, the rocks were the size of bowling balls and watermelons, growing larger towards the interior. A leviathan brooded at the center like a dead star in a grey solar system.

"Behold," Ozzie said, making an expansive two-handed gesture, like a carnival barker introducing his most astounding freak. "The Anvil."

Rose squinted at it, mentally comparing its square footage to her apartment. "That's a big rock all right," she said.

They continued along the path as it wove among the rocks. Branches and spurs exited from both sides as if they were in a petrified hedge maze, but the main trail was wide and well-worn and Rose didn't think she would've had any trouble finding her way to the middle even without Ozzie's assistance. A skirt of bare earth girdled the Anvil, three or four feet wide, hard-packed dirt angled slightly downward toward the center. Ozzie turned left and went around a corner and they came to a spot where a pile of smaller stones had been jammed into a cleft in the Anvil, forming a rough slope that reached almost to the top, ten or fifteen feet overhead. A knotted rope dangled from above to help intrepid explorers achieve the summit. "As you can see," Ozzie said, "this is the usual route folks take to get up there." Rose eyed this setup, considered the prospects, and gave Ozzie a pointed look. He laughed and patted his belly with both hands. "Unless you've got a crane in your purse, I won't be doing any climbing today. You feel free to go on up if you want to, though."

"Right," Rose said. She slung her camera around her shoulder to her back, then grabbed the rope and used it to haul herself up the makeshift ramp. A few of the rocks turned under her feet, but they were just rotating in place; overall, the structure felt surprisingly sturdy. At the top, she found that the rope was tied to an iron piton hammered deep into a crack near the edge. The broad and barren moonscape atop the Anvil was uneven but mostly flat, broken into a network of weathered slabs. It reminded her of a long-abandoned parking lot. She could see the remains of a few stumps where small trees had been removed, as well as a couple of natural depressions that had been repurposed as fire pits. Old half-burned logs and ashes, wet from last night's rain, hunched in them like dull shadows. She took pictures of the surface, and a few of the surrounding stones, then circled the Anvil, listening for spectral noises. Nobody was humming or singing or talking today. She returned to her starting point. Below, Ozzie leaned against a rock the size of a small car, arms folded behind his head, eyes closed, blue-shirted belly sticking out between his red suspenders. Just for the hell of it, she took a picture of him, too.

He opened his eyes. "Don't print *that*," he said. "You'll scare off all your readers."

With Sandy giving directions, Pedro drove them to one of the newer developments in town, then along a network of tree-lined back streets, with a little park and a creek and a man-made pond in the middle of it. Pete's house was a split level towards the back of the neighborhood. Pedro parked along the curb in front of it. Sandy retrieved her shopping bag and they headed around back. The yard sloped sharply downward, allowing for direct access to the basement via a door in the foundation. It was unlocked; she opened it and they went inside. The cellar was done up like an ersatz hunting lodge, with wood paneling and tartan upholstery and pictures of deer and ducks and turkeys on the wall. Pedro didn't see Pete, but Glenn was there, sitting in a folding chair at a game table in the center of the room, beneath a dangling chandelier made of antlers that were too uniform to be real. The lights were turned down low. When they entered there were three chairs around the table, evenly spaced. Glenn looked at Sandy, then at Pedro, then went and got another folding chair out of a narrow cabinet and rearranged the seating into quadrants before sitting down again.

"Are we playing poker or something?" Pedro said.

"Or something." That was Pete, coming down from the upstairs, carrying snacks and a case of beer. "Hey Pedro."

"Hey."

Sandy frowned. "I thought we said no alcohol."

"This is for after." Pete put the beer in a refrigerator that was disguised as more paneling, left the snacks on the counter next to it, then went to the game table and sat down opposite Glenn.

"After what?" Pedro said.

"This." Sandy pulled a box out of her shopping bag and put it on the table. The glowing bulbs reflected a halo off the plastic shrink-wrap of a ouija board. Pedro stared at it for a second, then looked at Sandy. She gave a little shrug. "I saw a movie once where they used one of these."

"So did I," Pedro said. "Somebody got possessed and killed a bunch of people."

After a moment Sandy said, a bit stiffly, "I think that was a different movie."

"Yeah, but yhe people didn't know which movie they were in until it was too late."

"Come on, Pedro." She sat in the third chair and pushed the last one out with her foot. "Four players is better than three."

"It is?"

"Sure. Four points of a compass, right?"

"Four sides of a square?" Glenn offered.

"Four Horsemen of the Apocalypse?" Pete said. Sandy smacked him.

Pedro was pretty sure Sandy was just making that up about the number of players, but he settled into the fourth chair anyway. "I'll just watch for now," he said.

"Okay," Glenn said. "You can make sure the spirits don't steal our beer."

Sandy tore off the plastic wrap and set up the board, with its spooky lettering and a plastic triangle with a hole in it that Glenn, who was reading the instructions, said was called a *planchette*. When they were ready to start, Pete and Sandy put their fingers on the planchette and Glenn started asked questions, trying to elicit responses from the spirits. The planchette never moved. After several minutes had gone by, Pete said: "This thing doesn't work."

Sandy shushed him. "You'll disturb the spirits."

"There's no spirits to disturb."

Pedro had no idea why they thought they might find ghosts hanging around a house that had only been built eight or nine years ago, but still, Sandy asked Glenn to call them again. He loudly repeated his invitation for any available spirits to come and say hello. More minutes passed with no results. Finally Pete took his fingers off the planchette and pushed back his chair. "All circuits are dead," he said. "Time for beer and chips." He got up and headed for the refrigerator. A moment later Glenn stood up, stretched, and wandered over to inspect a rack of videotapes, pulling them out and looking at them and putting them back.

Pedro, still in his seat, was watching Sandy. Her eyes were wet; she was crying, *crying*, over the failure of a tawdry chip of plastic and a board full of letters to dial up a ghost on demand. Pedro leaned forward and said, "What's wrong?"

"I wanted to talk to Pop-Pop," she said, her voice barely above a whisper.

And suddenly Pedro understood. Her grandfather had passed away a few months earlier, just before the end of the school year. His death had been sudden and unexpected; Pedro remembered sitting with a tearful Sandy in the dugout at the ball field behind the school as she sobbed and told him how Pop-Pop would never see her graduate, how she hadn't even gotten a chance to say goodbye. And now here she was, trying to grab for an opportunity she had missed.

Words came out of Pedro's mouth, unbidden, before he had a chance to think about them. "Maybe we should take the board someplace else."

All three of them looked at him.

Sandy said, "Like where?"

Wishbone Road was long and straight and narrow, paved with old asphalt that had decayed into broken sheets of blacktop brownies. Trees stood thick on either side, tangling themselves up in the telephone lines. In the distance the land humped up in rather sharp hills; they were stubbled with an older, taller, darker forest, growth that had never been cut for farmland or timber. The road climbed gently and curved to the right and then they emerged into open land, acres of it, rolling up in a gentle grassy slope surrounded by woods and scrub. The pavement decomposed into a gravel driveway and split in two. The wider branch ran along the edge of the field toward a large, square, plain house and detached garage that abutted the woods; the other branch quickly dwindled to two slender, parallel ribbons of crushed grey stone almost hidden by grass and low, broad-leafed weeds. It ran across the field to a prim little barn, bright red with white trim, apparently converted from its former use into a guest house or something.

"The Arvidsson homestead," Ozzie said, pointing at each structure in turn. "Former farmhouse, former stable, and renovated barn."

"What was the barn renovated into?"

"Apartments. Two, maybe three. I can't remember exactly. They were rented off and on, but nobody ever stayed very long—Enid used to advertise them in my paper, so I always knew when a tenant left—and she finally gave up on being a landlady to live in splendid isolation."

She parked in front of the Arvidsson house, eyed the place. *Splendid* was not an adjective she would have applied. The building rested, somewhat crookedly, atop a windowless foundation that consisted of slate and river rock mashed and mortared together. The roof sagged in the middle as well as at both ends, and had moss growing in the shade of the chimney. A long clapboard wall with faded, peeling yellow paint faced away from them at an angle, slightly warped, grimy windows and white lace curtains standing between the world and the unlit rooms inside. On the short side there was a small front porch, with wooden columns supporting a miniature peaked roof and settles for walls on the left and right. The high-backed benches had latches on their seats, secured with old padlocks. Storage bins. She wondered what was in them. Yard stuff, most likely. Tools. Pots. Outdoor toys, things Cassandra Weiss had played with, maybe. She surveyed the rest of the property. To the left of the house, a large three-stall garage stood. Instead of overhead doors, it had solid wooden gates that swung outward. Tall grass grew in front of all but one of the stalls. The door to that one hung slightly open. A red and yellow sign in front of it advertised the estate sale that she had missed. The sign had fallen over and was partially hidden in the weeds. Whoever had run the sale must have forgotten it when they'd packed everything up.

Rose reached in the back for her camera bag, then got out of the car. Ozzie got out, too, and wandered around without an apparent objective while she took a few pictures of the house and grounds. If there were ghosts here, they didn't oblige her by leaning out of the windows or gliding through the tall grass at the shadowed edges of the forest. She tried to picture what it would be like to live out here in Ozzie's so-called splendid isolation, but all she could imagine was her husband complaining about the upkeep. *Do you know how long it takes me to mow that grass every week? To clear that driveway in winter? The insulation here is crap. We have to replace all the windows. Why are you after me all the time to do things? Fix this. Fix that. I wish we had never moved here.*

"Shut up, Joe," she muttered.

Ozzie said, "Pardon?"

"Nothing." She glanced at him over her shoulder. "This place looks pretty old. Do you know when it was built?"

"I believe it's colonial," he said. "Actual colonial, I mean, not *in-the-style-of.* It could probably be listed as a historic building if anybody wanted to submit it."

"Has it belonged to the Arvidsson family the whole time?"

"Um, I'm not sure. Marjorie could tell you. That's my wife. She's an amateur historian about the area. Don't tell her I said *amateur.*"

"Noted." Rose moved away from the car and took pictures of the garage and the former barn, which was visible across the rise of the hill. Ozzie said something about retrieving Estelle's sign and ambled toward the garage. Rose went up onto the porch and tried to look through one of the tall, narrow windows bordering the door. It had an opaque curtain stretched tightly across it, top to bottom, and she couldn't see inside. Next to the window on the right was an ancient doorbell, a weathered brass hump with a black button on the end. She pressed the button, hearing a harsh buzz from inside the house, loud enough that she felt the vibration under her feet. Seconds passed. There was no answer, of course. She didn't press the button again.

Rose turned around. Late afternoon sun slanted in from the front of the porch, forcing her to squint as she peered out at the sprawling field, the forest, the sky, the looming tree-shrouded hills that obscured the horizon. The wind gusted, first from one direction, then the other, shivering the tall grass. The high-backed settles blocked the breeze so she couldn't feel it. The soft, plump clouds seemed frozen in the sky.

She heard a sound from her left. Faint. Like knuckles gently rapping on the backside of the settle.

"Ozzie?" she said.

Silence.

Then she heard the same sound from her right.

The two high-backed benches blocked her vision; she was unable to see in any direction except straight ahead, the slightly bowed steps down to the grass, her little blue car a dozen yards away on the gravel. It belatedly occurred to her that she was essentially cornered here on the porch, in the middle of nowhere, and that if someone happened to want to do her harm, nobody would see, nobody would hear, nobody would intervene, except for Ozzie. But he could have been waylaid out by the garage. Or he himself could be some kind of maniac. Big, jovial Ozzie, well-known proprietor of the local small press paper? Who would suspect him? She'd immediately pegged him as a harmless journalistic wannabe—otherwise she wouldn't have come out here with him—but it wasn't as if serial killers went around wearing special hats so you could recognize them.

She stood very still and listened for footsteps, whispers, laughter, anything. The wind blew, but not on her. The sun went behind a cloud. Its shadow flowed across the field like spilled ink.

Then lidded seats of the settles began to move, thumping from the inside, the padlocks rattling and shaking, as if the toys she'd imagined they contained had come to life and wanted to escape their confinement, to lurch at her with arms outstretched, demanding that she play mysterious games.

Rose bolted off the porch, down to her car, practically vaulted over the hood to get to the other side, and she stood behind it panting, listening to the blood pound through her ears. The noises from the porch had stopped, the shuddering lids stilled. She looked at the garage but didn't see Ozzie. The garage door was open wider than it had been when they arrived. She called his name but it came out as a faint, ridiculous croak. She called him again. Her voice was a little louder this time. A zephyr kicked up, stirred the grassy stalks, died down again. The old house groaned, a long, low, wooden sound, dry and dead. Something was here, she thought, in the house or out in the woods, somewhere it could see her. She could feel its gaze, cold, evaluating, marking her down in some kind of ledger.

"Ozzie!" This time it came out a proper shout.

Silence.

Then he appeared from inside the garage, placidly unperturbed, carrying a cardboard box full of stuff, with the estate sale sign tucked into his armpit.

"Sorry," he said. "Just doing some shopping."

5

AFTER STOPPING AT THE MOTEL to drop off her ridiculous little suitcase—he was going to have to find someone to box up all Janice's crap from her house and ship it to Virginia; maybe it would be fun to ask Richard to do it—Hank took his daughter out for pizza at the greasy dive near the airport. Apparently it hadn't occurred to the genius owners to decorate in a manner consistent with their name and location; you'd think it would at least have propellers on the wall or model airplanes dangling from the ceiling, but no. What it *did* have was this awful red and white color scheme and casino-style neon lights that made your eyes bleed. So stupid. At least casinos compensated for their hideousness with slot machines and short-skirted cocktail waitresses.

Either of those things would have been a welcome distraction, because the whole time they were at the restaurant, Janice didn't say two words to him; she just sat there holding Candy, her big creepy porcelain-faced doll. In fact, since giving him a perfunctory hug and introducing him to the doll—both of which she'd only done at the urging of the caseworker who'd met with Hank briefly ahead of time, then supervised the kid's transfer from police custody, a process that reminded Hank of a prisoner exchange in a Cold War spy movie—Janice had barely even acknowledged his existence. He probably shouldn't have been surprised; thanks to Beth, it had been years since the kid had seen him, so he was pretty much a stranger to his own daughter. Yet another reason for him to be pissed at the whole crazy Bartoski clan.

Once they finished up their pizza, they headed back to the motel.

Janice sat quietly in the back seat, staring out the window, clutching her stupid doll, giving monosyllabic answers to anything he asked her. That just made him ask more questions, increasingly difficult ones, in a louder voice. How had she liked kindergarten? What was her teacher's name? Where had her mother been working? Did her mother have lots of friends? How many of them were boys? Had she met any of them? More than once? Sometimes Janice professed not to know the answer, but after he asked the same thing three or four times, she usually came up with one. By the time they got back to the motel, the kid was looking a little teary-eyed, but she was going to have to get used to talking to grownups.

He pulled into an empty spot near the entrance closest to their room and got out. It took him a second to realize Janice wasn't following him to the building. He went back to the car and found her sniffling and fumbling with the seatbelt as if she had never been in a car before. "Jesus Christ, Janice, you just push the button," he said, leaning in and demonstrating. The belt released and snapped upward, the metal latch plate smacking him on the chin. It didn't really hurt, but it stung a little. Fucking piece of shit rental car. He hauled Janice and her creepy doll out of the car and slammed the door shut with his foot, making her squeak in surprise. After that she tried to mule it, planting her little legs on the pavement instead of walking like a civilized human. How the fuck had Beth been raising this kid? He gave her one chance to move under her own power and when she didn't he picked her up and carried her, screaming, into the motel. There was an old couple coming down the hallway, giving him disapproving old person looks. He grinned and tipped an imaginary hat to them as they went by, though the grin vanished as soon as they passed. He was still stewing about those judgmental fucks, about the squalling kid, about everything Beth and her family had done to him, when he reached the door of his room and realized someone was leaning against the wall next to it.

"Evening, Hank," Richard said.

Hank didn't look happy to see him, or about anything else. Janice was in the middle of a meltdown, slung over her father's shoulder, screaming in his ear. Richard wasn't sure if he would get invited into the room, told to fuck off, or socked in the face, but apparently even

Hank realized that getting into a fight while carrying a little girl was a bad idea, if only because it didn't leave both fists free for punching; after a few tense seconds of eye contact he grunted a greeting and set Janice down and unlocked the door. She stood there snuffling for a moment, then noticed Richard and came running over and latched onto him. He hoisted her into the air and followed Hank into the room for some awkward family reunion time.

Inside, Hank kicked off his shoes, lay down on the bed, and turned on the television. Richard went to the chair by the window and sat down, arranging Janice in his lap. They sat for a while as Hank watched local news that he obviously didn't care about. Finally Richard said, "So how are things in Virginia? I heard you work in a cave?"

"No, I work *for* a cave."

"What's that like?"

"Where I am, it's basically an office."

"Do you get to go into the cave for free?"

"Why would I want to go into the cave? It's cold and dark and wet down there."

"Is that what you tell people when you're doing public relations?"

"Of course not. But nobody is paying me to care what you think."

The phone rang. Hank picked it up and said *hello* like he was naming a color. Richard watched him listen and nod and say, "Yeah, actually, he's right here with me. You need him?" Hank listened a little bit more, then grinned and looked at Richard and said, "Did you forget to keep Detective Leeson informed of your whereabouts?"

"Shit," Richard muttered. Then: "Can you get his number? I'll call him back from my room."

"Anything to get rid of you," Hank said. He asked for the number and wrote it on hotel stationery and presented it to Richard with an ostentatious flourish. Richard set Janice down, ruffled her hair, took the piece of paper, and left. As he opened the door to his own room he heard a soft, whispery noise, like pages rustling, and then a faint slapping sound. He went in slowly, took a look around, but nothing seemed to have been disturbed; his hospital bag sat on the dresser, his spare clothes lay in a heap in the chair, and his father's notebook was on the nightstand where he'd left it. He closed the door. The clouds that had been gathering all day had begun to dribble, leaving stretched-out drops of water down the tall window. The wind was picking up a bit, teasing the rain into diagonal slashes. Maybe that was the sound he'd heard. He sat down on the bed, picked up the phone, dialed Leeson's number. Art's phone rang and rang and rang. Maybe he was busy arresting suspects. Finally a recorded voice told Richard the cellular customer was unavailable and that he should leave a message after the tone. Richard did so, then hung up.

He looked at the door and thought about going back to Hank's room, but decided not to push his luck; after all, Hank would be the one deciding if and when he got to see Janice for the next decade or so. He reached for the television remote, lifted it up, put it down without using it. He picked up the notebook instead, opened it to the first page.

The top line said, *The girl escaped today and Victor made me kill her.*

Ozzie must have thought Rose was nuts, the way she hustled him back into her car, telling him to toss Estelle's sign and his box of crap in the back seat instead of popping the trunk, then driving away from that farmhouse faster than she should have on the crumbling asphalt that returned them to Route 18. He didn't inquire why they were leaving in such a hurry or press her for a reason in the car, but once they were back on the sidewalk in front of his office he finally asked if she had seen something out there. And she told him no, she hadn't seen anything, but she had heard something and she had felt something and that had been quite enough to convince her it was time to leave. "Do you have any idea what Mrs. Arvidsson might have kept in the storage compartments on her porch?" she said.

"Afraid not," he said. "I can check with Estelle and see if she knows, though."

"Okay. Thanks."

"No problem." They made a little small talk and then Rose said she had to get going, at which point he invited her to follow him home—he said it was on the way back to Bentonville—and come in for coffee, talk some more about the old Arvidsson place. Rose remained slightly concerned that Ozzie might do something awkward, like proposition her or, worse, ask her to get him a job at the *Herald-Journal*, but she was pretty sure she could handle any such developments and accepted the offer.

She followed his car up Route 18, then onto a side road, then onto a private road with lots of long gated driveways. Ozzie stopped at a brown block fence with a black iron barricade that he evidently operated from a transmitter in his car. It rattled aside and they rolled on through. She watched in her rear-view mirror as it closed again behind them. The driveway went uphill between landscaped swells. Peaks and gables came into view, followed by the rest of a big stone house—a mansion, really—made of variegated brick, shot through with big windows, topped by a slate roof. The gate whirred shut behind her as she drove into a loop of the driveway and parked beside a front porch that could have sheltered a regiment from a rainstorm. Ozzie pulled his vehicle into a multi-car garage the size of a small house. She got out and stood there slack-jawed staring at the place. She stopped worrying that he might ask her for a job at the *Herald-Journal* and started worrying that he might buy it and become her boss.

Ozzie appeared, trotting along a flower-lined walk that led to the garage. Not saying a word, he collected his box and Estelle's sign from the back of Rose's car and started up the stairs to his front door, then stopped for a theatric glance over his shoulder. "I'm a wealthy dilettante masquerading as a small-town newspaperman," he said. "Do you still respect me?"

She laughed and said sure she did and followed him up the stairs. At the top, he paused again and reminded her in a not-entirely-joking tone to please not mention that he had referred to his wife as an *amateur* historian. She nodded and they went into the house, where said wife was already waiting for them. Marjorie appeared unsurprised that Ozzie had brought a stray home; apparently he had called ahead from the car. Rose and Marjorie chatted while Ozzie prepared the coffee, scooping aromatic black powder out of a bag with foreign writing on it to fill the basket of a gleaming appliance that looked like it had been taken out of a visiting spaceship. The machine emitted industrial-sounding noises for a few minutes and then Rose was sipping the best coffee she had ever tasted. She wondered if Ozzie would give her some to take home if she asked for it, but decided that whatever alchemy had produced the beverage here could not possibly be replicated by her department store coffee maker. Better just to savor it now than to besmirch the memory later.

Cups in hand, she and Ozzie and Marjorie retired to the dining room table to talk about the Arvidsson family's long history in the area, which was now at an end. Marjorie had evidently been briefed that this would be the topic, as she had gathered some material from her archives before they arrived. Despite his wife's being the historian, Ozzie did most of the talking, with Marjorie periodically correcting a piece of misinformation or steering him back on course when he veered off on a tangent, which happened a lot. Rose started to suspect that the main job for Ozzie's assistant at the paper was keeping him focused. Still, she did find out lots of local gossip about old Mrs. Arvidsson, the stories about her house and property, her husband's decades-old disappearance and her own recent passing. None of it really illuminated the events at the Potter Street house—Beth Bartoski's death, the apparition of the little girl—or Rose's strange experience out at the farmhouse, but she still jotted it all down in her notebook as pretend background for the article Ozzie thought she was writing.

As things were winding down, Ozzie offered to do some investigatory legwork into the old lady's land and family, and even volunteered to spend the night at the Anvil with recording equipment to see if he could capture any spectral voices. Both Rose and Marjorie tried to convince him that this was unnecessary and possibly even dangerous to his physical well-being, but he had latched onto the idea with a startling degree of enthusiasm and would not be dissuaded. By the time they said their goodnights and Rose drove off through the gate, which Ozzie operated from the front door via remote control, she had concluded that being a wealthy dilettante who masqueraded as a small-town newspaperman must be boring and he was looking for a way to liven things up.

If only she could have such problems.

Richard sat in a motel armchair that was the same color as a raw carrot, and almost as soft. He had the desk lamp on and the drapes closed to shut out the greying afternoon light as he read his father's spindly script, scrawled with blue ink in a shaky hand. *I don't know how the girl escaped,* it said. *The rope holding her to the water pipe should have been tight, but my fingers aren't as sure as they used to be. She must have worked herself loose.*

I heard the stairs creaking when she came out of the basement. I must have forgotten to set the latch on the door because when I got there she was at the front door, holding Elizabeth's old doll, trying to work the deadbolt. She saw me and ran upstairs. I have trouble with the stairs now but Victor would have been very angry if she got away so I climbed them as fast as I could on my hands and knees. I found her in the front room. She had managed to open the window and was trying to climb out, but I caught her and pulled her back in. She squirmed and fell and hit her head and lay still. Then Victor was there, telling me to put my hands around her throat, and I did. He told me to squeeze, and I did. The whole time, she never let go of the doll.

Victor told me what to do next. We went through the woods so no one would see. I brought the books. He carried the girl's body. I had taken her keys, so I could have let us into her house, but the back door was open. They must have left it unlocked in case she came back without her keys. The bedrooms were upstairs, just like in my house. Her parents weren't there. We put the books under their bed and the girl's body in her own closet. Her room reminded me of Elizabeth's room when she was young. Victor told me not to think about that.

We hid outside until the girl's parents came home. Victor followed them into the house. He told me it wouldn't take long and it didn't. They came back out and put a garden hose in their car and drove away. After they were gone, Victor came out with the books we had put in their room. Then we took gasoline and paint from their shed and splashed it all around the carpeting and the walls and set it on fire.

When we got back to my house, I found the doll on the floor in the front hall. I don't know how it got there. I took it into the basement, the books too. I locked the books in the old sea chest, all except this one. I was going to lock the doll in there too but she was looking at me with those eyes and I couldn't do it. I hid her in a box instead.

After that, the ink switched from blue to black. Richard wondered how much time the change of color represented. Hours? Days? Where had the old man been when he had written this next part? How close was he to his death?

Victor said this book was mine, for me to write in. He said it would make me forget, but first I had to change the pattern on the cover, make some new lines with my arc welder. I told him it would destroy the book but he said it wouldn't, not if I was careful. He told me what to do. While I was doing it I swear I heard things, saw things, reaching out for me. The basement got so cold. I put down the welder and ran out of the house and fell asleep in my car for a while. When I went back in, everything seemed normal. Victor was waiting. He told me to start working again, but I couldn't. I took the book and brought it up to my room.

The ink color changed again. Now it was red.

Victor is so angry with me for not finishing the work. He called me names, the same names Edna used to call me. How does he know them? He tells me I'm a weak old coward and a fool. I say he tells me these things but really he screams them. I can hear him muttering all through the house. He comes into my room and walks around my bed and walks away and comes back. His mouth is so big. His arms are so long. His fingers are so cold. I tell him to be quiet but he only screams louder. Louder. Louder.

After that, the writing devolved into slashes and squiggles, as if someone had grabbed the old man's hand and there had been a struggle for control of the pen. Could be that was when the stroke had hit him. But then, after a few blank pages, the drawings started: Not just Beth's room, but all the other rooms of the house as well, the kitchen, the dining room, the living room, the bedrooms, all neat as could be, furnished and tidy, as if the occupants had just finished cleaning and stepped out for ice cream.

Two pages of scrawled rambling about kidnapping, arson, and murder, followed by some nice, sure-handed sketches of the house? It didn't make any sense.

Richard pitched the notebook onto the bed and sat there staring at nothing. Perhaps the old man had been losing his mind, writing fantasy and nonsense, drawing pictures of the house, memories of the past. But still. The vanishing girl he and Beth had seen in the old man's house. The burned and gutted ruins next door. The doll.

Art needed to see this notebook.

Maybe he would get in trouble for taking it out of the house; maybe it was worthless as evidence since it had been in his possession. Didn't matter. That wasn't for him to sort out out. He picked up the phone, dialed the detective's car phone again. *Ring. Ring. Ring.* The cellular customer was still unavailable. Where was Art? Why wasn't he answering?

Well, surely Art wasn't the only one working homicide. He would call the station, talk to somebody else, bring them the book. He picked the phone up and started to dial the police; their number was on a little card next to the phone, along with the number for the fire department, poison control, and other emergency services. While the phone rang, he glanced at the bed where he had tossed the notebook.

It wasn't there.

Maybe he'd tossed it harder than he thought and it had slid off the other side of the bed. He hung up the phone and went to look there.

No book.

A knock on the door drew his attention, one short quick rap. Businesslike. Maybe Detective Leeson had come to see him. He went to the door and opened it, but no one was outside. He looked left. Empty hallway. He looked right. Empty hallway. An unattended housekeeping cart stood a few doors up, outside an open maintenance closet. Puzzled, he stepped into the corridor. Maybe it had just been a kid running by, hitting doors for fun. He walked up to the closet. A hotel employee stood inside, gathering cleaning supplies in a bucket. Her back was to him. He started to ask if she had seen anybody in the hallway, then got distracted by the feeling that someone was next to him, hiding in the cart. He crouched down and started rifling through the folded towels and sheets and washcloths.

"Sir? Can I help you?"

He looked up. The housekeeper loomed overhead, bucket in hand. She was holding a spray bottle as if prepared to fend him off with spritzes of cleanser.

"Uh, sorry," he said, standing up. "I just, uh, I needed a new towel."

Without taking her gaze off him or lowering the bottle, the woman reached into the cart, took out a towel, and handed it to him.

"Thanks," he said.

"You're welcome." Her eyes flicked to his open door. "That your room?"

"Yeah. Um, thanks. Thanks again." He retreated up the hallway, back to his room, conscious of being watched the whole way. He glanced back at her and the cart just before the door closed behind him. She was fixing the stacks of linen that he had disturbed with his rummaging. For a second he thought he saw something, a sliver of blue, between the layers of fabric, but then it was gone and the housekeeper was looking at him with an expression that told him he wasn't going to be getting any fresh towels or sheets today.

Richard hung the *Do Not Disturb* sign on his knob and shut the door.

~~~

They went in two vehicles; Glenn rode with Pedro and Sandy rode with Pete. Pedro parked in his own driveway; Pete parked on the street. They regrouped next to Pedro's car, near the path into the woods. Sandy clutched the department store bag with the ouija board inside, peering with wide eyes at the darkening trees, the lengthening shadows. "How many people died at that house?" she said.

"Two."

"That you know of," Pete added.

"Um, yeah. That I know of. Three, if you count the guy who got electrocuted out in front."

Silence.

"We don't have to go over there," Pedro said. "We could do something else."

More silence. Pedro hoped Sandy would say that she had changed her mind; he'd been wishing he could reach into the past and slap the suggestion out of his mouth ever since he had made it. But then she took a deep breath, held it, let it out, and said: "No, I want to try it. We might have better luck." She looked at Glenn and Pete. "You're both okay with this, right?"

Pete nodded; Glenn said, in a singsong voice, "I ain't afraid of no ghosts."

"All right," Pedro said. "Follow me."

The path was narrow; leaves brushed at him, their light touch like damp fingers sliding over his skin and clothes. Beth Bartoski had come this way to talk to him. These same leaves had trailed over her body. He had sent her away unsatisfied. By the end of the day, she was dead. Now he was going over there to help Sandy communicate with the spirits. What if she raised Beth? What would *that* spirit have to say to him? The thought stopped him cold for a moment. Pete ran into him and said, "Dude."

"Sorry." Pedro started walking again, trying not to think about receiving accusatory messages from dead women. They soon emerged onto the broad expanse of blacktop that formed the parking area outside the old man's garage. The cop paraphernalia he had seen earlier was gone, but the station wagon was still here. Everyone stopped to look at the cracked windshield, the dented hood. They all knew what had been there. The house windows slept darkly, reflecting the gloomy trees and distorted images of the four of them standing there. Pedro eyed the window where he thought he had seen the girl, but it was no different from the others. He headed for the back door, with its square pad of concrete and single step up. The others crunched along after him. Gesturing at the pad, he said, "We can set the board up here, on the patio."

"Are you kidding?" Glenn brushed past him. "You bring us to a haunted house and you don't even want to go in?"

"I didn't want … I mean, I wasn't thinking we would actually do it *inside* the house."

Pete said, "Is it locked?"

Glenn opened the door. "Nope."

"Isn't this is breaking and entering or something?" Pedro said.

"What are you, a lawyer?" Pete said. He went into the mudroom. Pedro followed. Meanwhile, Glenn moved to the inside door, tried the knob, pushed it open. He peered into the dim, cramped, dingy space beyond. Even from here Pedro detected the stale odor of fried bacon and eggs and cigarette smoke. The combination made him a little bit sick to his stomach, like he had licked an ashtray.

"I thought there'd be more cobwebs," Glenn said.

"It's not a movie haunted house. Somebody actually lived here."

"Yeah, you said. A creepy old man, right? Maybe he's still here." Glenn pointed to a small table at the far end. It had two chairs, with room for one more. "Let's set up the board there and find out."

"Okay." Pete glanced back at Sandy. "You coming or what? This is your party."

She had been standing at the threshold of the back door, her face tight and drawn, but now she stepped away from it and bumped it closed with her hip. When she shuffled past Pedro on her way to the short steps up to the kitchen, he put his hand on her shoulder. "Are you all right?" he said.

"Yeah." She gave him a quick smile. "Yeah, I'm good. Let's do this."

They did a quick walk-through of the ground floor to see if anywhere was more suitable than the kitchen. The table in the dining room was bigger, but too loaded with crap for them to set up the board there without sweeping a bunch of stuff onto the floor, which no one was willing to do. Sandy pronounced the floor in the living room gross, with its dirty carpet and scattered newspapers. In the front hall, they looked at the stairs to the second floor and the open door to the basement, but decided not to explore either one. They returned to the kitchen. Sandy and Glenn set up the board on the little table in the nook, then took their places at the chairs. Pedro stood back and watched. It would be fine. The house was quiet. Nothing was going to happen. Nobody was going to go off alone and get killed. Angry spirits were not going to ooze out of the heating vents to clutch at them with ghostly fingers.

Pete went into the dining room and came back carrying a chair. He brought it to the table, then gave Pedro a glance. "You helping this time?" Pedro shook his head. Pete shrugged and sat down. Sandy reached out and tentatively touched the planchette. Pedro glanced into the living room, at the empty space at the table where the chair had been, at the window overlooking the driveway. The damaged station wagon sat on the other side of the shade, hidden from view.

"It moved!" Sandy's excited voice snapped Pedro's head around. "I just barely put my fingers on it and it moved!"

"Are you sure?" Pete said.

"Yes! Ask its name, find out who it is."

Glenn said: "Who are we talking to?"

Pedro heard the pointer swish across the laminated board. He moved forward a little, craned his neck for a better look. Pete and Sandy both had their fingers on the planchette, which slid around in loops and swirls for a second before landing on a letter.

Sandy said, "V."

The eyelike chip of plastic started swooping around again.

Plink.

Pedro looked at the sink. It had started leaking, a slow but steady sequence of watery metallic pings.

"I."

He looked back at the table. His friends' eyes and noses were darkly shadowed in the slanting light from the octagonal window, small and high up in the wall.

"C."

Plink.

Pedro went to the sink and turned both knobs. The hot water handle moved a little. The leak stopped, one final quivering droplet clinging pendulously to the mouth of the faucet.

"T. O. R."

The last droplet fell. *Plink.*

"Victor," Sandy said. She sounded disappointed. "Not Pop-Pop."

"Hey, Pedro," Pete said, "did somebody named Victor used to live here?"

"I don't think so. Not as long as we've been here, anyway. It was always just the old man. His name was Walter."

"Ask Victor if he can relay a message to Pop-Pop," Sandy said.

Swish.

Everyone looked at the board.

"It's on *Yes*," Sandy said.

Under the table, Pete kicked Glenn in the shin. "Did you do that?"

"How would I do that? I wasn't touching it."

"It's on *Yes*," Sandy said again. "He can talk to Pop-Pop. Come on, come on."

They laid their fingertips on the pointer, all three of them this time. It scurried around the board like something alive and looking for escape, not stopping anywhere, pausing for the barest instant here and there. Pedro couldn't tell if it was making words.

He heard something outside the house. Gravel crunching under tires. He looked towards the back door, but couldn't see who it was. "Guys," he said, "I think someone just pulled up."

"Go take a look," Pete said. "We're kind of on a roll here."

On a roll. Like they were winning at poker. Pedro crouched down and scurried to the back door, then peeked out. He saw a sedan parked alongside the station wagon. Who was it? Were they coming into the house? Pedro reached for the deadbolt, intending to set it, maybe buy them a little time to pack up and sneak out the front door; but then he noticed a vague shape coalescing in the air on the step outside. It was kind of an outline, a ripple, a grey sketch in the form of a human being. He saw something almost like a face, looking in through the glass, leering at him.

Behind him, the kitchen door slammed shut. Pedro spun and ran to it, tried to open it. Locked. He pounded on it a few times, but there was no response from inside.

Shit. Shit. Shit.

He returned to the back door, tried to open it. It wouldn't budge. He pressed his face to the glass to peer at the car. He could see a man behind the wheel, engaged in a very animated discussion with someone, maybe an argument, but nobody else was there. Pedro pounded on the door with his fists and hollered for help, and the man in the car paused for a second, as if hearing some faint, strange sound; then his hand came up and Pedro saw something black in his grip. Phone? Radio? Gun? He seemed to be struggling to control it, struggling against nothing. Pedro got a better look at the thing, its L-shaped darkness, and, damn, it *was* a gun. Pedro could almost see down the black barrel as the weapon swung around, the business end turning to aim at the side of the man's own head. Pedro heard a *pop* as the gun went off. A ruddy smear appeared on the driver's side of the windshield, along with a network of spidery cracks. A second later the back door and the kitchen door simultaneously blew inward. Pedro went sprawling on the mudroom floor. He felt something wash over him, a cold wind, like the winter blast when you stepped outside into a January storm. For a moment he couldn't move, as if frozen to the floor; then he wrenched himself to his feet and stumbled into the kitchen.

The faucet was leaking again, *plink plink plink.*

The chair Pete had brought out lay on its back, with the ouija board lying across it; the planchette was stuck point-first into the ceiling tiles above the table.

And the others were gone.

Richard searched his motel room, but couldn't find the notebook. Out in the hallway, the housekeeping cart was no longer in sight. Did he really think the book had been tucked in among the linens? How would it have gotten there? Had he shambled out and hidden it there himself? Wouldn't he remember that?

Maybe. Maybe not. After all, he couldn't remember what had happened in the basement that put him in the hospital, could he? And that wasn't the first time he'd done things he couldn't recall later, was it?

He tried to reach Art again. The cellular customer was still unavailable. He had the sense of a missed opportunity with the detective's question about what had happened to Richard in the basement, a life preserver Art had tossed that he'd let drift away. Leeson had been down in the cellar himself and had come back rattled. What had he encountered down there? Whispers and movements and suspect shadows?

It wasn't just Richard and Art who had been affected by the house. The kid next door, Pedro, he'd gotten nervous and evasive when old Mr. Colosseo dragged him out for questioning. Richard didn't believe it had anything to do with the imaginary theft of nonexistent valuables, but he might have seen or heard something he didn't want to think about. And Beth, she had seen the same vanishing girl as Richard; what had she seen before she died? What had she heard? What had come for her?

Maybe Pedro would be willing to talk to him without Mr. Colosseo acting as an interrogator. What was his last name again? Ortega? Orton? Ortiz, that was it. Richard got the big yellow phone book out of the nightstand drawer, looked up the number. He dialed, got a machine, hung up without leaving a message. He thought for a minute, then called the store where he'd run into Pedro, asked for the men's department, got a girl who said Pedro was gone for the day. Richard thanked her and hung up. He wasn't doing very well when it came to reaching people. Too late, too early, never the right time. Out brooding in the park when his mother took all those pills. Out shopping when Beth died. Far away and asleep while the old man lay in the hospital calling out for—

Victor.

The old man had been shouting for Victor in the hospital. Not for his wife, not for his children. For Victor. Victor, who whispered and wandered the house and told him to strangle children and called him horrible names because he had locked some notebooks in a chest in the basement.

Did those notebooks exist? Could they tell him anything more about what the hell was happening here?

Only one way to know for sure.

Go back to the house and find them.

"You sure you're up to this, Dad?"

"Sure I'm sure," Ozzie Heckles said, panting, as he attempted to reach the top of the Anvil. "Just give me a hand up."

"I think this calls for two hands." His son reached down and hauled Ozzie over the lip of stone, onto the broad flat surface of the

Anvil. Ozzie collapsed onto his back, staring up at the sky, breathing hard. Clouds had begun rolling in. Ozzie lay there and watched them creep across the sky. They had already smothered the setting sun and were now planning a final assault on the eastern horizon. It wasn't supposed to rain tonight, but that didn't mean much; Mother Nature didn't watch the weather report.

He heard his son move a short distance away and begin assembling the tent. Some enterprising soul had once hammered a network of iron spikes into the stone, giving campers a way to secure their shelters. Ozzie had delegated that task to Carl; after all, it was Carl's tent, so he ought to know how to set it up.

When he thought he could move without suffering a heart attack, Ozzie rolled over and sat up and dragged his satchel over to the tent, which had begun to look like something you could sleep in instead of something you found under the bleachers and didn't really want to touch. He rummaged in his bag and took out the camcorder and the still camera and the tripod and the tape deck. As Ozzie was affixing the camcorder to the tripod, Carl finished up and came over to watch. At length, he said: "So. Hunting ghosts, huh?"

"Yup."

"Which you don't believe in."

"Of course not."

"Yet you're willing to spend the night out here for that lady reporter."

"It's research."

"Research." Carl chuckled. "I have *got* to meet this girl."

"Sorry, Romeo, she's married." Ozzie sighed. "Too bad your mom didn't want to camp out with me. We could've necked under the moon like in the old days."

"Dad. Ugh."

"Don't *ugh* me. We were teenagers before you were. Is the tent all set?"

"Yep. Let me see your phone."

Ozzie handed it over and his son inspected it. "What's the verdict, doctor?" Ozzie said. "Is the patient alive?"

"It's on life support. You had reception at the road, but not here, so if you want me to come back and get you before tomorrow morning you'll have to climb down and walk until you get a signal."

"Climb down? On my own?" Ozzie eyed the rocks. "Guess I better make it through the night, then."

"Yeah, you'd better." Carl patted him on the shoulder in a *you're crazy but you're my dad* sort of way, then swarmed back down the rope. Ozzie watched him pick his way through the rocks and vanish into the twilight of the forest. Now he was alone with the spirits. Ozzie Heckles, dilettante newspaperman, meet Ozzie Heckles, dilettante spook-chaser.

He switched on the recorder. "Hello, ghosts," he said. "Anyone here besides me?" He let it run for a few seconds, then rewound it and listened. Nothing but the hiss of the tape, then his voice, then the flutter of the wind.

Well, if it were that easy to collect audio from The Other Side, everybody would be doing it, right?

Hank lay on his back. The parking lot lights knifed through gaps in the curtain, giving the far wall a striated look, preventing the room from getting totally dark. He stared at the ceiling. It appeared to be a crude attempt at stucco, tiny white stalactites pointing down at him. The glow from outside made the points look bigger and sharper than they really were, like fangs ready to bite. Rain hit the window with a constant ticking sound, the tempo varying with the rise and fall of the sighing wind. Janice was curled up next to him. She had fallen asleep there while watching television; he didn't want to wake her up and listen to her whining again, so they would both be sleeping in their clothes tonight.

He heard something come creaking up the hallway, *squeak squeak squeak*, a room service trolley or a maid pushing her cart; but room service at this place meant calling the pizzeria or the sub shop, and maids didn't generally roll their wagons around at this hour. The squeaking stopped outside his door. There was silence for a moment, and then the doorknob rattled. Hank waited a second, hoping whoever it was would realize they were in the wrong place and move along, but when it rattled again he went to the door and looked through the peephole.

Nobody there.

He had started to turn away when the knob rattled again. He put his eye back to the peephole. Still nobody there.

Rattle.

Okay, so this was some dumbass jokester, crouched below the level of the peephole or standing off to the side, playing with the door. And who in this hotel would just happen to pick *his* door to mess with? He could guess that in one. Hank put his face right up to the door and growled, "Go on back to your room, Richard. Don't think I won't come out there and kick your ass."

The door thumped once, hard, like Richard had kicked it. Hank took an involuntary step back, then moved forward again, reached for the knob, and—

"Daddy?" Hank paused, looked down and to his left. Janice stood next to him, clutching that stupid ragged porcelain-headed doll, looking up at him with great big sleepy eyes. "What's going on?"

"Well, Janice," Hank said, "your big dumb Uncle Richard is out there playing tricks on us." Then, louder, to the door: "Hear that, Richard? You woke your niece up. Proud of yourself?"

Janice looked at the door, then down at the doll, and then back at Hank. Now her eyes were even bigger. "Candy says it's not Uncle Richard."

"Candy's just a doll," Hank said. "She doesn't know who's out there."

"Yes she does," Janice said. "She says it's—"

The door shook under a sudden fusillade of frustrated pounding, making Janice jump. What the hell did that prick think he was doing? Had he spent the last few hours draining the minibar in his room, getting drunker and drunker until he decided to come bash his way back into their room?

No fucking way was Hank going to stand for that.

He knew he should just call the front desk, or the cops, but he would rather handle this situation himself. He picked Janice up and carried her back to the rollaway bed the hotel had provided for her and plopped her onto it. "You stay here," he told her. "Daddy has to go beat the shit out of someone." He returned to the door, Janice's little face staring after him. He got there just as the knob went through another spasm of rattling.

Great. He could catch Richard in the act.

Hank slipped off the chain and yanked the door open and charged out into the hallway and immediately collided with, yes, a housekeeping cart that had been left right in front of the door. He caught it with both hands and managed to keep it from toppling over, then shoved it out of the way. Fucking Richard. He looked left, looked right, spotted the nearest stairwell door just clicking shut. He ran to the stairs and up half the flight, around the landing, up the other half, crashed into the second-floor hallway. It was straight and empty and silent. No sign of Richard. He must have ducked into his room. Hank didn't know which one it was because the bastard had never told him, but it had to be pretty near the stairs for him to have gotten into it already. Hank was almost angry enough to pound on doors one by one until he found the fucker. Almost. Instead, he clenched and unclenched his fists a couple of times, then turned around and went back downstairs. He would call the front desk and make them roust Richard's ass for him. Proper channels and shit, as appropriate for someone who had just been handed a kid to take care of.

When he came out of the stairs on the ground floor, the housekeeping cart was way down at the opposite end of the hallway —how hard had he pushed it?—and the door to his room was closed. He went to it, tried the knob. Locked, of course. Fuck. And the key was inside on the nightstand or the table or the dresser.

Hank rapped on the door, waited a few seconds, rapped on it again. "Janice, open the door," he said.

Janice didn't open the door.

"Richard, if you're in there, open the goddamn door," Hank shouted.

No response.

He pounded on the door with his fist a few more times, kicked it, shouted at Richard again, then stormed off to the lobby to tell them he had locked himself out. A grumpy motel employee with a master key accompanied him back to his room to open it for him, and when they got back damned if that fucker Richard wasn't standing outside his door. Richard came toward them, saying, "Hank, listen, I need to tell you—"

Hank didn't let Richard finish, he just landed a right and a left to his head and down he went. The desk clerk said, "Jesus Christ!" and took off as Hank kicked Richard a few times, not quite as hard as he wanted to, which felt good at first, then less good as he remembered he was still locked out of his room and now he might be charged with assault. But Richard had had it coming.

He went back to the door, trying to keep his voice calm now, asking Janice to let him in. There was no response from inside. He knocked some more, kept trying the knob, which never magically unlocked. He considered kicking the door down but decided against it. The motel guy would be back with the key, eventually, and probably also with the cops. He couldn't think of anything else to do, so he sat down on the floor to wait.

Richard groaned and rolled over and sat up. "One day," he said. "You've been here *one day*, and you're already—"

"Shut the fuck up, Richard," Hank said.

It wasn't long before the desk clerk returned, this time with the police in tow. Hank told his story to the dubious-looking officers, the whole thing: The pounding outside the door that had prompted him to leave the room, the cart left in front of his door, chasing somebody up the stairs. He told them he'd been afraid Richard was staging an attempt to snatch Janice. Richard denied everything, of course. They kept asking him questions until finally Hank said, "Listen, my daughter is in the room alone. Can we continue this in there please?"

The cops looked at each other like this was the most novel idea they had ever heard, then nodded. The clerk unlocked Hank's door and the cops pushed it open. Hank heard the sounds of rain and wind and something fluttering. He followed them inside, then stopped short at the sight of the mess inside. Furniture was tossed every which way; the sheets from the bed were draped over the television set and the mattress was up on its side against the dresser. The lithographs which had been bolted to the wall had been ripped down, leaving chalky sores in the plasterboard. The window had been smashed and the rain drizzled in through the opening, spattering water across the table and the chairs and the carpet. The curtains fluttered in the breeze. To Hank, who had thrown one or two chairs in his day, it looked like there had been one hell of a domestic disturbance in here. He started forward, but the cops stopped him. "Just take it easy, Mr. Pritchard," one of them said. "Let us have a look around first."

Hank hardly heard him. He was staring at the window, at the one large jag of glass that was left, sticking up from the bottom side of the pane. That stupid doll, Candy, was impaled on it, the sharp triangle emerging from her chest, a tuft of stuffing stuck on the jagged edge. Her painted blue eyes stared up at the ceiling, wide, as if in death.

And Janice was gone.

Pedro tried to search the old man's house for the others, but something prevented him.

When he tried to go up the stairs to the second floor he felt some kind of resistance, a heaviness, like firm cold hands pressed on his shoulders telling him *no farther*. He hissed their names into the darkness overhead, but the darkness didn't answer. He moved to the basement but an upwelling of denial kept him from taking that first step. He called for them again and this time something chuckled at him from the dim space below. The pressure shifted, swirled around him to his back, and he braced himself against the sides of the door just as it tried to shove him down the stairs. He slipped and turned sideways and managed to flee, away from the basement, out the back door, into the woods, across to his own home. He called 911 from the phone in his kitchen and told them he had heard a gunshot at the house across the street—not a lie, technically—and gave them the old man's address. Then he went outside and hunkered down in the driveway until he heard the sound of sirens and saw the vehicles that made them, two police cars and an ambulance and a fire truck flying in a cloud of red and blue light. It wasn't long before the ambulance blew by again in the other direction, even faster this time. No doubt it was carrying cargo now.

He got up and walked down to the sidewalk, turned left, stopped in front of the old man's place. The police cars were parked at the curb. They had put up a new barricade at the end of the driveway. The lights were on inside and the front door was partly open, letting a yellow wedge spill out onto the grass. Neighbors had started to appear in their yards to watch another episode of *What's Happening at the Bartoski House?* He lurked on the sidewalk, closer than any of the others, looking at the woods. There were points of light moving around under the trees: Flashlights, carried by cops, searching the grounds. They must have found the ouija board, so they would know people had been inside. He hadn't even thought of clearing that stuff out. Maybe he wanted to be caught. This was his fault, after all. Even though he'd pretended to have convinced himself nothing was in the house, he knew better, always had. Wasn't that the real reason he had declined to sit and work the board? He had lined up Pete and Glenn and Sandy as targets, then ducked behind a tree.

One of the lights peeled away from the others and approached the sidewalk. Pedro stayed where he was, watching it get closer, keeping his hands hanging down at his sides where they could be seen to be loose and empty. The dark shape behind the light resolved into a police officer who didn't look much older than Pedro. "Evening," the cop said. "You live around here?"

"Yeah," Pedro said. "Over there." He pointed at his driveway.

"Have you seen anyone hanging around this house tonight? Lights inside, or people moving around?"

"No. Sorry. I heard the sirens and stuff and came to look. What's going on?"

"Not for me to say right now."

"I see."

The cop eyed him for a few seconds longer, then sort of shrugged and said, "We're busy here. You might want to get on home. And if you do notice anything suspicious, you'll call us, right?"

"Uh, yeah," Pedro said. "Sure. I will."

"Okay. Have a good evening."

Pedro nodded and started walking, conscious of being watched all the way up the sidewalk to his driveway. He wondered if he should have told the cop about the shadowy thing in the house. Would it have done any good? Was there any way to describe what had happened that wouldn't make him sound insane? Or get him arrested? Or both? If there was, he couldn't think of it right now.

Pedro walked up his driveway to the back door and went inside. The night was warm and thick and black as ashes. He sat down on the couch in the darkened living room to wait until it was safe to start looking for the others; cops talked to each other and he could only claim to be out for a walk so many times before they would get suspicious and start asking him harder questions. And maybe he would get lucky and the police would find his friends or they would come back on their own, safe and sound, telling him what a jerk he was for ditching them.

But somehow he doubted it.

By the time Rose got back to their apartment, it was nearly nine o'clock. She found a space next to her husband's car, wondering how pissed he was going to be at her tardiness. The first sentence out of his mouth would be, *Where the hell have you been?* and the second would be, *Who the hell were you with?* and the third would be, *What the hell were you doing?*

Bracing herself for it, she went inside.

He must have heard her key in the lock, because he was standing at the apartment door when she opened it, blocking her way into the kitchen. Not even waiting for her to step inside before he started up. But when he asked her where she had been, his voice was quiet, which was not what she had expected. It worried her. "I was out doing research," she said. "For the paper."

"No you weren't. The paper called here looking for you. They didn't know where you were or what you were doing."

"I don't always tell them where I'm going or why." He still hadn't moved out of her way. "Are you planning to let me into the apartment or not?"

He shook his head. "The police called for you after the paper did. You have to go."

"I do? Where?"

"The hospital."

She felt a dribble of cold water inching down her back; or maybe she just thought she did. She said: "Joe. Why do I have to go to the hospital?"

"It's your dad."

"What about my dad?"

Joe rubbed the back of his neck. He didn't seem to want to look at her.

"Joe. Tell me what happened."

"He shot himself."

She sagged sideways in the doorframe, lowered her head, took a few breaths, then looked up and said: "Did they say where?"

"In the head."

"No, I mean, where was he when he did it?"

He blinked at her a few times, then said: "They didn't say. What the fuck difference does it make anyway?"

"I don't know yet," she said, turning to leave, "but I'm going to find out."

Two ways to make sure it would rain: Wash your car, or spend the night camping out.

Ozzie sat on his son's sleeping bag in his son's tent with the tape recorder and the video camera and the still camera and nothing to do. With all the weather going on, he didn't think he was going to be capturing any usable material; not unless he wanted to make one of those nature sound relaxation tapes. *Summer Deluge on Forest Rock*, he could call it.

During a lull in the downpour, he lifted a flap to peer outside. Inky, rapidly-moving clouds had painted over the moon and stars with tumbling motion. He reached over and flicked on the camcorder light, sending a cone of illumination out the front of the tent. The broken stone gleamed wetly; its knobs and ridges and imperfections cast weird, long shadows away from him. It had been decades since he'd been up on top of the Anvil and he had forgotten just how big it was. Of course, the night turned everything vast, borders erased by darkness that went on and on and on. The flat grey surface had turned black, water gathering in little pools and flowing along fissures, a watershed of tiny lakes and rivers. The collected boulders sprawled beyond the Anvil's plateau, silhouettes in a variety of shapes and sizes and contours. He briefly amused himself by pretending they were people he knew. That tall and skinny needle would be his son Carl. That equally tall but refrigerator-broad obelisk would be his other son, Chris. He found one with a squarish protrusion on its side that he decided would be his wife carrying around her briefcase full of legal documents, and a shortish one, nicely contoured, that he decided would be his new friend Rose. And of course any number of big round bulbous ones could be him.

Ah, well. Ozzie patted his stomach and sighed. Let the kids worry about their profiles.

Something drew his attention back to the surface of the Anvil. Ribbons of light seemed to be crawling in the depths of the puddles, like radioactive crayfish leaving luminous trails. But the puddles didn't *have* depths, or crayfish to crawl in them, so what was he seeing? Reflections? Of what? The moon? Distant lightning? He leaned forward, peered at the sky above the tent. The clouds hadn't thinned at all; if anything, they had congealed further, covered the sky more completely, dark and soft and thick.

He dropped his gaze back to the Anvil. The lights he'd thought he'd seen were gone now. The water looked black and bottomless, the way water should in the dark. The wind shifted. The rain fell in diagonal slashes, creating clashing ripples in the surfaces of the interconnected puddles. He felt a spray of droplets on his face. Time to close things up again, before the inside of the tent got soaked. Ozzie switched off the light and zipped the front of the tent, shutting out the storm. That done, he put his hands behind his head and lay on his back for a while, contemplating the top of the tent. It was still too warm for him to want to smother himself in the sleeping bag, but with its padding and its built-in pillow it made for a decent mattress.

Just before he drifted off, he remembered the tape recorder. He fumbled around with it, managed to find the buttons to make it record. The soft hiss of running tape joined the patter of rain on fabric, wind in leaves.

Before long, his own snores were added to the mix of sounds. White noise.

6

ROSE'S FATHER WAS STILL IN surgery when she got to the hospital. Someone came out into the waiting room to talk to her, saying he had shot himself in the left side of the head, telling her stuff about Broca's area and the somatosensory and motor cortices, things they thought might have been damaged when the bullet burned a shallow furrow through Art's brain. It had popped out from the front of his skull and cracked the windshield before falling, spent, onto the dashboard of that old piece of shit car he drove.

She didn't understand it. To produce a wound that shallow, with the projectile traveling forward, you would have to bend your arm back at the shoulder, pull your elbow in tight, twist your wrist outward sharply. Even if, at the last second, finger squeezing the trigger, you changed your mind and started to turn your hand away, you would never make that angle. It was completely unnatural. Nobody would do it. People who shot themselves did it the straightforward way: Muzzle to the temple or under the chin or inside the mouth, and bang. No contortionist bullshit.

A couple of reps from the force showed up while she was waiting. They wanted to ask her a few questions, but first she pried information out of them. She found out somebody had called 911 to report the shooting, a neighbor, but they didn't know which one. When the cops and the ambulance had gotten there, they'd found Art sitting in his car in the driveway, motor running, doors locked, the radio turned up all the way and tuned to a hard rock station, of all things. Art didn't listen to hard rock. Art listened to jazz. The back door and kitchen door of the house had been hanging open. No one was around, but they'd found a ouija board in the kitchen. The pointer thing had been embedded in the ceiling like a ninja star, as if someone had thrown it hard, in a fit of frustration.

Then it was their turn to do the asking, and Rose could tell from the questions—*Did your dad seem gloomier than usual? Had he been talking a lot about your mom lately? Isn't the first anniversary of her death coming up?*—that they were thinking Art had shot himself because of untreated depression over her mother's passing. One of them even suggested maybe Art had brought the ouija board to the house himself to try to talk to her. That was a load of crap and she told them so. Her father was about as likely to use a surfboard as a ouija board. Dust it for prints and see, she said.

After the reps reiterated their condolences and left, she sat there thinking about what she had learned. Somebody had been there idiotically mucking around, trying to communicate with the spirits. Maybe Art had stopped by and rousted them and had fallen victim to whatever lived in that house.

No, not lived in it.

Occupied it.

The waiting room began to feel close and hot. She needed air. She got up and wandered down the long bright hallway until she found herself in the emergency department. Not much was going on there tonight. She stood in front of the windows for a while, staring at the black walls of glass between her and the night, at the glistening drops of water that clung to the other side, at the cars as they came and went, headlights like the cool eyes of angels, taillights like the hot eyes of demons. She was about to wander back to surgery and its rows of dismal chairs when a police car, lights flashing, pulled up outside. She stared at it, watched the pretty lights spin around and around and around. Two uniformed officers emerged and opened the back door and helped a man out. He didn't seem to be a prisoner, wasn't cuffed or anything, and they weren't tense in his presence. He looked kind of familiar. When they cane inside she recognized him as Richard Bartoski.

As the officers guided Richard to the registration desk, she sidled closer. They were talking in low voices but she heard enough to gather there had been a fight and Richard had gotten laid out. She wondered what it had been about. The guy behind the desk started to shoot her sidelong glances so she backed off until they finished. The cops headed for the coffee machine; Richard sort of stood there as if unsure where to go next.

"Hey," she said. "Richard."

He looked at her.

"What in God's name is going on at your house?" she said.

While the cops got themselves some of that terrible coffee, Richard walked over to the woman who had spoken to him, stopping a wary distance away. She looked pretty strung out: Dark circles below her eyes, hair a mess, makeup smudged. Under other circumstances, he might have thought she was going to hit him up for drug money and ignored her, but she knew his name and so he said, "Have we met?"

"Yes. My name's Rose. Rose Mancuso." Then: "You don't remember me."

"No. Sorry."

"I'm Art Leeson's daughter."

"Oh. Right. You're the reporter."

The side of her mouth quirked into half a mirthless smile. "Yeah," she said. "I'm the reporter."

"What are you doing here?" he asked. "Still working on your story? I'm still not giving interv—"

"My father's in surgery."

"What?"

"Art is in surgery."

"Oh … I'm sorry." He dropped into the chair next to her. "Is he going to be all right? What happened?"

"He got shot in your driveway."

"He, uh … What? *My* driveway? You mean at the house?"

"Yes."

"Who shot him? Does it … Do they think it has anything to do with Beth?"

"No. They think he shot himself."

Richard stared at her for a few seconds. She wasn't looking at him; she was looking at something that was somewhere outside the windows and probably didn't exist. "It sounds like you don't believe that."

"Well, I believe he was holding the gun. I don't believe he intended to do himself harm."

"You think it was an accident?"

"No. I think it was the house."

"The house?"

"Yeah," she said. "The house."

Richard said, in a carefully neutral tone, "Houses don't kill people."

She favored him with some side-eye. "That one does."

He said nothing.

"Come on, Richard. Tell me you don't know there's something strange going on there."

Richard looked at the cops, then back at Rose. "Why don't you tell me what you think is going on, and I'll tell you if I know it or not?"

She exhaled firmly and turned her head away, an expression of disappointment and annoyance and maybe fear on the side of her face he could see, and he remembered his regret, earlier, that he hadn't said anything to Art about the things he had experienced; but he couldn't just open up about ghosts and visions and scrawled murder transcripts in disappearing books. He thought she might get up and leave, but then she leaned in closer, lowered her voice, and said: "That house. It has something ... malevolent inside."

He said nothing. He knew she was right, and he said nothing.

"You need more? All right. Stop me when you've heard enough. You've got the ghost of a twelve-year-old girl in there, but she's trying to get out. Blonde, blue eyes, dressed in an old grey smock. You've got—"

"Who am I talking to?" Richard said.

Rose leaned back and blinked at him. "What's that supposed to mean?"

"It means, am I talking to a reporter, or to Art's daughter?"

"Fuck, Richard, do you think I'm here chasing a story?" Then, when he didn't respond: "All right. Fine. You're talking to Art's daughter." And when he still didn't say anything: "Lack of communication is getting people killed, Richard."

That made him think of Beth gently chiding him over not mentioning the girl, the very same girl, that Rose had seen. "Okay. Yeah. I saw her in the basement. She ran upstairs and disappeared. I went looking for her but she was gone. My sister saw her, too. In the kitchen. That time, she ran into the living room and, poof, gone." Then: "Where did *you* see her? You were never in the house, were you?"

"No. I saw her when I was in the front yard. She was trying to get out through an upstairs window but something came up behind her and grabbed her and pulled her back inside. What's wrong?"

He couldn't answer. The scene Rose had described mirrored the scene Richard had read in the vanished diary. The old man must really have done it. The shame of association made Richard want to just fold up and vanish himself.

"Richard?"

"She always seems to be running, doesn't she?" He could barely get the words out past something that felt like a stone in his throat.

"Sounds like it. Do you have any idea who she is?"

"I read something, just before I came here. Something my father wrote in a notebook about a girl he had, uh, taken, who … who died in the house. He didn't name her, but he said she lived next door."

"If she's who I think she was, she did," Rose said. "Her name was Candy Weiss."

He must have had the most aghast expression on his face, if it reflected the icy, sodden feeling that had started welling up from his stomach, flooding his chest, filling his mouth with slush. *Candy*. They had thought Janice was having imaginary conversations with her doll, but what if she been talking to the spirit of a dead girl? What had it told her that she hadn't told them?

Rose, watching him very closely, said: "That name means something to you, doesn't it?"

He nodded, but before he could find his voice to elaborate, she looked up to greet someone behind him. Richard twisted in his seat and saw that his police escorts—Bill and Gary—had come over, each holding a steaming cup of questionable coffee. "Sorry about your old man, Rosie," Gary said. "I hope he'll be all right."

"Me too," Bill said. "Everybody's pulling for him."

"Thanks," she said. "I appreciate that."

"Can we get you something? A coffee?"

"That's not coffee," Rose said.

Bill laughed, then said turned his attention to Richard. "How about you, sir? You all right? You look like you've seen a ghost. Got

179

any nausea or dizziness? Feeling sleepy?"

"No, I'm okay. Just worn out, you know?"

"You a doctor now, Bill?" Rose said.

"We wear many hats," Bill said.

"But we charge a lot less than they do," Gary added, encompassing the entire hospital in a gesture.

"That's for sure."

The cops made a little more small talk, asked him a few more times if he was okay, then excused themselves. Bad guys to catch, you know how it is. Richard thanked them for bringing him and watched them until they left the building, then turned back to Rose and told her about Janice's disappearance and his scuffle with Hank. By then, someone had come over to take him in for an exam. As he stood up, he said, "Listen, I'm at the Pine View Motel." He gave her his room number. "Call me tomorrow, we'll talk some more, maybe figure out what to do next about the book and stuff."

"Okay." Rose produced a little notebook and scribbled in it. "Call Richard tomorrow, about stuff." Then: "Good luck. Make this Hank guy pay for everything."

"Oh, he will," Richard said.

After Richard went off to get checked out, Rose sat there for a few minutes looking at nothing and thinking about less. Then she got up and headed back to the surgical waiting room, arriving just as they paged her on the overheads telling her to report there. The surgeon was waiting by the door. He told her the operation was over, that it had been as successful as such a procedure could be. The wound was clean, no bullet fragments, but they wouldn't know the extent of the damage until Art woke up and they could test his speech, sensory, and motor functions. See if he could still talk, in other words. See if he could move, if he could control his bodily functions, if he could feel it when they stuck a pin in his foot. That sort of thing. He would be in recovery for a while, the surgeon said, so maybe she should just go on home to get some sleep.

She thanked him and left and went home. Joe hadn't waited up; she could hear him snoring in the bedroom. Instead of joining him there, she plopped down on the chair in the living room and stared at the curtains drawn across the high, narrow window. It was still raining outside, a thrush against the wide glass panes, whispers on the wind like the voices of wandering ghosts trying to tell their secrets.

Rose sat there for a while listening, then got up and drove to the *Herald-Journal* building. It was pretty much dead there at this time of night; the only activity was in the basement, where the big presses were rumbling away. She let herself in through a side entrance, feeling the key vibrating in her hand as she stuck it in the lock and turned it. She went into the hallway and the door clanged shut behind her. She descended to the stacks, where they kept recent issues of the paper, and dug out Monday's edition. There was a short article about the accident at 136 Potter Street, when that woman had crashed into the telephone pole; her name was Barbara Whittington, of East Woodbury. With that information it would be easy enough to get a phone number tomorrow.

She sat down at a terminal in the stacks and logged into the system and sent Alan an email saying she wouldn't be at work for the next couple of days and explaining what had happened. Somebody else would have to think up a synonym for *feckless*. By the time she logged out and left, the rain had stopped, but it started again before she got home. This time Joe was awake, sitting on the sofa in the living room. "You came home and then you left," he said as she hung up her wet coat in the front closet.

"I did," she said. "You were awake?"

"Where did you go?"

"To the paper. I needed to look up something."

"Really. The paper." He watched her pour a glass of milk and drink it. "Is that to cover up the smell of booze on your breath?"

She put the empty glass in the dishwasher. "Of course not."

"Oh." Then: "Is it to cover up the smell of something else you had in your mouth?"

"Jesus Christ, Joe." She kicked the dishwasher closed. "Enjoy sleeping on the couch again."

He raised both hands, palms out in surrender. "It was a joke," he said. "Can't you take a joke anymore?"

Ignoring him, she went into the bedroom, and slamming that door shut between them was much more satisfying than slamming the dishwasher door had been.

~~~

The cops questioned Hank for hours, asking the same things over and over again. Did he actually *see* anybody in the hallway? Anyone lurking around? What made him think Richard had been involved? What did he think whoever had torn the room apart had been looking for? Did he have something hidden in there? Drugs? Some other kind of contraband? Was it possible someone had taken Janice to use as leverage to make him settle old debts? They mentioned more than once that the motel had wanted to kick him out, but they had persuaded the management let him stay in another room, and had also persuaded child protective not to immediately yank his custody of the kid once they found her, and wasn't he grateful, and wouldn't he like to be a sport and help them out? And he said, again and again, that he had no information that would help them.

They were going off his history, of course, trying to hang him with a rope braided out of his past. That was how cops thought. Once a perp, always a perp. But, fuck, was he stupid? Would he bring contraband on a plane trip to podunk Bentonville to pick up his daughter from social services? And as for settling debts, well, aside from the public servants in the BPD and social services, nobody knew he was in town except for Richard; and even if some local shithead was still sore at him after all these years and had spotted him driving around, would they really have followed him to the motel to stage that scene, grab the kid, and jump out the window with her? Of course not. It didn't make any goddamn sense.

But that didn't change the fact that Janice was gone.

They finally got it through their thick skulls that he was going to tell him nothing—although they took pains to make him understand that they still thought he *could* tell them something if he wanted to—and cut him loose after midnight. At nearly one-thirty, feeling like his head was full of sand, he parked in the motel lot and went into the lobby to get the key for his new room and fucked if Richard wasn't sitting there waiting for him in a chair just inside the door. With his head tipped back and his eyes closed, he might have been asleep, but Hank knew he wasn't.

Hank said: "You lock yourself out of your room or what?"

"I'm fine," Richard said without opening his eyes. "No serious injuries. Thanks for asking. You'll be getting a bill from the hospital, by the way."

"Good thing I went easy on you," Hank said.

"Uh-huh." Richard opened his eyes. "We need to talk."

"Here? Now? No." Hank shook his head. "I have shit to pack up and move to my new room. Then I have to sleep."

"Tomorrow, then?"

"It's already tomorrow. And still no."

"I've been told," Richard said after a few seconds, "that lack of communication is getting people killed."

Hank folded his arms and resisted an urge to kick Richard in the balls. "You trying to communicate with me now is going to get people killed."

Richard sighed. "Okay," he said. "Obviously we can't have a conversation at the moment."

"You're goddamn right we can't."

"We'll talk after you get some rest."

"Maybe. If I feel like it."

"Sleep well."

"Yeah, yeah."

"Try not to dream."

"Fuck you, Richard," Hank said, as he headed for the front desk and its sour-faced clerk. "Fuck you, and good night."

Dawn woke Ozzie Heckles from a restless sleep. Somehow, during the night, he had gotten turned around on the sleeping bag; his feet were on the pillow, his head was on the stone, and damn, did he have a stiff neck. He unzipped the front of the tent and peeked out. The sky was streaked with clouds, catching the hues of sunrise and smearing them across the sky. When was the last time he had seen a sunrise? He couldn't even remember.

He rolled over onto his side. God, he had to take a leak. He rolled out of the tent and stood up, stretching, scratching his back. He went to the edge of the big rock and relieved himself. The Anvil was surrounded by scraps of fog that drifted among the smaller stones, ensnaring them in coils of grey, obscuring the forest walls and turning them into vague dark barriers. Feeling much less pressure now, he returned to the tent and checked the tape recorder, which had stopped and rewound itself automatically after running out of tape. He played it back. There were the expected noises—birds, frogs, insects, rain on the tent, wind in the trees—and then he heard himself starting to snore and good lord was it loud. He'd always thought Marjorie was exaggerating a little. No wonder she wore earplugs to bed.

He left the tape playing while he sat in the tent eating a couple of granola bars he had brought along for breakfast. He nearly choked on one of them when the sound of a roaring wind sliced through the recorded drone of his snoring, followed by a rat-a-tat hiss like small, hard pellets of snow shotgunning the fabric sides of the tent, and, underneath all that, a low, guttural howl that rumbled through his entire body and pinned him to the ground until it stopped.

Jesus H. Christ.

Ozzie rewound the tape and listened to the sequence of noises again. Definitely not the soundtrack of any summer rainstorm he had ever heard. And that howl! What could have produced those bass notes? No animal that he knew of had a call like that. Nothing terrestrial anyway. The closest thing he could think of was whale song from a nature documentary, but that lacked the ominous undertones of what he had captured. He could only imagine what it would sound like through a halfway decent speaker. Ozzie rewound the tape to listen to it again, but when he pressed *play* this time the little wheels inside didn't turn. The recorder emitted a faint electric humming sound and went dead.

Huh.

He pushed the button to open the recorder. The lid only popped up maybe a quarter of an inch and stopped. He squinted through the gap. Glossy tape had unspooled inside, possibly wound around the spindle. Great. Now he would have to surgically remove the cassette without destroying the tape, which he wouldn't be able to do right now. Too damp, too dim. He needed to get it into the dry, air-conditioned environment of his kitchen or office, where he could extricate it and then retension it using a specialized tool like a pencil eraser. High tech stuff.

A voice called: "You're up early."

Ozzie raised his head from the tape recorder and saw Carl and Chris coming out of the woods, heading his way through the field of boulders. It was Carl who had spoken.

"You are too," Ozzie said. Then: "I wasn't expecting *both* of you."

"Well, we figured you might need some extra help getting down from there in one piece," Chris said, "what with all that gravity pulling on you."

"Very funny." Ozzie, still gently fussing with the jammed cassette, moved aside as the kids swarmed up to the top of the Anvil and started packing up his stuff for him. It was good to have free labor.

"How'd the tent hold up in the storm?" Carl said. "Mom was worried you might have gotten blown away."

"Or that your socks might have gotten wet," Chris added.

"The tent held up just fine. My socks are perfectly dry. So's my underwear."

"TMI. You see any ghosts?"

"Oh, sure," Ozzie said. "They came out in the middle of the night and did a waltz all around the Anvil. It was so awesome I forgot to videotape it. Hey, I don't suppose either one of you brought a pencil?"

His sons looked at each other.

"Sorry, Dad," Chris said. "We left our pencils at home."

"We didn't know there was going to be paperwork," Carl added.

The sound of the television jolted Pedro awake. He sat up in a panic, not remembering where he was until he spotted his mother standing nearby, wearing her fuzzy purple robe, holding the remote, changing stations to get to the weather report. She gave him a sidelong glance. "Fell asleep on the sofa? You're turning into your dad." His father's voice drifted in from the kitchen, denying he ever did such a thing. His mother responded with an amused snort.

Ah, crap. When Pedro had plopped down on the couch, he had planned to go back out and look for the others again after the cops finished canvassing the neighborhood, and instead he'd gone to sleep. He had *slept* while Sandy and Pete and Glenn were missing. He remembered dreaming about being in a car, an old car with tiny little windows and an interior that smelled like plastic. He'd been driving it like a chauffeur, with someone in the back seat, but he couldn't remember who it was or where they had been going, just that they had never gotten there.

Pedro jumped to his feet and darted out the side door—his father asked a startled question, which he barely heard and didn't answer—

and raced down the driveway to the sidewalk. The pavement and concrete were slick from a light drizzle. The cop car was no longer parked at the old man's house, but the driveway was barricaded, the whole thing taped off, just like after Beth Bartoski died. Pete's car was still on the street in front of the burned-out shell of the Weiss's place. He looked around, feeling like he was being watched, but there was very little activity in the neighborhood yet, so that was probably just his imagination. Probably.

Pedro headed up the sidewalk towards Pete's car, skirting the sawhorses and police tape in front of the Bartoski residence, casting wary glances at it as he hurried by. The place was closed up tight. The windows were dark. If anything was inside looking out, it chose to stay hidden.

Pete's car had a ticket under the driver's side wiper. Pedro pulled it out and looked at it. Street sweeping. He put it back under the wiper. The interior of the car was dim as a funeral parlor after the mourners went home. He put his face to the windshield and peered through, but nobody was inside.

He turned and went back down the sidewalk, passing the Bartoski place again. He noticed this time that the police tape between the barricades was torn, one end dangling and the other snaking along the pavement like a big yellow flatworm. Had it been like that when he came up? He didn't know. He had been focused on other things. He picked up the torn end and tied it back in place, then watched it come untied and flutter back to the ground. Leaving it, Pedro continued on to his driveway, went up to his car. The top was only partially closed—had he left it that way?—but the interior was mostly dry. Good thing it hadn't rained too hard. Having some vague notion that he would drive around the neighborhood until he found the others or thought of something better to do, he got in and started the car. The radio blasted music, making him jump. He fumbled to shut it off, then stifled a cry as a face reared up into his rearview mirror. It took him a second to realize it was Sandy. The noise must have startled her awake. She was all pale skin and disheveled hair, smudged makeup, a bruise on her forehead, a black line of clotted blood along a cut below her left eye.

He twisted around in his seat to face her. She was alone. No Pete. No Glenn. She looked at him, then looked away. Her eyes were unfocused, seeing something in the distance, or maybe seeing nothing.

"Sandy? Are you okay? What happened? Where are Pete and Glenn?"

"We got separated. I couldn't keep up." She spoke in a flattened tone, her voice coming out of her mouth like it had gone through the rollers of a press.

"You couldn't keep up?"

"Yeah. Stupid heels. Couldn't get them off. Kept falling."

Remembering the complicated shoes she'd been wearing at the mall, he craned his neck to check out her feet. She still wore them but now they were filthy, streaked with grass stains and mud. "Where were you going?" he said.

"To get rid of the books."

"Books?"

"Uh-huh. Books. From the basement. He gave them to us and told us to get rid of them because they were holding him back. But after I fell running away from the dog they took my books away and left me."

"Dog? What dog? A police dog?"

"Just a regular dog. In a yard."

"Did it bite you?"

She shook her head.

"The police were all around here last night. Did you see them?"

Sandy nodded. "He said not to get caught, so I kept moving and hiding until they were gone. When it started to rain I came back here but Pete's car was locked. Yours wasn't." Her gaze wandered off sideways. "I could only pull the top closed halfway. I think I broke it."

"That's all right. Who asked you to get rid of these books?"

She squeezed her eyes tight, shook her head.

"Sandy? Who was it? You can tell me."

"Victor." She opened her eyes. "He said he would help us talk to Pop-Pop, but he lied. He *lied*, Pedro."

"I know. Did he tell you where to take them?"

"Uh-huh." She gestured vaguely around the neighborhood. "Out there someplace."

"Are the others still there?"

"Don't know. Maybe."

"Okay." Pedro helped Sandy out of the car, steered her around to the front seat. She muttered some vague protests as he buckled her in, but was too lethargic to do much else. Whatever had happened last night seemed to have sapped all her energy. He got back into the driver's seat and started the engine and they rolled out of the driveway and into the street. Pete's car was still parked at the curb. That meant Pete and Glenn must still be around here somewhere, right? Trying not to get caught. Time to play hide and seek.

Ready or not.

Richard dreamed he was back at the house on Potter Street, standing in the driveway next to the smashed station wagon, Beth's body crumpled across the windshield. He moved to touch her but she suddenly flew upwards, falling in reverse. The vehicle repaired itself, the glass uncracking, the metal unbuckling. Beth somersaulted in mid-air and landed on top of the house and stood on the edge of the roof, looking down at Richard, calling him up to join her. He asked her how he was supposed to do that and she pointed at the drainpipe, still attached, sturdier than ever. He started climbing but then the house shuddered and uprooted itself from the ground and shot into the air, leaving him clinging to the pipe against the downrush of wind. In moments he was hundreds of feet off the ground, thousands, clinging to the pipe, clouds drifting all around him. Then Beth dove off the eave as if into a swimming pool, and instead of falling she flew, spread her arms and swooped and looped and glided like a bird before coming up to hover behind him, inviting him to take her outstretched hand. He reached out for her but just then the drainpipe pulled away from the wall, pitching him out into empty space. He fell and fell and fell while Beth spiraled around him, laughing, telling him he could fly, too, if he would only put his mind to it.

The bedside phone started ringing, jarring him awake just before he hit the ground. Good timing. He fumbled the receiver into his hand, said hello into the listening end, realized his mistake, turned it around, and said hello again.

"Richard? Is that you?"

"Yeah. Who's this?"

"It's Rose. Listen, I just got off the phone with that woman who crashed her car into the telephone pole in front of your house. Her name's Barbara Whittington. She didn't really want to talk to me, but —"

"Maybe she was cranky because you called her so early."

"Early? What time do *your* days start? It's after eleven."

Richard thought that couldn't possibly be right, but when he lowered the receiver and peered at the clock, yep, it was. Quarter after, in fact. Damn, he had really sacked in today. Didn't feel like it, though. Felt like he could sleep for another ten hours.

He lifted the receiver back to his ear. Rose was still talking. "… interesting stuff to say. The short version is that she saw our little blonde friend. You can hear the whole thing when we have lunch."

"We're having lunch?"

"Yep. Twelve-thirty at Airport Pizza. My treat."

"Airport Pizza. Right. Um, where is it?"

Pause. "At the airport."

"Okay. Got it. I'll meet you there."

"You'd better, or I'll come looking for you."

Click.

Richard sat up in bed, yawned, stretched. The crack in the curtains was bright as a naked fluorescent tube. Nearly noon. Damn. He picked up the phone and dialed the office. Tony answered on the first ring. "Richard," he said. "Have things gotten worse? Every time you call me things have gotten worse."

"Things have gotten worse." Richard filled him in on the current situation. Tony listened in uncharacteristic silence, then asked if he could do anything to help. "Yeah. But only if you don't mind. Beth's already been taken out to McWraith's funeral home. Can you call them and see when they can get a wake set up? I've just got too much shit going on here right now to deal with them."

"Sure, I can do that. Anything else I should know?"

"No. Wait. Yes. You remember Art, the detective investigating what happened to Beth?"

Tony's voice became wary. "I remember Art."

"Well, he's in the hospital now. He shot himself in the head in the old man's driveway."

"Jesus Christ, Richard. Be careful. And stay the hell away from that house, okay?"

Richard would have loved to stay the hell away from that house, but he had a feeling he was going to end up back there again. He said, "I'll try." Then he hung up and leaned back against the headboard, eyes closed. A little while later he got up and went into the bathroom and turned on the shower. The hot water came out scalding. He got under it and let it cook him for a good, long time. Afterwards, shaved and dressed, he felt almost human again. Almost. After giving the matter some thought, he called up Hank's room to see if he wanted to come along to Airport Pizza and hear what Rose had to say, but Hank said no, Airport Pizza sucked. Then Richard asked Hank if he had heard anything new about Janice and he said he no, hadn't. He was in the process of asking Hank to call if he did hear anything when Hank advised him to fuck off and hung up. Richard hung up too and flipped the phone the middle finger and left.

Out in the car, he drove around to the side and paused for a look at Hank's previous room. Yellow tape was stretched around a couple of sawhorses outside the window, blocking the sidewalk. Someone was working there, sweeping up the bits of broken glass that were spread in a wide delta across the pavement, as if the window had exploded out from the inside. Boom. Richard imagined Janice flying out the window, the doll slipping from her hand, falling, impaling itself on the jagged shard; then he imagined *Janice* being the one to fall onto it, and felt a little shiver run through his shoulders and down his arms. Thank God it had only been the doll.

The guy who was cleaning up the glass paused to wipe his forehead with his arm, then started casting glances at Richard's car, so he stepped on the gas and drove out of the parking lot.

He had already attracted more than enough attention for one trip.

Rose had arrived at Airport Pizza before the lunch rush and had taken the most undesirable table in the place, way in the back, wedged behind a building support and right next to the lavatories. She often met people at this booth for semi-clandestine yet public interviews; the bathrooms were screened from view by a fake ficus and a kitschy paper room divider festooned with plastic tomatoes, but still, every time somebody went in or came out, you got a nice whiff of tile cleanser and that blue shit that filled the toilet bowl every time you flushed. Yummy.

She checked her watch again. 12:42pm. Richard was late, but she wasn't really surprised; when she'd talked to him, it had sounded like he was about a half mile on the dark side of awake. She leaned forward to peer around the support at the front door every time she heard it open, which had been happening with such frequency over the last thirty minutes that she could probably count it as her abdominal crunches for the week. Finally the person entering was the one she was waiting for. Richard took a few steps in and stopped and looked around. The neon squiggles surrounding the door lit up his face in various shades of blue and green as he eyed the sauce-red wallpaper with its fuzzy pale orange pattern, the crimson tabletops, the vermilion upholstery, the checkerboard floor of maroon and white. He didn't seem to have spotted her. She stretched out and waved to him. He waved back and came over and squeezed past the support to settle on the bench opposite her. "Hi," he said. "Sorry I'm late."

"That's okay. You had a rough night."

"We both did."

"Yeah." A waiter materialized. He wore a red hat, red pants, white shirt, and red suspenders decorated with pins that looked like pizza toppings. He handed Richard a menu consisting of a single laminated double-sided page and promptly vanished again. "Any word on Art?"

"Still in a coma. The doctors say he'll live, probably, but they don't know how, uh, how he'll be. Thanks for asking. How about you? Any word on your niece?"

"No. Hank is waiting at the motel in case they call."

"Ah, yes, the jerk-ass father who gave you all those lovely bruises."

He self-consciously touched his face, dropped his gaze to the menu. "So, um, what's good here?"

"Nothing, really. I already ordered us a pizza. Pepperoni, sausage, and mushroom."

"Old school. I like it." Then, not looking up from the menu: "So you really think something at the house made your dad shoot himself?"

"Yes."

"You think the same thing made my sister jump?"

"We don't know what happened to your sister. *Did* she jump, or

191

was she thrown? If she was thrown, who did it? From where? How did she get there?"

"You sound like Art."

"Thanks." She took a sip of her soda. "So. The girl. The notebook. Fill me in. What didn't you have time to tell me last night?"

Richard looked up at her. His face was pale, shadows under his eyes. She thought he was about to say something, but then dropped his eyes to the menu again.

"Come on, Richard. I thought we worked this out yesterday. Cards on the table, face up."

He sighed and laid the laminated sheet down and looked past her, as if searching for squirrels in the fake ficus. "I found a notebook in my father's bedroom," he said in a voice drained of inflection, flat as week-old beer. "He wrote that he and somebody named Victor had kidnapped a girl and were keeping her tied up in the basement. Same place he used to ..." He trailed off, cleared his throat. "Well, anyway, she got loose somehow. He caught her on the second floor, trying to climb out a window. He hauled her back inside and she hit her head. I don't know if she knocked herself out or what. I guess she must have still been alive because Victor, uh, *encouraged* the old man to strangle her. Then they brought her back to her own house, the house next door, locked her in a closet, and burned the place down."

Rose didn't often find herself reduced to speechless, slack-jawed staring, but that did it.

"The old man said Victor did something to her parents," Richard added, filling the conversational void. "Made them put a garden hose in their car and drive away. I don't know where they went or what happened to them."

"I do." Rose cleared her throat. "They were found dead in their car in the cemetery up the street from your house with a garden hose running from the exhaust into the passenger compartment. Murder-suicide, is the theory."

"Jesus."

The pizza arrived, temporarily interrupting the conversation. A couple slices in, Rose said: "So where is this notebook? Did you bring it with you? Can I see it?"

"No. See, the thing is, it, uh, it disappeared from my room."

She frowned. "What do you mean, disappeared?"

"Well, I tossed it on the bed when I called Art to tell him about it. When I looked for it a minute later, it was gone."

"Could someone have taken it?"

"I don't see how. I think it took itself. But, listen. There might be more of them. The old man mentioned locking other books in a sea chest in the basement. He just kept out the one he was writing in, the one I found. Maybe they're still down there. I mean, he said he put the doll down there, and I found that."

"The same doll you went in to get while I was there?"

"Yes. Candy Weiss found it in the basement. She latched onto it and brought it with her on her escape attempt."

"She was scared and wanted a friend."

"Yeah, I guess. She was still carrying it when she, um, when she died. And Janice must have tried to hang onto it when she was, um, taken out the window, but she lost it."

"Your niece called the doll Candy."

"Uh-huh."

"That was Cassandra Weiss's nickname."

"So I gathered."

"That can't possibly be a coincidence."

"No."

Rose drummed her fingers on the tabletop. "Okay. What about this Victor character? Any idea who he is? Could he have been at the motel?"

"I have no idea. I don't know what he looks like or if he even exists. But the shape my father was in, unless he was faking his injuries—scamming disability, maybe—I don't see how he could have done it on his own. The things he talks about, I mean. He must have had help." He put his hands out in front of him, then turned them over and spread them apart. "There you go. Cards on the table, face up. What do we do next? Do we talk to the police?"

"No. What would we tell them? All we have is a dead perpetrator, a notebook we can't produce, and an unknown subject who may or may not exist. If my father were still in the picture I would take it to him, but …" She chewed on the end of her straw. "I think we should go to the house and find this hypothetical sea chest full of evidence. But first, I have something for you to listen to." She pulled a cassette player and a pair of headphones out of her purse and slid it across the table to him.

He looked down at it, then at her. "What's this?"

"I recorded my call with Ms. Whittington. About the accident. I want you to hear it."

"Oh," he said. "I thought maybe you made me a mix tape."

"Sorry, Richard." She took a sip of soda through her mangled straw. "We're not at the mix tape stage of our relationship yet."

Headphones on, Richard listened to the recording of Rose talking to Barbara Whittington. She had taped the whole call, apparently without letting Barbara know she was doing so. Richard wondered if that was legal. Maybe that was why Rose had been cagey about it on the phone.

He already knew that Barbara had seen the phantom girl, and was anxious to get to the good stuff, but first he had to sit through Rose convincing Barbara to talk to her at all. It was apparent from the other woman's tone and her clipped responses that she didn't really want to have this conversation, but Rose made it clear—without actually saying so—that she just might stop by Barbara's place of employment for an in-person interview should Barbara choose to hang up on her.

Finally he got past all that, to the point where Barbara started answering questions. She had been driving up Potter Street, she said, when a dog darted across the road and she slammed on her brakes to avoid it. The next thing she knew, she had lost control of her car, and, *crash*, her hood was crumpled against the telephone pole, and the wires came down, and she was trapped.

On the tape, Rose said: "I saw the police report. It says you took your attention off the road briefly, then saw the dog, stepped on the gas when you meant to step on the brake, panicked and swerved."

"I'm not some senile old woman whose license should be taken away. I know which pedal is the gas and which pedal is the brake."

"Of course. So what distracted you?"

"Well." The woman sounded a little flustered now. "There was a girl."

Recorded Rose said: "A girl? In the street?"

"No. In the house." Barbara proceeded to describe spotting a child trying to climb out the the second floor window of the house on the left, only to be pulled roughly back inside by someone in the room behind her. That was what had drawn her attention for the critical second. Not some song on the radio. Not lighting a cigarette. Not taking a sip of coffee.

Richard stopped the tape, looked at Rose. "Trying to get out the window? That's what she was doing when you saw her, right?" Rose nodded, but she didn't say anything; she just reached across the table and stabbed the *Play* button with her index finger. Her recorded voice asked Barbara what the girl had looked like.

"Blonde. Twelve, thirteen. Dirty smock. Like she was playing in a dusty attic."

"A kid trying to climb out a second story window is a little weird, don't you think?"

"She was probably grounded and trying to sneak out."

"Did you mention her to the police?"

"I'm sure I did."

"Did they follow up?"

"What would there would be to follow up on? A kid in a house. That's where kids are. If you saw the police report then you know more about it than I do. You tell me. Did they follow up?"

There was a second or two of tape hiss. "No, she isn't mentioned in the report."

"Then why is it important?"

"It probably isn't." Recorded Rose asked a few more questions, nothing particularly probing; Richard had the sense that she was just tossing sand now, covering up what had really interested her. After a few minutes of that she thanked Barbara Whittington for her time; the other woman muttered something unintelligible and hung up.

Richard pressed the button to stop the tape. Real Rose watched him take off the headphones and set them down on the table, then said: "So what do you think?"

"Sounds like she saw Cassandra."

Rose nodded. "Still trying to get out the upstairs window. Presumably the one where the notebook says your dear old dad caught her." She tapped the tabletop with her fingernail. It made a hollow *tk-tk-tk* sound. "What was going on in the house when Barbara crashed into the pole? Do you remember?"

"Sure. Janice had gone down into the basement looking for the doll. She said she heard it calling for help."

Rose's tapping finger stopped. "She probably did."

"Really? You think the doll talked to Janice?"

"Richard. Don't be silly. Dolls can't talk. It was the ghost." Rose took a sip of her drink. "I mean, think about it: Cassandra Weiss is imprisoned in your father's basement. She gets loose, finds the doll, grabs it, brings it with her. It wouldn't take long for a scared little girl to bond with a friendly face, even one that's made of plastic."

"Porcelain," Richard said.

"Ooh. Fancy. So Cassandra is holding onto the doll when she's killed. Let's say that causes her to become imprinted on it. Now the doll is haunted. Your father puts it back in the basement before he dies. Then you guys show up. You're a big scary guy, Cassandra just runs away from you, but your niece hears her calling for help and goes downstairs and finds the doll. Let's say this triggers the escape attempt to start replaying upstairs. Barbara Whittington sees that drama unfolding, gets distracted, and crashes into the pole. Boom! Lights out. Later on I come along and I see it too. For all we know it's still running up there on an endless loop. Or maybe not. After all, the doll's not there anymore."

"True."

There was one slice left. He pointed at it and looked a question at Rose, who shook her head, so he picked it up and polished it off. It wasn't *good* pizza, but it was still pizza. Rose drained her soda, dark eyes on him, then said: "So. Now that I've plied you with food, what say we go for a drive?"

Back in his office at the *Mirror*, Ozzie sat behind his desk, his tape recorder on the blotter in front of him, the lamp pulled over to illuminate its innards. It had taken him the better part of an hour just to remove the cassette; it had unspooled its contents around the capstan and pinch roller and one of the the spindles, totally jamming the machinery. Even stranger, the glossy black surface of the exposed tape was festooned with tiny cream-colored flecks. He didn't know what they were or how they had gotten there, but they seemed to have bonded with the magnetic material. He had blown compressed air at it, without effect, but hadn't tried to scrape the stuff off, fearing he would destroy the tape.

After finally extricating the cartridge and winding it back up, he considered putting it back into the recorder, thought better of it, got a different tape out of his desk and popped it in and pressed *play*, and discovered that the device was dead. He put in fresh batteries and tried again. Still nothing.

Hmm.

Ozzie went out to his car and started to put the suspect cassette in the player, then thought better of it and drove out to the office supply store instead. He bought a new tape deck and a box of batteries and sat on a bench in front of the store, intending to conduct his tests there, but it was too hot and so he repaired to the air-conditioned bliss of his car. He unboxed the tape deck and loaded the batteries and played the tape. He heard some hissing and some popping but no real audio; then the little posts stopped turning and the unit hummed for a second and shut itself off. At the same moment, the car engine sputtered and died. He turned the key and the car roared back to life, but now the radio was on, tuned to some forlorn space between stations, a frequency filled with static and noise. He punched the button to turn the radio off, then picked up the tape recorder and popped open the chamber and inspected the cassette. The tape appeared to be intact. He closed the recorder and started playing it again. *Hiss hiss pop pop hiss.* Hum. Stop.

The car shuddered. The engine coughed and died. All the dashboard lights came on. When he started it back up, the radio was on again, blasting static even louder than before. This time, he had to push the button several times before it finally went off.

Okay then.

Handling the tape recorder like a piece of toxic waste, he removed the batteries and put it in the glove compartment, then pulled out of the lot and drove back to the *Mirror*, parking at the curb out in front. He brought the device with him when he went inside. Susan at the front desk, who hadn't yet arrived for work when he'd left earlier, looked up as he entered. "I have something for you, Ozzie," she said, holding up a big envelope.

"What is it?"

"The information you wanted about the auction at the Arvidsson place."

"Oh. Great. Thanks. Here, trade you." He took the envelope and gave Susan the recorder. She looked at it, then at him. "I want to send the whole shebang to Jake."

"Jake?"

"Yeah, Jake. At the place."

She raised an eyebrow at him.

"The tape restoration place."

She raised the other eyebrow.

"Where they restore tapes."

She laughed. "It's called Audiocraft. How is it you know everyone in town but you never remember the names of companies we do business with?"

"I don't run into companies at the diner or the park. Anyway, there's some kind of crud stuck to the tape. I'd like him to figure out what it is and remove it, if he can, and recover as much sound as possible."

"Okay."

Leaving Susan to package up the unit, he took the envelope into his office, opened it, flipped through the contents. The auction had been open and public, as per Mrs. Arvidsson's specification, so he had a complete list of bidders and purchases and prices paid. Nothing about it leaped out as of immediate interest, though of course he didn't really know what Rose was looking for. Hoping for guidance, he called her at the paper, but got voice mail. He left a message, then called back and pushed the button for the operator, who told him Rose had unexpectedly taken some time off for a family emergency. That didn't sound good. He called her at home and got a machine. He left another message and hung up.

Ozzie sat there for a minute, just thinking, then looked through the items again. All the usual stuff you would expect to see up for auction from an old farmhouse: Antique tools, antique furniture, antique rugs, antique ledgers. He flipped to the sign-in sheet, scanned the names of the attendees. He recognized several of the bidders as local dealers, as well as a few private citizens from around the area. Others he didn't know. One caught his attention, a Robert James, from Bentonville. Maybe Rose would be interested in him. He set the sign-in sheet aside and flipped through the high bids to see if Robert James had purchased anything. He found a single winning entry, which he circled. Then he called, "Susan!"

His assistant stuck her head into his doorway. "Yeah, boss?"

He put his hand on the auction documents. "Can we fax this to the *Herald-Journal* in Bentonville?"

She eyed the stack of papers. "What, the whole thing?"

"Yeah."

"Did they ask for it?"

"Not exactly."

"Then no. They'll kill you if you send an unsolicited fax that big."

"Okay." He held up the sheet with the purchase he had circled. "How about just this page?"

"That, we can manage," Susan said.

Rose followed Richard back to the motel, where they left his car in the parking lot and took Rose's back into town. She didn't seem to be in the mood to talk, which was fine with him; he stared out the window as the scenery scrolled by, trees and houses, people on the sidewalks walking dogs or jogging, a flock of teenagers on inline skates, a shirtless old man watering his lawn, kids playing in their yards. Normal things people did in a normal summer. Things Richard himself might have been doing, in a different life, a different universe, where his father hadn't been such a bastard, their family hadn't fallen apart, his mother and sister weren't dead, his niece wasn't missing. What a wonderful world that would be.

Potter Street was coming up on the left. As Rose turned onto it, Richard said, "Stay with the car while I go inside, okay?"

"Why?"

"Just in case I don't come out."

"Okay." She glanced at him. "And if you don't come out, what do you want me to do, exactly?"

"I don't know. Call in an air strike, maybe."

The other houses on Potter Street went by on either side; then came the thick stand of trees that insulated the old man's house from its neighbors; then came the old man's house itself, ramshackle, floating on a cloud of crabgrass and shrubbery. The telephone pole out front that Barbara Whittington had run into, still awaiting replacement, tilted slightly despite having been reinforced with straps and angled two-by-fours. Rose parked near it. Richard sat there for a little while looking up at the house, preparing himself. Finally Rose said, "Are you sure you don't want me to—"

"I'm sure." Richard got out and headed up the walk, taking deliberate steps, scanning the upstairs windows. If Candy Weiss was still trying to escape, she wasn't showing herself right now. He climbed the stairs to the front porch. The steps creaked a little bit. The boards groaned as he crossed to the front door. He found the key on his chain, big and heavy and tarnished. He stuck it in the lock and turned it. The deadbolt opened with a bang. The door swung inward with an easy sound, a sort of sigh, welcoming him home. He looked back at the car. Rose had gotten out and was standing in the filtered green light, leaning against the passenger side, arms folded, watching him. He gave her a nod and went inside and shut the door behind him.

The foyer was dim; the curtains on the narrow windows to either side of the entryway throttled the light that tried to get through. To his left was the living room, wide and empty. Ahead were the stairs to the second floor, the little smudge from Beth's final cigarette plainly visible on the old, dry wood. To his right was the closet. And there was the basement door, unlatched, slightly open. He went to it and reached out, but the door swung outward on its own before he touched the knob, as if pushed by some dank flatulence from the bowels of the house.

He swallowed, moved forward, put his foot on the first step. He felt a faint pressure pushing him back, like silken cobwebs stretched across the opening, touching his face. He shook his head and the imaginary threads fell away. He went down the stairs. The cool, stale air smelled like mildew and earth and standing water. Piles of crap stood everywhere. He wandered among the mounds of junk, a lost nomad in search of a rumored oasis. Then he spotted it, at the bottom of a pile of boxes, half-covered by an old winter coat: The sea chest. The hasp was visible and he could see a padlock hanging from it, but it looked breakable. He went to the workbench and picked up the biggest hammer he could find, a mallet with a rough wooden handle and a massive iron head, flat on one side, round on the other. He tested it, feeling its weight, running his thumb along the rusted metal. That ought to do it. He turned to go back to the sea chest, froze.

Something had taken shape behind him.

An indistinct, roughly humanoid curl of smog, narrow at the bottom, widening on top, it stood between him and the rest if the cellar. It reminded Richard of pictures he had seen of distant wildfire plumes on days when high-altitude winds smeared smoke in tendrils like arms across the sky. He could feel its regard, its disdain, its cool hostility.

Was this the thing that had hurled Beth out the window? Richard hefted the hammer, as if he might be able to bash the vaporous entity with it, and said: "Are you Victor?"

The smoke didn't answer.

It just swirled around him, ignoring the sweeps of the hammer, to pick him up and hurl him across the basement, into the small room, head-first at the cinderblock wall.

Rose leaned against her car and watched the house and the robin's-egg sky above. A few high thin clouds scraped across it, scarring the otherwise monotonous expanse of blue. A light, intermittent breeze blew, rustling the leaves, its subtle coolness the first hint that summer was ending. Somewhere, for no good reason, a bird warbled its appreciation of this cartoonishly beautiful day. But it wasn't a beautiful day for Candy Weiss, or for Beth Bartoski, was it? Neither of them would see another beautiful day, not ever again. It wasn't a beautiful day for Art, lying there in the ICU. She wondered if he had regained consciousness. She should be there with him when he woke up, but she needed to figure out what was going on here, and stop it before it harmed anyone else. He would understand the need for that. He would support it. She just hoped that one day she would be able to tell him what had happened, that he would still have the mental capacity to understand, to speak to her, that he wouldn't be—

Suddenly a car screeched up to the curb on her left, coming in fast and stopping short, facing the wrong direction. It was a convertible sedan, blocky yet sporty and muscular, the way old cars of a certain vintage could be. Fuzzy dice swayed on a string from the rearview mirror. A kid sat behind the wheel, with a girl slumped in the passenger seat next to him, half-asleep, or maybe stoned. The driver's gaze flicked from his passenger to the house to Rose to the house again, conveying a level of apprehension that you wouldn't expect from a random person who didn't have any reason to be worried about parking on a public street. Maybe he had stolen the car or the girl, or both. Or maybe he didn't like being this close to the house.

Rose circled the car and looked down at the driver. He was older than she had thought at first, eighteen, nineteen maybe. She glanced at the girl, whose head lolled from one side to the other and back again; her lips were moving, but if words were coming out she couldn't hear them. "You know, you can get a ticket for parking like that," she said.

"Are you with the police?"

"No. I'm a reporter."

"A reporter? Are you working on a story?"

She shook her head. "Waiting for a friend. My name's Rose. Who are you?"

"I'm Pedro. This is Sandy. Who are you waiting for? Mr. Bartoski?"

"Yeah. You know him?"

"Only a little."

"You a neighbor?"

"Uh-huh. I live next door." The kid looked past her, at the house. "Mr. Bartoski … Is he inside?"

The way he said it, *Is he inside?*, reminded her of the way you might ask if someone was dead when you were pretty sure they were. "Yes, he is."

"What's he doing in there?"

"He's looking for some books," Rose said. The kid started at that, cast a sidelong glance at his companion, then tried to cover it up by pretending to adjust his rearview mirror, causing the fuzzy dice to start swaying again.

Interesting.

"You swooped in here like somebody with a purpose, Pedro," Rose said. "Why not tell me what it is?"

He eyed her in a manner she recognized from years of asking questions people didn't really want to answer; he was trying to decide whether or not to talk to her, how much to say. Sometimes prodding such specimens loosened them up. Sometimes it backfired. If you went with prodding, you had to do it the right way, find the right levers to operate.

In Pedro's case, Rose figured, the key to unlocking his mouth was riding shotgun in his car.

"Your friend," Rose said. "Is she all right?"

"She's, uh, she's just really tired. She had a rough night."

"Mmm," Rose said. "That's all? Up too late? Didn't sleep well? Having nightmares?"

"Uh, yeah, sort of, I guess—"

"Have you been inside the house?"

Pedro didn't respond, but the expression on his face answered the question.

"Were you two here with a ouija board last night, by any chance?"

His mouth fell open, then closed, then opened again. "How much do you know?" he said.

God. Not this again. "There's obviously something going on here, Pedro. I'd like to help you, and your friend, but I can't if you make me play guessing games."

He looked at Sandy, then at Rose, then at Sandy again; and then he told her about the disastrous session with a ouija board that he and his friends had idiotically brought into the Death House. Rose mostly just stood and listened, letting him talk, asking no questions, even when he got to part about Art shooting himself in the driveway. He explained how he found his friend Sandy in his car the next day, what she had said about the books, how his other friends remained unaccounted for. When he finally wound down, Rose said, "The guy who shot himself. Could you hear anything he was saying?"

Pedro shook his head.

"Okay. How did he do it? Did he just raise the gun, like this?" She mimicked shooting herself in the head with her finger.

"No, he was waving his hands around the whole time."

"Was he just *waving* them, or did it look like he might have been struggling with somebody?"

"Struggling?"

"Uh-huh. Like, fighting for control of the gun?"

Pedro looked thoughtful. The fuzzy dice had finally exhausted their pendulum energy and he absently swatted them to get them moving again. "Um, it did kind of look like that. But there was nobody else in the car."

"Just because you didn't see anybody doesn't mean nobody was there." She turned away from him, towards the house. "You know enough about this place to know that, don't you?"

"Yeah, I guess I do." Pause. "How long has Mr. Bartoski been in there, anyway?"

"Too long. I'm going to go get him." If the books were gone, Richard was in there wasting his time and putting himself at risk for no good reason. "After that let's regroup, track down your missing friends and the books they took. All right?"

"Okay."

Rose turned to go up to the house.

"Wait!"

She stopped, looked back at Pedro over her shoulder.

"What do you want me to do if, you know, you don't come back?"

"I'm not entertaining that possibility," Rose said.

Richard managed to take the impact with his hands and arms to avoid bashing his head in against the cement, but the swirling fog-thing immediately started trying to half-shove, half-drag him sideways through the narrow passage between the furnace and the wall in the utility room. It had hold of both his feet and his shoulders in a way that should have been impossible given the tight quarters, but things like that didn't matter when you were made of mist. Richard's fingers scrabbled uselessly on the rough wall and smooth metal, failing to get a good grip on anything. He popped out into the back corner and his head collided with the metal pipe that ran into the floor near the sump, making him see stars. Sick, cold, blurry stars. The water lay black and gritty and quiescent in its receptacle. In the dim light that filtered in from the other room he could see ashen streaks extending from the hole, as if something had dipped long fingers in the oily liquid and then dragged them along the floor. Or maybe something had climbed out of it.

The hands on his shoulders shifted and pushed downward, roughly shoved his head towards the sump. He managed to plant his hands on either side of the opening and wrenched sideways to keep his face from going into the water. The entity wasn't superhumanly powerful; he could resist it when he had leverage, a place to brace himself, but when it sort of flowed down his arms to his wrists and started trying to pry his hands apart he didn't have the strength or the purchase to prevent it. Instead he brought his knees in close and kicked off the wall, shoving his back into the water heater. It clanged like a dull, thick gong. His insubstantial assailant tried to regain its hold on him while he squirmed and twisted and somehow wormed his way into space between the water heater and the wall. It clutched at his feet and moved up his shins but he kicked loose. Seemed like the thing could shove and it could push but it had trouble with tight grips. Maybe that was why the ghostly fucker hadn't just picked up a screwdriver and stabbed him with it; maybe that was why it hadn't strangled Cassandra Weiss itself instead of goading his father into doing it.

Richard hauled himself out from behind the water heater and scrabbled away from it. He spotted the hammer nearby and snatched it up, stood and spun and held it out in front of him as if he could beat the phantom into submission with it. He banged its iron head against the cinderblock wall with a clang that reverberated in the empty room. "Come on," he said, breathing hard. "Try me again."

Unexpectedly, the overhead light came on.

A small, dark figure stood in the doorway to the big room, finger on the switch.

"What's with the hammer, Richard?" Rose said. "We building a fort?"

Pedro sat in the driver's seat and stared at the front door. A few minutes after Rose went inside it creaked open, but nobody came out. Pedro slid out of the car and went to the bottom of the walk. The door swung wider and stayed there for a moment—long enough for him to see that nobody was moving it, as if the house were taunting him—and then slammed shut with such force that he took an involuntary step back. He turned to say something to Sandy and discovered she had climbed out of the car and taken off running, heading for the gap between the two houses opposite the old man's place, booking it like the high school track star she was. Her complicated heels didn't seem to be slowing her down now. He called her name but she didn't stop, didn't even look back. After one last backward glance at the house he went after her, chasing her into the downward-sloping joined backyards across the way. She vanished into the overgrown strip of forest that grew along the ravine; the brush shivered and then there was no trace she had ever been there.

Pedro followed, failing to notice a tie-out cable snaking through the grass until he caught his foot on it and fell, sprawling face-first on the soft ground. As he picked himself up, the dog at the other end of the long leash—alerted to his presence like a spider who'd felt the twang of its web catching a fly—came out of its house to stand growling, feet spread, hackles up, staring at him. The line was hooked to a thick leather collar around its neck; the grey plastic-clad cable looped out into the yard where Pedro had tripped over it, then returned to the doghouse, where it was secured to a shiny metal ring attached to an equally shiny metal plate screwed into the wood.

Pedro had often encountered this dog roaming the neighborhood. The two of them weren't on especially good terms. He had never seen it tied up before and the animal didn't seem particularly happy with the situation. As he got carefully to his feet, the dog took a threatening step forward, body tense. Pedro backed away slowly. The dog didn't charge, but kept pace with him. When Pedro thought he was close enough to the edge of the yard to make his getaway, he turned and bolted, which of course set the dog off. It came galloping across the grass, barking madly. Pedro plunged into the bushes, crashing through the thorny, reddish growth, while somewhere behind him the dog emitted a little yelp as the cable jerked it to a halt. A moment later it started yammering in furious frustration.

He pushed on through the bramble thicket. The woody barbs scratched him everywhere he had exposed skin and a few places he didn't. By the time he made it to the other side, where milkweed and sumac grew, he was bleeding from a dozen little cuts. In the yard behind him, the dog was still at it. Pedro heard a distant door bang open and somebody hollered at the animal to shut the hell up already, which it did after a few more grumbly complaints, just to show it *could* keep barking if it chose to.

Pedro crouched and scrambled under the thin, arthritic, ash-grey sumac branches. Beyond, larger trees took over and the underbrush grew sparse. Sandy was nowhere in sight, but the forest floor consisted mainly of needles and rotting leaves, easily disturbed by passing feet, and he quickly spotted a line of brown humus that had been churned to reveal rich dark earth beneath. He followed her trail away from the houses, towards the gully. As the slope grew steeper he came upon a big black smear on the forest floor where she must have slipped. It went almost all the way to the edge of the ravine. He hoped she hadn't fallen in. It wasn't super deep but the bottom was hard shale and you could easily break a leg in a short fall, or your neck, if you landed head-first. Just ask Beth Bartoski how that worked.

Getting on his hands and knees, Pedro crawled forward and peered down the wall of jagged, broken rock to the stony creek bed below. Sandy wasn't down there. He looked left and right and spotted a line of footprints along the lip of the drop-off; it looked like she had caught herself on the saplings that grew in the sunny space along the edge and had headed north, towards where the ravine began, at a culvert beneath Cemetery Road. Relieved, he picked himself up and followed her trail. In places where the bushes and scrub vegetation grew too thick, the tracks veered away from the edge, but always returned to it, as if she were looking for something. A safe way down, maybe. Farther up, he recalled, an old knotted rope had been tied around a sturdy maple and tossed into the ravine as a climbing aid. It had been in place for so long that the trunk had swallowed the rope, the bark enclosing it like lips over teeth. He doubted Sandy was aware of the rope, but if she came across it she might use it to get down.

He kept going and soon spotted a rope up ahead, but not the rope he remembered; this one was canary-yellow nylon, and it was in the wrong place, looped around a thick oak branch that extended out into the empty space above the creek. The two ends of the rope hung straight down into the ravine, stretched tight, as if supporting heavy weights. They swayed in the breeze with a gentle creaking sound. Pedro couldn't see what was hanging from them. He moved forward and peered down, saw what was there, gasped, recoiled, slipped on the loose soil, and went over the edge. The shale wall scraped at his back as he fell. He landed feet-first in a heap of scree that absorbed some of the impact and slid down it to the bottom. Now he was lying on his back looking up at Pete and Glenn suspended overhead, each dangling from a noose. The lemon-colored coils around their necks stood in sharp contrast to their purple faces and their swollen, blackened, extruding tongues.

Pedro scrambled away from the dangling bodies, scuttling backwards until he splashed into an eddy of the stream. Something floated half-submerged nearby, stuck on brush and sand: A book, soaked and thickened, discolored by the dark water. He reached out and picked it up but it was disgustingly slimy and he let go with a little grunt of dismay. Freed from its tangle, the book began to drift away.

"We got the rope from the house. Glenn was carrying it."

"Shit!" Pedro spun around and spotted Sandy crouching near the edge of the ravine, beneath an overhang formed by the roots of the oak tree. Mussed and filthy and all scraped up, she stared at the swaying corpses the way you might regard a hornet's nest that you weren't sure was occupied. "Sandy?"

"It was in the basement," she said, "down there with the books. Victor said we would need it. He didn't say what for." Her voice was distant, detached, as if she were talking on the phone while preoccupied with something else that was more important.

"Did you ... Did you come this way looking for them?"

"I don't know. I don't remember. Maybe. I guess if I hadn't fallen behind last night, I would be here too." She sounded a little disappointed, as if she had missed out on a particularly fun party, and Pedro wondered what sort of suggestion Victor had planted in her, in the others, that would make them carry a rope without knowing why and then hang themselves with it when they were finished with the chores he had given them, and if it was still active.

Pedro sloshed over to Sandy and hauled her to her feet and led her away upstream. She kept looking back over her shoulder as he hustled her along the shale floor of the ravine. "I should stay," she said. "I have to—"

"You don't have to do anything," Pedro said. "Let's just get out of the ravine and call the police."

"No," Sandy said, squirming, trying to pull away from him. "No no no, Pedro. No police. Victor said."

"Okay, shh, okay, no police. Okay. Just come with me, all right?"

She stopped resisting and the gentle curve of the ravine soon took the bodies out of view, although the spreading foliage of the oak remained visible for some time, green and innocent. After a little while Sandy stopped looking back. They passed the spot where the old knotted rope had been. Pedro looked for it but it was gone, moldered away to nothing; all that remained was a ring around the trunk, a scar like lips in the bark, as if the tree might split open and start shrieking at them.

At this point, Pedro wouldn't have been surprised if it did.

Art opened his eyes.

Lifting the lids was like raising fifty pounds of bricks. The room was dim but light rushed in and assaulted his retinas, each photon a tiny jackhammer. He was lying down. His head hurt, as if somebody had stabbed him in the skull with an icepick. It was all bandaged up. His left arm hurt, too; a needle was stuck in it near the elbow, attached to a tube, securely taped to his skin. A piece of plastic with a wire coming out was clamped to his finger. Something was making noise, beeping in the same sort of way his metal detector beeped when it found a bottle cap or a dime buried under the soil, only more persistent. Something else rattled in the distant background, like a dot matrix printer running, spitting out lines and lines of text. *Bzzzzzzt, bzzzzzzt, bzzzzzzt.*

He couldn't seem to turn his head, so he moved his eyes for a look around. His vision was blurred but he discerned that he was in a dim room with a front wall made of glass and covered by curtains, partially drawn. A glass door by the wall stood open; beyond was a brightly lit area of desks and counters.

This was ICU. He'd been in ICU before, but never as a patient. How had he ended up here?

Oh. Right. Bullet to the head. In the driveway. At Potter Street.

Why had he gone back to the house? A worry, a premonition, a hunch that something was happening that he needed to stop. But as soon as he'd arrived, eased his car in beside the damaged station wagon, he'd known he was too late. A presence bulged from the windows and the doors like rancid dough swelling out of a pan, keeping him in the car, pressing him into the seat with the weight of every awful thing he'd ever witnessed, every crime scene, every victim. He'd glanced at Beth Bartoski's car and suddenly her body had fallen out of the sky and crashed onto the hood of *his* car, face-down on *his* windshield, red hair spreading in a coppery bloom, head twisted at an angle incompatible with human life, staring directly at him with big wide dead eyes. But then those eyes had flicked to look to Art's right, and he had realized something was sitting in the passenger seat, a shape, dark and long and spindly. It had grabbed for his gun, yanked it out of his holster, and they had struggled, just like in the basement. Except this time, the gun had gone off.

Art became aware that a person had appeared in the room, big and tall and with an odd circle around its head like a dark halo, standing at the foot of the bed. He could make out the outlines of the hospital monitoring machines through the figure, could see the blinking lights, the overhead fluorescents out in the hall. Not a nurse, then, unless nurses were spread so thin these days they had become translucent.

"Good afternoon, Detective Leeson," the visitor said. "I'm glad you're finally awake. I've been waiting. Before we begin, please accept my apology for what happened to you at the house. Things have gone far beyond what was intended, and I am being required to take steps."

Art tried to say something but his tongue slid around helplessly in his mouth, garbling his words. They sounded like gloppy pulp burping up from the bottom of an orange juice carton and squelching into a glass.

"I can see that you are inclined to argue, but there's nothing to be done. The matter is out of my hands. Surely you of all people must understand how a single unanticipated action can lead to catastrophic consequences. No doubt many of the crimes you've investigated began that way. Choices are made that reduce choices available. The path narrows. Tragedy becomes inevitable." The shape moved to the side of the bed, leaned in. Its voice became a whisper. "I have come to set you free."

Suddenly something cold and heavy lay in Art's hand. The feel of it was familiar: A gun, his own sidearm, in fact. It couldn't possibly be here, but Art knew the pattern on the molded grip, the ridges in the metal. Now he felt cold hands on his arm, moving it, pushing it, pulling it, bringing it into position; now he smelled the weapon, oil and metal and old gunpowder; now he felt it on his lips, the cold steel of the barrel; now he tasted it on his tongue. Fingers caressed his hand, positioned it on the trigger.

When they squeezed, his own finger squeezed with them.

And without a sound, the room went black.

PART THREE

7

ROBERT JAMES SAT IN AN Adirondack chair on his balcony, high in the densely wooded hills northeast of Bentonville. His eyes were closed, but he was not napping.

He was on his way back from the hospital.

Giving his card to that investigator had served his own purposes; he needed to find out what the police knew, what they thought, what they suspected, and the card, being crafted from his own special materials and imbued with certain radiant energies, was as good as one of those electronic bugs seen in spy films. Better, in fact; it allowed two-way communication, both sending and receiving, under the right circumstances. In this case, he'd only intended to receive, but then Leeson had returned to the house and gotten himself shot and the connection had gone black.

Fortuitously, the card had remained in Leeson's possession— forgotten in a pocket or a sack of clothes in his hospital room, perhaps—and when the man regained consciousness, James had sensed it, and used the card to pay him a visit and shuffle him out of the deck in a way that would look like a natural outcome, given his condition.

That task complete, James opened his eyes. His home—a two-story converted mill, built of rough-hewn logs cut from the surrounding woodlands—was also his shop, the only destination on a gravel road once trafficked by horse-drawn logging sleds. The road ended at an unpaved parking lot, currently empty. A car was coming, though; he could hear it in the forest stillness, could see a cloud of dust rising out among the trees. Soon it hove into view around the last gentle curve:

A green sedan, big as a boat and twice as loud. Such a vehicle seemed unlikely to contain a customer. He watched it pull off to the left, listened to the motor sputter and die. The door opened and his assistant Barbara emerged; this jalopy must be a loaner she'd gotten while her vehicle was being repaired. He waved to her and she waved back, then disappeared onto the porch beneath him.

Robert James got out of the Adirondack chair, stretched, and went into his second-floor apartment. His hat and jacket hung on a peg near the stairs down to the store. He put them on before going down. One had to maintain one's standards, after all, even—*especially*—in the face of such distress as the last few days had inflicted.

The steps made little noises under his feet as he descended. The bottom of the stairwell was screened by a curtain of wooden beads that clattered as he brushed through. The shop was dim; he preferred to illuminate the showroom with scattered oil lanterns, only using the overhead lights while cleaning or when a customer wanted to examine an item more closely. Surrounded by old chipped dressers and handmade chests, overstuffed chairs with faded upholstery, black iron candelabra that still held the nubs of greasy tapers, dark paintings of blustery seashores, inky bookcases supporting and permeated by the odor of aged books, potential customers would be transported into another era; whenever possible, he tried to prevent the cultivated impression of antiquity from being intruded upon by modern conveniences.

His assistant had settled down behind her desk, an enormous secretariat near the front door. The hulking cabinet concealed a computer, keeping all its components out of sight, including the monitor. He hadn't a clue how to run the thing; it had been set up years ago by a former employee who had decided things needed to be modernized around here. His last several assistants had been telling him the system was out of date, but it kept his accounts just fine and he saw no reason to replace just because it was obsolete.

"Good morning, Barbara," he said, touching the brim of his hat. He knew she found that a charming affectation. "Welcome back."

"It's good to be back." She said it a little tightly, though, and without really looking at him. "I hope you've been managing all right without me."

"I always manage, but it's better when you're here, of course. Is something wrong?"

"No, I'm fine. Here, let me give you back your key." She opened her purse and rummaged in it briefly, then took out a loose key. It opened the outside doors at the house on Potter Street. He had obtained it by subterfuge from the late Walter Bartoski; although James could pick a lock, his assistant could not, and he had no interest in answering the sort of questions that offering to teach her that useful skill would invite. Much easier to misappropriate a key and tell her it had been given, that they had permission to enter and take what needed removing.

"Thank you," James said, pocketing the key. "Are you sure you're all right? You seem tense."

"I am, a little. A reporter called me this morning. She kept asking questions about why I lost control of the car, like she was looking for someone to blame for ... for what happened."

She must be referring to the electrocution of the utility worker. "You are hardly responsible for that man's death," James said.

"I know. I know. It's just, I mean, I already talked to the police. Why should the paper harass me? It's not right."

"I'm sure whatever interest they have will wane soon. There's always another tragedy for the papers to chase."

"I suppose you're right." Then: "Seeing that girl in the window ... She was weird. Spooky. I don't know what—"

The crunch of tires on gravel outside interrupted. Barbara stopped talking and her head swiveled to look at the front door, then back to James, lips pressed tight. Sitting at her desk, she couldn't see the parking lot, but he could. Reading the unspoken question on her face, he said, gently, "Customers. Not reporters or police."

"Oh thank God. I'll go greet them." She slid down the top of the rollup desk to hide the computer, then got up and headed for the door.

James watched her go, running his thumb along the toothy ridge of the key in his pocket, wondering what girl she had seen, and in what window.

Rose took a few steps forward, looked around appraisingly at the cell-like chamber. "So this is it? This is the room?"

"This is the room," Richard said. "This is where the old man liked to put me when he wanted to punish me. Guess he thought it would be a good place to hold a kidnapping victim." He pointed at the corner. "She would have been tied to that big pipe next to the sump."

"God." She found she was hugging herself, peering into the dark space behind the machinery. "Is it always this cold in here?"

"No. Sometimes it's colder." Then: "We should leave. Something's … lurking."

She looked at him, noticed for the first time that he had some fresh scrapes on his arms and his face, and his clothes were streaked with grey grime. "What happened? Did you squeeze back there?"

"Not intentionally. Come on." He led her out of the small room and into the basement proper, threading through the field of boxes. She thought they were going to head for the stairs, but instead he pointed the hammer at something on the floor, a sea chest that sat amid the wreckage, secured with a padlock. "There it is."

It looked like a movie prop, something full of rum and doubloons and blood-red jewels. "You didn't open it?"

"Not yet," he said. "I got, uh, interrupted."

"Interrupted how?"

"Something attacked me before I could bash the lock. A shape, like what you saw grab the girl away from the window upstairs. Probably the same thing that killed Beth. It flung me into the utility room and dragged me into the corner and tried to drown me in the sump."

"Jesus." She looked around. "Is it still here?"

"No doubt. But I don't think it's strong enough to take us both on. Physically, I mean." He tapped his temple. "That's why it tries to get inside your head and make you do its work for it."

"Like with Candy Weiss's parents."

"Yeah," Richard said. "Let's find out what's in this chest and then get the fuck out of here, okay?"

She was pretty sure what he would find—nothing—but he needed to see for himself. "Okay," she said.

He knelt down in front of the chest and raised the hammer, then paused, chuckled a little, and lifted the padlock so she could see it. A small key stuck out of the bottom; it wasn't even locked, just rotated to the closed position. Richard removed the padlock and stuck it in his pocket. "That was too easy," he said, lifting the lid.

Empty.

He peered into it for a few seconds, then started feeling around inside like he was hunting for a hidden compartment, a false bottom. Rose leaned forward for a better look at the interior of the chest. It was papered with old parchment on which strange symbols were scrawled in rust-colored ink. Some of the material had been torn away, leaving streaks of old dry paste behind.

Richard banged the lid shut, looked up at her. "Maybe they're hidden somewhere else," he said. "We'll have to search the house."

"No," Rose said, "they're gone. And I know who took them."

"You ... what? How—"

"While you were in here getting manhandled, I met one of your neighbors. A kid named Pedro. He and some buddies had themselves a session with a ouija board here last night."

"*Here?* At the house?"

"Mmm. Sounds like the place opened its doors and invited them in. They contacted a spirit named Victor who proceeded to get inside their heads, just like you were saying. Maybe he had an easier time because they were trying to communicate with him. My father arrived while this was going on. Pedro saw him in the car before he shot himself. He was arguing with nothing, then struggling for control of the gun—presumably against Victor—and that was when he got shot. After that their little soiree broke up and Pedro managed to lose track of all his friends, but he found one again today. Girl named Sandy. She's still pretty out of it, but she was able to tell him that Victor made them take books out of the basement and get rid of them."

"Get rid of them where?"

"Unknown. Sandy got separated from the others before the mission was completed." Rose gestured at the chest. "We came here looking for books. They're gone. Time to clear out."

"Right." Richard tossed the hammer aside and followed Rose up the stairs into the cool dimness of the front hallway. He closed and latched the cellar door, then pulled the padlock out of his pocket and put it on the latch. Rose watched as he tested it, making sure it was secure; then he inserted the key and snapped it off. That would hardly contain whatever lurked down there, which Richard surely knew, but if he gained some kind of psychological boost from symbolically locking it in then who was she to point out the futility of his action?

They went out onto the porch and proceeded down the sidewalk to the street. Pedro's convertible still sat at the curb in front of her car, but no one was in it. Rose broke away from Richard and ran down to the sidewalk and put her hands on the door and leaned over the interior, peering at the floor, as if the kids might be curled up down there, hiding from the house. Which they weren't, of course. She smacked the door with the heel of her palm just as Richard arrived, shoes crunching on the sidewalk behind her.

"Problem?" he said.

"My witnesses are gone." She looked up and down the street. "Damn it, I told him to wait for me."

"Did you give him a lollipop?"

She spun around to glare at Richard. The side of his mouth quirked up in an almost-grin and she couldn't stop herself from laughing, a mirthless little stress-bark. She clamped down on that before it got out of control and turned into something else. "No, but maybe I should have," she said. She put her hand on Richard's arm and steered him down the sidewalk. "Come on, Mr. Comedian. Let's go see if Pedro took his girl home to meet his mother."

Barbara stood on the front porch of the antique shop and waved at the retreating SUV. The couple had paid the asking price, in cash, for a Victorian dresser with a mirror, both of which were wrapped in moving blankets and ensconced in the back of their vehicle, and had put a deposit on a matching armoire. Robert James watched her through the front door, then came out and folded himself into one of the Adirondack chairs. "A lucrative afternoon," he said.

"I'll say. I can't believe they paid the full asking price."

"Those who are accustomed to shopping retail are often unaware that in a place like this, everything is negotiable, and bargaining is expected. I feel no compulsion to educate them."

She laughed. "Neither do I. Besides, I hate haggling."

"Most people do. But we all have to strike bargains from time to time."

"I suppose so."

As the dust from the vehicle's departure settled back to earth, Barbara sat on the step just within the shade of the porch. After a few minutes James said, "Before the customers arrived, you mentioned a girl in the window. Was that the Bartoski woman's daughter?"

"What? Oh, her. I don't know. I suppose so. A little blonde thing. She was trying to climb out an upstairs window onto the porch roof. Her father or somebody pulled her back into the house."

A little blonde thing. Not the Bartoski girl, then. "You saw the father?"

"Not really. It was dark in the room. He just looked like a shape." He watched her tilt her head back to look up at the sky, pure blue, a sapphire lens stretched above the earth. Her gaze traveled down to the trees, tall and straight, flush with late summer growth and the recent rain. Dragonflies buzzed and flitted above the gravel. "Hot today," she said.

"Indeed." He stood. "Let's take a walk up to the pond. It'll be cooler there."

"What if customers come?"

"They'll wait."

James turned the sign around from *Open* to *Closed* and set the hands on the cardboard clock to indicate they would be back in thirty minutes. He offered Barbara a hand and pulled her to her feet, and the two of them headed across the lot to the path that led to the old mill pond. It sloped gently upward, covered in pine needles, dark green overlaying brown, giving it a soft, spongy surface, padding that made no sound as they walked on it. Rainwater glimmered in the old ruts left behind by the ATV a previous assistant—Barbara's immediate predecessor, or maybe the one before that; it was difficult to keep them straight—had driven to the shop when the weather was pleasant, spending his lunch breaks and summer evenings after work careering through the woods, breaking trails, disrupting the quiet. James had not been at all sorry to send *that* young man on his way when the time came.

He and Barbara came to the rocky, pebbled, muddy shore. A few large boulders flanked the trail where the beach began. To the left was the trail to the weir; to the right, up a short, steep slope, an old concrete bench overlooked the water from the shade of a massive willow. The opposite shore was boggy, cat's tails and rushes growing thick, duckweed skimming the surface, and trees pressed in close.

They went up to the bench and sat down. Barbara kicked off her shoes, put her feet in the grass and squeezed it with her toes. Unseen birds warbled and insects thrummed in the woods behind them but no mosquitoes bothered them here, no frogs croaked in the shallows, no fish rippled the surface with flicks of their tails. They chatted a little, but mostly just enjoyed the quiet. He could do that much for her, at least.

After a sufficient period of time, James stood and stretched and said that he really must get back to the shop. Barbara made to stand too, of course, and accompany him, but he motioned for her to stay and enjoy the afternoon a bit longer. As she relaxed on the bench, James walked partway up the track, then stopped, scuffing his shoe along the surface.

Ah, well. It had to be done, and he had to do it. That was part of the bargain.

James turned and silently crept back down the path towards the beach.

No one answered the door at Pedro's house, and a quick walk through the neighborhood failed to turn up any sign of him or the girl. Rose and Richard retired to Rose's car, started it up, turned on the air, and waited. The kids didn't return, and eventually Rose pulled away from the curb, executed a three-point turn, and drove up Potter Street toward the burned-out remains of the Weiss house. She slowed as they went by and they both looked at it, but neither of them spoke.

At the intersection where Potter Street ended at Cemetery Road, Rose turned right. They drove across the culvert where the gully had been filled in. Richard looked down into the ravine as they crossed over it, at the inky grey stone of the stream bed, the water black as pavement, almost invisible through the trees. He remembered wandering around down there when he was young, exploring the darkly wooded slash through the center of his neighborhood. Did kids still do that sort of thing these days? He doubted it.

On the other side of the ravine they entered a seedy commercial area, run-down shops kept afloat by nostalgia and cheap rent. He saw two tattoo parlors, a dental office offering inexpensive braces to straighten your teeth and treatments to whiten them, a row of tired stores selling flowers or secondhand clothes or used books or off-brand medical supplies, a to-go pizzeria where he remembered standing on the sidewalk eating gooey slices of thin-crust pizza off oil-soaked paper plates. At the end was a sad little place advertising consignments and antiques. It was closed, perhaps for good, judging by the layer of dust on the wares displayed in the front bay window: A cracked cabinet radio, an iron coat rack, a faded loveseat on which sat a mannequin wearing a black suit and a fedora. As they passed, Richard found his head swiveling to stare at the dummy's uncanny featureless face, the outdated clothes, the string tie, the hat.

The *hat*.

"I have an idea," Richard said.

"I would love to hear it."

"There was this guy, Robert James. He came around the house a couple of times claiming he used to buy stuff from the old man. He mentioned books. The one I found looked exactly like he described. Maybe he can tell us more about them."

"Okay," Rose said. "Where can we find this guy, Robert James?"

"Um. I think he has a shop. But I don't know where it is."

"Do you have his number?"

"No. He gave me a business card, but all it had was his name."

"Do you still have it?"

"Um. No. I threw it away."

After a moment, Rose said: "So far none of this is incredibly useful."

"Yeah. Sorry." Then: "Do you have a cell phone? We can call directory assistance and see if he's listed."

"No. Dad had one, but it belonged to the department and they took it back already." She steered into a gas station at the corner, pulling up to the pump. "You can use the pay phone while I gas up."

Richard did as instructed, and was informed that directory assistance had no business or residential listing for anyone named Robert James. He made another call, leaving a message on Tony's voice mail, and returned to the car just as the pump clicked off. She glanced at him, nozzle in hand, and said, "Any luck?"

"They don't have a number for him."

Rose grunted and replaced the handle. "All right," she said, screwing the gas cap back on, "I'm officially suspicious of this character." She straightened up, brushed off her hands on her thighs.

"Let's go down to the paper. I might be able to dig up something there."

"Sounds good."

Richard paid for the gas and then they drove to the *Herald* building downtown, wedged in with the banks and the churches and the Bentonville convention center, which had a sign out front saying it was closed for renovations. Small, sluggish shops surrounded it, outposts in a wasteland of cracked sidewalks and lonely parking meters and weedy verges. Rose pulled into a tiny parking lot off a narrow alleyway, gloomy in the perpetual shade of tall buildings on every side, and hung a permit from her rearview mirror like a talisman. They went in through a side door and up a dim stairwell that smelled of old wood and lacquer. At the third floor landing they went into a large room, desks and files and putty-colored computer workstations scattered around, harshly lit by banks of fluorescent lights in the ceiling. It looked just how Richard imagined a newsroom would, except there weren't any reporters rushing around waving copy or typing up their stories or trying to coax information out of contacts over the phone; there were just a couple of kids, interns maybe, pecking away on their keyboards. In the corner a bearded guy in a fishing hat was writing something longhand on a yellow legal pad. Only the guy in the hat seemed to notice they had come in; Rose waved to him and he tipped the end of his pen toward her in acknowledgment.

Richard trailed along after Rose to her desk, a massive, scratched old wooden thing in the back corner of the big room, screened from sight behind a fabric-covered partition. "What's with the wall?" he asked as she settled down behind her desk, studying her phone, where a little red light was flashing

"Nobody wanted to look at my ugly mug, so they put me behind a screen."

Richard snorted. "I find that hard to believe."

She smiled without looking at him. "Actually, I bring ordinary people here sometimes for interviews, and the news room makes them nervous. Too much activity."

"Too much activity?" He made a show of looking out at the quiet newsroom. "Really?"

"Well, there's not as much activity as there used to be. Layoffs.

They swear it's finished now though. Hang on." She picked up the receiver and pushed the flashing light and listened. Voice mail, Richard surmised. After a moment she grinned and pressed a different button on the phone, and Richard heard a voice start up in mid-sentence. "... the information about the auction at the Arvidsson's," it was saying. "I've got a list right here of who attended and what they bought. I faxed you a page that I thought you'd find interesting. Call me if you want the rest of it." He gave a number and the message ended.

Rose pressed a button to stop the playback and smothered the mouthpiece with her hand, even though she wasn't actually talking to anybody. "That was this guy, Ozzie. He puts out a little local paper out in Massalacqua. Makes us look like the *Times*."

"Nice of you to put him on the payroll."

That elicited a snort from her. "Payroll? Fuck, no. I'm pretty sure his net worth exceeds the value of this building and everything in it."

"Oh. I see." Pause. "Does he need an accountant?" Another snort. "So what's the deal with the auction?"

"Candy Weiss's grandmother lived in Massalacqua. She died not long ago and they had an estate sale, auction-style. I asked Ozzie to find out who was there and what they bought."

"Why?"

"Because something unusual happened while I was at the Arvidsson residence. I'll tell you about it after I call him back." She dialed the number Ozzie had left. There was a pause, then Richard heard a muffled *hello* from the other end of the line. A brief conversation ensued, the upshot of which was that Ozzie would bring all the documentation he had collected about the auction, in exchange for which Rose would treat him to dinner at an excellent Italian restaurant she knew. Richard hoped she didn't mean Airport Pizza.

After they hung up, the voice mail button was still flashing. Rose pressed it again and a new message unspooled from the speaker. "Mrs. Mancuso, this is Dr. Pacula at Highland Hospital," it said. "I left a message at your home as well. Please call me at your earliest opportunity. It's about your father."

Rose regarded the telephone as if it had just reached out and slapped her.

"Oh, Jesus," she said.

Having finished up his business with Barbara at the pond, Robert James returned to the very darkest corner of his darkened showroom, a space shielded from the lights—and from casual traffic—by a deliberately confusing arrangement of antique room dividers and tapestries. A massive oak hutch with solid wooden doors stood back here, sporting a tag labeling it, falsely, as sold. He unlocked and opened the hutch, revealing three tiers of shelves that supported a number of notebooks. The interior was papered on all sides with his special parchment, scrawled with handwritten runes. Before taking what he needed, he examined the lining to make sure it was fully intact, the writing crisp. Couldn't have energies leaking out into the shop and affecting the environment in undesirable ways. Everything was fine. He ran his fingers along the spines of the books, then reached towards the top shelf, where he kept the volumes that had not yet been charged. Only a few remained; he would need to make more soon, once the raw materials upstairs were completely dry.

James slid an empty volume out. The leathery blue binding felt cool in his hands, the black pattern inlaid in its cover icy. He flipped through the book, checking its pages. Creamy, blank, unlined, no creases or tears. Good. He closed the hutch and brought the notebook back to the pond to wait for Barbara to emerge. Sometimes it took hours for them to come back; sometimes they never did at all. Barbara, however, had returned while he'd been gone, lingering silent and motionless on the gravel beach, looking confused and unsure. As well she might. He touched the brim of his hat in greeting, then felt a little foolish when she just stared at him. Of course such niceties were meaningless now, when she stood there in the August sun with neither breath nor shadow and the pond and the trees and the cattails were visible behind her as if through rippling, semi-opaque ice.

He opened the notebook wide, turned it towards Barbara, showing her the featureless interior. She looked at it, then at him. James said, "What do you see?"

Her wide, blank eyes stared at it.

"Barbara? Do you see anything written on the page?"

The eyes moved up to look at him, back to the book, back to him.

She shook her head slightly, a fraction to the left, a fraction to the right. He let out a relieved breath. In rare cases, returnees saw invisible words scrawled across the paper: Messages carried back from the water. Instructions, requests, information. Threats, sometimes. These they would read to him in a dead intonation, the voice of something inhuman, like daggers of ice scratching against a gravestone.

"Good." It was always a relief when they saw nothing. He closed the notebook and held it out to her. "This is for you."

She stared at it.

"Go on." He gave the book a little shake. She lifted her eyes to look at him. "Take it."

Her eyes, wide and filmy and fish-belly white, stayed aimed at him as she slowly reached up and grasped the notebook with both hands. He let go of it as the black iron inlay on the cover turned dull red, then white. The book hummed in her hands as tiny brilliant flecks began traveling along its labyrinthine pattern, moving from her hands towards the center of the pattern. Barbara made no sound as the notebook pulled her inside, soaked her up like liquid into a sponge, and then she was gone. The light faded and he stood alone on the beach, the book drifting in front of him, its cover fluttering like butterfly wings. The black maze on the cover had turned to gold. He reached out and took hold of the newly empowered book, brought it close, checked the interior. The pages were now lined in red, ready to be inscribed for the purposes of influence or incantation or enchantment or whatever needed to be done.

James brought the book back to the shop, to the hutch where he stored them. He unlocked it and opened it again and took a step back, frowning at the empty space where the volumes he'd left at that accursed house should have been. After receiving his instructions, recited in a nightmare voice by the returned spirit of a hitchhiker James had picked up along Route 18 and delivered for trade—and who had then turned and vanished back into the pond, not even granting the boon of a freshly energized book—James had spent some months grooming Walter Bartoski, first ingratiating himself by stopping to admire the man's prized antique automobile at a neighborhood car show, then paying a series of visits to his home and vastly overpaying for kitschy artifacts and pieces of furniture that went straight to the heap of unsalable junk in the backyard of the shop. On each occasion, James had contrived to leave behind a book or two, gradually poisoning the atmosphere of the house, until finally the proper constellation of effects had been achieved to induce the old man to take the steps that were required of him.

And then things had started to go wrong.

Nearly every time he stopped by, James could not escape without first listening to a litany of complaints, chief among them that Walter Bartoski's children wanted nothing to do with him, that they wouldn't care if he lived or died, indeed, that they would treat news of his death as a cause for celebration. Certainly he would have been shocked to learn that it had, in fact, brought them to his door. Would the old man have found that gratifying?

Perhaps. But look at all the trouble it had caused.

James selected a few more books, then closed and locked the hutch, sat down at a nearby desk with Barbara's volume, and began writing himself an ending.

For the second time in as many days, Richard found himself at Highland Hospital. He held Ozzie's fax—plain paper, not that awful onionskin crap the fax machine at his office spat out, which never stayed flat and gleefully transferred black stains to your fingers at the slightest touch—as he sat there waiting for Rose to come back. He kept looking at the item Ozzie had circled on the list, down near the bottom. It read, *James, R., set of 5 notebooks, $350, cash.* Underneath that, Ozzie had written, *Thought this might interest you. Somewhere in Bentonville zip code. Don't know address.*

Oh, yeah. Richard was *very* interested in that one.

He looked up as Rose came into the lobby, carrying a paper sack with twisted handles. He could see the elbow of Art's jacket hunching up from the top. She walked toward him, looking bewildered and exhausted. Richard stood up, but before he could ask her anything she said, "He's dead."

Richard, who already knew that, said: "I'm so sorry." Then, into the ensuing silence: "Do, uh, do they know why?"

"Brain hemorrhage. Probably. They told me it might happen. Because of the surgery. His injury." She rubbed the back of her head. "I heard them talking. When I picked up Dad's stuff in ICU. One of them said he was making a gun with his hand. It was in his mouth when he coded." She made a finger-pistol, put it to her temple. "Bang."

Richard had no idea what to say about that. "Is there anything … I mean, do you need to stay? Because——"

"No. There's nothing I can do now."

"Okay. Come on, let's go." She still had the finger-pistol pointed at her head as if she were holding herself hostage. He took her hand and lowered it and guided her through the double glass doors and out into the parking lot toward her car. He still had hold of it when he heard a sharp voice from behind them say Rose's name. They both turned. A man approached them, walking purposefully from closer to the hospital. He was shortish, stout, with a little black beard and little black eyes. He looked almost like a pirate, Richard thought. A pirate in a suit.

He heard Rose mutter, "Great."

The guy stopped in front of them, flicking his gaze back and forth. Richard saw the man's eyes note his grip on Rose's hand, and self-consciously released it.

"Rose, there was a message on our machine saying to come to the hosp——"

"Art's dead," Rose said.

"What happened?"

"Brain hemorrhage."

The man nodded, scrutinized her for a second, tilted his head at Richard. "Who's this?"

"This is Richard. He's helping me investigate something. Richard, this is my husband, Joe."

Richard proffered a hand to shake. Joe didn't take it. "You're a reporter?" he said.

"Accountant."

"An accountant?" Joe looked at Rose. "What are you investigating? Tax deductions?"

"Murders."

He gave her a blank look. "What?"

"Murders."

"You're kidding."

She shook her head.

"Whose murders?"

"A little girl's. His sister's. Art's, now."

"For God's sake. Rose. Art shot himself. What makes you think he was murdered?"

"I have my reasons."

"So you know better than the police, is that it?"

"I've been looking at things and drawing my own conclusions. I'm a journalist. That's what I do."

Joe snorted. "What you do. Yeah, I know what you do. Anything for a story." He looked Richard up and down. "Or anyone."

Rose stood there for a moment, saying nothing; then she turned to Richard. Her face was even paler than usual, and her eyes were furious. She handed Richard her keys and said, "Go wait in the car."

"Are you sure you—"

She shook her head. "Go wait in the car."

Richard went to wait in the car.

"What the hell's going on with you, Rose?" Joe said. "You disappear for a whole day, not a word, nobody knows where you are or how to reach you—"

"How is that different from any other day when I'm out working on a story?"

"—and then here you are at the hospital with that guy without even bothering to come home first, and it's different because you're *not* working on a story, I called the paper and they said you were taking a few days off, which you didn't think I needed to know, I guess, so—"

"This isn't for the paper," she said. "It's for Dad. Maybe you should—"

"Don't hand me that." He pointed at her with two fingers, the other two curled under, thumb up in the air. The double-barreled point. She fucking hated the double-barreled point. "This is for Art? You're deluding yourself. Nobody murdered Art. He shot himself. Okay? And you should've been here with him—"

"Don't tell me what I should be doing."

"—not running around town doing who-knows-what with some goddamn *accountant*—"

"We're not running around town doing who-knows-what. I told

you, Dad was murdered, and I'm trying to——"

"Bullshit. That's bullshit. If that's what you think, go to the police. They would *love* to nail the person who shot one of their guys. But you're not going to the police, are you? Because *you've got nothing to tell them*. Because *it didn't fucking happen*." Joe glanced at her nearby car, where Richard sat hunched in the passenger seat, conspicuously not looking at them. "Where'd your friend get the shiner? He have to fight somebody for the privilege of getting a ride from you?"

Rose stared at him for a second. "I'm not having this conversation with you again, Joe. Not here. Not now. Not ever." He opened his mouth to say something else but she shook her head, held up her hand, palm out, forestalling his next comment. "We're done."

She pivoted and headed for the car. She could hear his feet on the pavement as he walked after her. "Yeah, that's it," he said. "Go on, take off, pretend to look for your imaginary murderer. Hey, when you find him, give me a call. I'll get out the thirty-aught-six and take care of him for you. Sound good? Don't get in that car, Rose. We're not finished."

She paused at the door and gave Joe a hard look. "Oh, we're finished, all right."

Joe blinked and took a step back and raised both hands in that way he did when he realized he had gone too far. He started talking again but she didn't care to hear him and switched off her ears. She got in the car, slammed the door, engaged the locks. Richard seemed to be trying to disappear into the passenger seat, but at least he had started up the engine and turned on the air. Rose put the car in gear and backed out of the parking space and drove away. Joe stood where she had left him, watching them go.

"That looked like it went, uh ..." Richard trailed off, tried again. "Listen, if you two need to talk some more, I can——"

"No. I tried to explain what we're doing, but with him, nothing is ever the way you say it is. There's always an angle. That's something he picked up in law school."

"He's a lawyer?"

"Was going to be," Rose said. At the end of the row she turned right instead of left, heading for the exit on the far side of the lot because it would get her away from Joe faster and remove the temptation to run him over. "He's failed the bar a total of seven times. Currently he does paralegal work for the Angelo Group on a contract basis."

"Well, that's—"

"It's his fifth paralegal position in as many years, is what it is. He keeps getting fired. He says it's because attorneys only want pretty young female paralegals. I say it's because his kind of bitterness has a way of showing up in your job performance. Not to mention the rest of your life."

"Oh," Richard said.

"Yeah," she said. "Oh."

They exited the lot, turned onto the road.

Richard said: "So, uh, where are we going now?"

"Dad's house," Rose said. Then, to clarify: "*My* dad's house, this time."

Arthur Leeson had lived in a compact white clapboard home not far from Potter Street. It had a fenced-in front yard barely big enough for the tree that was growing there and a narrow driveway that consisted of parallel rows of concrete slabs, one for each car tire, leading to a doghouse of a detached garage. Richard could see a small back yard, also fenced, that contained an epic clothes-drying apparatus, as if a spider had gotten tired of constantly repairing her web and had decided to redo it permanently in wire and metal. Rose roared partway up the drive and stomped on the brakes, jerking them to a stop. He was pretty sure she had failed to stay on the slabs, but she hadn't said a word since leaving the hospital behind and he wasn't about to break the silence by suggesting she had parked improperly.

Rose cut the engine and got out and strode to a gate in the fence. She reached down and unlatched the gate from the inside—the fencing was nominal, with peeling pickets that only came up to Rose's waist; Richard could have stepped over it—and proceeded to the front porch, where she flung open the screen door and tried to unlock the wooden door behind it. Richard caught up with her as she stabbed at the lock, missing the keyhole a few times before scoring a hit. She opened the door and went inside. Richard followed her into a cramped hallway that ran straight back to a kitchen. Steep stairs ascended on the right; archways opened to either side, one to a small living room, the other to an even smaller den. Rose was already on her way up to the second floor. Feeling like a foundling puppy, Richard trailed after her. The stairs terminated in a stubby hallway with a closed door on the immediate left, a bathroom directly ahead, and a bedroom on the immediate right.

Rose went into the bedroom. Richard wasn't sure there was space in there for both of them so he stayed in the hallway. The twin bed was unmade, the partially pulled-out dresser drawers overflowed with socks and undergarments, the half-open closet was a jumble of hangers and shirts and haphazardly folded pants. In the corner, a little desk supported an old computer. He wondered what Art had used it for. Writing letters? Keeping track of clues? Working on his detective novel? A miniature coffee maker, jug of water, and various accoutrements necessary for brewing occupied a card table next to the workstation. On a stand opposite the bed, a little television squatted like a dozing sentinel. "This reminds me of my old dorm room," Richard said.

"It was practically the only room in the house he used anymore, since Mom ..." Rose didn't finish the thought. Instead she shook the paper sack from the hospital out onto the bed. Clothing tumbled forth, a dress shirt and pants and socks and shoes and a jacket, all falling together in a heap on the bed. He noticed that the jacket and shirt were stained on the collar and shoulder with blood. Richard assumed it was Art's.

Rose mechanically began stuffing the garments into a wicker hamper that already overflowed with clothes. "Honestly, Dad, you would never do your laundry if I didn't remind you," she muttered, as if Art were standing shame-faced in the corner with nothing to wear but boxers and a T-shirt and mismatched socks. She picked up the last item, Art's jacket. It was a little threadbare, Richard realized, patched at the sleeves, with one mismatched button. The patches were beginning to wear through. He hadn't noticed its condition when Art had worn it. Well, he supposed that when talking to a homicide detective in his official capacity, you probably weren't too concerned about the state of his attire.

As she added the jacket to the hamper, Richard spotted a stiff, cream-colored card with lavender lettering on the bed where the small pile of clothes had been.

"Rose," he said.

She turned. Her gaze followed his pointing finger, landed on the card. She picked it up by the edges and read it aloud. "Robert James, Antiquarian." She looked from the card to Richard, then back to the card. "Him again."

"Something's written on the back," Richard said.

She frowned and turned it over. "It's a phone number. And an address. Mill Pond Road."

"Where's that?"

"I don't know."

"Do you think that's James's number?"

Rose was silent for a moment.

Then she said, "Let's call it and find out."

All the telephones in Robert James's home and shop were big, heavy, rotary models, black and shiny like giant beetles. When they rang, the building shook with the clangor of proper mechanical bells rather than the electronic bleats of modern telephones, which he detested.

They didn't ring often, but they were ringing now.

The last person James had given his number to was Arthur Leeson. It could not be a coincidence that, a few hours after the detective's passing, he should be receiving a call. Perhaps some other policeman had gone through the man's personal effects, found the card, and decided to dial the number on it. James did not want to talk to another policeman, but better to take the call than ignore it and have one of them show up at his shop; and if the card remained nearby, he should be able to use it to glean some information about who was on the other end of the line.

He picked up the handset, held it up to his ear, and closed his eyes. After a moment, a woman's voice said: "Hello?"

James said nothing. He didn't need to. The card was there; the woman held it in her free hand. Information began to flow down the wires, rewarding him with knowledge.

This was not a policeman calling him; this was a policeman's *daughter*.

He hung up the phone, but of course the infernal device rang again almost immediately. He picked up the handset, cradled it, picked it up again to engage the line, giving himself some peace while he considered the situation. So: The police did not have his card, but Arthur Leeson's daughter did. No doubt she had discovered it among her father's belongings. This should be a time of mourning for her, of shock and grief, so what had prompted her to dial an unknown number on a business card? Did she have suspicions? Why?

Well, it hardly mattered. She was a threat.

He gave it a little while, then cradled the handset. When the telephone failed to ring immediately, he went downstairs to get a notebook, one intended to induce a hazy sense of bonhomie and a desire to accommodate; he had several of these hidden around the shop, encouraging visitors to browse longer, purchase more, and not wish to haggle. They were fairly old, and while they remained effective in these close quarters, he required a fresher one for what he intended to do next. Back to the hutch he went, collecting another book from his dwindling supply of prepared volumes. He took it into his office at the back of the shop, where another black telephone squatted. He slipped the notebook underneath it and waited a few minutes for its whispers to permeate the device, then picked up the receiver and dialed a number. After a couple of rings, a voice came on the line. "Bentonville Police."

"Hello," he said, summoning his most pleasant salesman's tone. "My name is Robert James. May I speak to Arthur Leeson, please? He is a homicide detective."

"One moment." There was a delay, then several clicks and pauses as the call was transferred. Then a new voice came on. "Homicide, Don Eckhardt."

"Hello, Mr. Eckhardt. My name is Robert James. Is Arthur Leeson available?"

"I'm afraid not. Can I help you?"

"Well, I don't know," he said. "Let me tell you what it's in reference to and we'll see. I'm an antiques dealer, and Mr. Leeson had recently purchased a Victorian mirror from me as a gift for his daughter. He requested a few minor repairs before taking delivery and asked me to call him here when they were finished. To maintain the surprise, you understand?" Eckhardt grunted, and James pressed on. "Those repairs are now complete, and the item is ready for him to pick up."

"Oh." Pause. "Well, um, I'm sorry, Mr. James, but Art passed away this morning."

"Oh! Really? But he seemed in such good health." James waited just long enough to convey the impression he was deciding not to ask what Art had died of, then said: "The item is already paid for and I would be happy to ship it to his daughter, along with my condolences, but I do not have her address. Is that something you could give me?"

One second passed, then another. James began to worry that the notebook had not done its work. But then Eckhardt said, "Yeah, I don't see why not. You got something to write on?"

"I most certainly do," James said.

Hank had gotten pretty damned tired of hanging around his hotel room waiting to hear from the cops, so when they finally called, he might have been a little bit surly on the phone. It didn't improve his mood any when, instead of telling him they had found Janice, or at least had some kind of a lead on her, they invited him down to the station to answer a few more questions, as if he might have held something back during the previous session, which of course was exactly what they believed. When he got there, they parked him in a waiting area for over an hour, with nothing to do but watch the hands on the clock move while the local criminal element passed by, all the drunks and petty thieves and subpar prostitutes. He kept his head down and didn't see anyone he knew, which was a relief; the last thing he needed right now was some former acquaintance starting in with him while every cop in Bentonville was looking on.

At last, a uniformed officer came over and asked Hank to follow him. As he stood, Hank said, "Nothing new on my daughter?"

"I'm afraid not. If you'll please step this way—"

"Maybe If you spent more time looking for her and less time dragging me in here to answer questions—"

"Just take it easy, Mr. Pritchard. Rest assured, we *are* looking for her. We just want to clear up a few things about what happened the night she disappeared."

"I already told you everything I know."

"We just want to clear a few things up." The guy repeated it in the sort of slow voice you used on your kid when she kept asking why she had to clean her room and you were just about done explaining it to her. Hank knew what came next when cops used that tone, so he nodded and followed his escort into one of their tiny windowless airless interrogation rooms where some new guy, who introduced himself as Detective Eckhardt, was waiting, a stack of manila folders on the desk in front of him. Eckhardt ran him through another marathon question and answer session, during which he was made to repeat the previous night's events five different ways, and forced to concede—again—that he never actually saw Richard do any of the things he thought Richard had done; and Eckhardt told him that although they still didn't know what had been used to break the window and still hadn't located any witnesses who had seen it happen, they did know it had been broken from the inside; and then Eckhardt mentioned how they had found fingerprints from at least one known local drug dealer in his room, and was he *sure* he had been alone in there with Janice, and that he didn't know what the person or persons who had torn his room apart had been looking for? And Hank reminded Eckhardt that it was a hotel room, not his own personal house or apartment, and that all kinds of people, including known local drug dealers, might visit and leave fingerprints in hotel rooms, all the time, for all kinds of reasons; and he reiterated quite vigorously that the only ones who had been in the room since he had been there were himself and Janice and Richard and, of course, cops. Hank must have gotten a little bit worked up about what Eckhardt was insinuating, must have raised his voice a little, which was a mistake, because that got Eckhardt talking about his temper, and his history with Beth, and why she might want to kill herself, and what kind of relationship she had with her brother, and what kind of relationship *he* had with her brother, and blah blah blah, until finally Hank said, "Look, why are we going over all this again? I already answered these kinds of questions for Detective Leeson."

And then Eckhardt got this strange expression on his face, a look that Hank wasn't used to seeing from cops. "Detective Leeson shot himself in the driveway of your former father-in-law's house," Eckhardt said. "He passed away last night. I'm taking over the investigation that involves you, your daughter, and the death of your ex-wife." He put his hand on the folders. "I have Detective Leeson's notes, of course, but I'd like to get it from you again, first-hand."

"Oh," Hank said. Then: "Jesus. Yeah. Sure. Okay."

And so Hank answered more questions from Eckhardt about Beth and Richard and their whole nutty family, and the more questions they asked the more apparent it became that this was the real reason they'd asked him to come down. It wasn't about Janice; they were hunting for a reason for Leeson to have chosen that house as the best place to put a bullet in his head, which Hank, of course, couldn't provide. Didn't stop Eckhardt from coming at him from every angle he could think of.

When they finally cut him loose it was pushing five o'clock. A whole day wasted, telling cops things they already knew. Not an inch closer to knowing where Janice was or who had taken her. Which meant he was still stuck in fucking Bentonville. Goddammit. He should have just told them to put Janice on a plane so he could pick her up at Shenandoah Valley Regional.

When he got back to his rental car in the police station parking lot, he sat there for a little while with the air conditioner blowing in his face and his once-favorite local station playing drivel on the radio. While he'd been away they had changed their format, and now aired crap he wouldn't listen to in a million years, normally, but it was still the same deejay he remembered from back then and he was suffering through the shitty playlist out of nostalgia for days of better music and wide open possibilities.

He put the car in gear and pulled out of the lot. He didn't give much thought to where he was going, so when he found himself rolling up to 136 Potter Street, he was a little bit surprised at himself. Must be all that talk about Beth and Richard had got him thinking about those times spent in the old place, and it had drawn him back, just to take another look.

But he was just here to look, why was he parking on the street in front of the house? Why was he getting out of his car, standing at the curb looking up at it? Why was he walking up the steep, crumbling driveway? Why was he going around back, into the shadow of the peak? He didn't know, couldn't say. Maybe he just needed to see the spot where Beth had taken her header onto the car. He stood there for a little while, eyeing the station wagon—it looked like it had run into a small flying deer—and thinking and remembering, before a flicker of movement behind the black panel of glass overhead drew his attention. Was someone in there? A squatter? A transient? A neighborhood kid?

Richard?

He heard something, the faint scrape of wood on wood, and then the window above the station wagon opened, sliding upward, leaving a black gap into the unlit space beyond. Whoever had lifted it stayed out of view, though. Just like when somebody had been pounding on his door at the motel while avoiding the peephole. Which made him think it must be Richard in there, whack-job Richard, returning to the scene of various crimes, taking advantage of Hank's fortuitous appearance to fuck with him some more.

"Richard," Hank said, "come on. Enough already."

No response.

Hank took a few steps back, hoping to get a better look into the darkened room, maybe spot the crazy bastard lurking inside, but no, nothing. He imagined Richard holding Beth like a battering ram, running at the window, flinging her out. Was that even possible? He glanced at the broken windshield, back at the house. The upstairs window was closed now but the door to the mudroom was open, inviting him to step inside.

Hank stood there for a few seconds staring at it, wondering what the fuck Richard was playing at.

Then he slowly moved forward and went into the house.

Robert James parked his little black car up the road from Wood Hill Estates, the rather pretentiously-named apartment complex where Detective Leeson's daughter lived. For today's outing, he had chosen to wear a black suit and sunglasses, white shirt, black tie, black shoes. He still wore a fedora—one couldn't go out without one's fedora— but this one was the color of charcoal, with a grey band. He carried a shiny briefcase of the sort that might contain various sorts of wares or samples. He could be selling knives; he could be selling encyclopedias; he could be selling brushes. One thing was certain: In this garb, no one would want to talk to him, or even acknowledge his existence.

He strolled downhill along a curving sidewalk that followed the loop of the main avenue between the buildings. They did not look like estates to him; they looked like any other squat, square, drab communal hive of humanity. Soon he reached his destination, building twenty-two. A sign indicated that visitors had to buzz to enter, but someone had thoughtfully left the door propped open with a cinderblock, so after buzzing his target apartment and getting no answering crackle, he went right in. Leeson's daughter lived on the ground floor, at the end of a short hallway; the door was underneath a flight of stairs, in a dim corner of the building, illuminated by a dusty fluorescent halo ensconced in the underside of the steps. He went to the door, took a look around, knocked, waited, got no response. He knocked again, waited some more. Still nothing. There was no sound except the rumbling of a nearby laundry machine and, somewhere overhead, the faint noise of a television program.

Confident that no one was home, he set down his briefcase and removed a set of tools from a hidden compartment within. Less than a minute later he was inside the apartment. The place not large and not bright, the furniture neither old nor new. Its few windows were wide but not tall, situated high up along one wall, barely above ground level. He could see grass and untrimmed weeds and the bottom of the building across the greensward. Like living in a cellar. How horrid.

He opened the briefcase and took out several thin blue notebooks, in which he had scrawled incantations of violence. Where to put them? He eyed the sofa, which faced a small television. There was a definite sag to it, making him think of a sad horse that had been ridden too far and too long. He slipped the notebook beneath the cushion directly in front of the television and moved on, passing through a darkened doorway into a dim bedroom. The bed was unmade, sheets thrown back, pillows in disarray. They would never notice if he disturbed the mess. Kneeling, he slipped another notebook in between the mattress and the box spring, up near the headboard.

That should be sufficient, given the small size of the apartment. He returned the other notebooks to his briefcase, which, like the armoire in his shop, was shielded to block their effects. One had to be careful with incantations such as these. They tended to spread.

James did a quick search of the rest of the apartment, checking the tiny bathroom and the galley kitchen, but he could tell his card wasn't here. Pity. He had hoped to remove it from circulation. He let himself out and used his tools to lock the apartment behind him.

Before he could depart, though, he heard a door open somewhere overhead. For a moment the sound of the television grew louder, then the door closed and muffled it again. Footsteps came down the stairs, accompanied by off-key whistling of what sounded like a hymn. There was no way James could avoid being seen, so he simply knocked at the apartment door, as any visitor might, and pretended to wait for an answer while a plump man descended into view. He wore a T-shirt and pink shorts and carried a bright blue laundry basket with nothing in it. The man glanced at James and pursed his lips, then went through a swinging door just up the hall, briefly exposing a washer and dryer crammed into a room the size of a closet.

James knocked at the apartment door again, as if he still hoped its occupants were home, and stood there a little while longer. He turned away just as the swinging door bumped open and the man emerged, his basket now full of jumbled fabric. This time the he stopped and said, "How did you get in here? That ass left the door propped open, didn't he?"

Seeing no point in denying this, James said: "The door was propped open, yes. So I entered."

"Every time I call him on that, he uses something bigger to do it. What was it this time? A brick?"

"A cinderblock."

"That's it. I'm reporting him to the property manager again." The man shook his head, shifted his basket to his hip, as if it had grown too heavy to hold. "So what church are you from?"

"I beg your pardon?"

"You're handing out pamphlets, right? Or selling Bibles? I know a Bible salesman when I see one."

Well, why not?

"Yes," James said. "I am a Bible salesman."

The man nodded. "I knew it. You don't have to stop by my place. Third floor, 22G. I've got all the Bibles I need. But 22A could use a lesson or two from the Good Book. Do unto others and such."

22A. That was the apartment James had just broken into. No doubt it was the residence of the ass who kept propping the door open with ever-larger objects.

"Words to live by," James said, touching the brim of his hat.

~~~

It took them a long time to reach the culvert, because Sandy was moving so slowly or because it was farther away than Pedro remembered or both. That was the opposite of how it was supposed to be, wasn't it? When you went back to someplace you knew as a kid, everything was supposed to seem smaller, tighter, closer together.

Not this time.

The walls stayed high and steep as the ravine narrowed and the crowns of the trees met overhead, sealing them up in a verdant tunnel. Then it widened again, the stream slowing and deepening, the splashes and burbles of tiny waterfalls giving way to broad pools that reflected the greenery above. Leaves skimmed the surface like origami ships. Pedro clung to the edges of the gully, half dragging Sandy along behind him, trying to find secure footing on the shifting scales of stone.

At last the culvert came into view, an oblong slant of mossy, weathered concrete protruding from the embankment, cracked and crumbling, fronted by a large, deep pond flanked by retaining walls that shored up the slopes and protected them from erosion when the creek flooded. The walls were streaked with whitish mineral deposits and old muddy smears. Cemetery Road crossed at the top of a nearly vertical grassy slope thirty or forty feet high. The sides of the ravine along the street were decorated with junk; it was within easy tossing range of the sidewalk, so people freely dumped bulky items that they would otherwise have had to pay the city to remove. Out of sight and rarely cleared, stuff just accumulated year after year into a small trash glacier, slowly flowing down to collect at the bottom: Rusty shopping carts and smashed wooden crates, a mattress or two, tires, plastic bags ripped open by animals or elements. A few of the more unusual items—a broken pink claw-foot bathtub half full of scummy rainwater; a disembodied picture tube onto which someone had scratched a series of stick figures, anorexic and immobile pornographic actors—jogged dim memories of long-ago excursions to this end of the ravine. Someday this whole thing would be an archeological dig.

They edged around the pool toward the culvert, picking their way over shoreline garbage. Pedro almost fell in when an old door tilted under his feet and slid into the water and drifted off like the last remnant of a torpedoed houseboat, but they eventually reached the concrete retaining wall. Here, they had to sidle along a narrow lip of cement through shin-deep water, but the ledge was rough and nubby beneath the black water and provided good traction despite the slimy growth underfoot. They arrived at the mouth of the culvert, water running out around their ankles. The dark passage seemed menacing, like the entrance to some damp underworld. The retaining walls stood taller than Pedro, but he knew that the ones on the other side, which had to catch and channel water rushing down the steeply sloped hill, were even taller. The ravine was deep and narrow across Cemetery Road, a knife wound through the graveyard, with several small waterfalls; they would have to scale those and do a rock scramble nearly to the summit before they would be able to climb out. There was no way he could drag Sandy through that obstacle course in her half-dazed condition.

"Listen," he said, "I'm going to get on top of the wall, then I'll pull you up. Okay?"

"Okay," she said.

Standing on his toes and stretching up his arms, he could just reach the top of the wall. He braced his fingers on it and hopped. His sneakers scrabbled on the rough cement and he scraped his forearms and elbows on the old, rough concrete as he hauled himself up. He rolled into a crouch and reached down. Sandy took hold of his wrist. He pulled; she jumped and caught his other wrist. Now she was partway up the wall, feet braced against it. He leaned back and pushed with his legs to pull her up, but she didn't come. In fact, she seemed to be actively resisting.

Their eyes met. But hers seemed to be seeing something that wasn't him.

He said: "Sandy—"

She opened her hands and let go of him and dropped back to the lip of concrete. With the sudden loss of weight he popped up and fell off the wall onto the trash-strewn slope. The back of his head hit something, a rock or a hard piece of refuse. The blow sent a numbing shock through his body, down his arms and legs into his hands and feet, and left him teetering on the edge of a strange, thin darkness.

Then he splashed down into the water, and everything went black.

~~~

241

Robert James, Bible salesman, pulled up to the curb and sat in his little black car for a few moments, his gaze flicking back and forth between 136 Potter Street and the vehicle parked in front of it. The car had a license plate frame from a rental company that operated out of the airport. What did this mean? Could it be that yet another out-of-town relative had unexpectedly materialized at the Bartoski residence?

Well, he wasn't going to find out from here.

James got out of the car and carried his briefcase up the sidewalk to the front door and, like any other visitor would, rang the bell. There was no response. He rang the bell again, then knocked. Nothing. He reached into his pocket and felt the house key that Barbara had returned to him earlier, then let himself in as if he were someone who lived there. In the foyer, he called out a few times. No one answered. Perhaps whoever had come in the rental car had gone to a different house, up the sidewalk, across the street. Perhaps they were dead in the basement. In any case, it seemed he had the house to himself for the moment. Except for Victor, of course, but Victor would not be able to ply any influence on him.

He stood in the foyer for a few moments, looking around, trying to sense where his books might be. He had left them in various places around the house but it seemed they had been moved. His gaze strayed to the cellar door, which had a latch on this side, secured with a padlock. That was new. Perhaps the books were downstairs. He went to the door, rested his head against it. Yes, he definitely sensed an emanation from the other side: Victor, trying to hide from him, knowing he was immune to whatever phantasms might be deployed against him.

James lifted the lock to look at the bottom. He could have picked it easily enough, except that some contrarian had snapped the key off in it. The whole assembly would have to be removed. Fortunately he had tools for that too. He got out a screwdriver set and went to work. Soon all the screws were removed and the lock assembly clattered to the floor. He picked it up and pocketed it. And at last, something in the house spoke to him.

Robert? Is that you?

"Yes, Victor, it's me."

Are you here to take me back?

"I am," James said, as he reached for the knob.

Good, good, good.

Suddenly the closet door flew open and a large man burst out, plowing into James, knocking him over. Beefy hands closed around his throat and squeezed.

I've been waiting for you.

Pedro gasped and sputtered and opened his eyes.

His head throbbed. He was surrounded by dirty chipped pink walls. It took him a few seconds to realize that he was lying inside the broken bathtub at the end of the ravine. He took hold of the cool, curled edges of the basin and hauled himself to a sitting position and looked around. He was alone. He remembered trying to pull Sandy up onto the wall with him, how she had deliberately let go and left him overbalanced so he fell over backwards. He had lucked out by landing in the tub instead of in the pool; the filthy rainwater hadn't been deep enough to drown him, just to soak his clothes.

Where had Sandy gone? He had a suspicion, and he didn't like it.

It took him a couple of tries to make it out of the tub. Stumbling to the bottom of the trash slope, he inched his way back to the ravine proper, then squelched through the thickening shadows towards the tree where they had found Pete and Glenn. He paused at the last curve before that spot, steeling himself, then stepped around the corner. They still swayed overhead, bluer and duller in the fading daylight, but Sandy wasn't there.

Pedro stepped back to put them out of view, exhaled a breath he hadn't realized he'd been holding. She wasn't there. But then where was she? She wouldn't have gone back to the house, right?

Right?

Shit.

He returned to the Cemetery Road end of the ravine, threaded his way to the culvert, jumped and scrambled to the top of the wall from which he had fallen earlier. The effort made his head throb and he spent a few minutes lying on his back on the concrete before scuttling up to the street. Once on the sidewalk, he clung to a light pole for a few minutes, waiting for his head to stop spinning; then he trudged to the Potter Street intersection and turned left, lurching back into his neighborhood.

Now that he was in the shade, his wet clothes started to leach his body heat, making him shiver. He plodded along like a zombie that had hauled itself out of a graveyard and slogged through a dirty pond in search of delicious brains. Houses and yards went by. He passed the burned-out husk where the Weisses had lived—it still stank of smoke, wet and stale—then the stand of trees between it and the Bartoski residence. There was his car, right where he had left it, facing the wrong way. A parking ticket underneath the windshield wiper waggled at him like a disapproving finger. The reporter's car was gone and a different one had taken its place. The license plate frame identified it as a rental. Somebody from out of town. Another unknown Bartoski relative, maybe.

Pedro finally forced himself to look up at the house. The front door was open a crack; he could see a vertical line of interior darkness between the wood and the frame. He headed up the walk. The house seemed to swell, inflating from within, looming over him, trying to shove him back down to the street. He took hold of the railing and hauled himself up the steps to the porch. He stepped across the threshold and nudged the door closed behind him. In the foyer, he found the closet open wide, its door hanging half off its hinges. The cellar door was open, too, just a couple of inches. A few coats, some still on hangers, lay strewn across the dull wooden floor. A briefcase sat in front of the stairs, overturned, silvery tools scattered around it. There had obviously been a struggle here, but between whom? And for what?

As Pedro stood there taking in the scene, trying to figure out what might have happened, feeling like he had entered a schoolyard in the aftermath of a bully fight, he heard something from the cellar door: The faint sound of water splashing, then a whimper, like a scared person trying to avoid detection by stifling sobs or being prevented from crying out for help by a hand over their mouth.

He hesitated, then opened the cellar door the rest of the way. The stairs were dark but a light was on somewhere below. He flicked the nearby wall switch up and down. Nothing happened. He took the steps slowly, hand lightly touching the old wooden railing, just a raw beam nailed at an angle to some posts. It pricked at his skin, promising splinters if he wasn't careful. The dimly lit room at the bottom was filled with crap, boxes tipped over every which way as if kicked over in an extended burst of rage.

The light he had seen emanated from a small, barren room, ahead and to the right. There was a fairly clear path heading that way so he took it, stopping in the doorway. A bare bulb overhead glared on a cement floor, block walls. An old furnace and a water heater huddled in the back left corner. If anyone was in here, he didn't see them.

Then he heard the water noise again, a splash, like someone ladling out punch. He went over to the appliances, peered into the space between and behind. Sandy crouched there on the dirty, dusty concrete, next to a hole full of dull liquid. She had a big glass jar beside her, like the kind Pedro's grandmother used for pickling eggs and vegetables. It contained a quantity of dark, gritty water. The banded glow of the naked bulb illuminated bits of stuff drifting and swirling in the grey slurry, like the world's worst snow globe. Sandy stared straight ahead, tears glistening on her cheeks. In her right hand she held a kitchen ladle. As Pedro watched, she used it to scoop water out of the hole and into the jar, pausing to take a sip as it went by her face.

Pedro choked back a gag, which got Sandy's attention. She set down the ladle and said, without turning, "What are you doing in my house?"

"*Your* house? Sandy, what—" He broke off because her head suddenly swiveled in his direction, giving him a look he had seen before. Like he was throwing earwigs at her.

"You," she said. "I remember you."

"What did you do to her?"

"She came here on her own. Sneaking in. *Trespassing.*" She sounded peevish. "She was looking for Victor, but he's gone. He's finally gone! So I *borrowed* her. Why shouldn't I? It's my house, not Victor's." Her voice was harsh, gravelly, as if the gritty stuff he'd seen her sipping had coated her throat to come out in her speech. Pedro realized his hands had become fists and willed them to relax, because what was he going to do? Punch the old man out of her?

"You're trespassing too." Sandy put the lid back on the jar, screwed it down. "You can help me." She picked up the jar, brought it through the gap between the water heater and the wall. Her clothes were filthy from the ravine, from scraping through the narrow, grimy space. "Take me to him. Then I'll give you your friend back."

"Take you to who? Victor? I don't know where he went."

"But I do," Sandy said.

8

DESPITE HAVING A MAP, WHICH Richard had purchased at a gas station near Art's house, they missed the turn for Mill Pond Road twice, and would have missed it again if Rose hadn't slowed to fifteen miles an hour and driven along the shoulder, hazard lights flashing, cars and trucks and tractor trailers whizzing by to their left. This time Richard spotted the overgrown sign, leaning against a tree, some of the the paint worn away, so that it read *ill Pond R ad*. Another sign, almost as weathered, stood nearby; it said *Seasonal Limited-Use Highway*. "There," Richard said, pointing behind them. "We passed it."

Rose stomped on the brake and glanced over her shoulder, then put the car in reverse and backed into the turn-off to Mill Pond Road. Running straight in for ten or fifteen yards before hooking sharply to the right and vanishing into the thick woods, it looked more like a trailhead parking lot or a wide shoulder where the cops would set up a speed trap than a street.

"All right," Rose said. "Here we go."

She cranked the wheel hard and goosed the gas pedal. Gravel crunched under the tires as she guided the car onto Mill Pond Road. Full, dark pines closed in quickly, screening the interior of the woods from sight. Grey grass and late summer flowers proliferated along the edges of the street, taking advantage of the open sky afforded by the gap in the trees; goldenrod grew in clumps, while here and there, sumac extended thin, knobby arms out of the tight wall of evergreens, beggars supplicating for scraps of sunlight. The road curved back on itself like a snake. They crossed an old wooden bridge that spanned

247

the broad, shallow carved by a black stream. The bridge had a driving surface of thick planks turned sideways and railings of unprocessed logs, everything fastened together with large, rusted bolts. After the bridge the trees pressed in closer than before as the road went into a lazy leftward curve. The razor-sharp peak of a dark roof came into view ahead and they soon entered a gravel lot in front of the building. Half-buried tree trunks demarcated where visitors were expected to park. Rose pulled up to one and stopped the car.

Richard eyed the the building. Made of hefty logs interlocked and stacked into a tall, broad A-frame, it reminded Richard of a small hunting lodge or a large cross-country ski trail warming hut. The top third or so of the wall that faced them was sided with dark-stained shakes. A rustic porch with log-and-branch railings ran the length of the building at ground level, studded with tooth-white Adirondack chairs, tables made of tree stumps, and a couple of sawn plank benches. The roof of the porch formed the floor of a small second-story balcony. He could see a couple more Adirondack chairs up there and a sliding door beneath a green metal awning. An empty carport stood on the left side, while on the right, a massive white pine shaded a stretch of lawn that was equal parts grass, dirt, moss, and fallen brown needles. An old pickup truck was parked under the tree; beyond, a palisade fence of thick, dully-tapered tree trunks enclosed the backyard. A stretch of tire-tracked gravel led to a wide padlocked gate in the section of fence between the tree and the building.

The front door of the shop was wood and glass with a bamboo shade unrolled behind it. A sign hanging from a hooked suction cup between the glass and the shade said the shop was closed. The sign had one of those cardboard clocks with positionable hands; it indicated that they had about three hours left before the proprietor's intended return. Rose went up onto the porch and tugged on the door. It didn't move. She glanced back at Richard, who had gotten out while she was doing that. He gave her a *what did you expect?* shrug. She stuck her tongue out at him and came back to the car. "What now?" Richard said. "Do we wait for James to come back?"

"Let's try snooping around first," Rose said.

Their initial round of snooping didn't turn up much of anything; from outside, squinting through the small windows, the place looked like any other rustic shop peddling antiques and collectibles. No ghosts peered back at them from the darkened interior, and any mysterious books inside weren't kept within view of the porch.

They ended up under the white pine near the stockade fence. It was too tall to see over and too tight to see through, so Rose, being the lighter one, was elected to climb up into the bed of the pickup truck—it was littered with fallen needles and pine cones—and then up onto its roof. From there she could see the top of a green tarpaulin nearby and, in a far corner, the peak of a large shed or small outbuilding, but not much else. The back of the shop, which faced away from them, wasn't visible at all. She slid down from the truck and joined Richard, who had his eye up against the narrow gap around the padlocked gate. "See anything interesting?" she said.

"Not much. It's like trying to look through a mail slot." He stepped back from the gate. "What now?"

"I'd really like to get into the yard and take a look around. Who knows? Maybe the back door is unlocked."

"Okay," Richard said. "You want I should rip the gate off its hinges for you or what?"

"Settle down there big guy." She squeezed his bicep, then tilted her head towards the fence. "If you feel the need to perform feats of strength, how about you give a girl a boost instead?"

"I can manage that."

They picked a spot a little way from the house, where the nubs on top of the logs seemed especially blunt. Richard got down on one knee, shoulders forward, palms up, fingers linked, giving her a place to step. It was a practiced movement, Rose thought, something he'd probably done a hundred times for his sister and would never do again. She put one foot in the cup of his hands and shifted her weight forward as he lifted, stepping up to stand on his shoulders. From this position she could easily see over the fence. Gripping the tapered ends of the logs, Rose leaned forward to survey the huge back yard. Rectangular and hemmed in by forest like a fort undergoing a long-term tree siege, it had to go back at least three hundred feet on the long sides. The back of the shop had a ground-floor patio of weathered brick and a small second-story deck. There was a barbecue grill on the patio, along with a couple of green plastic Adirondack chairs, and another chair on the upper deck. Each level had its own entrance to the building. The green tarp drooped nearby, bowed and stained where dark rainwater had collected, fallen leaves drifting like shipwrecks in the dingy puddles, and the distant roof turned out to belong to a big prefabricated shed of the sort you could get at any garden center. She noticed a power line dipped from the shop to the shed, roof to roof, like a cable that might be used as an escape route by a cornered spy.

Interesting.

She looked at Richard's upturned face. "Hold steady, okay? I'm going in."

He nodded and she scrambled over the fence and dropped to the ground on the other side. Her feet shot out from under her on the slick grass and she thudded down on her butt. She picked herself up, muttering, swatting imaginary debris off her backside. Good thing she wasn't wearing white pants.

From the other side, Richard said: "You all right in there? That sounded like a hard landing."

"Yeah, I'm fine. I have padding." He responded with something that sounded like *I've noticed*, in a low voice she wasn't sure she'd been meant to hear. "Excuse me?" she said.

"Uh, I said, now what?"

She grinned and shook her head. "Now I go exploring. Stand by."

"Okay."

She headed for the shop, stepping up onto the brick patio. She briefly pondered the Adirondack chairs. The seats were festooned with ancient forest debris: Fallen maple helicopter seed pods, tough leaf stems, bits of bark and grit. She wondered if James ever sat in them. She lifted the lid of the grill, looked inside. The stainless steel wire rack gleamed, unmarred by deposits of congealed fat or drippings or any sort of food material; there was only a layer of charred, flaky residue, not unlike burned paper. She scooped a little bit up and it disintegrated into ebon dust in her hand. She rubbed the ash between her fingertips, leaving them blackened, like she had just given her prints after being booked.

Rose closed the lid and wiped her fingers on her pants, then checked out the shop door. Locked. It had a window but there was a curtain on the inside and she couldn't see anything through it. She climbed the stairs to the second-story deck, which creaked unsettlingly but didn't seem likely to pull loose or collapse. Yet. She tried the door—also locked—then turned and put her hands on the railing and regarded the trees around James's shop. Mostly pines, they covered the rolling hills that surrounded them like gentle waves. If the forest knew any secrets about this place, it kept them to itself.

After a minute or two she descended the steps to the yard and headed for the green tarp. It was attached to the fence along the back, open in front, with side walls made of wooden lattice and corrugated metal. Supporting poles at the corners, in the middle, and along the edges lent it the peaked appearance of a shabby circus tent. It sheltered an assortment of outdoor items: Old patio chairs, disembodied window frames, and knickknacks—bird baths, dry fountains, lawn ornaments on a spectrum from kitschy to racist, rusted weather vanes, stacked planters still full of black dirt—along with several pieces of furniture that didn't look like they really belonged out in the elements and had suffered warpage, fading, and peeling as a result of their exposure. A dusty, bug-eyed ATV was parked next to the tarp, incongruous as a lunar lander. Maybe James liked to indulge in roaring expeditions through the forest in his spare time.

She was about to head for the shed all the way at the back of the yard when a small voice from the shadows said, "You gave me a lollipop."

Holy shit.

She oriented on the voice and crouched down to peer into a tunnel formed by a stack of patio bricks, a heap of rolled-up canvas, and some old doors being stored horizontally as tables for bric-a-brac, and there she was, the missing girl, way at the back, smudged and wide-eyed, clutching a blue notebook. A narrow black gap at the end of her bolt-hole gave access to the uncharted recesses of the junk pile, and she was obviously ready to vanish through it the moment any scary grownups made any scary moves.

Rose eyed the notebook with the wariness normally reserved for a weapon, then put on her friendliest reporter face and said, "Well, hi, Janice. What are you doing in there?"

"Hiding."

"Like hide and seek?"

She shook her head. " Just hiding."

"How did you get here?"

"Mommy brought me."

"Your … your *mother* brought you?"

"Uh-huh."

"From your daddy's room at the motel?"

"Uh-huh."

"How did she do that?"

"Carried me."

"She carried you?"

"Uh-huh. Through the air."

"Through the air? You mean, like, flying?" Janice didn't answer, just gave Rose a deeply skeptical look, as if starting to have serious doubts about her mental capacity. Rose took a deep breath, told herself to stop asking stupid questions that just parroted what the kid was telling her. "Listen, Janice," she said, "your Uncle Richard is here with me. So how about you come out of your hole and we'll go find him, okay?"

Janice shook her head.

"Are you hungry? You must be hungry. My purse is in my car. If you come out, I'll give you another lollipop, then we can go get pizza. How does that sound?"

Another head shake. "Mommy says it's not safe."

"Sure it's safe. We won't let anything happen to you."

Suddenly the little girl pivoted and slithered through the opening at the end of the tunnel, disappearing from sight.

"Janice."

Silence.

"Janice, come back."

Nothing. Janice was gone, as if she had never been there. Her presence altered the situation, though; now they had grounds for summoning the authorities. They would come in here and turn James's shop upside-down and shake it like a cartoon mugger holding his victim up by the ankles.

Keeping one eye on the tarp, Rose went to the spot where she had gone over the fence. "Hey Richard," she said, "you'll never guess who I just found."

He didn't answer.

"Richard? You there?"

No response. Fuck. Where had he wandered off to? "Great timing, Richard," Rose muttered. She stepped back, examining the fence, and tried a few half-hearted hops that didn't come close to putting the top within reach. Well, getting back out of the yard had always been kind of a weak point in her plan. She went over to the gate and tried to do as Richard had done, putting her eye to the gap, but she mostly just saw a narrow strip of the shop wall and her own eyelashes.

Okay. It was okay. James had to have a phone in the shop, and now she had a legitimate reason to break in and use it. There was plenty of junk under the tarp; she could find something to smash the window on the back door, let herself in, and call the cops, and then she would find Richard, and—

She heard the back door of the shop bang open. She pulled away from the gate and looked in that direction, expecting to see maybe Richard, maybe the mysterious Robert James, maybe both, and maybe having to explain her presence in the backyard. Instead she saw a big man running straight at her. He caught her before she could react, picked her up and spun her around and slammed her face-first into the stockade fence, one arm across her waist and one pressed up hard against her throat. Her vision filled up with blotches, red and black.

Red and black.

Black.

While Rose had been poking around in the backyard, Richard had heard a car approaching the shop, tires crunching on gravel. He headed back to the parking lot just as Robert James's low-slung black car slid into it like a wedge in search of a door, late afternoon sun glaring off the darkened windows. It veered in his direction and stopped near the side of the house. He had walked towards it, cooking up a lie to explain his presence, thinking he could say he had finally decided to sell James the books and the car and anything else he wanted to buy; but then the driver's side door had burst open and Hank had flown out, his eyes wild but his expression vacant, all fists and knees and clutching hands. Before Richard could react, or even shout a warning to Rose, Hank had gotten an iron arm across his throat and choked off his breath until everything went dark.

When the lights in his brain flickered and came back on, Richard was surprised to discover he was no longer at the shop. Instead, he was lying on the sofa at the old man's house on Potter Street. He sat up, looked around, marveled at a living room that was not half-empty, with furniture that didn't look ready for the curb or smell like it had already been out there for a while, a floor not strewn with newspapers, a carpet that didn't reek like the inside of an old ashtray. There were easy chairs and a coffee table and a television set and an area rug, end tables and a mirror on the wall and a stereo in the corner, everything neat and orderly and recently dusted.

He got up off the sofa and stood there for a minute, puzzled and indecisive, then went into the dining room. The table was clear of crap, polished, reflecting the glow of the ceiling fixture that hung above it. Three place mats were out, each set with gleaming dishes and silverware and tall clear glasses. He stared at them. The pattern on the plates—a sheaf of wheat in the center, ears of corn around the edges—stirred memories of tense family dinners from long ago. He picked up a fork, inspected it, put it down, picked up a knife, looked at his reflection in the flat shiny metal blade. He set it back on the table and continued into the kitchen. The counters were clean, no cracks, no filament tape. Fresh flowers sat in a vase on the table in the nook. It smelled so strongly of cookies in here that he checked the oven, but nothing was baking; the interior was spotless, as if it had never been used. Vaguely disappointed, he turned, and spotted a little yellow note stuck to the refrigerator with a plastic watermelon magnet. It said, *Come upstairs. We need to talk.—Beth.*

Richard stared at the note for a while, then headed back through the dining room, through the living room, into the front hallway. Like the rest of the house, it was neater and tidier than he ever remembered, with a little marble-topped table and another vase full of fresh flowers and a brightly-colored octagonal rug in the center of the floor. He went to the front closet, opened it, looked inside. Jackets hung in an orderly fashion; sneakers and boots were lined up in a rack underneath. An umbrella leaned against the side wall. Nothing was dirty or threadbare or crusted with suspect mud.

"Richard?" Beth's voice floated down from above. "I hear you moving around down there. Stop dawdling."

She was really here. He shut the closet door and went upstairs.

When he reached the upstairs hallway he found both ceiling globes alight. He glanced out the window. Instead of the front yard and the street he saw a drifting mist, as if the house were encased in dense fog. It left tiny droplets on the glass in strange patterns, like runes he didn't know how to read.

The door to his sister's room stood open. He went over to it. Inside, it looked the way it had when they were younger, adorned with posters of cute big-haired boy bands and cuter big-eyed animals and a rainbow streamer tacked up high, where the walls met the ceiling. On top of her dresser, next to a frilly unicorn lamp that he remembered, sat a cage containing a gerbil—or maybe a hamster?—whose name and, indeed, very existence he had forgotten. The little creature stood on its hind legs, clutching the bars with its miniature hands, staring at him with gleaming black eyes, and he suffered a sudden, vivid recollection of their father tearing open the cage, pulling the tiny animal out, and hurling it against the floor, while Richard had stood in the doorway hanging on to Beth so she didn't fly in there to save her pet and become the target of the old man's rage herself.

He closed his eyes, shook the memory away, opened them again. The small rodent was still staring at him. There was a mirror behind its cage. In it, he could see a reflection of Beth—her grown-up self, not the teenage version he'd been half-expecting based on the decor—on the bed, lying on her stomach, reading something. She still wore the clothes she'd died in. As if sensing his gaze, she closed the book and set it aside, then rolled over and met his eyes in the mirror.

"Come on in, Richard," she said. "I won't bite you. Gertrude might, but that's why she's in the cage."

Rose woke up somewhere dim and stuffy, sprawled on a warm, hard floor. The front of her head ached where it had been shoved into the fence, and her throat hurt where it had been squeezed. She swallowed a few times just to make sure she still could, then squirmed herself to a sitting position and looked around. She was inside the big shed. Where there should have been tools and supplies and equipment, there was only empty space. No shovels, no rakes, no bags of soil, no lawn mower. What light there was came from a small, filthy bulb at the vertex of the roof, encased in a wire shell. It provided enough illumination for her to spot a camera mounted in a high corner, the lens gleaming blackly. The walls were reinforced with beams and crossbeams and heavily soundproofed.

This wasn't a shed. This was a holding pen.

As her head cleared, she became aware that she was not alone in her little prison; Richard lay on his side next to her, facing the wall. She stretched out her leg, gave him a little nudge with her foot. He rolled onto his back and lay still, but she didn't think he was dead.

"You must be the detective's daughter."

The voice startled her. It came from a third person, who sat in a back corner. He wore a black suit and a black hat pulled low over his face, blending into the shadows like a corporate ninja. She swiveled on her butt to face him. "Yes, I must. Robert James, I presume?"

"The very same." Fabric rustled as the man doffed his hat to her.

"Did you kill my father?"

"My dear girl, how could I have killed him? I was nowhere nearby."

"That's not a denial." Then: "He had your card."

"If I killed everyone who had my card, my shop would get very little business."

"Also not a denial."

"Your father shot himself. His hand held the gun. His finger squeezed the trigger."

"I believe he was operating under false impressions."

"But is that not something we all do, all the time? How could any of us function without our illusions?"

"There's a difference between our illusions and illusions imposed on us by someone else."

"Ah," James said. "Well. Perhaps you do understand a few things after all."

"Not as much as I'd like. What is all this? The shed? The camera? I'm guessing this isn't the first time people have been locked in here. Although it's probably the first time *you* have."

"Indeed." James grimaced. "This is where I keep inventory, on occasion, when trading is unavailable. Finding myself here is ... unexpected."

"Inventory? Trading? Explain."

But James just smiled at her, and said nothing.

Rose heard a muffled clattering sound from behind her as someone fumbled with the latch. A moment later the door swung open to reveal an enormous figure standing there, the man who had attacked her earlier, silhouetted against the darkening sky by the big lamp on the distant back wall of the shop, amber-pink, throwing long inky shadows, distorting his features. Or maybe that was just rage. He stepped forward and Rose shrank back, but he wasn't coming for her; he grabbed James roughly by the arm, twisted around and tossed him out onto the grass, then withdrew and kicked the door with a massive foot. It slammed with the solidity of a bank vault. She heard the bolt scuff back into place.

And then, silence.

Instead of going south to pick up the Interstate, Ozzie had decided to take Route 18 to get to Bentonville; he had plenty of time, and it was a nicer drive. It passed through small rural towns and villages, places where downtown was a bar and a post office and a gas station that doubled as a grocery store, but for most of its length it cut through open country, an uncluttered ribbon of blacktop rising and falling with the folds of the land, piercing mottled forests, the evergreens like stains amidst the deciduous trees whose leaves were beginning to turn. He had the radio on, stations fuzzing in and out depending on where he was in relation to the hills and plateaus and transmitters. In some stretches he found pleasing music of the collegiate alt-rock variety; in some, he had to settle for Top 40; but many benighted locations offered nothing but twanging country and thundering religious incantations that sent him scanning the empty frequencies across both the FM and AM bands in search of something that wouldn't make him want to drive his car into a tree.

It was in one such stretch, where he had settled for a while on an AM news station broadcasting from Bentonville, that he learned that Rose's father—a forty-year veteran of the police department, they said, twenty-five of those in the homicide department—had passed away at Highland Hospital. When she called from the paper she'd mentioned her dad was in the ICU, but Ozzie had figured he must be stable since she was still working on her story. Evidently he'd been wrong.

He reached over and opened his glove box and dug out his cell phone. He hadn't put her number in the address book yet—or, more accurately, hadn't yet gotten one of his sons to do it for him—but it was scrawled on a card clipped to the top of the stack of papers and photos from the auction. Keeping one eye on the road and one hand on the wheel, he flipped the phone open with his thumb, he dialed the number, then waited as it rang and rang and rang. He was about to close the phone when someone finally picked up the other end. They didn't speak; all Ozzie heard was breathing in his ear. So he said, "Hello?"

After a moment, a man's voice answered. "Yes?"

"Is this the Mancuso residence?"

Another pause. "What do you want?"

"May I speak to Rose?"

"Rose isn't here."

"Could I leave a message for her?"

"Don't play games. I know she's with you."

Ozzie took the phone away from his head and held it in front of his face, as if that would tell him something about the mental state of the other party on the call. He knew Rose was married but she hadn't talked much about her husband, who, he assumed, was the other party to this conversation. If *conversing* was what you wanted to call what they were doing.

He put the phone back to his ear. "I'm not sure who you think I am, sir, but I can assure you Rose isn't with me. I—"

"You're a liar. You tell Rose I've got my rifle. Tell her I'll be waiting for her."

The line went dead.

Rifle? Shit.

Ozzie dialed directory assistance and had them connect him to the Bentonville police. The dispatcher listened to his story and said they'd send a car around to Rose's apartment to make sure everything was all right. He thanked them and closed the phone and frowned at it as he tried to figure out if there was anyone else he could call, any other way to get word to Rose, warn her what her husband had said. As far as he knew, she didn't have a cell phone—and, really, what kind of newspaper didn't provide cell phones for its reporters? Maybe he should acquire the *Herald-Journal* and rectify that situation—so he had no way of reaching her directly. But maybe she would be at the hospital. He called directory assistance again, got connected to Highland Hospital, had Rose paged, and spent some time waiting on hold while she didn't answer. Next he tried the paper. Not there either.

He hung up and spent the next mile or two driving with the phone in his lap, drumming his fingers on the steering wheel, until finally he decided there was nothing to do except keep going, stick with the original plan of meeting her at the paper, and hope she would show up without getting herself in anyone's rifle sights. He picked up the phone and went to stick it back in the glove compartment, fumbled and dropped it instead. It bounced off the front of the passenger seat and was swallowed up by the pool of darkness on the floor. Keeping one eye on the road, he leaned sideways and felt around for the phone. There it was. He picked it up and straightened in his seat, phone in his hand, just as he came around a bend, and *shit!* A jackknifed semi sprawled sideways across both lanes right in front of him, with a passenger car wedged in beneath the trailer, its roof peeled back like the top of a sardine tin.

Ozzie stomped on the brake, but it was too late. He went into a tire-screeching skid and plowed into the back of the stuck vehicle. His airbag deployed and he experienced the miracle of near-instantaneous deceleration into a gas-filled balloon. He stayed put for a moment, stunned and panting as he registered the fact that he had emerged more or less unhurt from his brief foray into stuntman life. The airbag sagged in his lap like a gigantic spent prophylactic. The broad corrugated steel wall of the trailer loomed a foot or two away from his windshield like the wall at the end of an alley. The accordioned roof of the other car, now completely detached, lay crumpled on his hood. The car itself was gone, shoved the rest of the way under the trailer by the impact.

His hand shaking, Ozzie fumbled with the door handle. It moved but the door wouldn't budge. He unbuckled his seatbelt and slid across to the passenger side. That door opened, with some reluctance. He clambered out, fell down, used the mirror as a handle to haul himself back to his feet. He caught a glimpse of his reflection in the glass. His nose was bleeding from both nostrils and the left side of his face was red and puffy, like he'd been pummeled in a slapfest. He didn't feel any pain yet, but he knew he was going to once the shock wore off.

The crash had done something to his right knee and he limped a little as he moved away from the wreckage. He hobbled around the back of the trailer. What was left of the other car had popped out the other side and ended up on the narrow shoulder, nosing into the trees that lined this stretch of the road. Whatever it had been before, it was a convertible now, with no windshield and the top permanently down. He could see a shape strapped into the driver's seat. The shape was human, as far as it went; the top third or so was missing. Jesus. He toddled in that direction, then stopped. What did he think he was going to do over there? Perform CPR on what was left of the body?

Ozzie turned around, looked at the tractor-trailer. The driver's side door of the cab hung open. It didn't look like anyone was inside. Had the trucker gone off to find help? Why not just use the CB radio? Weren't they always talking on those things, going good buddy this and what's your twenty that and has anybody seen a smokey around here and hey we could really use an ambulance right now.

He limped over to the truck and peered inside. Yep, there was a radio mounted on the ceiling, mike clipped to the side, within easy reach of whoever was behind the wheel. Unfortunately Ozzie was on the ground, and also short. He took hold of the shiny grab bar and hauled himself up onto the running board. The seat loomed in front of him, absurdly high. He still couldn't reach the radio. There was another grab bar bolted to the roof just inside the cab, but he couldn't reach that either. These things were built for giants.

Ozzie jumped for the upper grab bar, missed, and landed badly, with only one foot—the one attached to the hurting knee, of course— on the running board. Fresh pain shot up his leg as he slipped off the narrow platform and landed on his ass on the pavement and discovered that he was looking up at somebody he assumed to be the trucker. The man stood over near the enormous gas tank on the side of the cab. He held a road flare in one hand and a blue notebook, a mileage log maybe, in the other. He peered at Ozzie with the slightly stupefied expression of someone who hadn't quite finished waking up yet and was wondering how they had ended up in the middle of a highway.

Ozzie managed to get himself to his feet and brushed himself off. "Hi," he said. "I'm Ozzie. Is this your truck?"

"It's the *bank's* truck."

"Right. Okay. Is help on the way?"

The man shrugged, turned away, and set the notebook down on the running board. Then he removed the cap from the flare to expose the striking surface. "I hate long-haul driving," he said.

"Pardon?"

"Hours and hours on the road."

He struck the flare, but it failed to ignite.

"Barely getting by."

He struck it again. Sparks, but no flame.

"Pretty sure my girlfriend gets busy when I'm not around."

"I'm, uh, I'm really sorry to hear that," Ozzie said. The man grunted and struck the flare again. It caught this time, shooting out a red-hot jet like a tiny rocket. "Do you have more of those? I can help … What are you doing?"

Holding the flare out sideways as sizzling globules pinged and popped and dribbled from the fireworks end, the trucker had taken some keys out of his pocket and unlocked the cap on the fuel tank. Now he was unscrewing it.

"Whoa, hey hey hey." Ozzie took a step forward. "That's a bad idea."

The trucker pointed the business end of the flare at Ozzie. "You stay there," he said.

Ozzie stopped. What was he going to do? Rush the guy, beat him up, and take his flare away? The trucker had at least ten years and eight inches of height on Ozzie, and while Ozzie might have occupied a heavier weight class, it wasn't because he bristled with muscles.

"Listen," he said, backing away from the truck, "I realize this is a bad scene, okay? But it was an accident. Insurance will cover it. You must have insurance, right?"

The gas cap came off.

"Wait! I have money! I can pay for—"

"Fuck the insurance," the trucker said, "And fuck your money."

He let go of the flare.

Ozzie scrambled away and had just reached the shoulder when the gas tank detonated, sending an orange-yellow bloom into the sky behind him. Something big and flat flew past his head. He thought it might be a mirror or mud flap blown clear by the blast, but no, it was the blue notebook, spinning through the air like an ungainly butterfly. The gold inlay on the cover reflected amber light as it whizzed by. He stared after it for a few seconds, then thought of his cellular phone. He made his way back to his car and poked his head inside, but he couldn't see the handset. He'd been holding it when he crashed. It could have ended up anywhere. And now the trailer was becoming engulfed. He had to back off before he roasted or his own car blew up. No phone. No way to summon help.

He'd just have to wait for the giant signal fire to do it for him.

Richard took a few steps into his sister's room, gestured at their surroundings. "What is all this, Beth?"

"Are you having memory problems? It's Potter Street."

"Potter Street hasn't been like this in a long time. I'm not sure it ever was."

"Yeah. Well, it wasn't like this when I got here, either. It was ..." She shook her head. "Never mind. You don't want to know. The things I found." She turned and sat on the edge of the bed, planted her feet on the floor. "Anyway, I changed it. Drawing over the bad stuff. Making it like I remembered. Or like I wanted to remember, anyway." She looked away from him, at one of the boy band posters, or maybe at nothing. After a few seconds, she said: "I know you want to ask. So ask."

"What happened to you? At the house?"

"We were going to leave, I swear to God, Richard, we were going to leave right then. Janice refused to come in the house. I went upstairs to get our shit, but first I just *had* to go into Dad's room. The book ... It was in the drawer. It came out, trapped me in there. There was something inside it. Or around it. I'm not really sure. Whatever it was, the fucker opened up the window, carried me out, and threw me at the car. Next thing I knew, I was where it had been."

"Inside the book."

She nodded. "Inside the book."

"I saw them, I think. Your sketches. In the book. I figured maybe the old man did them."

"No. That was me."

"Why didn't you leave me a message or something? Let me know you were there?"

"I was pretty messed up. Disoriented. Being killed is a traumatic experience. Don't give me that look. Have *you* ever gotten murdered, Richard?"

After a moment, he said: "Not yet."

"Well if it happens and you're perfectly fine afterwards, you be sure to let me know, all right?" His face burning, all Richard could manage was a nod. "Sorry. I didn't mean to snap at you. It's just … Listen, I can tell what's going on around the book. I can see things. Hear things. I know you were talking to Hank. Why is he here? Did you call him?"

"Me? Call Hank? Fuck no. Social Services located him after, you, uh … Well, you know. After. He came up here to get Janice and take her back with him, but then she—" He broke off, realization dawning. "Disappeared," he finished. "She and the book, they both disappeared, because you were in the book and you took her."

She shrugged.

"Jesus Christ, Beth. Where is she? Is she all right?"

"Of course she's all right! I may be dead, but I'm still her mother. I'm not going to let anything happen to her. And I'm damn sure not going to let Hank have her." She put her hand on the notebook as if swearing on a Bible. "I can still do things out there in the real world. It's kind of like operating one of those stupid claw machines, but I've snagged my share of toys for Janice that way. As for where she is …" Beth sighed. "I didn't think that through. I mean, where could I take her where she'd be safe? Not back to your room. That's the first place they'd look. And not back to Potter Street. I never should have brought her there in the first place. So we stayed near the motel while I tried to come up with a plan. Then I sort of felt something *tugging* on me, so I went with it, and we ended up here." She picked up the notebook and turned it towards him, opening it wide. Scrawled across the pages, as if on a faded screen, he saw the backyard and looming rear wall of an A-frame log building. "And now you're here too. So you tell me. Where's Janice?"

"At Robert James's shop," Richard said.

"Seriously? The annoying antiques salesman?"

"The annoying antiques salesman. He's involved in all this

somehow. Rose and I tracked him down and came out to talk to him, but he wasn't here, so we poked around a little. But then Hank showed up, and—"

"Yeah, I know. When he was dragging you through the backyard, I freaked out. Just a bit." She closed the book and set it down. "I didn't really mean to bring you in here. I just wanted to wake you up. Next thing I know you're sacked out on my couch and you *still* won't wake up." She smirked at him a little. "Typical guy."

"Typical guy. That's me. But what I don't understand is, why is Hank even here? When I invited him to come meet Rose with me he told me to go fuck myself. So how did he find this place? And why did he come at me like that?"

"Hank hardly needs a reason to be an asshole. But that thing from the house? The thing that threw me out the window? It's here now too. Hank brought it with him. I felt it all around him. It's riding him like a pony."

"Really? Shit. And Rose has no idea. I didn't even have time to warn her." Richard went to the window, lifted the curtain, peered through. The nothing outside was still nothing. He let the curtain drop and turned around. "How do I get back?"

Beth cocked an eyebrow at him. "Back to Rose?"

He felt his face burning again, for a different reason.

"Richard's got a *crush*," Beth said. "How cute."

"Is this really the time for that?"

"It's *always* the time for that," Beth said, but then she got serious again. "It's a good question though. How do you get back? I'm not sure. Open the door and walk out, maybe?"

"Could it be that simple?"

"Why not? I mean, I know *I* can't do it. I've tried. I open the door, there's, like, an invisible wall keeping me in. But maybe *you* can leave, since you're, you know, still alive and stuff." She picked up the notebook and stood. "Let's go find out." She brushed past him, patting him on the shoulder as she went by. He trailed after her into the hallway and to the top of the stairs. Beth started down, but he paused at the window that overlooked the misty nothing surrounding the house. Something flickered and moved far out in there in the grey, a half-seen shape in the indeterminate distance, huge and branching, like a massive barren tree using ice-covered branches to drag itself across the sky. Without thinking, he put his hand on the glass. Instantly another hand appeared on the other side, a hand at the end of a long, spindly white arm that trailed off into the fog. Narrow fingers splayed across the other side to match the spread of his own. He jerked away, leaving behind a frost-rimed outline of his palm on the glass. The hand on the other side scratched on the glass a few times, making a faint rasping noise, leaving behind long razor-thin trails of ice; then it withdrew and vanished into the mist.

Richard stared at the window for a moment, then called, "Hey Beth?"

From below, her voice came back. "Yeah?"

"Don't open the front door just yet," he said.

Rose was pretty sure she wouldn't be able to bash down the reinforced shed door but she tried anyway, charging across the short space of floor and hitting it with her shoulder right where it met the wall. She might as well have been trying knock down a concrete wall. It barely even shuddered under the muted *thump* of her impact. She tried a few more times and then her shoulder told her she needed to stop. Frustrated, Rose collapsed to the floor and looked at where Richard lay, wishing she could pick him up and use him as a battering ram.

Then she heard something at the door, a faint scuffing sound. The bolt again. She retreated to the back of the shed and flattened herself against the far wall. She was prepared; she would charge the bastard, take him by surprise, get past him, get out into the yard, and then ... Well, she would figure something out. But when the door swung outward this time, it was Janice doing the opening. One of the Adirondack chairs from the deck stood nearby; she must have dragged it over and stood on it to reach the bolt, which would otherwise have been too high for her. Just like stealing cookies from a jar on the counter, right? Resourceful little monkey.

"Thanks, Janice," Rose said, stepping out into the yard, looking around the yard. Empty, at the moment. "Good job."

The girl stood nearby, watchful, saying nothing, the harsh glare and black shadows of the sodium lights making her look like a freckled, pallid little ghoul.

"Listen, Janice. The man who put your uncle and me in the shed.

He could come back any time. So I need you to—"

"That was my daddy," Janice said in a near-whisper. Then, in a harder voice than Rose typically associated with kids her age, she added: "Something's wrong with him."

So that was Hank, Richard's infamous ex-brother-in-law. How had *he* ended up here? Had he stopped by Potter Street and gotten himself dragooned into the service of whatever was haunting the place? Robert James had suggested as much.

Well, that was a question that could be answered later. She had other concerns right now. "Did you see where your daddy went, Janice?"

"Uh-huh. He took the other man inside the house. Then they let the books out."

"They … They did what?"

"They let the books out."

"They let the books out?"

Speaking slowly, as if her suspicions that Rose might be a bit dim had now been confirmed, Janice said, "They went in there." She pointed a stubby finger at the back door of the shop, which now hung partway open, exposing the darkness inside. "I followed them and peeked. There was a big wooden thing with books inside. My daddy made the other man say some words and then the books came out and flew away."

"They flew away?"

"Uh-huh. Right over my head."

"Which, uh, which way did they go?"

"That way." Janice gestured in the general direction of Route 18.

Rose thought about Pedro's story, how the thing in the house had made his friends remove some notebooks. Now it had apparently gotten hold of Janice's father and used him to force Robert James to do the same thing, except this time he'd had the books remove themselves.

That couldn't possibly be a good thing.

"All right. Janice. Listen. Your daddy isn't feeling well. I'm glad you followed him and saw what they were doing, but it was dangerous and you shouldn't do it again. So I need you to go back to your hiding place and stay there until I come get you."

"But I want to stay with Uncle Richard."

"Uncle Richard wouldn't want you to stay with him. He would want you to be safe. He would want you to go hide and be quiet. Can you do that? Can you go hide and be quiet?"

"Quiet like a mouse?"

"Quiet like a mouse. And don't come out for anyone." Janice opened her mouth to say something but Rose talked right over her. "Not for *anyone*, Janice. Okay?"

Janice hesitated, but then she nodded and scurried back under the tarp, vanishing amid the piles of patio furniture and lawn ornaments and other crap. Once the girl was out of sight, Rose found an old iron weathervane with a broken arrow and a pineapple on top. She hefted it, swung it around a little. Unwieldy, but it was the closest thing to a weapon she could find on short notice, so she took it with her.

She went into the building, entering a small, cramped office. Separated from the rest of the shop by an open doorway and a curtain made of polished wooden beads, it looked like the cubby of some put-upon nineteenth century bookkeeper who spent every daylight hour sitting on this unpadded wooden stool, shuffling papers into and out of those ancient filing cabinets that lined the walls, stuffing bills of sale into the pigeonholes of that small roll-top desk. A massive rotary phone sat on a columnar stand next to the desk, its matte black surface soaking up all the light that touched it. She picked up the phone, put it to her ear. No dial tone. She rapidly pushed and released the cradle as if sending an emergency message in Morse code. Still no dial tone. She hung up and moved to the bead curtain and pushed aside a few strands to peer into the shop. It appeared to be unoccupied. The front door hung open, so she stole across the shop for a look out front. She spotted heavy footprints and parallel scuff lines in the gravel, heading for the trail that opened from the opposite side of the parking lot. Hank, she thought, dragging Robert James along with him. She wondered where they were going. James had referred to his victims as inventory to be traded: Not high-value prisoners being swapped between governments, but goods being bartered. That suggested the existence of an exchange floor. A trading post.

Maybe it was at the end of the path.

She spotted another phone on a desk near the front door and

picked it up. No dial tone. Hank had probably ripped the lines out at the box or something. She scurried out the front door and went to her car. She had left the keys in the ignition and of course they were gone. Hank might have them in his pocket; he might have tossed them into the woods. No keys in the other vehicles either. The only way she could summon help would be to run up that long driveway to Route 18 and try to flag someone down. At this hour, traffic would be light, and while she was out there trying to get someone to stop, Hank would be at liberty to do whatever he wanted.

Fuck.

Slinging the weathervane over her shoulder like a cartoon caveman's club, Rose ran across the parking lot and followed the drag marks into the woods.

"So something came at you when you touched the window upstairs?" Beth said.

They were together in the front hall now, shoulder to shoulder, looking at the front door. It was outlined with cold white light seeping in from outside. "Yeah," he said. "A hand. Sort of. Not one I would want to shake."

"I've opened the doors. I've been to the windows. Nothing has ever come at me."

"Yeah, but maybe it's different for me. Like you said, I'm alive and stuff, and you're …" He dragged his finger across his throat.

"Very nice." She sucked her lower lip under her teeth, then said: "Okay. You need to leave, but not through the door and not through a window. What are you thinking? Going up the chimney like Santa?"

"Not up. Down."

"You won't fit through the toilet."

He pointed at the cellar door.

"There's no way out from the basement."

"Maybe there is." Richard opened the door, then stood at the top of the stairs, peering down into the dimness. Beth came up behind him and gave him a little push to get him moving. She clomped along behind him. The cellar wasn't cluttered like it was in the real world; it was as he remembered it from years ago, organized shelving along the walls, tools arranged in an orderly fashion on the workbench.

The washer and dryer sat cold and white and gleaming in their nook beneath the stairs, unsullied by fabric softener seas with detergent powder shores and lost button archipelagos. He headed for the utility room, where he had suffered through so many dark, cold hours sitting on the floor in the corner tied to the rough, rusty pipe that ran up the wall near the sump. When the old man used to put him down here, Richard would pretend the sump was a way out, that if he could get loose from the rope, he could dive into it and surface someplace else. But when he got there he saw that Beth's recreation of the house hadn't included the sump, or even the furnace and water heater; the little room was unbroken concrete from wall to wall, corner to corner.

He probably should have guessed it wouldn't be there; his sister hadn't spent the time down here that he had. The old man had punished her in other ways. This room, those appliances, that puddle of dank water, they contained little significance for her, so when she had drawn the place the way she remembered it she had left those details out. As he turned away, he became aware of a sound, something scratching against paper. Beth had sat down on the floor behind him, notebook out and opened, pencil in hand, sketching furiously. He circled around so he could see what she was drawing. A bare, square room. Cinderblock walls. A dangling light fixture.

A hole in the floor.

In the corner where the sump should have been, lines appeared and spread across the concrete, joining together, forming a square. Crosshatching spread across the inside of it, then faded. A cold breath burped out of it, a curl of mist, as the square became an opening, three feet on a side.

Beth snapped the notebook closed and stood up. "One emergency exit, made to order," she said.

He went to look at it, five or six inches of smooth concrete dropping to swirling pale fog. A sense of impending separation settled over him like a shawl on his shoulders, like how it felt when you went to the airport and boarded your plane, friends and relatives waving goodbye from the gate. But this went beyond an airline departure. When he found his way back from here, he would be leaving Beth behind, presumably forever, in this strange little world she'd drawn for herself inside the book. He crossed back to his sister and pulled her into a long, hard hug. She felt warm and solid, like a real person, not like a corpse or a spider web or a sack of clouds or however you might expect it to feel when you embraced a ghost. Into her ear, he whispered, "Has anyone ever told you you're amazing?"

"No, now that you mention it." She pushed him away and punched him lightly on the shoulder. "About time you did."

Not trusting himself to speak, Richard nodded and went to the corner. She had drawn the opening more than big enough for him to fit through. He crouched down, sank his hand into the mist. It felt cold and slightly viscous, but didn't offer any real resistance. Nothing grabbed his wrist or ripped his arm out of its socket. He looked back at Beth.

"Go on now," she said. "Shoo. Go help your niece, you big lunkhead. And your new friend Rose."

Richard pushed himself off the edge and slipped into the grey.

9

THE TRAIL THROUGH THE WOODS ended at a couple of tall, narrow stones with a clearing beyond. Rose flattened herself against one of the rocks and peered around it. She saw that the clearing was actually a pond, the water cold and still and black in the near-dark. Most of the perimeter looked marshy, but on this side there was a rocky beach. To the left a path ran along the water's edge to another gap in the trees, possibly an outlet stream; to the right a grassy slope rose and crested into a high, flat bank. A concrete bench squatted up there beneath the overhanging branches of a massive weeping willow. And Hank stood in front of the bench, a few yards back from the edge, holding on to Robert James.

She jerked her head back, but he was looking at the water, not the path, and she didn't think he had seen her. After a few seconds she risked another glance. Hank hadn't moved; he remained broad and immobile, as if he were a statue that had come to life, grabbed a passerby, and reverted to marble. His expression as he stared at the pond was inscrutable. He might as well have been watching the mortar set in a brick wall. She couldn't see James's face but she didn't imagine he would look particularly sanguine right now.

She returned her gaze to the water, which had begun to glimmer. Narrow things moved in the shallows, white and gleaming, wriggling and squirming and crisscrossing each other. Reflections on the surface? Light catching the scales of esoteric fish? She didn't think so. The dim, cloud-smeared moon was too low and the water too still to account for what she was seeing. No, these were animate things, eel-like creatures with a filamented mouth that opened and closed and opened again like grasping fingers. They increased in density in front of the high bank, gathering like eager koi that had noticed a human and were hoping for a treat.

Hank dragged James forward, closer to the overhanging edge of the bank, maneuvering him into what was obviously a throwing position. James flailed and squirmed but it didn't do him much good. Hank shifted his grip and bent at the knees the way you were supposed to when you were going to lift something heavy.

Now.

She rushed at Hank just as he raised James off the ground and hurled him into the pond. The antiquarian hung in space for a moment, arms and legs akimbo, then splashed down. Dark water closed over his head. At the same time, Rose reached the top of the slope and swung the iron pineapple at Hank as hard as she could.

It shuddered and stopped before it hit him, like she had smacked an invisible wet sandbag.

Before she could react to this unexpected development, the metal shaft twisted out of her grip and was wrenched away, tossed among the humped roots of the willow tree. She ran after it but Hank caught up with her and swept her off her feet, bringing her around in front of him, his arms like iron bands around her body, and dragged her back towards the water.

Ozzie felt useless, just standing there watching the truck burn. Worse than useless: Responsible. Like he could have stopped this if he had been more careful, had thought faster or said something better when the trucker was striking that flare. There was nothing he could do about the fire—he was fresh out of extinguishers or water hoses or aircraft that could drench acres of land with smothering foam—and he had no idea how far he would have to hobble to find a house or business where he could call for help. *Somebody* had to come along soon, right? Somebody with a car phone. Somebody who would stop and let him in and drive him to a place with a pay phone. Somebody. *Anybody.*

But nobody came, and he had just about decided to start trudging north when a vintage sedan erupted out of the burning wreckage on the far shoulder, trailing smoke and licks of fire. It blew past him, not even slowing down; all he could do was watch his own astonished visage goggling back at him from its windows as it went by. He turned and stared as it vanished around the turn, and he was still staring, wondering what sort of idiot could possibly be in such a hurry that they would plow through such a scene and just keep going, when he noticed that sirens were approaching from the south.

Finally.

He stumbled a little way up the hill so he could look past the blaze and see what was coming: A fire engine, its lights sending rock-concert swirls of red and blue through the drifting smoke, trailed by a posse of police cars and an ambulance. Two of the police cars peeled away, looping back and turning sideways to block the road. Their occupants jumped out and went around to open the trunks, rummaging around inside, looking for reflective triangles or flares or shotguns or whatever it was cops pulled out of their trunks in situations like this. The ambulance stopped a prudent distance from the flames and paramedics tumbled out of the rear doors, heading for the decapitated car. The fire truck shuddered to a halt close to the burning rig and disgorged its helmeted crew. They started hooking up equipment to deal with the fire, which had begun to spread into the damp woods along the southbound lane.

That left one more police car, which kept going, sneaking past the fire along the same route the old sedan had taken, albeit with considerably more caution. Ozzie headed in that direction, intending to intercept the car when it came out the other side. As he toddled forward, made gimpy by his stiffening knee, he noticed dark shapes entering the dome of firelight. It took him a few seconds to realize what they were.

Notebooks.

Covers extended, pages rippling, they glided into the open doors of the fire truck, the back of the ambulance, the trunks of the two police cars. Others floated in lazy circles around the people who had come to work the scene. Ozzie slowed, then stopped, watching as the books settled into positions above the men and women, one per person, sometimes two, hanging above them like docked dirigibles. The emergency responders faltered in their tasks, seeming to forget there was an emergency to respond to. The cops closed their trunks and got back in their cars and headed south; the paramedics abandoned the destroyed car, returned to their ambulance, and drove away, leaving the rear doors to flap and bang; the firefighters piled back into their truck, executed a multi-point turn, and trundled off, dragging the hose along behind them like a dog's broken leash.

Ozzie stood there slack-jawed as his brain grappled to make sense of what he had just witnessed. The books had *flown in on their own*. They had *made everyone leave*. How was that possible?

He thought about the notebook the truck driver had been holding. Had it been hanging around the road waiting for a victim, then fluttered through the window of the cab and forced him to jackknife his trailer? That probably wasn't so difficult. Just make the driver see something in the road—a kid, a stalled car, a herd of deer—that would cause him to stomp on the brake at just the right moment and, bam, instant roadblock. Okay. But getting him to blow up his rig? And himself with it? That was taking influence to a whole different level. And what was the point? Why crash a truck and set it on fire? All that did was attract the attention of cops and firefighters, who had then been sent away with …

Books.

They had been sent away with books.

Lying in wait like a gang of highwaymen, they had swarmed in as soon as the emergency vehicles opened their doors. It was a dispersion tactic; the goddamn things had built themselves an ad hoc distribution network. He did the same thing with his little paper. Print out a run, divvy it up between the boys and himself and, if she had nothing better to do, Marjorie, and off they would go in different directions, delivering the bundles to all the places around town from which the *Mirror* could customarily be acquired.

His earlier smart-ass thought that the burning truck would act like a signal fire for the authorities now seemed exactly right. Maybe the books could move on their own, but they were slow, ungainly. Butterflies dipped in cement. Emergency vehicles were fast, and they could go as far as their gas tanks would take them, and they had sirens and spinning lights that said nowhere was off-limits. Who knew where they would end up? The ambulance crew might scatter books around a hospital. The fire truck might fill the shelves at a library. The cops might leave them lying around in the station, the jail, supermarkets, schools. Anywhere people could come into contact with them. And then what?

Chaos.

While he'd been standing there in a fog of dawning comprehension, the last police car had cleared the crash. It pulled up in front of him and parked sideways across the center line, blocking the road. The officer behind the wheel eyed Ozzie while her partner twisted around to examine the wreckage. He pointed at the accident scene and said something Ozzie couldn't hear. Maybe he was telling her everyone else was gone. The driver turned to her partner, then looked back at Ozzie, then past him, squinting into the night. She reached for the handle and started to open the door.

The red and blue lights across the top blinded Ozzie to his surroundings, but he was willing to bet a few more books lurked in the vicinity, waiting for the chance to dart in and hijack this one too. He couldn't allow that.

And so, not thinking about what he was doing, Ozzie reached out and pushed the door shut.

The officer stared up at him. "Sir, please let go of the door."

"Listen, there are things out here that—"

"Sir. Let go of the door and step away from the vehicle."

And what was he supposed to do? Order her to stay in her car? Ozzie released the door and moved away, hands raised, palms out, but before the driver could get out the radio started squawking. Reaching for the mike, she told her partner, "Better put up some reflectors, Cam." He nodded and popped the trunk. While the driver engaged in a murmured conversation with the person on the other end of the radio, Cam got out of the car and headed around to the back. He got out a set of reflectors and put them on the ground, then went back in for something else.

And Ozzie, once again reduced to the status of impotent bystander, could only stand there and watch while a trio of books— two blue, one red—fluttered into the trunk. Cam stiffened, then stepped back, closed the trunk, went around to the driver's side, pulled the door open, and bodily hauled his partner out of her seat, tossing her to the pavement. He took her place and a moment later he was gone, tearing off up the road, lights flashing, siren wailing, like a sheriff's kid going joyriding in the patrol car.

The remaining cop stared at the taillights of her vehicle as it disappeared into the darkness, then turned and looked at Ozzie with a confused expression and said, "What the *fuck* just happened?"

"I've been asking myself that all evening," Ozzie said.

Hank hauled Rose to the edge of the bank and then stopped. Down below, Robert James hadn't surfaced yet. The glowing things were in chaotic motion—a feeding frenzy?—around the spot where he had disappeared. Now and then they hunched into view; breaking the surface, they resembled nothing so much as thin pallid arms trailing silvery threads of something that wasn't water. Each ended in a long-fingered hand. She could swear she saw brittle cellophane skins of ice forming and vanishing whenever the things breached.

Where was James? Had they dragged him to the bottom? Was this the trade he had talked about?

A round dark shape appeared amid the glowing spirals, appearing, for a moment, like the pupil of a baleful, luminous eye; then it swirled and bobbled and floated away, and she realized what it was: Robert James's black hat, upside down, a tiny black ghost ship adrift on a foaming sea.

The air filled up with a faint, confused muttering. There was somebody here she couldn't see, and whatever was going on in the pond was not what he or she had expected.

"Victor?" she said. "You're Victor, right? Something is wrong, isn't it? What you expected to happen isn't happening."

The muttering turned harsh as she spoke. Victor didn't want to be interviewed. Hank moved, dragging her forward in a shuffle-step, turning to position her between him and the pond. Rose struggled, nominally, enough to make him fight her but not enough to really slow him down, until they got to the edge and she felt his grip begin to change as he prepared to lift her. Then she corkscrewed herself around, slipped down a little, found the earth with her feet, and pushed as hard as she could in the direction he was already going. The added impetus caused him to over-rotate and she swung out into space. The pond gaped beneath her like a mouth full of luminous frothy spit. Off-balance, Hank tried to toss her away, but she locked her legs around his waist and pulled him after her. They fell together and splashed down into the icy water. She immediately felt light, experimental touches running along her arms and legs and flanks as the many-fingered things caressed her in a manner that felt weirdly preoccupied. She thrashed away from them, squirming towards the nearby beach. She heard Hank doing the same behind her but didn't look to see if he was finding his own way out.

When she felt mucky ground beneath her feet, she half-swam, half-waded, half-crawled—give it a hundred and fifty percent, Rose!—up the pebbly shore, scrambling out of the pond. She stumbled up the loose gravel to the grass near the two big stones, fell against one of them, looked back at the beach. Distended arms were withdrawing into the water, spasming fingers leaving icy furrows through the damp gravel. Hank had managed to clamber up the embankment; below his kicking feet, greedy digits scraped frost-encrusted claw marks into the muddy sides. Something at the top was helping him, a vaporous shape in the dim moonlight, best seen through peripheral vision. It knelt at the edge, long vaporous arms curled around Hank's wrists, pulling him away from the things in the water. When she looked straight on, it wasn't there, and Hank seemed to be rising on an invisible line.

She had little time before he reached the top. Certainly not enough to get up there and reclaim her ersatz weapon.

Hoping he would look for her back at the shop, she pushed herself off the boulder and ran up the trail that skirted the pond.

While they awaited the arrival of more emergency vehicles to replace the ones that had left, Ozzie and the last remaining officer—the name embroidered on her shirt was *Lucia*, but she told him everyone called her Luce—placed the reflectors on the far side of the blind curve, setting them up in a line across both lanes, then spent their time making sure the few drivers who came this way respected the barrier and turned around. Luce did all of this work herself; she was uniformed and authoritative and mobile, whereas Ozzie was just a rumpled and rather battered civilian, and gimpy to boot.

When not shooing away cars, Luce tried to raise her runaway partner on her little portable radio. These attempts grew increasingly irate as Cam continually failed to respond. More than once, she wondered aloud what the hell had gotten into him and everyone else, why they had all driven off like that. Ozzie kept his mouth shut on that topic. None of the cars that came near the crash site were attacked by the notebooks, so Luce never had the opportunity to see what he had seen, and he could hardly explain it to her without sounding crazy.

As time passed, the radio began to squawk out bursts of staticky dialogue with increasing frequency. Ozzie had trouble understanding what was being said but he gathered that emergency services was getting slammed down in Bentonville, with police and fire and ambulance crews lurching from one crisis to another as they tried to respond to an escalating number of calls coming in from all over town. Not being an aficionado of the Bentonville scanner scene, Ozzie didn't know how many calls they usually got in an evening, but this couldn't possibly represent a normal level of activity. Luce confirmed his suspicion by informing him that reinforcements were being called in from neighboring communities and that was why no one had arrived yet to take over the accident scene and put out the fire. So they kept up their vigil on the lonely road, shooing away the occasional bit of traffic, while the glow to the south slowly intensified. Ozzie was glad it had rained recently and wasn't a windy night.

Finally a new set of emergency vehicles screeched in from the north, heralded by a tide of sirens and flashing lights. When they arrived he saw they belonged to the sprawling town of Birch Creek, which serviced mountain hamlets to the north and east and also dealt with the occasional threatening wildland fire. Ozzie had a camp out that way and more than once had gotten stuck behind one of their articulated trucks as they noodled along winding wilderness roads in no apparent hurry to get anywhere. They were definitely in a hurry now, though, and got right to work attacking the blaze. This time things proceeded the way they were supposed to: The cops barricaded the road, lining up their cars and putting up flashers; the firefighters hosed down the burning truck and nearby trees; and after the flames were beaten back sufficiently, the ambulance crew inched past the wreckage to evaluate the decapitated car and what was left of its driver.

As the situation settled down, Luce excused herself to go talk to one of the officers, an older guy who seemed to be in charge of the new arrivals. Ozzie sidled closer to them as they chatted, but started drawing interested looks from various parties before he got close enough to properly eavesdrop over the noise of the scene and was forced to remain ignorant until the discussion was concluded. Luce stomped back over to join him by the side of the road. She didn't look very happy.

"What's the good word?" Ozzie said. "*Is* there a good word?"

"I don't know, Ozzie. Is *fuck* a good word? Pardon my Anglo-Saxon." Luce scowled at the diminishing glow of the fire. "They didn't see Cam or my car on their way down and that ass would rather crack jokes about women forgetting where they parked than do anything helpful."

"So, what?" he said. "We just stand around?"

Luce glanced at him, looked away, glanced at him again. "Why? You got someplace to be?"

"Well, yeah, kind of. I'm worried about a friend of mine who I was supposed to meet in Bentonville. I tried to call her not long before the accident and got her husband. He sounded ... irrational. Making threats."

Luce arched a lacerating eyebrow in his direction. "A *friend*, huh?"

"It's not like that. We're colleagues. Reporters. We've been working on a story together."

"Okay. If you're really concerned the husband might harm your friend—" Luce tapped her badge. "—then the thing to do is call the police. Do not attempt to intervene in a domestic matter yourself. It's dangerous enough when we do it."

"I know, and I did call the police, but I haven't ... Hey, maybe you can find out if they went around to her place? Ease my mind?"

"I can inquire. What's your friend's name?"

"Rose," he said. "Rose Mancuso."

Luce had been reaching for her little radio, but now she stopped, frowned, and said, "Rosie Reporter?"

"Uh, all right. Do you know her?"

"Her dad worked homicide. Everybody knows her, or at least *of* her. But I don't know the husband." Still frowning, Luce made the call, listened to the response—which sounded to Ozzie like so much static—asked if they were sure, listened to that response, looked at Ozzie while saying his name into the radio, said okay she would, and holstered the transmitter. "Well, they did respond to your call. They are in fact still at her residence. Some folks at the scene have indicated they would greatly appreciate it if you might come down and have a word."

"Okay," Ozzie said. "I'm kind of stuck here with a burned-up car though."

"Right. Hang on." She went for another chat with the officer who was running the show. Gesticulation ensued, then Luce handed the man her radio, which he alternately talked at and listened to, while casting sidelong glances in Ozzie's direction. Ozzie feigned a sudden interest in scuffing pebbles around the pavement with his shoe. Then Luce came back over and told him they would be getting a ride; before long a police car rolled to a stop in front of them. Luce opened the back door and gestured Ozzie inside. He clambered in. She shut the door and headed around to the passenger side. The officer behind the wheel introduced himself as Mitch and apologized for not shaking hands: A joke, given the metal grid that separated them.

Luce settled herself in the shotgun seat and looked back at Ozzie. "You okay back there?"

"Sure. I never rode in the back of a police car before." Then, trying to inject a sneer into his voice: "You got nothing on me, coppers!"

"Oh yeah," Mitch said. "That's exactly what everyone says when we put them back there."

The path along the edge of the pond quickly shrank to a strip of packed dirt between the sharp-limbed evergreens of the forest and the cattail-infested shallows. Rose stayed close to the slashing branches, dodging and ducking when necessary to avoid getting whipped in the face; even though she didn't see any of those glowing menaces worming through the gloomy stalks, she wanted to keep as far away from the water as possible. Suddenly the sound of her footfalls changed to a hollow *thunk*; she had transitioned from earth to the top of a wooden weir twenty or thirty feet across. At its center was a stone block structure, like a tiny roofless castle, anchoring both sections of the dam. Planks groaned and creaked underfoot but she reached the platform without anything collapsing. Its floor consisted of a rusty iron grille, through which she could see water pouring over the top of a lift gate. The gate was set into a geared track that could be operated by a wheel on a shaft that stuck up through a slot in the floor. She guessed this had been part of the water control system back when there had been an actual operating mill out here. That must have been decades ago, but the controls still seemed to be intact. She ran her fingers along the gearing, then gave them a sniff. Oil. The mechanism was still being maintained.

Interesting.

Rose leaned over and peered at the stream flowing away from the dam. Most of it came over the top of the lift gate but there were also small leaks here and there where water found its way between the variegated boards of the dam. The resulting stream appeared devoid of glowing grabby hands. It flowed in a gentle leftward curve, pooling in front of the mossy stone foundation of a small collapsed building, then splitting around it on both sides to continue along its way. Assuming this was the creek they had driven over to get here, she should be able to follow it back to the driveway and maybe make it to Route 18. If she could stay ahead of Hank.

There were rough stairs on the side of the platform and she slid down them to the shallow current. It burbled cold around her ankles. She sloshed downstream, following the lazy arc of the stream bed. It was littered with large stones and blackened half-buried branches that lurked below the surface, waiting to trip the unwary; brush grew thickly along the banks and across the wash where water didn't currently flow. She avoided the sandy areas, sticking to the water, hoping to leave no trace of her passage in the vegetation or the loose soil. As she neared the split she heard running footsteps thumping on the wooden dam. She darted forward and ducked behind the hunched remains of the building, peering between the ferns and weeds that sprouted from the fallen beams and ruined shingles. She saw Hank moving along the top of the dam, a silhouette in the moonlight. Her heart hammered rusty nails into the back of her throat as he reached the platform where she had been a few minutes before. He paused there to look around, swinging his head left and right. He seemed to be studying the stream bed. Rose stayed as still as she could, even stopped breathing, until at last he turned and headed back the way he had come.

So much for leading him away from the shop.

She waited a few minutes to make sure Hank was gone and then moved out, staying low, taking care to avoid slipping or splashing. He might be listening. When she had put some distance between herself and the pond she straightened up and and started moving faster. The channel narrowed and became a small ravine as the downward slope of the land increased and the current picked up speed. Tree limbs tufted with needles stretched in from each side and met overhead. The ravine curved gently to the right, then straightened and opened up into the shallow wash she remembered. Not far ahead, she saw the outline of the bridge. When she reached it she found rough steps cut into the bank on the left side, cut logs placed horizontally and secured with stumps of rebar. She scrambled up them and turned right and headed towards Route 18, but hadn't gotten far before headlights came blazing at her from around a curve, moving way too fast for the road. She threw herself to the side to avoid getting hit, rolled in the dust a few times, and pushed herself up on one elbow, sharp gravel grinding painfully into her skin, to watch the vehicle roar on down the driveway away from her. It was a giant, ancient thing, all curves and chrome with fins on the back and tall narrow taillights that stained the dirt red, and damned if she didn't recognize it as the ass end of the car that had been parked at the Potter Street house. But what the fuck was it doing here? And who the fuck was driving it?

For some reason, her mind went to Pedro and the girl, and stayed there.

Shit.

Rose hauled herself to her feet and ran back towards the shop.

Richard gasped and opened his eyes, lying on a floor, alone, feeling half frozen to death on a warm August night. His limbs felt heavy and unresponsive, as if he'd been buried in a snowbank and needed time to thaw out.

Escaping from Beth's dream house via the exit she had created in the floor had worked, but the transition had not been instantaneous. Not even close. He remembered, in some dim way, what felt like months spent slogging through grey mist that filled an unformed landscape, a ribbon of some solidified white substance under his feet; and icy water constantly dripping from the featureless sky, dead chalky things that may have once been trees, boulders like giant chunks of crumbling talc; and a distant, giant, many-limbed tree-like thing, constantly moving along the horizon, sometimes closer, sometimes farther; and skeletal hands that waggled on the ends of bony extensions, thousands upon thousands of them, reaching and waving, clenching and unclenching, many clutching transparent tattered things like pieces of leather, leather with arms and legs, heads and hair and empty eyes and gaping mouths, fluttering and flapping, skin flags in a frozen wind; and when the wind was just right, oh, how those lipless, lidless holes would whistle and shriek. Finally he'd come to one giant screaming face, stitched together from dozens of smaller screaming faces. This one was stretched across the road he walked, its mouth staked and sewn into a low archway. He'd crawled through it on his hands and knees, careful to avoid any contact with the grotesque leathery barrier, and that was when he woke up here.

At last Richard had shaken off enough of the chill and disorientation that he was able to sit up and survey his surroundings. A small building, or maybe a large shed, but empty as a freight elevator in a condemned building. He stood up, nearly collapsed, leaned against the wall until he felt like he could move without falling down. Then he stumbled out into the yard. Deserted. Remembering that Beth had said Janice was here, he called her name a few times, then Rose's, then Janice's again. No one answered. There was a pile of crap under a tarp nearby and he went to it, peered underneath, saw nothing. An ATV was parked beside the tarp; he clambered up and stood on the seat, giving him a view over the fence. There was the pickup under the pine, Robert James's car parked at the gate, Rose's car in front of the shop. She must still be here, then, but no one was in sight. He climbed down, stepped back, looked around. The back door of the shop was ajar. Richard headed up the gentle slope and nudged his way into a small, cluttered office with a telephone. He tried the telephone. No dial tone. He tapped the cradle a few times, but that didn't change anything, not that he really expected it to. He pushed on through a bead curtain and into the shop itself. It appeared to be deserted. A flight of stairs stood off to the right, guarded by another bead curtain and a small sign that said *Private*.

Private? Fuck that. Up he went.

The stairs emerged in a living room with angled walls and a peaked roof, crisscrossed by dark rafters and angular beams. It smelled of pine cleaner and wood and old fabric. The amber-pink glow of the big sodium lamps seeped in from outside and gave the place a funhouse cast, made it grotesque and garish. Along the front wall, facing the second-story porch, he saw large windows and a sliding door, mostly blocked from view by curtains. The back part of the space was occupied by a galley kitchen that ended in the door to the second-story deck. Darkly varnished cabinets sucked in the light and stainless steel appliances shone dully and marble countertops glimmered with a liquid sheen. He could see a bedroom through a half-open door in front of him. It didn't appear to be occupied. He crept over to poked his head into the bedroom. Empty. Everything was perfectly made up, sheets tight, pillows fluffed, neat and proper and clean as a hotel room waiting for its next guest. Somewhere, he heard a fan blowing. A bathroom opened from the right side of the bedroom; fixtures gleamed from the darkness within.

The apartment appeared to be just as empty as the shop and he began to wonder if he was really back in the real world or if this was another layer of the vacant realm he'd found himself in earlier. Where *was* everyone?

Richard went into the bedroom, then the bathroom, which was perfectly ordinary, except that part of what he had taken to be shadows turned out to be overlapping vertical panels of black vinyl or rubber hanging from a track in the ceiling. As far as he could see this room had no windows to give away his presence, so he reached over and flicked the wall switch. An overhead light flared into harsh blue-white life. He parted the panels. The area beyond was floored, walled, and ceilinged with subway tile. Strange machinery hulked across much of the space; cubbies and bins occupied the rest. He stepped forward and studied the equipment, an amalgamation of flat surfaces and bars and arms and teeth and rollers. One of the cubbies held empty blue covers, while the others contained rolled-up sheets of material in shades of pink and grey and brown, reminding him of the scrolls in some medieval library. A wide, shallow refrigerator with a locking handle hummed in the corner and a stainless steel tub stood off to the left. A shelf above it supported big plastic bottles, glue and bleach and an unlabeled one, bigger than the rest, containing fluid the color of glacial ice. Beside the tub was a large bin, divided down the middle, with fine sawdust on one side and heaps of powdery off-white grit on the other. A heavy-duty electric grinder was bolted to the wall above the tub, discharging into a white-streaked chute. A wooden drying rack stood between the tub and the binding equipment. Swatches of translucent leather, or something like it, hung from several of the horizontal rods of the rack. They made him think of the things he'd seen flapping in the spectral wind.

He moved closer to the tub, sniffed above the grey powder, blew on it and watched it flutter around its bin. He started to reach out, intending to pick up some of the grit and rub it between his fingers, see what it felt like, but then he heard the movement from the ground floor. The bead curtain rattled and heavy footsteps came up the stairs. Richard scuttled out of the rubber-sheeted alcove and killed the bathroom light just before Hank, carrying some kind of club over his shoulder, climbed out of the stairwell. Hank didn't seem to have spotted Richard; he plodded across the creaking floor and passed out of view, heading for the front wall. Richard heard a door slide open and figured he had gone out onto the balcony.

Crouched there in the dark, Richard debated what to do. Could he sneak out of the apartment while Hank was there? Hang a left, crawl through the kitchen, exit into the backyard? Would the creaking floor give him away? Before he could make up his mind whether or not to attempt it, another shape emerged from the stairwell, a much smaller one this time, light and silent.

Janice.

She stopped at the head of the stairs and stood there looking around, obviously undecided where to go next. How could he get her attention? If he called to her or ran out and grabbed her, Hank would hear. After a moment he reached up and flicked the bathroom light on, then off. On, then off. The third time he did it, Janice looked his way. He flicked the light on again so she could see him and motioned her forward. She darted into the bathroom and he scooped her up, swung her around, bumped the door closed with his hip. Then he set her down and held her shoulders so he could look at her. "Are you all right?" he said.

"Uh-huh."

"Where have you been? Were you hiding in the backyard?"

She nodded.

"Did you hear me calling you?"

"Yes."

"Why didn't you answer me?"

"The lollipop lady said I had to be quiet. Like a mouse."

"The lollipop lady?" That had to be Rose. "Where is she?"

"Don't know. She said to wait for her but she didn't come back." Janice sniffled, wiped her face with her arm. "I stayed quiet like she said, but after you went away I was scared to be alone so I followed you. Are you mad?"

"No, sweetie, I'm not mad." He shifted his grip to a hug, rocked her back and forth in his arms. "But listen. Your daddy is out there in the other room, and he *is* mad. At you. At me. At everyone. So we have to hide for a little while, just until he leaves, or until I figure out how to make him not be mad anymore. Okay?"

Janice nodded against his face.

"Okay. To make sure he doesn't find us, I'm going to turn the light off. Will you be all right in the dark?"

"Uh-huh."

"Okay. Here we go." Richard reached up and flicked off the light, then brought Janice through the muffling rubberized panels into the back of the bathroom where the weird stuff was. They huddled silently in the darkness for a few minutes, Richard listening for sounds from the other room. He didn't hear anything, but that didn't mean Hank was gone. He could just be waiting. But for what?

In his ear, Janice whispered, "Uncle Richard?"

"What?"

"Can you turn the light on?"

"How come? Are you scared of the dark?"

"No," she said, "but I have to pee and I can't see the toilet."

When they got to the parking lot, Pedro pulled up alongside the building, driving into the hazy illumination of a big peach-colored light up near the roof. He parked parallel to the porch and looked sideways at Sandy. He had been sneaking glances at her the whole time they were driving here. Sometimes, like in the glow from that burning truck, he could see the old man's thin, pinched, pickled apparition stretched over her like a translucent Halloween costume; sometimes he just saw her. Here, in this light, in this place, he got his best view yet of Mr. Bartoski. The upper half of his body was bare, with shriveled skin stretched over a rickety framework of ribs and collarbones, thin grey hair smeared across the chest, man-breasts sagging toward the indistinct lower half, which was a geometric jumble suggesting bunched corpse-wrap spread like sheeting to catch paint or other, less savory fluids. His head was turned towards the house, while inside, Sandy continued to stare straight ahead.

"Okay," Pedro said. "Now what?"

The ghostly visage swiveled to face him. Underneath it, Sandy's head didn't move. Its mouth opened. Hers didn't.

Before the spirit said anything, the entire car bucked as a figure crashed onto the hood, a man carrying some kind of spiked club. He brought it down on the windshield as he landed and it smashed partway through the glass. The spikes got stuck, curls of black iron a foot from Pedro's face. The guy ripped the windshield right out of the frame and sent it sailing across the parking lot as Pedro cursed and fumbled with the clutch and shifter, trying to peel out backwards, but he did something wrong and the car shuddered and coughed and died. The guy on the hood raised his weapon, and Pedro stared at him, and all he could think about was that the club was a *weathervane*, a weathervane with a *pineapple* on top, and how ridiculous it was that they were going to be killed by somebody wielding a *piece of fruit*.

And then the old man bunched himself up and launched himself forward like he had been fired out of a cannon. Simultaneously the lid blew off the container in Sandy's lap. Revolting grey gritty liquid erupted out of it, splattered him and Sandy and the interior of the vehicle. The ghost enfolded him and he fell off the hood, landing on his side in the gravel, rolling and squirming as the old man swirled around him like grey mist. He stumbled and scrambled across the parking lot until he found his footing, then ran off up a path into the woods with the shriveled phantom in pursuit. Pedro stared after them in bafflement, then turned at the sound of retching. Sandy vomited up a cup or two of the same nasty stuff as had filled the container, hacking and coughing and spewing it over herself and the seat and the dashboard. She coughed and spat and coughed again, and looked at him, and he had never seen her face so angry, hadn't known it could contain such an expression.

"That *thing*," she said. "That *thing*, it got in there and it made me —"

Suddenly someone appeared at the passenger side window behind her. That reporter from the Bartoski house was there, breathing hard, face bloodied, interrupting Sandy by rapping her knuckles on the glass to get their attention. She motioned for them to roll down the window, then noticed the missing windshield and leaned around it instead. "What are you two doing here?" she said. "Why are you in that car?"

Sandy shrank back and Pedro realized she didn't remember her. He put a hand on her shoulder, hoping to steady her, and murmured, "That's Rose. We met earlier." Then, louder, so Rose could hear: "The old man made us drive him here."

"Old man?"

"Mr. Bartoski," Pedro said. "His … ghost, or whatever. He did something to Sandy. Like, possessed her. He said he would let her go if we brought him. So we did."

"He's here now too?" She straightened, looked at the path. "Did he chase Hank off?"

"I guess so, he … Wait, you know that guy?"

"I don't *know* him. I've run into him. He's not himself right now, and I've been told that even when he is himself he's not very pleasant." Turning back to Pedro, she said, "Does this jalopy still run?"

"I can't get it to start."

"Smells like gasoline. You probably flooded the engine. Give it a few minutes before you try again. If it starts, don't wait for me. Just go and get help before Hank comes back."

"Don't wait for you? Where are you going?"

"I left somebody behind. I have to go look for them."

"But—"

"Don't wait," she said, punctuating each word with a two-fingered tap on the hood. "Just go."

"All right. Don't wait. Got it."

Rose nodded and went into the shop. Pedro and Sandy watched as the door closed behind her. Then Sandy turned and punched Pedro in the shoulder, hard. "Ow," he said, rubbing it. "What—"

"That was for suggesting trying to reach Pop-Pop at that *fucking* house," Sandy said. Then she grabbed him by the ears, pulled him in close, kissed him hard on the mouth, and pushed him back into his seat, leaving him gaping at her in bafflement.

"And so was that," she said.

~~~

Rose ran through the shop and into the backyard, first to the shed—no Richard—then to the pile of crap beneath the tarp—no Janice—then back to the patio, where she stood for a few seconds looking at the yard, wondering what had happened while she was gone. Best case, Richard woke up and found Janice and got her to safety. Worst case … Well, there was probably plenty of room at the bottom of that pond.

She went back into the office, tried the phone again. Still no dial tone, of course. She pushed through the bead curtain and into the shop. To her immediate right a flight of stairs, marked *Private*, went up to what must be James's living quarters. She could see the battered car out front, coughing exhaust vapor into the calm air. The kid had gotten it started. She hesitated, looking at the car, then at the stairs. Could Richard and Janice possibly be up there?

Fuck. She had to check.

Up the stairs she went.

The apartment was dead quiet, no sign of a struggle, everything neatly in place, like it was ready for a photo shoot for *Little Cabin Apartments Quarterly*. Kitchen, bedroom, everything was dark. She went out onto the balcony. Below her, the car idled, surrounded by a cloud of its own mist. Only some of the emissions came from the tailpipe; it was also drooling vapor from underneath the dented hood. That couldn't bode well. The kids had opened the trunk and were rummaging around inside. As Rose watched, Sandy pulled something out of it: A tire iron, lug nut wrench on one side, pry bar on the other. She took a few steps away from the car and swung her prize a few times, as if bashing an invisible assailant. Rose was pretty sure this was just a practice swing and not an actual defense against unseen attackers. She brought it over to Pedro and showed it to him, and he nodded and put a protective arm around her shoulders.

Ah, young love.

"Hey," Rose called.

The kids froze, looked around, finally spotted her up on the balcony.

"Sorry to interrupt," Rose said, "but I'm coming down."

A minute later she was out the front door and into the back of the car. The kids had already returned to their seats. As Pedro put it in gear and swung around the lot in a broad circle to get them aimed at the exit—apparently he didn't trust himself to shift into reverse—Sandy twisted around to look at her. "Couldn't find them, huh?"

Rose shook her head.

"Maybe they got away on their own," she said.

"Yeah," Rose said, turning away, her voice tight as she pictured Hank heaving an unconscious Richard into the pond, picking up his own daughter and flinging her far out over the water. "Maybe."

As Hank ran up the path, the stream of gritty liquid that had surged into his face and forced itself down his throat, up his nose, felt like acid in his stomach, in his brain, like thousands of tiny knives chiseling at him from the inside. He couldn't make them stop, couldn't prevent them from manipulating his body, making him run, awkward as a puppet, back to Victor.

He stumbled between the two big stones where the path widened into the grassy bank. Victor was still there on the beach near the pond, staring at the striated glow of the luminous shapes that swarmed beneath the surface. The thing riding him turned him in that direction. As he approached, he felt Victor's attention shift towards him, felt his puzzlement but no real concern as to why Hank was running right at him. It wasn't until they had almost collided and the stuff inside Hank came boiling out—an eruption of awful liquid turning into a coherent, moving cloud of vapor—that he felt Victor's understanding, his sudden, blinding panic. The two entities merged into a blur the color of ash and bloodstained paper, swirling together like the currents of meeting rivers. They slid across Hank's skin like thin scraps of damp ragged fabric. He heard angry sounds that could have been enraged shouts far away or harsh whispers right beside him. Momentum carried him forward and he dragged them along with him in a smoky eddy as he splashed into the pond where those coiled things lurked and waited. They were ready for him, took hold of him, icy bands around his ankles, his shins, his arms, his legs. They used him as a scaffolding to clamber up and snatch at the squabbling vaporous figures, catching them, sinking into them like grappling hooks.

Hank heard a howl from all around him, a screech of rage and fear as Victor attempted to escape the clutching, clinging, digging fingers;

and he might have been able to do it if not for the other one, hanging on, pulling him along after Hank, out into the water. The hands were strong and they were many and despite all his thrashing they would not let him go. They dragged Hank out and down into murky water. The water closed over his head and suddenly Victor's presence was gone from his mind, snuffed out, leaving behind an icy cauldron of lingering rage that had always been there, always simmering, leaking out; and in that instant Hank understood that Victor had tapped into that to get him to him do the things he had done, and, oh, how easy it had been, and how he had enjoyed being granted license to do them.

Deeper, deeper. Ragged shapes shot by on all sides, unearthly barracuda circling prey. Down and down into depths so dark and cold it hardly seemed like they could still be in the pond. They must be somewhere else now. The only light came from the swarming wormlike things, and in the dimness Hank could see human remains all around him, bodies ranging from swollen corpses to mere bones. Some were complete, some were skinned, some were missing limbs or heads; and they were *moving*, all of them, being rearranged and repositioned and played with. Arms and hands sprouted from the muck like a forest of sinister kelp.

Then the hands turned him and he came face to sightless milky-eyed face with a dead woman, a cloud of hair floating around her head. Several of the spectral arms twined around her limbs, manipulating her like a marionette, bringing her up to Hank's face, opening her mouth, tilting her head to the side. Hank screamed as they pressed the dead lips to his for a kiss. The bubbles of his breath rose through the tight space between their faces, up towards the unseen surface, glimmering ornaments in the light emanating from below that passed unhindered through the two spirits that had been dragged down with him. Here in the water they were revealed for who they were, or had been: First Victor, a young man, nondescript, no one Hank would have noticed or remembered if they met on a street, then Walter Bartoski, a spindly geriatric version of Beth's thuggish father, garbed in a gown of morgue-table plastic, glaring down with hate in his eyes at Victor or Hank or both of them.

Hank finally reached the muck of the bottom. The hands held him there, pressing him into the mud. Silt rose in little eddies around him.

They pulled Victor and Walter Bartoski down even farther; the two spirits disappeared into the sediment, leaving Hank to writhe alone and breathless in the cold and the silence, until the hands reached in and pulled something out of him and carried it away, and the water faded to murk.

10

THE OLD CAR COUGHED AND sputtered its way through the darkness, white vapor drifting from underneath the hood. Rose doubted they were going to make it all the way to Route 18 without overheating, but it wasn't like it was *her* vehicle they were running into the ground. Sure enough, just before they reached the bridge, the car sighed like an old dog that had found its favorite bed, then shuddered to a halt. Pedro tried a few times to start it up again, but no luck. The ride was over.

They abandoned the car and gathered in the road. The night air was warm and moist. As they crossed the bridge, Rose paused to look at the ravine. The creek, black and burbling, sang a cheerful little melody as it ran beneath them. Her thoughts wandered upstream, to the levee, the sluice gate, the wheel, the water.

The water.

Her gaze strayed to the dead car, still surrounded by the last scraps of steam—its engine had been shut down by escaping water—then back in the direction of the pond. The wooden dam was kept patched and repaired, to keep the water in; but the lift gate was kept in working, providing the option to let the water out.

Was the gate some sort of kill switch? What would happen if she opened it all the way?

She turned to the others. They were both staring at her and she realized she had been mumbling *the water* over and over again. They probably thought she was losing her mind. Sandy held the tire iron with both hands at one end as if ready to club her. Rose pointed at it and said, "Can I have that?"

Sandy only clutched the pry bar tighter. "What for?"

"This stream flows out of a mill pond. There's an old sluice gate keeping it full. I want to open it. I might need the leverage."

"Why do you want to open it?"

"Something's in the water," Rose said. "Something to do with the ghosts, or whatever they are. I think draining the pond might stop all this."

"How do you know that won't just make it worse?"

"I don't. Not for sure. But everything I've seen tonight says the pond is important. So if there's no pond ..."

The kids exchanged dubious glances. They leaned in close to each other and had a murmured conversation. Finally Sandy handed over the tire iron. "What do you want us to do while you're trying to hit the kill switch?" she said.

"Keep going to Route 18. Get help. I'll catch up, if I can."

The kids nodded and started walking. She watched them go, then made her way down the rough stairs to the creek. She splashed upstream through the cold, shallow current until the dam came into view. The boards were rimed with frost, steaming in the warm night air. Beyond it, the pond was covered in mist, and it was *glowing*. What did that mean? Did it always happen after people were thrown into it? Was it what Victor had been waiting for?

Rose approached the dam—she could hear the wooden planks creaking and groaning, like a ship under stress from arctic ice—and scrambled up the steps to the platform with the wheel. She could hardly see the pond through the drifting vapor. There were shadows moving through it that made her head hurt. Turning her back on them, she rammed the pry bar between two of the spokes of the metal wheel that controlled the sluice gate and heaved.

The wheel moved, just a tiny bit.

She heaved again. It moved a little more. Twist, grunt, pause. Twist, grunt, pause. Her hands and wrists and shoulders were already getting sore. Nothing at the gym had prepared her for this kind of workout. Where was Richard when you needed a big lunk to put some muscle into turning a wheel?

Not in the pond, she hoped.

After several turns the wheel started to loosen up, making quiet grinding noises as the gears remembered they were built to turn, the teeth that they were built to mesh. She started walking in a circle around the wheel, pushing the tire iron. Water stopped flowing over the top of the gate but wasn't flowing out from under it yet. She kept walking, faster, faster. The gate clicked higher. At last, sludge began to ooze from beneath the door, a thick slurry of mud and debris, sticks and branches and rotten leaves, all the shit that you would expect to find at the bottom of a pond in the middle of the woods. Maybe some of the branches were bones. She couldn't tell. They were too blackened, and covered in slime.

The wheel stopped turning so abruptly that she rammed her abdomen into the tire iron, nearly flipping over it. She tried to move it more but the gate would go no higher. Was it enough? She went to the edge of the platform and leaned over to look upside-down at the gate just as a thick layer of jagged ice abruptly crystallized all across its surface. A moment later it erupted into a horizontal geyser. The creaking of the surrounding planks crescendoed and the dam on both sides of the block construction froze, shattered, and let loose a wall of water.

Over the roar, she heard a voice behind her.

It said, "You have no idea what you've just done."

She whirled. Robert James stood on the platform, soaked, bedraggled, with wild hair and wilder eyes. His skin was even paler than before, scarred with streaks of crimson all across his face and neck and hands, as if he'd endured a lashing from a thin whip made of ice; the whites of his eyes were reddened and leaking, like he'd stared for too long into a stinging wind.

They regarded each other for a moment; then Rose lunged for the tire iron, which was still wedged into the wheel.

But his arms were longer, and they shoved her off the platform before she could reach it.

The thick hanging barriers and log walls muffled sound from the rest of the building; Richard had no idea if Hank was still out there or what he might be doing, and so he stayed put with Janice until she finally fell asleep, her breathing becoming soft and regular. Then he carefully laid her on the floor, pushed through the rubbery panels, cracked open the bathroom door, and peeked into the master bedroom. Empty. He crept out, carefully pulled the bathroom door shut behind him, ventured to the bedroom door. Now he could see the rest of the apartment as well as most of the balcony. No sign of Hank or anyone else. He moved into the living room then out onto the balcony. Leaning on the railing, he looked over the parking lot and the surrounding woods. Nobody around. Not one single person. But he could see, some distance away, a glow among the trees, a foggy and mysterious illumination directly in line with the trailhead that exited from the opposite side of the parking lot, as if someone had arranged a bank of floodlights around a smoke machine.

What was it? Might Rose be there?

Richard went back to the bathroom, flicked on the wall switch. Janice was still in the back, squinting at the light and grumbling. He told her he had to go for a little while, that she had to stay here and hide and keep quiet. Janice, predictably, objected, grabbing him with her little arms and refusing to let go, but he finally pried her loose and got her settled into the dark space between the stationary tub and the wall. It reminded him of where the old man used to put him for punishment, but he pretended it didn't.

Leaving the light on, he closed the door, then ran down the stairs and out of the shop and up the rutted path into the woods. It took him to a pair of tall boulders, beyond which lay a beach and a little hill and a pond that was rapidly draining through the broken remains of what looked like an old wooden dam off to his left. The illumination he had seen from the shop, and the fog—both of them were now dissipating—emanated from the water, which swarmed with spindly arms and grabby hands thick as noodles in a horrid soup. He had seen those phantom limbs before, scratching at the windows of the house Beth had built inside the book, and in the wintry, half-remembered wasteland he'd wandered through after slipping out through the sump.

He stayed well back from the water, watching, wondering what had happened to destroy the dam. He must have only just missed the event, given how quickly the pond drained. Within minutes it had become a black canker full of inky mud and stones, filthy puddles, a trickling current, dead leaves and tree limbs, and ...

Bodies.

They were scattered all around, in varying states of decay, a few more or less intact, most utterly decrepit. He spotted Hank, out towards the middle, lying on his back, water pooled in his open mouth and the hollows of his eyes, and right next to him a woman, nearly as fresh; the rest were grotesqueries barely identifiable as having once been human. He didn't see Rose among them. He hadn't realized how afraid he'd been that he would find her drowned and bedraggled in the muck until he didn't.

A breath of wind stirred the air, wafting noisome odors Richard's way. He raised an arm to cover his nose and mouth, then trudged up a small grassy slope to stand beneath a willow tree. From here he had a better view of the ghastly contents of the weeping sore that had once been a pond. He could see that the glowing arms squirming through the shit-colored phlegmy sludge were manipulating the bodies, tugging at them, moving them around, apparently arranging them into a pattern not unlike a labyrinth. A shape began to form and grow in the center, like a bud slowly unfolding itself to reveal strange geometries within its petals, a space that simultaneously comprised a pit and a tower, a tunnel and a bridge, a gate and a road. A road through a wintry wasteland. And down that road, in the far distance, something massive dragged itself forward in lurching fits and stops, digging fingers into splintered ground to haul itself forward.

The unnatural angles and frozen light emanating from the hateful flower began to hurt his eyes and his brain and he had to turn away. Whatever they were doing, whatever pattern they were designing, it needed to be disrupted. But how? He looked at boulders he had passed through to get here, at the beginning of the path beyond.

The *rutted* path.

An idea took shape.

Richard ran back to the shop to put it into action.

Ozzie held on tight as the patrol car careered along the side and back roads north of Bentonville, racing at unsafe speeds on surfaces of broken asphalt and dirt that he would have taken for the driveways of summer camps or survivalist compounds. He had no idea where they were until they abruptly bounded across a shallow washout—if he hadn't been buckled in his head would have bounced off the roof— then passed between a couple of sawhorses, knocked over a flashing *Road Closed* sign, and somehow ended up back on Route 18. They were well south of the accident now, barreling down into the city. As they descended from the plateau, which offered a panoramic view of Bentonville and its small suburbs, Ozzie could see a number of fires burning down below, the flashing lights of emergency vehicles, entire blocks without power, columns of smoke that transitioned from black to grey as they rose into the moonlight. It was as if some giant monster had stomped through the valley, leaving ruin in its wake.

The radio squawked with an alert. It had been doing this the entire trip and Ozzie could never understand a word of it. He figured they must offer a class in cop school on how to interpret police band gibberish. Luce answered the call, saying something that sounded affirmative. After she cradled the handset, she looked back at Ozzie. "That was an update on the situation at Rosie Reporter's apartment."

"Is she all right?"

"Unknown. She has not been located. However, her husband was taking potshots with a rifle from the balcony of a third-floor apartment that does not belong to them. Word is he and the resident of that particular unit—who has been found shot dead in the laundry area—had a longstanding history of squabbling over minor apartment building neighbor bullshit. No idea if that's what set him off. He's not telling us."

"Refusing to talk?"

"Incapable." Luce turned away. The road bottomed out in the valley and they zoomed into Bentonville, a wailing, sparkling street-meteor, ignoring traffic signs and signals and other cars. Ozzie found his belly kept bulging in one direction and then the other as they whizzed through turns and around corners. Traffic flashed by going the other direction, blurs in the darkness. Ozzie couldn't remember ever going this fast in a car. He wasn't even sure he had gone this fast in a plane.

Finally they climbed a hill, made a left into an entrance, and bounded down into an apartment complex, squat buildings scattered around a looping driveway lined with parking areas. He figured Rose's building must be the one surrounded by barricades and cop cars. Their lights illuminated the pale pink walls of the surrounding buildings with a weird flickering disco effect. He saw no bystanders.

They screeched to a stop at the back of the phalanx. Mitch cut the siren and they idled there for a minute. Ozzie eyed the other cars. A number of them looked to have been shot, with little windshield perforations decorated by spiderwebs of cracks or silver punctures in their paint or shattered door mirrors. Figures crouched among the vehicles, some sheltering under cover, others moving fast and low towards the building.

"Are we getting out?" Ozzie said.

"Negative," Mitch said. "Something's wrong. Luce, can you find out what's up?"

"On it." Luce picked up the mike and tried several times to raise someone, without success. Suddenly Ozzie heard a sharp, distant *crack* and the plastic casing of the light bar on the car nearest them exploded in a shower of blue and red fragments.

"What was that?" Ozzie said.

"That was a rifle," Mitch said. "There isn't supposed to still be an act—"

There was another *crack* and suddenly their own windshield had a hole in it, surrounded by a roughly circular pattern of jagged lines that glimmered in the parking lot lights. Mitch made a noise. Ozzie discovered the he had thrown himself off the seat of the car, which was a pretty neat trick considering he was still strapped in. The belt held him just off the floor; he was eye level with a petrified piece of chewing gum that somebody had stuck to the bottom of the barrier between him and the officers. He popped the buckle and fell the rest of the way to the floor, then peeked over the back of the seat. Luce and Mitch had somehow switched places while he'd been communing with the nether regions of the vehicle. Luce was looking over her shoulder, not at him. The car began moving in reverse. "You all right back there, Ozzie?" she said.

"I think so. What's going on?"

"Mitch took a bullet and can't drive, not that he could before—"

"Very funny," Mitch said, his voice tight.

"—so I'm getting us out of this shooting gallery."

"But who's shooting at us? I thought—"

"I don't know. But I'd advise you to stay down until—"

Just then a shot grazed the side window; one moment it was clear glass and the next it sported a diagonal white groove where a bullet had skimmed its surface. An instant later it shattered into thousands of tiny glittering pieces, bedazzling the seat and floor with jagged little cop car window jewels. Ozzie found himself back on the floor with his hands covering his head, and stayed there until he felt the car go through a three-point turn. Figuring Luce wouldn't be doing that if they were still in the line of fire, he hesitantly pulled himself onto the seat, and saw that they were nearly back to the exit from the complex.

"Yeah, you can get off the floor now, Ozzie." Luce flicked the siren on. "And I'd suggest you buckle up. We're taking a little trip to the hospital."

When the flood abated, Rose found herself washed up in a shallow eddy off to one side of the creek, soaked and shivering. She sat up, then rolled onto her hands and knees and threw up a thin stream of water, then fought her way upright and stumbled upstream until the splintered remains of the wooden dam came into view. The stone platform was the only part of the weir left standing, looking sad and ridiculous with its raised lift gate, a barrier without a barricade. Beyond it, the pond appeared to have drained completely, but some kind of weird shit was going on in there; she could hear grotesque squelching slurps, and could see a bizarrely coherent cylinder of mist in the middle. She took a few halting steps forward, slowed, stopped. Whatever was going on in there, she had very little left in reserve for dealing with it; and Robert James might still be lurking nearby, now armed with Sandy's tire iron. She would be so pissed.

Fuck.

Opting for strategic retreat, Rose staggered off downstream. She had to go easy on her right foot, which was reporting a serious throb in its ankle region, so it took her a while to get to the bridge. When she arrived, she spent a minute eyeing the crude stairway, wondering if she could make it up. Finally she tackled it, crawling more than climbing, using the iron rebar to haul her battered ass to the top. The old car hunched where they had left it, silent and inert now, settling into its new role as a roadblock. Rose wished she could crawl inside and just go to sleep on the big bench seat, but settled for leaning up against it for a brief rest. Then she pushed herself off and started hobbling towards Route 18, hoping she would get there and find that the kids had flagged down some serious help.

Because she was starting to think that she had, in fact, somehow made things worse.

Richard ran through the shop and into the backyard. There was the shabby canopy with all the crap underneath it and, parked beside it, the ATV. He hadn't ridden one in years—not since that disastrous family vacation when Hank had glommed onto Beth—but they'd all taken lessons then and surely the machines couldn't have changed all that much, right? Wheels and a handlebar. Just like riding a bike.

He looked the thing over quickly. It sported a big cargo basket on its back end and a smaller one in front, complete with bungee cords for holding things down. Dried mud speckled its flanks and fenders. A silver key gleamed in the ignition. He climbed into the seat and inspected the handlebars, with their big brake flippers and cables, like a steroidal ten-speed. He managed to disengage the brakes and the ATV rolled forward slightly along the slope of the ground, then stopped. That was progress, sort of, but he needed to make the thing move under its own power. There was a big red switch near the handlebars. It reminded him of the button on a cartoon detonator. In the dimness, he could barely make out a white circle with a vertical line on the button. Some wag had enhanced the circle with dabs of paint, turning it into an abstract rabbit head. He pushed the switch and turned the key. The engine coughed and sputtered, coughed and sputtered, died. He tried it again, then again. No luck.

Come on, rabbit. Run.

He gave it a minute to think about life then turned the key again and this time the engine caught and roared and vibrated like a wood chipper full of rocks. He found the headlamp switch and flicked it on, lighting up the interior of James's stockaded yard with harsh white light. Unexpectedly, something drifted into the glare: A blue notebook. It flapped around in front of him and fluttered into the basket. He stared at the book for a second, then leaned forward and strapped it down with the bungee cords. These were stiff with age and made soft crackling noises as he stretched them, but still performed their intended function.

Having thus secured the book—welcome aboard, Beth!—Richard leaned back and looked for the clutch. A lever down by his foot resembled the shifter on a motorcycle; he nudged it upward with his toes and the tenor of the engine changed and the ATV leaped forward, bucking up onto the pallet to its left, crushing some small cardboard boxes full of blown glass plant-waterers. He managed to stay in his seat as the vehicle bounced to the ground on the other side, its big knobby wheels scraping grass and mud off the surface of the lawn and converting it into a filthy spray. Then he did something wrong and the engine sputtered and died. Hoping it wasn't out of gas, he located the fuel tank, checked it. Nearly full. Good. He returned to the seat and after a little bit of cajoling he got the thing started again.

"Hang on, Beth," he murmured. "Here we go."

Richard drove down to the far end of the yard, swung around in a tight arc, and gunned it straight at the gate. He braced himself in the seat as the ATV crashed into the gate, knocking it off its hinges and onto the hood of James's low-slung car, turning it into a ramp. He went briefly airborne and like a dilettante stunt driver made a glancing landing on the back of the trunk. The ATV pitched off sharply and for a second he thought he was going to flip over. He shifted his weight as far back as he could. The rear tires touched down and the vehicle lurched forward, bouncing from wheel to wheel to wheel, skittering at an angle like an epileptic crab. Dirt and gravel pinged everywhere. The headlights swept across the forest and lit up the trailhead. He wrenched the ATV in that direction and roared into the woods. The machine bumped and rumbled and coughed and spit. The knobby tires bounded over rocks and irregularities in the ground. The big suspension springs sent one wheel bouncing into the air, then another. Richard clung to the handlebars and kept his knees locked against the chassis and did his best to keep the thing from plowing into the trees on either side until he managed to bobble between the boulders that marked the end of the path. The crunch of metal told him he had left some paint behind.

He couldn't bring the vehicle around in time to get it to the beach and bounced up the grassy slope instead. Wrenching hard to the left to avoid crashing into the concrete bench or the willow tree, he ran out of runway and sailed over the edge of the bank. He held on tight and wished for wings. The front wheels hit the muddy, rocky bed hard; the ATV bucked and nearly pitched him over the handlebars. Adjusting his grip, he steered into the field of corpses, tearing through the remains, spewing crud and bones and mutilated flesh from beneath the wheels as he chewed his way along, trying to think of it as disrupting the design and not as shredding the bodies of the dead.

The inlay on Beth's book had begun to glow. Sparks flashed at the burnt spots in the pattern. Richard noticed this only obliquely, while fighting through a sliding curve, and didn't have time to wonder what it might mean.

Wheels slipping and squelching in the muck, the ATV spiraled in towards the center of the pattern. He chanced a look at the gate, hoping to see it faltering, seeing instead that the gigantic dragging thing had arrived on the other side. It lashed out at him as he passed, the long pale arm emerging from the gate, fingers like clawed tree branches stretched and splayed. He steered hard away from it but it caught his rear bumper and the ATV flipped into a barrel roll. Richard lost his grip and was flung from the saddle. He landed face-down and plowed a furrow through the disgusting muck, sliding to a halt on the pebbly shore like a shipwrecked castaway. He scrambled to his feet, caked in mud and gobbets of stuff he didn't want to think about, and staggered the rest of the way up the beach, then turned to see what was happening behind him. The ATV lay on its side, filthy, the bumper half-torn off, but it was somehow still running, the engine sputtering. Beth's book was still strapped into the basket, held tight by the bungees, glowing like a little star. Beyond, the thing in the gate extended itself again, reaching for the vehicle. It didn't look like it could possibly fit through the opening but who knew how those strange angles worked, what manner of eldritch origami allowed it to fold itself across from one side to the other?

Before it made contact, the ATV quivered and flipped itself back onto its wheels. The engine coughed and roared. The tires spun, spraying muck behind it, and it lurched into motion, narrowly avoiding the clawed grip of the giant hand, and Richard could see, backlit by the book and the gate, a faint ripple in the driver's seat, like a misty heat shimmer, coiling around the handlebars, working the pedals.

Beth, he thought, guiding the machine back into the pattern.

Just like riding a bike.

Rose hadn't gotten too far past the bridge when, rounding a bend, looking back instead of forward—a small, loud engine had just started up from the direction of the shop, making her think of the ATV in the backyard—she found herself sprawled across the hood of a low-slung sports car that had been driving down Mill Pond Road. Fortunately it had been moving too slowly to run her down. She pushed herself off of the hood and smacked it with her palm, then went to the driver's side as the tinted window scrolled down, revealing an expensive-looking haircut, then the man it belonged to. She said, "Why don't you look where you're going?"

At the same time, the driver said, "Are you Rose?"

Well, that was unexpected.

"Who wants to know?" she said.

"I'm Tony. I work with Richard. I just met a couple of your friends up at the end of the driveway and they told me—"

"You work with Richard? And you just happened to, what, come out this way for a drive?"

"Fuck no. Richard left me a message earlier today, said he and somebody named Rose had tracked down a guy who might be involved in what happened to Beth, that he would get back to me with an update, and that if I didn't hear from him I should call the cops and send them to this address. Not being the guy who waits around for things to go to shit, I called the cops right away, but they didn't even pretend to be interested in what I had to say. As far as they're concerned Beth was a suicide, and they've got other things to worry about besides crackpot theories—their exact words—and so like an idiot I got a map and drove all the way out here myself." He gave the driveway an unfriendly look. "If Richard had mentioned it was a goddamn dirt road in the middle of nowhere I would have rented a Jeep."

"We didn't know it was a goddamn dirt road in the middle of nowhere until we got here." She looked back towards the shop. The engine she had heard earlier didn't seem to be coming this way; it sounded like it had headed off into the woods. Maybe Robert James was making his escape into the wilderness. "All right, yeah, I'm Rose. Sorry. I wasn't expecting to run into the cavalry. Richard forgot to tell me he called it. You talked to Pedro and Sandy?"

"I didn't get their names. Nice kids. Couldn't tell me very much though. They don't seem to know what the fuck is going on. I hope you can do better."

"I don't know what the fuck is going on either. We found Richard's niece, but—"

"Janice? You found *Janice* out here?"

"Yeah, she's—"

"Is she all right? Where is she? Where's Richard?"

"She was all right last I saw her. Things got a little, uh, crazy and I lost track of her and Richard. They—"

"You *lost track* of them?"

"This will go faster if you stop interrupting me." She pointed up the driveway. "I think they're still at the antique shop, maybe hiding."

Now he looked baffled. "Antique shop? Did I hear that right?"

"Yes. Listen. Tony. There's all kinds of weird shit going on out here that I don't understand. The smart play would be to turn your little sports car around and take it back to the highway where it belongs and drive it someplace that has cops and bring them back here."

"Hmm." Tony seemed to consider that for a long moment; then he reached into the vestigial storage space behind his seat and got out, carrying a big heavy flashlight which he slung up against his shoulder and a pistol which he tucked into the waistband of his expensive-looking slacks. "The cops had their chance," he said. "I'm here and I've got nothing better to do, so I'm going to go to this antique store to find Richard and Janice and maybe pick up a nice dresser. Are you in?"

Richard had summoned a cowboy. Wonderful.

She pointed at the pistol. "You know how to use that thing?"

"Haven't had any complaints yet," Tony said. "Oh, you mean the gun? I know how to use that, too."

A cowboy *and* a comedian.

Even better.

Richard had moved up the bank to the concrete bench, wanting to get a better view as the ATV churned through the muck, dodging ponderous swings from the thing beyond the gate. The book glowed so brightly now that he couldn't look directly at it anymore; it was like watching a nuclear explosion spiraling through a toxic waste dump, picking up fuel as it went along. He could see luminous currents of energy siphoning into it from the bodies and from the gate itself, reminding him of those storm globes they sold at the novelty stores, the ones that sent lightning to your fingertips when you touched the glass exterior. And, in fact, when the clawing hand finally connect, something like an electrical blast caused it to recoil and retreat into the gate like a sea polyp into its tube.

Whatever that energy discharge was, it had definitely done damage. The impossible angles that made up the gate in the center seemed to be crumpling in on themselves, losing depth and width and other strange proportions that should never have existed in the first place. The thing on the other side thrashed and flailed in obvious frustration, but had become flat, unidimensional, a monstrosity projected onto a screen. Despite that, Richard felt each blow as a subsonic thrumming in his gut, a vibration traveling through the ground and up the cement bench and into his gripping fingers, and he wasn't at all confident it wouldn't find a way through again.

Maybe Beth wasn't either. Maybe that was why she circled in close to the gate, becoming connected to it by writhing tendrils of plasma, then slingshotting away to the edge of the muddy expanse until, with a sliding bootleg turn, she reversed course and headed straight back at it.

She was going to ram it.

With a sudden realization of what might happen when the four-wheeler collided with the gate, Richard ran to the giant willow tree and flattened himself against the rough bark on the opposite side just before the entire world detonated silently behind him. An icy white blast passed by, breaking on either side of him with the fury of a winter hurricane. He heard the bank explode and collapse behind him. The willow tilted a little bit towards the pond. Then the shockwave reversed direction, drawn back inward on itself. He heard branches cracking overhead.

Then it all stopped. The clattering, skittering sound of sliding dirt ceased. Everything was quiet again.

He stayed where he was for a few seconds, then peered around the side of the listing tree. Everything that had been on the pond floor was gone. No ATV. No gate. No bodies. No glowing arms. No muck. All that remained was a solid flash-frozen crust, steaming, ice already sublimating into vapor. The water in the shallow stream bed that ran through the basin had crystallized but new water was already flowing in, drawing a black line across it. The bench and most of the bank was gone. Half of the willow's roots now stuck out into space. It would probably topple over in the next stiff breeze.

Was it over? He thought it might be. At least for now.

With a last look at where his sister had disappeared, Richard left to collect her daughter.

Tony and Rose walked towards the shop, moving at the slow hobble that was all Rose could manage. The engine noise had moved off to their left, in what she thought was the direction of the pond. Tony asked her what it was and she could only shrug and say she didn't know. He carried his gun a little higher after that. As they passed the broken-down vehicle Pedro and Sandy had arrived in, she noticed him eyeing the dented hood, the missing windshield, the drying grey stuff all over the interior, and could see him formulating more questions she would be unable to answer. To forestall this, she said: "So do you always carry a gun around in your car?"

"Sure. Don't you?"

She couldn't tell if he was kidding or not. "No. Should I?"

"If you're planning to keep doing things like this? Probably."

"I'm not planning to do anything like this ever again."

He nodded and seemed like he was going to say something else, but then there was a sudden sharp flash from out in the woods, in the same direction as the engine noises, which ceased immediately. They both stopped, staring off into the darkness. "What the fuck was that?" Tony said. "Wait, let me guess. You don't know."

"Nope."

"Of course not." Then: "All right, well, come on. We can't let Richard have all the fun."

They started walking again, and soon neared the bend that would put them in the parking lot and its dome of pink light. She spotted a figure coming from the direction of the shop, tall and broad and carrying something, or someone. She lifted her flashlight to see who it was: Richard, cradling Janice, her arms around his neck and her face buried in his shoulder. He held up a hand to shield his eyes. Rose lowered the light. "Richard?" she said. "Is Janice okay?"

"She's fine," Richard said. "Just sleeping."

"And you?"

"Alive. Tony, what are you doing here?"

"What am I … you left a message for me, remember? *Tony, I'm gonna do something dangerous now.* Ring a bell?"

"Yeah, but I just meant for you to call the cops if—"

"Oh I called the cops, but they weren't interested in what I had to say so I came myself. Lucky for me, since that's how I met my new future wife, here." Rose snorted. "See? She knows it's true."

"How many future wives does one guy need, Tony?"

"What kind of a stupid question is that?" Tony shook his head. "Richard. You've got all these new friends. You're visiting antique shops unsupervised. Things are exploding in the woods. I feel left out. You mind telling me what's been going on out here?"

"You'll never believe it. Nobody would."

"She says she doesn't know, and now you say I wouldn't believe it."

"That's because it's the truth."

"Well then you'd better start thinking up some plausible lies," Tony said.

The driveway seemed a lot longer on foot, in the dark, carrying an exhausted six-year-old. When had Janice gotten so big and heavy? You lose track of a kid for a day or two, they come back gigantic.

As they walked, Rose filled Richard in on what had happened while they'd been separated: Finding Janice, her run-in with Hank, Robert James getting thrown into the water, Pedro and Sandy showing up in the old man's car, James returning to attack her after she'd drained the pond, meeting Tony—"Her future husband," Tony interjected—on the driveway. He could tell she was leaving things out, and expected to get a full accounting later, when it was just them.

Then it was Richard's turn. He told them about finding the book-binding equipment in James's bathroom, the empty covers, the raw materials, and after some discussion he and Rose agreed that James had been making books out of human skin and ground-up human bone and who knew what else. By the time they were finished, Tony was looking at them like they were both insane. "Making books out of *people?*" he said, his voice oddly plaintive. "Why would someone *do* that? Did he think he was a fucking necromancer or something?"

Richard and Rose exchanged glances, and then Richard said, "That's where the plausible lies come in."

"I'm not sure I even want to hear those," Tony said.

They crossed the bridge and came to Tony's car, where they paused. Spinning blue and red lights had become visible up ahead, illuminating the low, misty clouds that had begun drifting in. "Looks like Pedro and Sandy managed to flag down the police," Rose said.

"Good," Richard said. "Let's go see what—"

"Hold up a second." Tony took out a handkerchief and wiped his pistol thoroughly, then went to the side of the bridge and reached underneath it, hiding the weapon in a crook of the support beams.

Rose raised an eyebrow at him. "I take it you don't have a permit for that."

Tony gave her an innocently puzzled look. "A permit for what?" He opened the passenger door of his car and gestured for Rose to have a seat. She settled in, then pointed at Janice and patted her lap. Richard passed her down. The little girl mumbled something but didn't wake up, curling into Rose's lap. He shut the door and stepped back while Tony started up the engine and adjusted his mirrors and started driving in reverse. Richard walked alongside as they slowly rolled the rest of the way to Route 18. When they got there, they found a Bentonville patrol car parked sideways across Mill Pond Road, blocking the entrance. Its trunk was open and its hazards were flashing, the lights on top spinning lazily. Pedro and Sandy leaned against it, standing next to a police officer. The name *Cam* was embroidered on his uniform. He stood with his hands behind his back, watching them approach; then he raised one hand, palm out. They stopped and he motioned for Tony and Rose to get out of the vehicle, which they did. Rose passed Janice back to Richard as the three of them assembled in front of the trunk of Tony's car.

"The kids here were telling me about your situation," Cam said, looking them over. "Everyone accounted for?"

Richard and Rose and Tony exchanged glances.

"Yeah, as far as we know," Richard said.

"You all okay?"

"More or less."

The officer nodded. "Glad to hear it."

Then he stepped forward and brought a shotgun out from behind his back and fired it into Tony's stomach.

Tony fell backwards, eyes wide, the front of his body a blooming mass of crimson. Rose screamed and stumbled sideways into Richard. He caught her with his free arm, swung her around, pivoted to shield her and Janice with his body. In the black mirror of the windshield he saw Cam level the gun at his back.

Pedro lunged at the officer. He knocked the shotgun aside with his forearm just as it belched smoke and fire. Pedro spun away and went down, blood splattering the white paint of the police car. Sandy shrieked and leaped on Cam, punching and kicking, fouling his aim. Richard thrust Janice into Rose's arms and launched himself off Tony's bumper. He grabbed for the weapon but missed, felt the backs of his hands slide along the hot barrel and down the stock, just as Cam smashed Sandy in the jaw with the butt of the shotgun. It boomed once more, unexpectedly, dizzyingly loud, and most of Cam's head evaporated in a spray of red and white and yellow-grey. He slid to the ground, leaving a grotesque smear along the rear passenger-side window and door.

Richard found himself staring down at Cam's ruined skull, ears ringing, skull throbbing like a struck bell. Off to his left, something small and dark and rectangular emerged from the trunk, drawing his attention. It resembled James's notebooks, but the pattern was different, and the cover was red. It hovered there for a moment, as if inspecting them; then it fluttered off into the night. Richard watched the book disappear into the darkness. So did Rose. "That's one of Gustav Arvidsson's books," she said. She turned to Richard. "It's not over. We have to find Robert James."

From the ground, in a voice gritty with pain, Pedro said, "Can we call an ambulance first?"

11

MORNING.

Rose sat in the round-backed chair in her motel room and stared out the window as the light crept up over the distant airport, glinted off the darkened windows of the control tower. Last night, she'd been sure she wasn't ever going to see the sun again. Yet here she was.

They had called for help using the radio in Cam's cruiser, and even saying there was an officer down didn't get them assistance right away. Everyone was stretched crazy thin. It had been a full moon night, the kind of evening when half the population seems to go crazy, when suicides and murders and crimes of all kinds spike, cars crash into each other, houses burn and fuel depots explode and the phones ring off the hook with calls from crackpots and wackos and frantic people reporting that long-leggedy beasties are out in their yards eating their dogs. But finally help had arrived; she and Richard had been taken to police headquarters and the kids had been whisked to the hospital, Pedro with his shotgun-blasted shoulder, Sandy with her broken jaw and cheekbone. Tony and Cam had been left where they lay because, at least temporarily, they weren't people anymore; they were part of the crime scene. Evidence. Camera fodder.

So many crime scenes right now. Her apartment was one of them. That was why she'd taken a room at the Pine View motel, when she and Richard had finally been turned loose in the early hours of the morning. There had been seemingly endless questions, mainly about what had happened with Cam, which, at least for now, overshadowed their finding Janice at the shop; but she and Richard and the kids all told the same story about the incident, and none of the civilians had been armed, and a little girl had been in the line of fire. The optics were terrible. Rose wouldn't want to be the departmental flack charged with finding a justifiable reason for Cam to have started shooting, especially in light of his bizarre behavior earlier that evening.

She had found out about *that*—and all the other weirdness they had missed—from Ozzie, who had shown up while she and Richard were at police headquarters; Rose had spotted the portly newspaperman talking with Luce Sabbatini, Cam's partner and a patrolwoman she knew slightly. Rose had managed to wrangle a short conversation with him, which started out with his saying he was sorry about her husband. She'd given him a blank look, and he'd turned red as his suspenders and started stammering. It had fallen to Luce to fill Rose in on what her husband had gotten up to while she'd been out at James's shop. Rose digested this story and gave a statement to the effect of no, she hadn't had the faintest idea Joe might be about to go off the deep end, then asked Luce if they'd found her husband's journal. A blue notebook, she said, with gold inlay on the cover. About the size of one of those marbled pads from high school. Maybe it'll give you a clue why he had done it, she said. Luce told her that they had indeed found such a book, two of them, in fact, hidden in odd places, one under the mattress and one under the seat cushions of the sofa; she'd heard they contained gibberish that might be some kind of code. Did Rose have any idea how to read it? Rose said no, Joe had never let her look in them. Luce said okay, she would let the investigators know the books were Joe's journals, and excused herself from the conversation to go do that.

James must have learned she was getting close to him, decided to stop her, and laid a trap at her apartment that had snared Joe by mistake. Or maybe not by mistake; maybe that had been his plan all along, to make one or both of them go blind with rage and kill or maim each other. That seemed to be the bastard's preferred method of operation.

A knock on the door interrupted her thoughts. Just as well. She didn't need to do any more thinking right now. She stood, watched the sun a moment longer. The red on the horizon was fading, the purple in the sky lightening to blue with just the faintest trace of high-altitude clouds, like acid etching across the atmosphere. Looked like today was going to be a scorcher.

Another knock. She closed the curtains and went to the door, walking carefully on her injured ankle, mummified in sports wrap. Although she was expecting Richard, how stupid would it be, after everything that had happened, to throw open the door and find James standing there, grinning and disheveled, holding the tire iron, come to finish her off? But a squint through the peephole showed her it was Richard, of course, looking haunted and exhausted and very well scrubbed. She imagined him spending hours in the shower, trying to wash off the events of yesterday, the stinking mud, the blood, the things he told her he had seen at the pond after she'd drained it. No quantity of soap and water could ever remove all that.

She opened the door. "Hi," she said.

"Hi." He was holding Janice's big doll, which had been returned to him while they were at the police station last night. The gash where it had been impaled on broken glass had been stitched up with thick black thread, as if it had been autopsied and sewn back together with no regard for those who would view the corpse afterwards.

"Did you sleep at all?"

"Not really. You?"

"Nope."

"I figured not." Then: "Ready?"

"Ready." Then, pointing at the doll: "Are you, uh, are you bringing that thing?"

"This?" He held it up, looked at it as if he hadn't realized he was carrying it. "Yeah."

"Why?"

He hesitated, then said, "Maybe so Candy Weiss can be there for the end of it. If that's what this turns out to be."

"Really? You think she's still in there?"

"Something is." He tucked the doll into his armpit. "Let's go. Ozzie will be waiting."

When they arrived at Main Street in Massalacqua later that morning, Ozzie was sitting on the grass in front of the headquarters of the *Mirror*, as arranged, hiding from the sun beneath a roadside maple. He got up as they rolled to a stop along the opposite curb, crossed the street, and clambered into the back seat. "Morning," he said.

Rose told him good morning; Richard grunted a hello. He stepped on the gas and they pulled away. The buildings of Main Street went slowly by.

"How're you dealing, Rose?"

She looked at Ozzie over her shoulder. "By not thinking about it."

"Fair enough. How's the little girl, Richard?"

"Still at the hospital for observation. She'll be all right, just hungry, tired, and dehydrated. I should be there, but … Well. Things to do. You know?"

"I do know. " Pause. "You take the interstate to get here?"

"Uh-huh."

"You talking just to hear yourself talk, Oswald?" Rose said. "Trying to keep yourself distracted?"

"Yeah, maybe," Ozzie said.

"Is it working?"

"Not really. Gonna keep doing it though." And so he did, pointing out landmarks and historic buildings, telling them what notable figure had slept here or died there, interspersing all that with instructions to Richard about where to turn and how far they would go before they turned again. They exited town and soon reached Wishbone Road, bounced along the broken, desolate street. It suddenly struck her, the similarity between this approach and the way to James's shop, both of them out in the woods at the end of a long, long driveway. Isolation suited the strange business the proprietors got up to.

Soon they emerged into the open area around the Arvidsson house, where the driveway split into a Y. Richard drove up to the house and stopped the car, but didn't shut the engine. A battered pickup was parked near the porch, the driver's side door hanging open. There had been a pickup out at Robert James's place, Rose remembered, but this was a different one. She looked at the porch, where the hollow spaces beneath the settles had been ripped open, freshly splintered wood showing pale against the older, weathered surfaces. Growing uncomfortable, Rose shifted around in her seat, slumped down a bit. Maybe then the house wouldn't be able to see her.

"I'm gonna take a look around," Richard said. He got out and poked around in the truck, put his hand on the hood as if feeling a feverish child's forehead. He proceeded to the porch, where he looked in the storage compartments and tested the front door, then stepped off and headed for the side of the house. She found herself growing tense when he disappeared from view and didn't relax until when he reappeared and returned to the car and got back behind the wheel. "What'd you find, Sherlock?" she said, trying and failing to keep her voice light.

"Engine's still warm. It's not James's truck. There's an insurance card in the glove compartment with somebody else's name on it."

"That might not be his truck but I guarantee he stole it and drove it here," Rose said.

"I'd assume so. The bins on the porch are empty. He pried them open, but it doesn't look like he tried to force his way into the house."

"Nothing in the house he wanted," Rose said. "Just in the bins."

"Yeah." He drummed his fingers on the steering wheel, looked around at the broad, empty yard. "I wonder where he is."

"If the engine's warm, it can't have been here very long," Rose said. "He couldn't have gotten far on foot."

Silence.

Then Ozzie said, "Maybe he went to the Anvil."

Ozzie directed Richard to turn the car around and take the other fork of the driveway, following it out to an overgrown gravel lot in front of the tarted-up barn, then along a rutted path that went behind it, stopping in the dusty grass where the ground began to slope downward into the surrounding woods. They all got out of the car and gathered at the front bumper. The heat had arrived; the air felt like a sauna just after someone had poured a fresh ladleful of water over the stones, as if steam were rising from between the blades of grass, blanching them bright green.

Ozzie came to stand beside Richard, pointed at a barely-visible gap in the trees. "That's the path. Just stay on it and you can't miss the Anvil even if you try."

"You'll know it when you see it," Rose added.

Richard glanced at her, then at Ozzie. "You aren't coming?"

"She's got a bum ankle and I've got a bum knee, and I'm fat and no sprinter even when I don't. We'll follow you, but you're the only one who might catch him."

"Assuming he even came this way."

"Yeah," Ozzie said, "assuming. Hey, if I'm wrong, we'll have a nice quiet walk in the woods, and then we all go home and pretend none of this ever happened."

"That'd take a lot of pretending," Richard said.

"I know," Rose said. "You'll be okay on your own until we catch up?"

"Sure." He went to the trunk and came back carrying the grotesquely mutilated doll. "Besides, I won't be on my own. I'll have Candy."

Leaving the others behind to exchange glances, Richard headed into the forest. It was cooler in the green shade of the trees, the light dappled, the air laced with scents of bark and leaf and earth and fallen rain. The path obviously hadn't been used much in recent years; it was threatened from both sides by twisting creepers and the low-hanging arms of young trees. The ground was broken by the protruding crania of rocks and exposed roots like the hunched spines of buried serpents. Some distance in, Richard paused at the top of a ridge, leaned up against a tree, looked back the way he had come. He could see a little way through the woods before everything became an undifferentiated mass of foliage. He imagined the others back there somewhere, both of them hobbling along, Ozzie huffing and puffing. What a trio they made. He wondered, not for the first time, if they were doing the right thing, coming after Robert James on their own. They'd given the police his description, of course, and had identified him as Janice's captor, but hadn't aired Rose's theory that the man would be coming to the Arvidsson estate. There was no way to properly prepare anyone for what the books could do, and the last thing they wanted was a bunch of cops coming out into the woods and shooting each other.

He started moving again, heading down the ridge. It was fairly steep and the trail cut at a rightward angle along the slope, following a lip in the face of the hill: An old cart track, maybe, rutted and overgrown with ferns and spongy mosses. Below him was a wide, flat tract of land, the flood plain of a creek that curved away to the left. He figured it must be one of the fields Ozzie said the Arvidssons had once tended. At the bottom the path turned away from the ridge and ran straight for a while, then hooked sharply to the left and climbed again. Soon Richard found himself standing on a dry, crumbling embankment, with a garden of stones below him. At its edge the rocks were small, but they grew larger farther in, surrounding a behemoth of a boulder that could only be the Anvil. Tall grasses and sumac and milkweed and raspberry brambles grew between them, taking advantage of the sun that fell unimpeded to the stony ground.

Had James come to this place? What for? Was the field of stones equivalent in some way to the pond back at the shop? There was a suggestion of a pattern there, the layout of the rocks reminding him, to a certain extent, of the labyrinth of bodies in the muck.

The main path to the center was clear and obvious. Richard descended the slope and went in among the rocks. The smaller ones around the perimeter could have been gathered by the Arvidssons when they cleared the land for farming, but the bigger ones must be the droppings left behind by retreating glaciers thousands of years ago. He thought again of the writhing things in the pond, their gigantic counterpart on the other side of the impossible opening, and he wondered if they had fond memories of the ice.

He reached the big rock in the middle. It was twice as tall as he was, patchy with moss and lichen in the shady spots, cracked by eons of weathering as it slowly crumbled into rubble. There was no grass around its base, only hard-packed bare brown earth. He put his hand on the ancient surface. It felt warm under his palm. He began to move slowly along the ring of dirt, keeping his hand on the boulder, following its gentle curve until he came to a corner. He heard a clanking, clacking sound—metal on stone, stone on stone—from up ahead. He listened for a moment, then leaned forward for a peek. This side was raw and jagged, as if the Anvil had been shorn from some other, even more massive protrusion. It ran inward at an angle, then bent out again; in the vertex of the crook Richard saw a sort of crude ramp made of rocks, almost like the side of a large cairn. Robert James was busily dismantling it with a tire iron. Displaced rocks littered the ground behind him like stone cabbages.

Richard inspected the formerly natty antiquarian, now sodden and decrepit, his shock of white hair hanging tangled and unkempt from beneath his misshapen hat. His shirt was partially untucked, revealing the slack, pallid flesh of his stomach; his hands were rough and dirty from digging. At the moment he appeared to be nothing more or less than a sad, injured, destitute old man, someone in search of a hot meal and a safe place to sleep.

But, of course, he wasn't.

Why was he excavating the rocks? Was he digging up something he had cached earlier? More books, maybe? He had a small collection of them, a pile of crimson spines—no blue ones—that sat haphazardly stacked on a medium-sized boulder to his left. Maybe those were the ones he had taken from the storage bins on the porch.

Richard waited until James stretched forward to pry loose another rock, then darted across the open space between the Anvil and a large boulder that hunched and brooded nearby, putting himself a few yards closer. He pressed himself flat against the rock and listened to the quiet clattering of James's excavation project, waiting until he was convinced the other man hadn't seen or heard him. Then he slid into a crouch, set Candy against his knees, pulled apart the black stitching that held her stomach together, and carefully withdrew Tony's gun from inside the doll.

After they'd finally been let go from the police station in the early morning and taken a cab to the motel, he'd escorted Rose to her room, then went to his own, where he'd sat for a little while staring at nothing on the television. Then he'd turned it off and gone back out again, heading out on Route 18, passing the scene of the accident Ozzie had told them about—blackened pavement and withered greenery were all that remained of the fire—stopping a mile or so south of Mill Pond Road. From there he'd snuck into the woods, found the stream bed, and followed it north to the bridge. The dome of light from the investigators who were still working the scene of their confrontation with Cam had been visible through the trees, but the bridge had been deserted, with no one to see him creep underneath and slip the pistol out of the crook in the beams where Tony had hidden it. He'd felt tense and squirrelly the whole way back to the city, carrying that dull L-shaped lump of metal. Once back at the hotel, he'd crudely stitched the weapon up inside Candy, using a sewing kit he'd obtained from an all-night drugstore. Better the others should think he was crazily clinging to his niece's doll than know he was toting a sidearm; that way they wouldn't be accessories to whatever he might do with it or, worse, try to take it away from him.

A loud, dull *thud* jolted Richard back to the present. Realizing that the scuffing and scraping and clanking noises had stopped, he peered around the boulder. Robert James's efforts had uncovered a hole in the stone, a downward-facing cleft partway up the side; a large flat rock, chiseled and shaped into a capstone—that must have been the source of the thud, Richard thought—lay on the ground behind him, along with the discarded tire iron. As Richard watched, the antiquarian climbed up to the opening, dropped the red notebooks through, and slipped in after them.

Richard waited a minute or two to see if James was coming out before going to the truncated heap of rocks. He left Candy on the boulder where the notebooks had been and hauled himself up to the hole. It turned out to be a rocky chute descending into a tight stone box, from which a dark opening led deeper underground. James was out of sight. Tucking the gun into his belt at the small of his back, Richard swung his feet around and lowered his body into the hole, holding himself there for a moment. Was this a good idea?

Probably not, but he let go anyway.

He slid down the chute, landing on packed earth. It felt like being swallowed. The air smelled of dirt and dust and old rocks. He cast a glance up at the jagged circle of blue sky visible above him, them moved into the tunnel. It was short and sharply angled and deposited him in a large, irregular, oblong chamber. The ceiling was rock, too low for him to stand fully upright; the floor was dirt, hard-packed in the middle, though it looked looser along the edges. He could see tool marks where the Anvil had been chipped away, hollowed out. Old, dry wooden beams and braces supported the sides and roof. A lit lantern hung from one of them, battered and ancient, like an artifact recovered from a long-shuttered mine. It cast a soft amber light around the space. Alcoves had been cut into the stone between the supports; grey bones lined the niches, skulls turned outward, reminding Richard of pictures he'd seen of medieval catacombs. James crouched before one of them, arranging his notebooks within like a librarian shelving returns.

Richard took out the gun and pointed it at the antiquarian's back and briefly contemplated just shooting him. Instead he said the man's name. James ignored him, so he said it again, louder. This time James stiffened, paused, then slipped the rest of the notebooks into the alcove before turning to regard Richard with eyes that looked yellow in the half-light. After a moment he gave a little sigh and slid to the floor, sitting with his back against the stone and his knees drawn up towards his chest. "Richard Bartoski," he said, dragging his fingers back and forth in a semicircle through the soft earth in front of him. "What are *you* doing here?"

"I was going to ask you that."

"My apologies," James said, "but you must speak up a little. Recent events have left my senses a bit damaged."

Richard gestured with the gun and said, loudly, "Whose bones are these?"

James laughed a little, then coughed a little, spitting watery phlegm into the dirt at his feet. His traveling fingers mixed it with the earth and made a little bit of mud. "You think *I* know?" he said. "This was Arvidsson's place. Look to his ledgers for an accounting of these dead, not mine."

"What does that mean, Arvidsson's place? What is it? A family crypt?"

"Hardly." James scrutinized him with those jaundiced eyes. "Just tell me what is it you want, Richard, that you didn't simply shoot me. After all I've done, surely a bullet in the back is no more than I deserve."

What *did* he want? Richard considered it. Finally he said, "I want to know why."

"You want to know why? Can you really have no idea, at this point?"

"I know about the books made out of people. I know about the things in the pond. I know—"

James shook his head, turned his gaze to the floor. "All of that is *what*, Richard, not *why*."

Richard stared at the man. So bedraggled, so pathetic. He looked mostly dead himself. "My friend Tony asked me if you thought you were some kind of necromancer. What do you say to that?"

"I say your friend Tony has quite an imagination."

"Had. He's dead."

"How unfortunate."

"The person who killed him is dead, too. My sister. Rose's father. Her husband. All because of your books."

"Ah. Is that what you believe? That the books are mine? They are not. They never have been."

"If they're not yours, then whose are they?"

James smiled thinly. "Finally," he said, "an intelligent question."

Suddenly something clutched the back of Richard's neck in a burning cold grip. His body instantly went numb. The gun slipped from his hand; he didn't feel it, but he heard it thud heavily to the floor. Hand-like things began to emerge all around him, pale fingers wriggling in the earth like icy sprouts germinating, and he knew it was one of those that had slung itself out of the floor and caught him in its paralyzing grasp.

"But, sadly, asked too late," James said.

Rose and Ozzie stood at the top of the slope, peering down into the field of stones.

"I don't see him," Rose said. "Do you see him?"

"No. Maybe he's around the other side."

"Maybe. Let's go."

They circled the rocks, staying on the ring of tramped earth along the outer perimeter. As the snub-nosed front of the Anvil rotated into view, Rose spotted something. She put her hand on Ozzie's shoulder and said, "Wait. Look there."

He stopped. "Where?"

"There." She pointed at one of the tall rocks near the center, on which a tiny figure lay sprawled. From a casual glance it might have been an infant sacrificed on some rough altar, but it wasn't; it was the doll Richard had brought with him, lying on its back, porcelain face blank as the sky above it. Even at this distance Rose could see that the black stitching had been torn open, exposing a cavity in the sad, stuffed body. She wondered what had happened to it, imagined Robert James getting the drop on Richard, clubbing him with the tire iron, tearing the doll apart in a fit of rage.

As she scanned the surrounding stones, a translucent shape began to unfold itself from the gash in Candy's abdomen: First an arm, then another arm, then a leg, then another leg. It hauled itself out and stood over the eviscerated form of the doll, coltishly unsteady, gaining poise and solidity as it coalesced into the waifish figure of a girl. Blonde hair. Blue eyes. Bare feet. Dirty smock.

"Ozzie," Rose said, "do you see that?"

"Yes. Do you?"

"Yes. That's why I asked you."

"Right." He dragged a hand across his face. "You know who that is?"

"Cassandra Weiss," Rose said.

The girl stared at them for a few seconds, then skipped through empty air towards the Anvil. Rose realized that a number of the stones had been dislodged from the pile of rocks she had climbed when Ozzie had brought her here, revealing a hole in the rock, black as Robert James's hat. Cassandra Weiss stopped at the opening and glanced back at Rose and Ozzie with an expression of grim satisfaction, a smile that spoke of imminent revenge for some longstanding crime.

Then she slipped into the opening and was gone.

Richard could only watch as the glow from the emerging polyp-like creatures suffused the interior of the Anvil, casting weird shadows upward from floor to ceiling. The spot where James sat, the little semicircle of earth demarcated by the line he had drawn in the floor, remained undisturbed, but everywhere else the floor was alive. What Richard had taken to be idle scratching had obviously been much more than that.

Jaw set, teeth gritted, Richard kept trying to compel his body to move, his legs to work, his arms to rise, but nothing happened. He might as well be frozen up to his neck in ice. James observed his efforts with amusement, as if watching the performance of a sweet but incompetent child. He glared back at the antiquarian, who shuddered theatrically and said, "If looks could kill."

Richard could still speak, with effort. "Why haven't you?" he said.

James raised a ragged eyebrow. "Why haven't I what?"

"Killed me?"

The antiquarian's thin lips quirked into a bloodless smile. "Richard. I don't intend to kill you. I intend to *trade* you."

"Trade me? What are you, a colonist exploiting the natives? Trinkets for furs?"

James shook his head. "You have it backwards. *They* are the colonists. *We* are the natives." He ran his spindly fingers through his thin grey hair, cast his gaze around the stone cavity. "There are factions out there, you know, in the places beyond our experience. They contend and jockey. When Arvidsson's contingent sent him back, mine instructed me to deal with him, and I did. They wanted the books that were hidden here, and I obtained them. But then Victor rebelled somehow, and tried to trade me—and believe me, I was punished for my carelessness in allowing that to happen—and you and that woman managed to destroy my outpost, and as you can see, I am in no state to perform the rituals to create a new one. Fortunately, Arvidsson's was available, thanks to the kind efforts of your father."

"So you brought those things from the shop?"

"No, Richard. They do not travel with me in a satchel. I called them, and they came, which is why your timing was so fortuitous. Surely it must be fate. If you were not here, I would have nothing to offer them but more apologies." He cast a glance around the subterranean chamber, as if wondering when the next subway train was going to arrive. "The only thing I don't understand is why they have not taken you yet. It's almost as if they're waiting for … something …" He trailed off then, lifting his gaze to the ceiling, then returning it to Richard. Fear lurked in the corners of his yellow eyes. "What have you done?"

Before Richard could say he hadn't done anything, a small, translucent shape dropped out of the ceiling and settled onto his shoulders, feet dangling down in front of him. He experienced a flash of disorienting brightness, a sense of walking along an endless, icy road.

Then he stood before the Arvidsson farmhouse. It looked younger, cleaner, freshly whitewashed, no sag to its roof, no skew to its walls. Off to one side, another building, burned-out blackened timbers wet with rain, leached thin smoke into the air. Robert James stood nearby, much younger but still recognizable, dressed in clothes that were decades out of date. He held something in his hands, a big book loosely bound in leather, which Richard instantly recognized as an accounting ledger.

Then walking through fields beneath gloomy skies, Robert James ahead of him, still carrying the ledger, trudging across rolling terrain that had been woods before and would be woods again. Ahead of them, in a back pasture, down in a hollow out of sight of house or barn or workers, he saw the field of rocks, and the Anvil at its center.

Then up on top the Anvil, the two of them, facing each other, near the black opening that led to its interior. Off to the side he saw the same capstone James had pried loose to gain entrance. In hands that were not his own, Richard held a red notebook. He gestured James forward, and James came; but then he pulled a thin knife out from the pages of the leather volume, dropped the book, leaped forward. The blade came down once, twice, three times. Richard, trying to turn away, felt a series of sharp, stabbing pains in his chest, his stomach, his side.

Then floating up above the weathered, flat-topped stone, looking down at a body as its blood flowed along the jagged cracks in the surface, soaking into the rock, dribbling into the cleft. Robert James crouched over him, feeling his throat, his wrists. He shoved the corpse into the opening. It tumbled down and disappeared. The red notebook lay where the dead man had dropped it. James picked it up, looked around, fled. Richard continued floating, even as it began to rain, washing away the blood; even as day became night and a furtive shadow returned, piling up rocks to block the cleft in the Anvil, sealing up the barrow, making it a cairn.

Then, finally, Richard found himself back in the space beneath the Anvil, feeling cold and drained. The icy band around his neck was gone. He stumbled backwards and sprawled on the dirt. The line that the antiquarian had drawn in the dirt had been breached, stomped and scuffed and stamped by the imprints of footprints the size of Richard's shoes. On the other side, Robert James cowered against the stone, looking up at the transparent figure of Cassandra Weiss. He had pressed himself so small that she towered over him even though she was barely half as tall as he was.

The glowing hands and arms surged forward, through the gaps in the line. They passed through Candy and seized James, taking him by the feet, the hands, the arms, the face. He writhed and gibbered and screamed as his skin frosted and crackled and an icy sheen glazed his urine-colored eyes.

Cassandra Weiss—or was it Gustav Arvidsson?—observed this with a posture that spoke of vast satisfaction. When she glanced back at Richard, her eyes were swirling white pits. She cocked a half-smile, showing the curve of translucent teeth, then turned her attention back to Robert James.

Richard took that as a dismissal, or maybe a momentary dispensation, and scuttled out of the chamber like an insect fleeing the light.

Despite her bad ankle, with a boost from Ozzie, Rose managed to haul herself up the slope of loose stones to get a look at the opening into which Candy Weiss had disappeared. It turned out to be a short chimney leading down to a cavity beneath the boulder. The air welling out of the hole felt oddly cold, as if vented from a deep cavern full of icy water. She heard something from down there, a voice, faint, desperate, pleading. Was it Richard? She couldn't tell. She leaned forward and put her head into the hole just as a horrible gurgling scream echoed out of it, amplified by the rocky throat. She recoiled, looked down at Ozzie, who was staring up at her with wide, round eyes.

"Should I go down there?" she said.

"After *that*? Are you kidding?"

"But what if—"

She broke off as Richard scurried on hands and knees into the chamber below. He used the stone walls to pull himself to his feet and leaped for the chimney, fingers scrabbling at the rock, but it was too steep and he slid back to the bottom. Then he noticed her looking down at him and his eyes widened. "Rose?"

"You were expecting someone else?" She wedged her knees into the walls of the cleft on either side of the hole and reached down with both hands. He reached up, but their fingers ended far apart. "Come on, jump."

"I'm too heavy. I'll pull you down."

"I'm stronger than I look. Jump!"

He jumped. She caught his hands and, damn, he nearly did pull her down, but she was well-braced and managed to hold on until his feet found some purchase. She pulled. He scrambled. That was enough. She shifted around, pushed with her legs, and hauled him up. One of his hands found a hold near the top of the chute, then the other one got a grip on the edge, and then he was out, crammed into the crevice right next to her, covered in dirt and dust, sweating, yet radiating an odd chill. "Thanks," Richard said, breathing hard.

"Any time," Rose said.

They skittered and slid down to the bottom to join Ozzie. "What happened down there?" he said. "Did you find James? Did you see Cassandra Weiss? She—" He broke off when the flat, roundish rock he had been standing on began to quiver. He jumped off it with a yelp as it spun and slid up the Anvil and settled like a lid over the hole where Richard had been.

"Yes and yes," Richard said. "Come on. We need to leave. Now."

They fled, Richard half-carrying both Rose and Ozzie, and didn't stop until they had reached the top of the ridge. From here she could see that a thick mist had begun to ooze out of the hole, bubbling around the edges of the cover, dribbling down to pool in the ring around the bottom, spreading out from there. The smaller boulders were in motion, shivering, shifting like corks in water. The fog bank spread until it encompassed the entire field of rocks, obscuring everything with coils of seething vapor. Even from here she could feel the cold.

Then, abruptly, mist retreated, sucked back into the Anvil. The pile of rocks that blocked the entrance had been fully rebuilt, as if James had never dismantled it. The chill vanished from the air. Steam rose from all the rocky surfaces as frost sublimated in the heat. And still they watched, until all of that was gone, and the birds had started singing again, and the insects buzzed, and there was nothing to indicate that any of it had ever been disturbed.

"That's it," Ozzie said, "no more parties at the Anvil. I'm going to buy it and fill it with cement. Oh, and, here." He thrust the ghoulishly disemboweled remains of the doll into Richard's hands. "You forgot something."

"What am I supposed to do with this?" Richard said.

"Fix her up and give her back to your niece," Ozzie said. "I know a guy who repairs old toys."

"Of course you do," Rose said.

Epilogue

THE FAMILIAR HISS OF THE school bus brakes brought Richard out onto the porch. The big yellow vehicle disgorged his niece and pulled away, its windows full of little heads and faces looking outward and forward to the next stop. Janice came running towards the house, her school bag flying along behind her.

"You forgot to get the mail again, kiddo!" Richard called.

Janice stopped short with a chagrined expression on her face, pivoted, scampered to the mailbox, opened it, pulled out a wad of envelopes, then dashed to the porch and bounded up the steps. As she handed over the mail, Janice said: "Hey Uncle Richard, did you know eighty minus eighty is zero?"

"No way."

"It is! And a hundred minus a hundred is zero too!"

"The things they teach these days." He went to the wide hanging rocker on the right side of the porch and sat down. Janice climbed up next to him, reciting more mysteries of subtraction, as the glider gently oscillated back and forth. Half-listening to his niece, just in case she happened to say something that required an actual response, Richard flipped through the mail. Mostly it was bills, but there was also a thick brown envelope that bore a Bentonville postmark and Rose's new return address.

He set the bills aside, but didn't open the package right away. Instead he sat on the bench and looked across the yard. To the right and left, trees curved to the road in two gentle arcs. The leaves were well into their autumn colors, red and orange and gold sweeping away the green of summer. The big, twisted oak in the front yard was surrounded by a puddle of fallen foliage. Across the street the field was fallow, its yearly crop of corn harvested and taken away, leaving churned earth behind. Beyond that was the distant line of the forest, dark and indistinct on this hazy October afternoon.

He glanced at Janice. She wasn't paying any attention to him; she was staring off into space and reciting subtraction equations set to the tune of the theme song of her current favorite television cartoon. He opened the brown envelope. A letter and part of a newspaper fell out. He looked at the newspaper first. There was a picture of Robert James's shop on the front page; the article below it was circled in blue marker. Rose had written *Thought you might find this interesting* next to the story. She was right. It said the police had discovered a stockpile of body parts in a large stainless steel refrigerator in the proprietor's apartment, and an undisclosed number of remains scattered around the rest of the property. Richard figured this meant the former pond and thereabouts. A manhunt was now on for Robert James, though of course they wouldn't locate him. Not unless they looked beneath the Anvil. And Richard wasn't sure they would find him even then.

He wondered if they'd discovered any traces of the ATV that Beth had been piloting through the pond. He doubted it. The explosion that wasn't an explosion had probably obliterated it. Still, he liked to imagine it had found its way to some other direction, not a frozen wasteland of mist and ghosts and screaming faces but a countryside of trees and hills, of ponds and fields and faded fences, Beth in the driver's seat, her auburn hair billowing out behind her in a spectral wind.

Richard set the clipping aside and read the enclosed note. Like most of Rose's letters, this one was terse. *Dear Richard,* it said, *I hope this finds you and Janice well. Things have mostly returned to normal here. I'm back to work at the paper. I wrote an article about what happened in August and showed it to Ozzie. We agreed it was pretty accurate. Then we burned it in his fireplace. Speaking of Ozzie, he finally got back the cassette tape he recorded out at the Anvil. His guy at Audiocraft managed to recover the audio, but it's just rain and forest noises and Ozzie snoring. He swears there were screams and voices on it when he first played it back. I believe him, but whatever he heard is gone now.*

Pedro and Sandy say hello. They stopped by before heading off to school. They're still together, but we'll see how long that lasts now that they're at different colleges. You know how long-distance romances are. Or do you?

I went up your street today. The developers already tore down your old place and are bulldozing the forest on either side. I think they're putting up four new houses. How much money did you say you got for selling all that land? Can I have some?

She followed that with a smiley-face, to show that she was only kidding. Mostly. He smiled at the smiley, but that faded when he read the final paragraphs.

Ozzie really did buy the Arvidsson property. It's all posted now. He told me the rocks have moved again. The hole into the Anvil is open. We don't know what that means. He didn't go inside. Even if he wanted to he wouldn't fit. He still says he's going to find a way to get a truck out there and fill it with cement. I'm not sure if he's kidding. I kind of hope so. I can only imagine what would happen if he really did it.

Beware of strange men bearing books, Richard.

He put down the letter and stared up into the branches of the oak tree. The remaining leaves flickered in the autumn wind in a doomed effort to hang on to their accustomed places, while others blew in swirls around the yard.

The Anvil had opened. Did that mean Gustav Arvidsson had come out? Or something else?

Janice said, "I'm hungry."

He looked at her, ruffled her hair. "You're always hungry."

"I'm a growing girl," she said.

Richard laughed. "Okay, growing girl. Come on, let's find you something to eat."

They went inside. Leaves carried on a gust of wind swirled in from the trees, glanced off the closed door, and blew sideways across the porch, making a sound like distant whispers. Janice skipped off down the hall to deposit her backpack and wash up and fetch Candy, now good as new, thanks to the efforts of the toymaker Ozzie had recommended. While she did that, Richard headed into the kitchen and set down the mail. He noticed that he'd missed something at the bottom of the big envelope, and shook it over the counter. A cassette clattered out, did a little spiral dance, and landed with the top facing him. He reached out and picked it up. It was labeled *Alt-Rock Blend For Richard.*

Well, how about that.

A mix tape.

About the Author

James V. Viscosi is the author of several horror and fantasy novels. An expatriate New Yorker, he currently resides with his wife and various finned and furry animals in sunny Southern California, where he spends most of his time hiding beneath a very large hat. Visit him at www.jamesviscosi.com.

www.ingramcontent.com/pod-product-compliance
Lightning Source LLC
Chambersburg PA
CBHW050009120726
47903CB00006B/1704